SHATTERED

By Kevin Hearne

Hounded
Hexed
Hammered
Tricked
Trapped
Hunted
Shattered

Iron Druid Chronicles Novellas

Two Ravens and One Crow
Grimoire of the Lamb

SHATTERED

THE
IRON
DRUID
CHRONICLES

KEVIN HEARNE

DEL REY • NEW YORK

2015 Del Rey Mass Market Edition

Copyright © 2014 by Kevin Hearne

Published in the United States by Del Rey, an imprint of Random House, a division of Random House LLC, a Penguin Random House Company, New York.

DEL REY and the HOUSE colophon are registered trademarks of Random House LLC.

Originally published in hardcover in the United States by Del Rey, an imprint of Random House, a division of Random House LLC, in 2014.

ISBN 978-0-345-54850-4
eBook ISBN 978-0-345-54849-8

Printed in the United States of America

www.delreybooks.com

9 8 7 6 5 4 3 2 1

Del Rey mass market edition: April 2015

To Nicole Peeler and Jaye Wells,
the original Laser Vaginas, and to all honorary
members of the band. Pew! Pew! Pew!

PRONUNCIATION GUIDE

I think it's cool if you read the unusual names in my books however you want. There won't be a test afterward and I'm not going to withhold a Twinkie from you if you pronounce any of them incorrectly. You're supposed to have fun here, after all, and it's usually not fun if someone tells you that you're doing it wrong. But I like to provide these in case you want to master those names and enjoy the Druids' globetrotting. So here we go; caps-lock bits indicate stressed syllables. . . .

OLD NORSE

Erlendr = EHR len dur (Not quite AIR lend ur, but close. A bit more like a short *e* on that first syllable.)

Freydís = FRAY deece

Hildr = HILL dur (Female name still used today in Iceland and Norway, but in modern spelling they go ahead and indicate the last vowel, like *Hildur*.)

Ísólfr = EES ol vur (The first syllable should rhyme with *fleece*, not *ease*. The *o* is a long *oh*, you know. And an *f* in the middle is kinda soft, so it sounds like a *v*.)

Krókr Hrafnson = KROH kur HRABn son (Hrafn = raven. Difficult to get this right in English. There's that aspirated *Hr* at the beginning and then the problematic *fn*. In modern Icelandic it's pronounced like a *bn* or simply a *b*, but we're unsure precisely how it was spoken in Old Norse. In the old days it may have been HRAV son. From poetry scanning we know that there wasn't a vowel sound between the *f* and *n*, so this is supposed to be a two-syllable word, but maybe with a hint of *n* in the middle.)

Oddrún = ODD rune (Female name still used today in Iceland. Bonus points if you roll the *r* a bit.)

Skúfr = SKOO vur (Again with the soft *f* thing.)

ÍRÍSH

Creidhne = CRANE ya
Flidais = FLIH dish
Fuilteach = FWIL tah
Goibhniu = GUV new
Granuaile = GRAWN ya WALE
Fragarach = FRAH gah rah
Luchta = LOOKED ah
Orlaith = OR lah
Scáthmhaide = SKAH wad juh
Siodhachan = SHE ya han

HÍNDÍ

Dabāva = da BAHV (Translates into *pressure* or *compression*. Last vowel is dropped in pronunciation.)

IRON DRUID CHRONICLES

THE STORY SO FAR

Atticus O'Sullivan, born in 83 B.C.E. as Siodhachan Ó Suileabháin, has spent much of his long life as a Druid on the run from Aenghus Óg, one of the Tuatha Dé Danann. Aenghus Óg sought the return of Fragarach, a magical sword that Atticus had stolen in the second century, and the fact that Atticus had learned how to keep himself young and wouldn't simply die annoyed the heck out of him.

When Aenghus Óg finds Atticus hiding in Tempe, Arizona, Atticus makes the fateful decision to fight instead of run, unwittingly setting off a chain of consequences that snowballs on him, despite his efforts to lie low.

In *Hounded,* he gains an apprentice, Granuaile, retrieves a necklace that serves as a focus for Laksha Kulasekaran, an Indian witch, and discovers that his cold iron aura is proof against hellfire. He defeats Aenghus Óg with an assist from the Morrigan, Brighid, and the local pack of werewolves. However, he also severely cripples a witches' coven that wasn't exactly benevolent but was protecting the Phoenix metro area from more-menacing groups of predators.

Hexed, book two, forces Atticus to deal with that, as

a rival and much more deadly coven tries to take over the territory of the Sisters of the Three Auroras, and a group of Bacchants tries to establish a foothold in Scottsdale. Atticus cuts deals with Laksha Kulasekaran and Leif Helgarson, a vampire, to earn their help and rid the city of the threats.

In book three, *Hammered,* the bills come due for those deals. Both Laksha and Leif want Atticus to go to Asgard and beard the Norse in their mead halls. Putting together a team of badasses, Atticus raids Asgard twice, despite warnings from the Morrigan and Jesus Christ that this would be a terrible idea and it might be best not to keep his word. The carnage is epic, with heavy losses among the Æsir, including the Norns, Thor, and a crippled Odin. The death of the Norns, an aspect of Fate, means the old prophecies regarding Ragnarok are now unchained, and Hel can begin to work with very little opposition from the Æsir. However, a strange coincidence with the Finnish hero Väinämöinen reminds Atticus of a different prophecy, one spoken by the sirens to Odysseus long ago, and he worries that thirteen years hence the world will burn—perhaps in some altered form of Ragnarok.

Feeling the heat for his shenanigans and needing time to train his apprentice, Atticus fakes his own death with the help of Coyote in book four, *Tricked.* Hel does indeed make an appearance, thinking Atticus might like to join her on the dark side since he'd killed so many Æsir, but she is brutally rebuffed. Atticus is betrayed by Leif Helgarson and narrowly escapes death at the hands of an ancient vampire named Zdenik, but the book ends with a modicum of assurance that Atticus will be able to train Granuaile in anonymity.

In the novella *Two Ravens and One Crow,* Odin awakens from his long sleep and forges a truce of sorts with Atticus, enlisting the Druid to take on Thor's role in Ragnarok, should it come to pass, and perhaps take care of another few things along the way.

After twelve years of training, Granuaile is ready to be bound to the earth, but it seems as if the Druid's enemies have been waiting for him to emerge in book five, *Trapped*. Atticus must deal with vampires, dark elves, faeries, and the Roman god Bacchus, and messing with the Olympian draws the attention of one of the world's oldest and most powerful pantheons.

Once Granuaile is a full Druid, Atticus must run across Europe to avoid the bows of Diana and Artemis, who took exception to his treatment of Bacchus and the dryads of Olympus in book five. The Morrigan sacrifices herself to give him a head start and Atticus is *Hunted* in book six. Running and fighting his way past a coordinated attempt to bring him down, he makes it to England, where he can enlist the help of Herne the Hunter and Flidais, the Irish goddess of the hunt. There Atticus is able to defeat the Olympians and negotiate a fragile alliance against Hel and Loki. At the end of this volume, he discovers that his archdruid was frozen in time in Tír na nÓg, and when Atticus retrieves him, his old mentor is in as foul a mood as ever.

Also, along the way, there may have been some talk of poodles and sausages.

SHATTERED

CHAPTER I

Few things trigger old memories so quickly as authority figures from our youth. I'm not saying those memories are necessarily good ones; they're simply old and tend to cast us back into roles we thought we grew out of long ago. Sometimes the memories are warm and blanket us like a mother's love. More often, however, they have the sting of hoarfrost, which bites at first, then numbs and settles in the bones for a deep, extended chill.

The ancient man who was pushing himself up into a sitting position in front of me triggered very few memories of the warm sort. Apart from being brilliant and magically gifted, my archdruid had frequently been abusive and had made few friends during his life—a life that, until recently, I thought had ended millennia ago. After he bound me to the earth prior to the Common Era, I'd seen him only a couple more times before we drifted apart, and I'd always assumed he'd died, like almost everyone else I knew from my youth. But for reasons unknown, the Morrigan had frozen him in time in Tír na nÓg, and now he was about to confront the fact of his time travel—with, I might add, flecks of spittle and bacon around the edges of his wrinkled lips.

I hope that if I ever travel two thousand years into the future, there will still be bacon.

His voice, a sort of perpetually phlegmy growl, barked a question at me in Old Irish. He'd have to learn English quickly if he wanted to talk to anyone besides the Tuatha Dé Danann and me. "How long was I on that island, Siodhachan? You still look pretty young. By the looks of ye, it can't have been more than three or four years."

Oh, was he in for a surprise. "I will tell you in exchange for something I'd like to know: your name."

"My name?"

"I've never called you anything but Archdruid."

"Well, it was right that ye should, ye wee shite. But now that you're grown a bit and a full Druid, I suppose I can tell ye. I'm Eoghan Ó Cinnéide."

I grinned. "Ha! If you Anglicize that, it's Owen Kennedy. That will work out just fine. I'll call Hal and get you some ID with that name."

"What are ye talking about?"

"That's a question you'll be asking a lot. Owen— I hope you don't mind me calling you that, because I can't walk around calling you Archdruid—you've been on that island for more than two thousand years."

He scowled. "Don't be tickling me ass with a feather, now; I'm asking seriously."

"I'm answering seriously. The Morrigan put you on the slowest of the Time Islands."

Owen studied my face and saw that I was in earnest. "Two *thousand*?"

"That's right."

He flailed about for something to hold on to; the number was too huge to register, and the stark fact that he had been uprooted and could never go back to his old earth was a deep, dark well into which he could fall forever. He opened his mouth twice and closed it again after uttering a half-formed vowel. I waited patiently as he worked through it, and finally he latched on to me, having nothing else in front of him. "Well, then, you were on one of those islands too. She must have set us there around the same time."

"No, I didn't get to skip all that time in an eyeblink. I lived through it. And I've learned a few things you never taught me."

He grunted in disbelief. "Now I know you're pulling me cock. You're telling me that you're more than two thousand years old?"

"That's what I'm telling you. You might as well brace yourself. The world is far bigger and far different than it was when you left it. You've never even heard of Jesus Christ or Allah or Buddha or the New World or bloody buffalo wings. It's going to be one shock after the other."

"I don't know what a *shock* is."

Of course he didn't. He'd never heard of electricity. I'd thrown in a modern Irish word with my Old Irish.

"But your lack of hair is certainly a surprise," he said, gesturing at my close-cropped skull. It was starting to fill in from when I'd had to shave it all off—a consequence of a recent encounter with some Fae who'd tried to chew off my scalp—but to Owen's eyes it must look like an unnatural cosmetic decision. "And what in nine worlds happened to the rest of your beard? Ye don't look like a man. Ye look like a lad who had a rat die on his chin."

"It works for me," I said, dismissing it. "But look, Owen, I'm wondering if you can do me a favor."

"Do I owe ye one?"

"You'd still be on that island if it weren't for me, so I'd say so."

My archdruid huffed and wiped at his mouth, finally dislodging the bacon bits that had rested there. "What is it?"

I raised my right sleeve over my shoulder, revealing the

ravaged tattoo at the top of my biceps. "A manticore destroyed my ability to shape-shift back to human, so I can't shift to any of my animal forms until it gets fixed. Would you mind touching it up?"

He scowled and flared up. "I fecking taught ye how to tame a manticore, didn't I? Don't try to tell me I didn't! That isn't my fault."

"I didn't say—"

"And I remember ye complaining about it too." He affected a falsetto to mock me. " 'When am I ever going to meet a manticore?' ye said. 'Why do I have to learn Latin? When are we going to learn about sex rituals?' "

"Hey, I never said that!"

"Ye didn't have to. There was a year ye couldn't sneak up on anyone because your knob would peek around the corner first and everyone would say, 'Here comes Siodhachan!' and then the rest of ye would follow. Ye remember that?"

Desperate to return the conversation to more recent scars—a much safer topic than my uncomfortable puberty—I said, "The manticore struck first, and taming him was never an option."

"It's always an option."

"No, it's not. You weren't there, and you've never had to deal with manticore venom. It requires all of your attention to break it down, trust me. And once I managed to do it, I was so weak that I'd never have been able to survive another dose. I was severely wounded and unable to confront him without leaving myself open to another shot. Any attempt to tame him would have been fatal. I was lucky to get out of there alive."

"All right, fine, but why me? Can't ye have some other Druid do it? I have some catching up to do."

I carefully neglected to mention that he and I were two of only three remaining Druids in the world. Time enough for that later. "That's true, you do. We have a lot to talk about, and I have a new language to teach you if you're going to get along. And the other Druid I'd trust to do this is busy working on another project."

Granuaile was training her new wolfhound, Orlaith, to speak and was also taking care of Oberon in the meantime. I didn't want her talking to Owen anyway, until I'd had the chance to teach him modern manners. If he spoke to her the way he spoke to me, there would be blood in short order, most of it his.

My archdruid winced, sighed, and rubbed at his temples as if he had a major headache. "Dagda fuck me, but I need something to drink. I don't suppose ye know where we can find something besides water?"

"Sure. I'll buy. Can you walk yet?" I glanced at his legs, which had been broken in the stress of removing him from the Time Island. He'd had some time to heal here, under the ministrations of the healer Fand, Manannan Mac Lir's magic bacon, and his own healing powers, but I didn't know if it was enough.

"I think so." He nodded. "Bones bind quickly, but it's the bruising to your muscles that always takes time. We'll walk slow and drink fast."

He leaned on me a bit for support and walked gingerly, but we made it off the barge and into the boat I'd taken out to the island. Once we reached the riverbank, it would be a short walk to a tree tethered to Ireland. We'd be able to shift to someplace with plenty of potables on tap and a comfortable spot to talk. In a strange way, I was looking forward to it. It felt strangely empowering to know something my archdruid didn't already know.

Somebody didn't want us to have that talk, however. No sooner had the boat ground into the gravel of the bank than an angry, high-pitched bark greeted us from downriver.

"Oi!" A hopping-mad Fir Darrig bounded toward

us—literally hopping and literally mad, as evidenced by the bulging of his eyes and the belligerent brandishing of his shillelagh—intent on accosting us at the least and teeing off on our skulls at the worst. Rat-faced, red-coated, and only three feet tall, Fir Darrigs have a five-foot vertical leap and a quick hand with the shillelagh; their single-digit IQs couple with that to make them think they are eight feet tall and four times as fearsome.

Usually you can just toss something shiny at them and they will stop to investigate, because they're greedy little goblins and tend to hoard anything that appears valuable. I had a quarter in my pocket and I lobbed it at him, making sure it caught the sun, but his eyes never wavered. He was determined to take a swing at me for some reason.

Another one bounced out of the trees downriver, spied us, and leapt forward. "Oi!" A second later, three more appeared. "Oi! *Oi!* Oi!"

"That's fecking strange," my archdruid said. And he was right. Fir Darrigs are typically solitary. You'd see two of them slamming their fists into each other every so often, which was actually their mating ritual, and if they didn't kill each other first, eventually they'd slam other things into each other and carry on the species. I'd never seen three together before, and here we had five coming at us.

"Oi! Oi! *Oi!*" Whoops. Make that eight.

The first one was obviously the most immediate threat, so I crafted a binding between the wool of his natty red coat and the silt of the riverbank and let the earth pull him to the ground. I wasn't quick enough to bind the coat closed, however, and he wriggled out of it and came at us nude, because Fir Darrigs don't wear anything except those red coats. He was filthy and ugly, and his yellow choppers gnashed out a series of incoherent snarls. Belatedly, I realized it would have been a better choice to bind his shillelagh to the riverbank. I drew my sword, Fragarach, from its scabbard and stepped forward, setting myself; there would be little time for other bindings.

Behind me, Owen began to tear off his ragged tunic and pants. He had no weapon; he *was* a weapon when he shape-shifted to his predator form.

"Stand back, lad, I can handle this."

I shot a quick scowl at him over my shoulder. "You're not in any shape to fight."

That fired him up, and he spat at me, "When a fight comes at ye, it's not going to ask if you're in shape for it! Ye have to be ready whenever it comes, and the day I'm not ready for a fight is the day I'm dead!" Free of his clothes, he shape-shifted to an enormous black bear and roared. That secured the attention of the first Fir Darrig, which roared back, hopped out of my reach to the left, then leapt up high in an arc that would end with his shillelagh crashing down onto Owen's skull. I turned and pursued like someone chasing down a Frisbee. Owen attempted to rise up on his back legs to meet the Fir Darrig, but those were the ones that had been broken and they weren't sufficiently sturdy to support a bear's weight yet. He got halfway up before they buckled and he came back down. The Fir Darrig had adjusted his swing to meet Owen's head up high but then couldn't recalculate in time once the bear fell to his feet. His feeble effort glanced off the top of Owen's shoulder but skipped along on the follow-through to clock him on the ear. It staggered Owen, and he bellowed as he reeled sideways, but the Fir Darrig never got another chance to swing. I caught up and shoved Fragarach quickly through his neck; as he fell, I turned to meet the other seven.

The leader was still forty yards away, and they strung out from there. About five seconds to impact if I waited for them to come to me, less if I went to meet them. Owen was still shaking off the first club to the head and probably wouldn't see the next shillelagh that brained him if I let them get close enough to take another swipe. So I charged, making plenty of noise to ensure they focused on me rather than the big bad bear. Owen wasn't ready for this, no matter what he said.

Sword held high as I went in, I slid low at the last moment, upending those who didn't leap up in an attempt to strike from the sky. The jumpers completely overshot me, but I wound up with three Fir Darrigs draped across my body, and once they came into contact with my cold iron aura, they were doomed as creatures of magic to death by disintegration. I didn't even have to slap them; they gave a startled cry as their substance unraveled and thumped the air inside their coats with a plosive cloud of ashes.

Scrambling to my feet as the final four landed and whirled around, I brought up Fragarach to defend my head from their next attack. One of them, the smallest and most agile of a small and agile group, had already launched himself at my midsection as I was turning to face them, catching me off-balance and plowing me back to the sandy gravel of the riverbank. He had puffed away into the wind by the time I hit the ground, but he'd set me up to be pounded to putty by his mates. They weren't bright; instead of approaching from the side and smashing down as if they were chopping wood, they jumped on top of me to keep me down and raised their shillelaghs high. Their clawed toes scratched me, and their heels knocked the wind out of me, but they got the worst of it. They came apart before they could swing, and the only wounds I suffered were from three shillelaghs and three foul red coats that fell on top of me. I coughed from the ashes in the air and checked on Owen, who was closer than he had been but still twenty yards away from the action. His ears were up, and his eyes were wide in an expression of ursine surprise.

The archdruid didn't give me any thanks for saving his hide or even comment that I had done well to take out eight Fir Darrigs all by myself. Fortunately, due to long acquaintance with him, I didn't expect either thanks or praise.

"What did ye just do?" he said upon shape-shifting back to human, his breathing somewhat labored. "They had ye all laid out for killing and then they exploded! Ye could have left me a couple."

I stood up, dusted myself off, and tapped my necklace. "One of the reasons I'm still around—*koff!*—is this amulet. It's cold iron and I've bound it to my aura, mostly for magical protection. But a useful side effect is that my aura kills Fae on contact. They call me the Iron Druid because of it."

"You're wearin' cold iron? And you can still cast bindings?"

"Aye. It took some experimentation, but the mass is low enough to permit it."

Owen grunted and waggled a finger at the rest of my necklace. "What's all that silver on either side?"

"Charms. They let me cast basic bindings with mental commands rather than using my voice. It's faster. Gives me an edge."

He grunted again and considered. "All the Druids are doing this now?"

"Just me. But that's pretty much all the Druids."

"What?" My archdruid's eyebrows, wild and white affairs that could do double duty as household dusters, drew together and folded his skin into grooves on his forehead.

"Not counting the Tuatha Dé Danann—and we can't really count them, because they're supposed to stay in

Tír na nÓg as much as possible—there are only three Druids left, including us."

"Shut your hole. How is that possible?"

"The Romans came for us. They burned all the groves on the continent and hunted us down. We couldn't shift planes and so they were able to trap us. You heard about it, I'm sure. Julius Caesar was in Gaul in your day."

Owen stiffened. "Aye, I remember. Did the Romans take Ireland?"

"No, they never made it there."

"Well, then, why are there only three Druids?"

"Because the pagan Romans eventually turned into Christian Romans. The Holy Roman Church did make it to Ireland, centuries later, and a man named St. Patrick converted much of the populace to his religion. The Druids died out for lack of apprentices."

He slumped, not understanding everything I said but sifting it for the essentials. "All the Druids died but you, eh? If this isn't all an elaborate joke—and if it is, I will ask Ogma to help me pound the living shite out of ye— how did ye manage to live on when all the others died?"

"I left Ireland a long time ago, at the Morrigan's urging, and learned to keep my body youthful. I've seen the world, Owen. It's much, much bigger than we ever thought back in our time. To the rest of the world today, Ireland is a tiny country, famous for its fighters and its alcohol."

"How tiny?"

"If the world were nine hundred sheep and a billy goat, Ireland would be the goat."

"Huh." He paused for a moment, trying to grasp the scale of it and orient himself, but it didn't add up for him. He looked at me through squinting eyes. "Still, lad, why so few? With two thousand years to work with, I'd imagine ye would train more than one apprentice."

"I was being chased by Aenghus Óg for much of that time."

"Oh, *him*. For a god of love, he's sure quick to hate and be hated back. He's a right bastard."

"He's a dead bastard. I killed him."

He raised a finger and tilted his head. "Is it the truth you're telling me now, Siodhachan?"

"Aye. And as soon as he was dead, I began to train an apprentice. I just finished binding her to the earth a little over a month ago."

"Ah, ye did? What's her name?"

"Granuaile."

"When do I get to meet her?"

"Later," I said. "We need to get you acclimated first. The world is so different that I'm worried you'll withdraw and hate everything."

"There's little chance of that," Owen said, a tiny grin tugging at the corners of his mouth. "I can't wait to see it all, to be truthful. And I'm sure the basics are the same. People still eat and shite and sleep, right?"

"Well, yes."

"Then it can't be all that different, can it? We'll just have to train some more Druids."

"I suppose so. But I have to caution you that there will be plenty of adjustments to make. We can start adjusting over a pint or five." It occurred to me that he might not know what a pint was, so I added, "Ready for that drink?"

"Aye. But I should probably put me clothes on again."

We shifted planes to Ireland—to the Kilkenny Castle grounds, actually, where there were some bound trees along the canal. From there I led him through the streets to Kyteler's Inn, a gray stone structure established in 1324. The interior would still be a jarring experience for him, but at least it wouldn't have giant plasma screens shouting about the latest football match. I expected a flood of questions on the way, especially once he saw the castle, but he didn't speak the whole way there; instead, he looked around with his mouth gaping open, staring at cars and streets paved in brick, stone, and asphalt, and at the concrete and steel of modern architecture mixed with the mortar and stone of older days. He stared at people too, whose clothing and shoes he found perplexing. The archdruid received more than a few stares of his own. No one made rags like the ones he was wearing anymore.

The bartender gave us an uncertain welcome. I must have looked like a university student buying a homeless man a drink. I pointed to an empty table where we would sit.

"Two Jamesons, neat, and two pints of Guinness, please?" I asked.

"Right away, sir."

Owen slid cautiously onto the upholstered chair after watching me do the same, his expression a mask of wonder at the feeling of padding. But horror suffused his face shortly afterward as he remembered what he'd seen on the way in, and he whispered his first words to me in the modern world, hunched low over the table. "They've covered up the earth, Siodhachan!"

CHAPTER 2

Atticus is off to confer with some crabby old man from the past—according to him, an unwashed, potentially explosive type, sort of like the human equivalent of a propane tank—while I get to hang out in Colorado with the hounds. I think I have the far better deal.

Oberon is so happy to have Orlaith here that the surfeit of his joy buffets me like the tide, waves of exultation wafted about by the swishing of his tail. He has taken to asking every morning if he can talk to Orlaith yet and is only mildly disheartened when I tell him no—we have all been running together in the forest after I climb out of bed, and that is such fun that it sugars over many disappointments. I bind myself to the shape of a jaguar, dark and sleek and liquid next to the bounding exuberance of the hounds, and we dance through the trees and let the crunch of leaves beneath our paws announce our good cheer to the forest. We chase squirrels and the occasional deer and smell things that tell us stories of life and death in the woods.

I am becoming more used to the smells and am not afraid of the form anymore. As with magical sight, the trick is in the filtering.

Orlaith is gradually acquiring language. Right now she speaks to me in short bursts of words, the simplest of sentences. Fluency and syntax will come later, though she knows how to ask for new words, and her meaning is always clear to me through our bond, a sort of emotional and image spillover akin to the communication we share with elementals.

She'd been at the rescue ranch because the newborn child of the couple that owned her turned out to be allergic to dogs. She misses them still and remembers how sad they were to give her up, but she is happy to be with us now. Her mental voice is a bit lighter than Oberon's, and she loves the trees here.

<Pine! Spruce!> she says as we run, excitement evident in her words and in the movement of her tail. <Town! Noises!>

Our mission today is to explore the small town of Ouray on foot. Surrounded on three sides by the San Juan Mountains and only a couple of square miles in area, it rests in a sort of natural bowl with egress to the north. Yesterday we dug a cache above the town and buried money and a set of clothes for me, along with collars and leashes for the hounds—for though Ouray is a very dog-friendly town, local ordinances require a leash at all times.

Burying things and digging them up again, of course, is half the fun.

Now dressed in jeans, sandals, and a black T-shirt announcing my affection for the legendary all-girl punk band the Laser Vaginas, I fold the paper bag that had protected my clothes and take it with me down the hill. The hounds gambol ahead, turning back frequently to check on my progress, since I am moving so much slower than before.

Ouray's economy largely depends on tourism. The majority of income derives from hotels, restaurants, and shops selling gimcracks, souvenirs, and the occasional artsy doodad. A glassblower and a blacksmith keep shops going in the summers, and one guy does some amazing sculptures with chain saws and tree trunks. Jeep touring companies make a killing as well, their income from the summer months supporting them for the rest of the year. Now that it's October and the temperature is dropping, the town is largely quiet and safe for Orlaith to learn how to conduct herself in urban environments. The opportunity to teach her new words would be invaluable too.

Lacking a jacket and feeling the chill, I use the binding Atticus taught me to raise my core temperature, then call the hounds over as we approach the Uncompahgre River, which marks the western edge of Ouray. As I fix the collars onto their necks, I say aloud, "Let's review the rules for behavior while we're in town. Oberon, you go first."

<We must not approach people but let them approach us.>

"Very good." I repeat Oberon's words for Orlaith's benefit and then ask her, "Do you remember any rules?"

<No poop! No pee!>

"Excellent. Make sure you take care of that before we cross the bridge. Anything else?"

Oberon says, <We mustn't sniff anyone's ass.>

<No woofs!> Orlaith adds.

"Good, good. And?"

<No jumping, no humping, stay next to you, and let you know if we want to stop to smell something,> Oberon finishes.

"Fabulous!" I repeat everything Oberon said for Orlaith but don't bother with the other way around. Oberon is an old hand at this.

Leashes in my fist and filled with insouciance, I take the dirt road down from Box Canyon Falls, cross the bridge, and enter Ouray near the Victorian Inn. We turn left up Main Street and slowly make our way north, pausing frequently when the hounds want to investigate something or when passersby want to pet them and chat. Some people cross the street when they see us coming; wolfhounds can be intimidating if you've never seen them before, and no doubt they think that I won't be able to hold on to one of them, much less two, if the dogs take it into their heads to run for it.

The pleasant morning is ruined as we pause outside a leather shop, though it's no fault of the leather's. The manager of the establishment, a grizzled man in his fifties with a brow furrowed in confusion, steps outside with a cordless phone and says, "Sorry, but would your name be Granny-Woo, by any chance, or something like that?" He completely bungles the pronunciation of my name, but I'm used to that.

Oberon and Orlaith swing around in concert to look at him, ears raised, and he flinches when he sees them. They hadn't been in view from inside the shop, so they take him by surprise when he steps across the threshold. "Gah. Those are some damn big dogs," he mutters.

<Woof?> Orlaith asks.

<If I barked at him right now, he would squeal,> Oberon says, and it's a struggle to keep my expression neutral when both dogs are thinking essentially the same thing. They are right: He'd probably stagger backward and hurt himself in his haste to get away, so I remind them to remain silent.

"Yes, I'm Granuaile," I tell him.

"Well, there's a phone call for you," the manager replies, holding out the phone to me. "They say it's an emergency. Life or death." I take the phone from him, and he says he'll be inside when I am finished. I'm not terribly surprised, since I'm aware that those of sufficient skill can divine my whereabouts if they wish, but I dread the bad news.

"Thanks," I say to him, nodding, then hold the phone up to my ear. "Hello?"

"Granuaile. It is Laksha."

"Laksha? Where are you?" I had not heard from Laksha Kulasekaran for more than a decade. The spirit of the Indian witch had shared space in my head once, and it was thanks to her that I learned of Atticus's true nature and became his apprentice. But after she found a body she could fully possess, we had spoken only a few times, as I began my training in earnest and she moved away to build a new life.

"I am in Thanjavur, India."

"Okay. I'm not sure where that is."

"It's near the southeastern coast, in the state of Tamil Nadu. I have been living in the region for several years. There is a problem here that might interest you, and I would appreciate your help even if it doesn't interest you. You are a full Druid now, yes?"

"Yes."

"Congratulations. Your skills could do wondrous good here, but especially if you are related to this man. Do you know of a gentleman named Donal MacTiernan?"

"Yes, that's my father's name. My real dad, not my stepfather."

"Is your father an archaeologist?"

The conversation was beginning to worry me. "Yes, he is."

"I was afraid of this. That is why I took the trouble to divine your location and call you. I believe your father is here. Did you know he was digging in India?"

"No, but that doesn't surprise me. He digs all over the world."

"I am afraid he found something that would have been better left buried. He unearthed a clay vessel recently and he opened it, either ignoring what was written on the outside or encouraged by it. It wasn't empty. The vessel contained a spirit that had been trapped inside for many centuries—trapped for very good reasons—and it immediately possessed him."

"*Possessed* him? Shit. How? The way you do it?"

"No, but it is similar. His spirit still dwells within his body, but the possessing spirit is dominant."

"What can you tell me about it?"

"I found the vessel at the site. Your father had dropped it, or perhaps shattered it on purpose. I pieced it back together in order to read the Sanskrit markings. They warned that there was a raksoyuj inside."

"I'm sorry, what was that?"

"A raksoyuj, which means a yoker of rakshasas. It's a type of sorcerer that I thought had been eliminated before I was born. They are capable of summoning demons and bending them to their will, and that is what he is doing. The rakshasas your father has summoned are spreading a pestilence throughout the region. People are dying."

"Wait, you're saying my dad is killing people?"

"The spirit possessing him is responsible, but it's his body. I can imagine that someone will be wanting to stop him soon, and they might not be very careful about how they do it."

"Oh, gods—"

"Yes, them too."

"Okay, I can be there in a few hours." I'd need to run back to the cabin and throw some things together and then find Atticus, but shifting around the world wouldn't take any time at all. "Where should I meet you?"

"Meet me at the entrance to the Brihadeeswara Temple. We are eleven and a half hours ahead of you, so it will be fully dark when you get here."

"See you then. Thanks for calling me." I thumb the OFF button, ask the hounds to wait, and dart into the leather shop to return the phone to the manager.

Oberon asks, <Is there something wrong, Clever Girl?> when I return outside.

Yes, I answer him mentally, then make sure to include Orlaith. *We have to return to the cabin quickly. Jog with me; no stopping unless I stop.*

<No more town?> Orlaith says.

No more of this town. We will go to a different one.

We turn around and eat up ground quickly, especially since it's downhill. People on the sidewalk move out of our way.

<I heard you say someone was possessed,> Oberon says. <You weren't talking about Atticus, were you?>

No, it was my father. Laksha says he's in India and he needs my help.

<Am I going too?>

Well—damn. I can't take both Oberon and Orlaith with me unless I make two trips. I don't have enough "fully furnished" headspaces for it, and a Druid needs a separate headspace for each being she takes along when hopping between the planes. We can slip our friends into the worlds built by scions of literature, splitting our consciousness into self-contained partitions. Atticus explained it to me like so: The tethers are roads, and Druids are the vehicles that drive on them. Headspaces are like seats for passengers. Thus far I have memorized only the world of Walt Whitman, and that would allow me to take one person—or hound—with me when I shift to Tír na nÓg and thence to India. It would be more practical to have Atticus join us if he could; he has six headspaces. He's like one of those old-fashioned boatmobiles, where I'm only a two-seat Smart Car. Well, scratch that. I'm more like a two-seat Jaguar F-Type. *I'm not sure, Oberon. I'll have to see if I can find Atticus.*

Once we cross the bridge over the Uncompahgre River that leads to Box Canyon Falls, we zip behind some undergrowth and I shuck off my clothes before shifting to a jaguar. I abandon my jeans and sandals but decide to carry my Laser Vaginas T-shirt back in my mouth. Those are rare, after all. We sprint back to the cabin together, the hounds enjoying every moment of it, unconscious of my worries—as they should be.

When we get home, they both head straight for the water bowl and I head for the bedroom to get dressed for a fight. I doubt that physical weapons will be of any use against a spirit, but the sorts of spirits who possess people tend to have ways to manifest physical threats. I throw on another pair of jeans and a nondescript T-shirt, a simple solid black. No customs agents, metal detectors, or anything like that will delay my travel, so I strap on two holsters that carry three throwing knives each and hide another pack of them between the waistband of my jeans and the small of my back.

Oberon and Orlaith, I'm going to find Atticus in Tír na nÓg. Hopefully it won't take long. Are you okay on food?

<That depends on how you define *okay*,> Oberon says. <I haven't had my morning sausage yet.>

<Sausage now?> Orlaith asks, and I smile despite my stress. They are two of a kind.

Okay, I hear you, I reply. *We must adhere to our priorities.* Forcing myself to take the time, I fry up some sausages for the hounds and toast some sprouted-grain bread for myself. While I hope this will be a quick trip, it could easily turn into something more lengthy, and I don't know when I'll have a chance to eat again—and, besides, I haven't had breakfast yet either.

Recognizing that the same uncertainty applies to the hounds, I haul out a bag of kibble and pour it into two gigantic bowls.

<You don't expect us to eat that, do you?> Oberon says.

"It's a backup plan," I reply. "Just in case. You're free

to hunt, of course, and there's all the water you want in the river. I hope I'll be back in a few minutes and none of it will be necessary. But you know how weird things can get when you expect Atticus to behave normally."

<Do I ever! Sometimes he eats vegetables!>

"The point is, you won't starve while I'm gone, and I'll be back as soon as I can."

We all make short work of our breakfast and I give the hounds hugs before I shift away to Tír na nÓg, the primary Irish plane to which the Irish gods have tethered all others, allowing us to travel as we wish. I check at Manannan's estate first, but Atticus isn't there. Nor is he at the Time Island; the boat he used is moored at the shore with a rope tied to a stake plunged in the ground. He isn't at Goibhniu's shop or at the Fae Court, and that exhausts all the places I know to look for him in Tír na nÓg. No one I ask knows where he and the old man have gone. I don't have time to waste looking anymore, so I shift back to Colorado and find the hounds playing down by the river.

Oberon! Orlaith!

<Clever Girl is home!>

<Granuaile! Race!>

There are no creatures better at making someone feel welcome than happy hounds. Though I had been gone perhaps only a half hour, their joy at my return was no less than if I had been gone half a year. I wish sometimes that humans could greet each other with such unreserved delight. Leaving out the face-licking, perhaps.

I can't play with them, however, and though it breaks my heart, I have to leave Oberon behind if I'm going to go to India.

"I couldn't find Atticus. I need you to stay here and explain where I've gone so that he can find me," I tell him. We enter the cabin, and I grab a pen and paper to scribble down a note.

<What do you want me to tell him?>

"Tell him I'm with Laksha; we're trying to find and help my real father, who's in trouble, and the details on where to find me are in this note I'm leaving. Don't forget to tell him about the note, okay?"

<I won't forget.>

"Good hound."

<Do you think it would be creepy if I had you tell Orlaith from me that I will miss her while you're gone?>

I smile and answer him privately. *You've seen too many human movies. Hounds are allowed to miss whomever they want at any point in a relationship without any creep penalties.*

<Oh, yeah! We have different rules.>

I will miss both you and Atticus, I say, picking up my staff, Scáthmhaide, and walking outside with Orlaith trailing behind. *I hope to see you soon.*

<You will!>

I put my hand on a tethered tree and ask Orlaith to put one paw on me and one on the tree. Orlaith says, <Bye, Oberon! Play later!>

I tell Oberon what she said, and then we shift away to India.

CHAPTER 3

"Why did they do it?" Owen asked. "Cover up the earth?"

"They would say it speeds their transport system, but I think primarily it's an aversion to mud. They don't feel the magic of the earth like we do, so it's not a moral decision for them. It's convenience."

"Oh, Siodhachan," he said, shaking his head in despair. "Are you going to tell me that everything's worse? Hasn't the world gotten better in two thousand years?"

The bartender arrived with our shots and beers, and I thanked him. "Some things have improved dramatically," I said, looking down at our drinks.

"What's this, then?" My archdruid scowled at the glasses, distrust writ large on his face.

"A sampling of Ireland's genius," I replied, and switched to English for the next sentence. "Whiskey and stout." I picked up the shot glass and returned to Old Irish. "Begin with this and toss it down. Then follow with a few sips of the dark beer."

"All right," he said, picking up the shot glass. "Your health."

"*Sláinte,*" I replied in modern Irish.

The whiskey burned precisely as it should, and the Guinness was a perfect pour.

Owen coughed once and his eyes watered. "Oh, thank

the gods below," he said, putting down the pint glass. "My people aren't completely lost."

We both laughed—a common enough occurrence, but one that I couldn't recall ever sharing with him— and then I answered a stream of questions about what he'd seen on the way to the inn. That turned into a stream of questions about what he saw inside the bar and what was this strange new concept called *science* anyway?

We talked through a couple more rounds, and the after-dinner crowd started to filter in. Owen became particularly animated at one point, and this amused some young toughs at the bar. They laughed and one of them aped him—an astoundingly poor decision, which meant that his night of fun with his mates was about to turn into The Night He Got His Ass Kicked.

"Shut your hole, you," Owen growled at him. It was in Old Irish, but the tone was unmistakable. The grin disappeared from the punk's face, and he put down his drink and did that jaw-flexing thing that some guys do because they think it makes them look tougher.

"Are you talking to me, old man?"

In the punk's experience, that was the point where most people backed down. He'd left room for Owen to say, "My mistake," and look away, and he thought that would be the end of it. But my archdruid wasn't the average senior citizen. He knew a challenge when he heard it, and he had never refused to accept one. Keeping his eyes on the punk and sneering the entire way through his next words, he said, "Siodhachan, tell him his mother makes badger noises when I tup her sideways."

I grinned but elected not to translate. There was no need; there was plenty of offense to be taken from Owen's body language and voice, and the punk was happy to take it. He balled his hands into fists and approached the table.

"Look, old man, if you want trouble, I've plenty to give you." He raised a fist and pointed at Owen when he got near. "In fact—"

That was it. Owen grabbed his arm, yanked it toward him, and head-butted the punk. He went down with a yelp and Owen stood up, kicking his chair away behind him. "Respect your elders, lad!"

The inn got quiet the way things will when shit gets real. The punk had four friends at the bar, who had just seen him lose in less than a second to a man who looked to be more than seventy and unable to pay for his drink. For a brief moment they had a choice regarding their mate: They could laugh at him and give him unending grief about it for the rest of his life, or they could back him up. Owen wasn't going to let them get a laugh out of it. He kicked the punk in the gut and beckoned the others forward.

"Come on and have your lesson, then," he said, and though they didn't speak Old Irish, his meaning was unambiguous. The dinosaur wanted a fight, and the huge grin on my face probably didn't help matters.

"Now, wait, boys—" the bartender said, but they all put down their drinks and rushed Owen. Pride and brotherhood wouldn't allow them any other choice. I didn't move but muttered words to boost my strength and speed in case they decided to involve me.

The first one came in with the intent to tackle Owen to the ground, the better to pummel him into submission. It wouldn't work out well; the archdruid used to have us charge him in just such a fashion for training, because it was a common tactic in unarmed combat. Owen feinted to his right, causing the punk to veer that way, then hopped left, slapping the outstretched right arm away to ensure he'd pass by. Pivoting as the poor bloke chugged past and keeping his fists near his sternum, the archdruid delivered a blow with his left elbow to the lad's temple and then kept spinning around, taking the charge of the next guy in the back and stunning him with a right elbow to his guts. The punk stopped, bent over, and Owen raised his right arm again, still cocked, and completed his turn, this time giving the man an elbow to the jaw. He lost some teeth on the way down to the floor.

The third bloke slowed down, deciding to search for a weakness, and the fourth chose to have a go at me, even though I had a sword plainly slung across my back. He came at me from my left side, fist cocked, and I waited for him to throw it at me. Once he did, I caught it in my left hand and took my cue from Owen: I headbutted him, using his own momentum against him. I smashed his nose and let him go down cradling his face.

The last guy rarely behaves as tough as he had with his mates still standing around him. Morale evaporates rapidly when you encounter something that's able to take out your friends in a few seconds.

He held up his hands and backed off. "Hey, our mistake. Sorry."

"What happened to all his piss, Siodhachan? He charged me and now he's thinking better of it?" Owen said.

"Wouldn't you, in his position?"

"I might think about fighting another day, sure. But only after I learned how to fight. These were hardly any fun."

"Fun's on its way," I said, pointing past him at the approaching bouncer. He was the tall hulking sort who could take a lot of punishment and patiently pound you on the head until you dropped. "It's that man's job to throw you out of here."

"Is he any good at his job?"

"You're about to find out." I pulled some money out of my pocket and switched to English to talk to the bartender. "Sorry about the mess. I'll leave enough for our drinks and then some." I didn't have anything but American dollars, but they could exchange those easily enough. There wasn't a lot of damage yet beyond some blood to mop up, but I figured that would change in a moment. Unlike the punks, the bouncer knew how to fight. He looked ex-military and at some point had been trained in Krav Maga. He introduced Owen to its finer points. The archdruid was down and under control, gasping for breath with his arm twisted behind him, in about twenty seconds. The bouncer was breathing heavily too, for Owen had gotten a couple of licks in, but both men were smiling bloody smiles.

"Grandpa's got some moves," he said, and spat blood on the floor before looking over at me. "You going to give me trouble too? You pull that sword on me and you'll have an issue with the law, not just me."

"Nah, I don't need my attitude adjusted. Thanks very much for adjusting his."

"Right. Out you go, then." He jerked his head toward the door. "I'll be right behind you with Grandpa."

I passed by, keeping my distance, and preceded them toward the inn's front door. Owen was laughing as the bouncer pulled him to his feet. "Siodhachan, tell this giant oaf I like him."

"What did he just say?" the bouncer asked, pushing Owen along. "He'll kick my arse later?"

"No, he said he likes you."

"Oh. Well, that's different."

"I'll kick his arse later, of course," Owen said, and I laughed.

"There it was."

The bouncer chuckled. "They always say that. Look, I'm kind of glad you came in here and laid those wankers out, because they're tosspots, but don't come back here again, guys, or I won't be so nice."

"No worries," I said, walking outside. He pushed Owen out behind me and closed the door.

"What was with all the elbows in there?" I asked.

"Oh. That. Fecking aches in me knuckles." He stretched, held his lower back, and winced. "Abuse my hands now and they won't open in the morning. Getting old is about as much fun as swimming in shite."

"I know; I tried it once."

"That so? How old were ye before ye started aging backward?"

"I was seventy-five when I met Airmid and she taught me the trick. That ache you're talking about, they call that arthritis now."

"Did I ask ye what they called it? I don't care, because I'm goin' to call it an ache in me knuckles."

"All right."

"So what's your secret to stayin' so young and fresh, eh? Did you get one of Manannan's hogs?"

"No, I drink a certain tea. I'm going to make some for you, in fact, before we arrange to get you a modern identity. How old would you like to be?"

"You're asking me seriously?"

"Aye."

"Well, I don't want to look as young as you. I know you're older than me now, but it doesn't *feel* that way, if you know what I mean."

"I do." I liked appearing young, however. It made everyone underestimate me.

"I suppose I'd like to revisit me forties. Young enough to be strong and active again but old enough to command some respect."

"Sounds good. Let's head back to the trees and we'll go get the necessary supplies. Your legs are better now, aren't they?"

"Oh, aye. Feel as good as they ever have in me dotage. That bacon Fand gave me was wonderful."

We began walking toward the grounds of Kilkenny Castle, and his stride was much more confident than during the trip in. I thought perhaps the drink and the fight had helped him as much as the healing powers of Manannan's miracle bacon.

"Ready to start learning the new language?"

"Aye. But ease me into it and begin with the cussing."

I began to teach him English, using my Irish accent, and he proved to have an excellent ear for it. His absorption of the language, of course, was Druidic. We shifted from Kilkenny to Flagstaff, Arizona, where it was just after noon and Winter Sun Trading Company was open for business on San Francisco Street. They had the necessary ingredients for Immortali-Tea, including teapots, and there was a forest nearby that Owen would appreciate.

Before walking in, however, I pulled out my cell phone and called my attorney, Hal Hauk, who was also the alpha of the Tempe Pack. Owen was so mesmerized by passersby and the sights of downtown Flagstaff that he didn't even notice I was speaking to someone with a small rectangular device held up to my ear.

"Hal! Need some ID."

"You're kidding. I just gave you some!"

"It's not for me." Granuaile and I had ditched our previous aliases—terrible names given to us by Coyote: Sterling Silver and Betty Baker—and now lived under the names Sean Flanagan and Nessa Thornton, though we never used them in private. She was still Granuaile to me, and I was still Atticus to her. "It's for someone else. Need a complete workup because he's never been around until now."

"Who's this?"

"An extremely old friend named Owen Kennedy. Listen, we're in Flagstaff and can't get down there quickly. Is there someone up here who can take the picture and the info and send it down to you?"

"Yeah. Go see Sam Obrist. Swiss fellow in charge of the gang up there. Ready for his address?"

I memorized it and thanked him, promising to bring Owen down to meet the pack when his ID was ready.

After picking up the necessaries in Winter Sun and making a quick trip over to Peace Surplus on Route 66 for a propane stove, a small mirror, some modern clothes for Owen, and one of those backpack shovels, we hiked up to Mars Hill with six gallons of water and hid ourselves in the ponderosa pines a few hundred yards away from Lowell Observatory. I mixed the blend of herbs and then performed the all-important bindings Airmid had taught me long ago to make this particular tea a miraculous rejuvenator instead of a mildly effective blend of antioxidants and detoxifiers. Then, since building a fire would be not only illegal but inefficient, I brewed the Immortali-Tea on the propane stove and told my archdruid to start chugging.

He scowled at the cup after the first sip. "Tastes like shite, lad."

"But it's good for you. You'll start to feel it soon."

He shrugged and threw it back, then drank several more cups until the first pot was gone. I began to brew another, smiling as I did so, and he spied mischief in it.

"What are you so pleased about?"

"I only drink a little at a time, like half a cup every four or five months, to maintain my current age. Half a cup has a mild laxative effect."

"What kind of effect?"

"Laxative. It means it loosens your bowels."

"Half a cup has . . . ? But you just had me drink a whole pot!"

"That's why I brought the shovel. By the time you finish digging yourself a hole, I imagine you'll be needing to use it. Here." I picked up the shovel and tossed it to him.

"You worthless spawn of a she-goat!" he roared, snatching the shovel out of the air. He shook it at me. "I should cave your skull in with this!"

"You won't be able to do that until you've drunk another few pots," I said. "You'll be flushing toxins out of your system until we're through, but they're nothing you'll miss. You'll be getting rid of that ache in your knuckles, for one thing."

A torrent of profanity gushed forth from my archdruid's mouth as he turned to choose a place to dig a makeshift latrine. He promised dire consequences for this humiliation.

"My, aren't we feeling spry already," I said. "Try to remember that I'm doing you a favor. Rapid cell regeneration and replacement and . . . Never mind, you don't know what any of that means anyway."

The shovel wasn't strictly necessary; my archdruid could easily move a bit of earth as needed through Druidry, but if he did it that way, he'd have to stop cursing me to speak the bindings, and I knew very well he wouldn't want to do that. I wouldn't want him to stop either. He had taken great pleasure in giving me grief for twelve years during my training, so I allowed myself to enjoy a bit of schadenfreude now.

"Oh!" he blurted, interrupting his cussing as internal convulsions rocked him. I heard him throw down the shovel and tear frantically at his pants. "Damn you, Siodhachaaaaan!"

Heck yes, I laughed.

Though he complained bitterly, Owen had to admit that the Immortali-Tea was working. I took out the mirror for him each time he returned from his exertions and got ready to drink another pot. The wrinkles gradually disappeared and the age spots on his hands faded away. His posture improved and his muscles began to fill out. I remembered going through the same process when I first learned how to make Immortali-Tea, but I had erased fifty-plus years instead of the thirty he was shooting for. When he came back after the fourth pot, his hair and eyebrows, as well as his beard, had begun to grow in dark again. All were growing faster than normal as his body shed the markers of age.

"We're going to have to visit a barber," I said.

"What's a barber?"

"Someone who cuts hair."

"Doesn't everyone cut hair?"

"No, a barber has been trained to do it, and he or she makes a living doing that. People have specialized their professions to a far greater extent than we used to in the old days. You'll need to choose a profession at some point."

"What are you saying? I'm a Druid. That's it."

"No, from now on you're *also* a Druid. No one will pay you for that now, and you need some way to generate income."

"Well, what have you been doing?"

"I've practiced many professions throughout the years. Most recently I was a silversmith. Before that I owned a bookstore that also sold herbs, like the one we visited in Flagstaff."

"What's a bookstore?"

"A merchant that sells books. Books are like bound scrolls, full of knowledge. It's how people absorb information these days, if they're still using paper."

"They learn things from books instead of from Druids?"

"That's right."

"Then they must be pretty stupid, am I right?"

"Some of them are," I admitted. "Mostly the ones

who don't read. But the advantage of books is that any knowledge is readily available to anyone. People who are currently ignorant of something can educate themselves at any time, on their own schedule, and the books never rap them on the head with an oak staff and tell them they're cocking it up again."

Owen frowned at the sudden turn to the personal. "Oh, I see," he said. "I wasn't delicate enough with your feelings during your training, is that it?"

"It wasn't pleasant," I said. "Nor was it necessary to use those methods."

"Wait, now, lad. Are ye a Druid or aren't ye?"

"Not only am I a Druid, I am *the* Druid, if you listen to the elementals of the earth."

"And have ye outlived all the other Druids?"

"Obviously I have."

He stabbed a finger at my face. "Then me fecking methods were brilliant. The fact that you're sitting here feeling your mushy feelings instead of feeding worms is a testament to the value of knocking some sense into ye."

I kept my eyes on the propane stove and the teapot and said nothing. Eventually he continued in a muted grumble that may have been his version of an apology. "I'm going to be your student for a while, it seems, and I'm sure it will be far more pleasant for me than it was when our roles were reversed. What's next?"

"Next you drink one more pot and deal with the side effects. Then we'll go into town, get you shaved and trimmed and fed, and I'll take you to see a werewolf named Sam Obrist."

"He's a what?"

"Werewolves are shape-shifters, but they only have the wolf form. Immune to magic and vulnerable to silver."

"Ah, I was wondering why you chose silver for those

charms of yours. Gold would conduct energy better, wouldn't it?"

"Yes, but I felt the trade-off in efficiency for protection was worth it."

"Are werewolves prone to attacking, then?"

"Not so much anymore. At the time I began to work on these charms, they were. They're much more civilized now, and the territory boundaries are firm. If you'd like to make some charms for yourself, I can show you how. But first we'll get the ID process started and then continue your language lessons while we fix my tattoo."

One last pot of tea and Owen looked and felt fortyish—which was outstanding compared to looking and feeling seventyish. I took him into town to get him cleaned up and buy him a late lunch at Lumberyard Brewing Company. The barber was confused by all the dark hair growing underneath the white, but he didn't ask any questions, since Owen favored him with a forbidding glare. Owen kept a full beard, albeit neatly trimmed, and his eyebrows were likewise shorn to acceptable standards. He looked as if he should be throwing something heavy into the back of a truck in one of those manly commercials where they talk about durability and payloads in deep bass voices.

Our server during lunch was a very pretty college student, and when she greeted us and smiled, Owen's expression warned me just in time.

"Wait!" I said to him in Old Irish. "Look at me!"

His leer melted away and he scowled. "What now?"

"I'm not sure what you intended, but this isn't a tavern wench from two thousand years ago. Smiling at you is not an invitation to grab her ass. If you touch her, she will have you thrown out at a minimum and maybe arrested for sexual assault."

"What?"

"Keep your hands to yourself at all times, and don't stare or stick out your tongue or wink or anything. Treat her like the king's daughter."

"Is she a noblewoman?"

"As far as you're concerned she is. Every woman is. Courtship is very different now, and it varies from country to country. Wait a minute and let me order for us. I'll explain."

He grunted and looked away. I apologized to the server, who'd been very patient, and ordered a couple of deli sandwiches on kaiser rolls, along with their craft-brewed Red Ale. Catching Owen up on what Oberon would call "human mating habits" occupied our time and frustrated us both.

"No one is as frank about sex as they used to be," I said.

"Why not?"

"Monotheism made everyone worry about being a slut."

Owen stared at me blankly. "I don't know what ye mean."

"People don't want to appear too wanton, so you have to take it slow. Plus there are plenty of genuinely creepy guys out there, and women are afraid you might be one of them."

"What?" He bobbed his head in the direction of the kitchen, where the server had disappeared. "She doesn't even know me."

"Exactly. And until she gets to know you, the possibility of a romp is out of the question. I know the behavior sounds strange and unnecessary compared to what you're used to, but there are reasons for it. Until you're comfortable with the language and the culture, the best advice I can give to keep you out of trouble would be to wait for the woman to make the first move. And a smile is not a move."

Owen passed a hand over his face and muttered, "Brighid grant me patience."

"Yeah, get yourself loaded up with plenty of that."

After the late lunch, I took him to the address Hal had given me and we met Sam Obrist, alpha of the Flagstaff Pack. Though I'd known there was a decent-sized pack in town, I'd never had occasion to meet him. He was a tall, blond, and square-jawed sort and wore a pair of glasses on his nose that were doubtless some kind of hipster affectation. His house was near the forest—go figure—and he shared it with his second, Ty Pollard, who also happened to be his husband.

"Hal told me you were coming," he said, and shook our hands briefly. His eyes flicked down to the silver charms on my neck, but he didn't react otherwise. "Please come in." He smiled and waved us through the door and offered us beers, on which we passed, having just finished a couple.

He weighed and measured Owen and talked as he wrote down details, like eye and hair color, for the ID. "I've heard you can shift to a wolfhound," he said to me.

"That's right." That always came up quickly whenever I met a new werewolf. The fact that I wore silver and shifted to an animal bred to hunt down wolves was understandably interesting to them, but it wasn't as if I had ever done it. Some werewolves took meeting me as a pleasing thrill of danger. Some took it as a challenge. Fortunately, Sam was inclined to the former.

"You ran with Hal's pack a few times, didn't you?"

"Yes, but that was some time ago. Back when Gunnar was with us."

"Oh, I see. Does he shift too?" he asked, indicating Owen.

"Yes. A black bear, among other things."

There were a few more questions—did we have specific names or occupations we wished Owen to have in his background? I told Sam to make up whatever names for parents he wished and to use outdoorsy occupations for his work history. Thinking of the nearby university's mascot, I said, "Maybe make him a lumberjack."

It wouldn't be long until we'd be free to begin work on my tattoos, but that would take us away for more than a week and I'd be off the grid the whole time. I thought it would be best to check in with Granuaile.

When I pulled out my cell phone, however, I discovered that I was already off the grid. My last call to Hal must have finished off my battery, and I didn't have a charger with me. I'd have to shift up to the cabin and tell her in person.

"Would you mind if I stepped out for a short time while you take his picture?" I asked Sam.

"No, that would be fine," he replied. "He seems harmless."

"Thanks." I turned to Owen and spoke in Old Irish. "I want to go check in on Granuaile really quick before we go back to the Old World, let her know we'll be gone and out of touch for a while."

"You're leaving me here?" he said.

"Only for a few minutes. They're just going to take your picture and let you drink beer. There's nothing to worry about."

"Don't be stupid! I don't know what a fecking picture is, for one thing! Why not wait and take me with ye?"

"Because I'd like to spend more time on your transition to the culture first."

"Not learning quick enough for ye, am I?" Owen looked at Sam and pointed a finger at me before uttering his first words aloud to another person in English. "Him. No balls," he said.

Surprised by Owen's sudden language switch and accusation, Sam and Ty erupted in laughter and I waved goodbye, confident that he'd get along with them just fine. The forest near Sam's house provided a convenient link to Tír na nÓg, and I was able to shift to our cabin in Colorado near sundown. Granuaile and Orlaith weren't there, but Oberon was.

<Atticus! It's about time! I've been here alone for days!> He bounded up to me, his tail wagging, and I petted him.

"Days? Are you sure about that, buddy?" It had been a long day for me, but I doubted it had been a full twenty-four hours since I had left.

<Well, I've taken several naps since they took off.>

"Where did they go?"

<Someplace in India. Granuaile's father got possessed, and Laksha called her to come help.>

"What? When did this happen?"

<I told you, days ago! But Granuaile left you a note on the table. You're supposed to read it.>

"Yeah, I think I will." A yellow sticky note waited on the kitchen table, and Granuaile's neat script in blue ink spelled out the news:

Atticus—
    Laksha called. Father possessed by something called raksoyuj. Going to meet her at Brihadee- swara Temple in Thanjavur. Will try to leave message there. Please come.

    —G.
    October 21, 9:10 a.m.

"Oberon, this wasn't written days ago. It was written this morning."

<Oh. Well, in my defense, I'm adorable.>

"She's been gone nine hours, and that's way too much

time to spend alone with Laksha. I don't trust her. Why does she have Granuaile's father in India?"

<I don't think Laksha actually has him. They sounded like they were going to go look for him.>

"So the whole thing could have been a ruse, and Granuaile just rushed off without knowing the situation?" I said, heading out the door.

<You mean kind of like what you're doing? Yeah.>

"What in seven hells is a raksoyuj, anyway?"

<If I had to guess, it sounds like marinated beef on a stick with a piquant dipping sauce.>

"Wait, you're right," I said, turning on my heel and reentering the cabin. "I'm rushing things. I should charge my cell phone and leave her a note in case she comes back while we're out looking."

<Hey, why are you here alone? Weren't you supposed to go get that old guy who was pointing at us on that island beach?>

"Oh, yeah. I got him. But he's in Flagstaff right now with a couple of werewolves. He'll be fine . . . I hope."

<You sound uncertain.>

"He doesn't know the language well, and he has a short fuse," I said, plugging in my cell phone and grabbing a sticky note to scrawl down the time we left.

<It sounds like he's qualified to be an action movie star.>

"He'll be ready for a fight sequence when we get back, but this can't wait. It's a potentially hostile situation, so I want you to stick close and be on your guard, okay?"

<Copy that, Red Leader.>

I adjusted Fragarach, more to reassure myself of its presence than to fix any discomfort, and strode outside toward our tethered trees. "I haven't been to India in quite some time. I hope there will be a tether somewhere close to Thanjavur."

<What's it like in India?>

"Oh, that's right, you've never been there at all. Well, brace yourself, buddy. More than a billion people live there, and the majority of them are vegetarians."

<Ha-ha, very funny.>

"I'm serious, Oberon. Cows are sacred. Nobody eats them."

<Are you trying to scare me?>

I grinned at him. "Sounds like a harrowing adventure, doesn't it? Come on, Oberon. Paws on the tree."

<Wait, Atticus, I think we should talk about this—>

CHAPTER 4

Dense air and pregnant clouds welcome us to India, promising rain. The croak of frogs and the drone of insects sing of cycles, of hunger and need and of satisfaction also, of turning the wheel and hanging on. My hound notices the change in weather right away.

<Air wet,> she says.

Yes, it's quite humid. Much of Thanjavur is surrounded by rice paddies and the occasional banana or coconut grove. It's into one of these groves that we have shifted, bunches of bananas hanging overhead, a few miles outside the city's boundaries. Even so, the tether was much closer in than I thought it would be. Back in what Europe called the Dark Ages, Atticus had traveled the world the slow way and tied as much of it as he could to Tír na nÓg, and once those tethers were established, Fae rangers maintained them by Brighid's order, popping in to make sure they still worked and creating new ones as necessary when trees died or were removed by humans. Some of those rangers were working for Aenghus Óg and looking for Atticus while they were at it, but all the Fae and Tuatha Dé Danann benefited from it.

The banana grove occupies a bit of high ground, and once I cast night vision, I can see a canal that winds into the city. A path or perhaps a road runs alongside, and I decide to follow it, gambling that we will find someone on the way to provide directions to the temple. Most people have already shut themselves in for the night, but I'm sure there are still a few wandering around. I cast night vision on Orlaith too, and she keeps pace beside me as I jog cross-country toward the canal, her tail communicating her joy.

<Fun! New smells!>

It is quite different, isn't it? I say. There is mown grass or hay somewhere, and spices pepper the air, whispering of decadent homemade curries and perfumed incense. We hear strains of sawn strings groaning over the rhythm of tapped drum skins and ringing cymbals as we pass a house with its lights on and windows open. Someone sings along discordantly with the recorded voice, unconscious and untrained and clearly uncaring.

We finally see some people once we hit the canal road. Orlaith, being a very large creature moving at speed off a leash, frightens a few of them. We witness tiny squeals and cringes and hear sighs of relief when we pass.

<People afraid. Why? Good hound, right?>

You're the sweetest hound ever, but they don't know that and you surprised them. Don't worry about it. Just stay close to me.

<Best human. Love Granuaile.>

A few raindrops fall, and I realize we had better ask for directions sooner rather than later. My assumption that the temple must lie in the center of town might be false. I spy a couple walking and let Orlaith know that I want to slow down and talk to them.

They draw up short as they see us approach, and the man steps in front to protect his wife or sister. I don't speak Tamil or Hindi or any of the dozens of other languages spoken in India, so I hope they will recognize enough of my English to help.

"Brihadeeswara Temple?" I say, holding out my hands in a gesture of helplessness. It doesn't register, because their eyes are fixed on Orlaith.

Sit for a minute and look cute and harmless, I tell her, and she does. Then I repeat my question and the couple finally notices me standing there. It takes two more repetitions before the man raises his arm and points in the direction we were traveling, because now that he's noticed me, he's wondering if I'm a bigger threat than the hound.

Why, yes, good sir, I am.

I've noticed that men have difficulty maintaining eye contact or even speaking to me since I got my tattoos. The Celtic knotwork isn't anything like what they're used to seeing; they sense that it's not merely decorative, and the mystery discomfits them. I think they want to ask what the tattoos mean, but something keeps them silent. In this case, maybe it's the knives strapped to my thighs and the fighting staff in my hand.

We were headed the right way, Orlaith. Let's go.

I deliver a shallow bow to the man and say thank you before resuming our run. The rain starts to fall with urgency, fat drops hinting at a serious shower and guaranteeing that Orlaith and I will be soaked by the time we reach our destination. The street clears of its remaining few stragglers as people dive under roofs, leaving us to slice through the dark alone—a blessing, really, that allows us to travel faster.

After ten minutes or so, the tower of the temple looms out of the dark to our left, its surface lit by spotlights from below and sheets of rain glittering in the beams. We cross the canal at a bridge and arrive shortly thereafter to discover that the tower is part of a larger compound surrounded by a high wall. The entrance is a massive stone interruption in the wall, thirty feet high or more and doubly wide; its soaring arch provides shelter from the pour. It is crested with sculptures of the Vedic gods and their deeds and makes one feel small in comparison to such a monument. A solitary figure waits there—not underneath the arch but underneath an umbrella, wrapped in a sari. As I draw near I see that it is Laksha, or at least the body that Laksha currently occupies; I never know how to think of her. She changes bodies the way Atticus and I change IDs, but for now she still wears the body of Selai Chamkanni, which she had taken years ago, after she moved out of my head.

She flashes white teeth at me as I approach, and I smile in return. Atticus would probably think me too trusting of her, but I doubt he fully understands what is between us. Back in the days when I was bartending at Rúla Búla, Laksha could have killed me at any time—in fact, it would have been simpler for her—but she chose not to. I know my life is safe with her, because my death would have been more expedient. And I know, too, because of the fact that she lived in my head. That requires an enormous amount of trust, and it's a relationship very few people can grasp, Atticus included. He thinks she could change her mind at any time, and in theory I suppose that is true. I do understand why she is to be feared by others; her power is the easily abused kind, and in the past she did abuse it, and may do so again. But I also know that I personally have nothing to fear from her.

"Laksha," I say, moving close underneath the umbrella. "I'd hug you, but I'm soaked and you're still somewhat dry."

"Hug me anyway. I have come to admire this custom, and it's been too long." I do so but feel guilty for ruining her clothes, which always look so much more elegant than anything I ever wear. She has swaths of red and yellow fabric draped around her from shoulders to ankles, in dramatic sweeps that are simultaneously modest and profoundly sensual. Her ruby necklace, which acts as both a focus for her power and a place of refuge for her spirit, rests beneath her collarbone in plain sight, and I notice that she is wearing a ruby bindi between her eyes these days.

"You look good," I say, noticing a few deepening crinkles around the eyes that indicate she has aged. She notices that I haven't aged at all.

"My thanks. But I do not look as good as you. What do the Druids know that I don't?"

"How to make the right kind of tea. What happened to Idunn's golden apple?" Atticus had gone to great trouble to get her one; she was going to use the seeds to plant her own tree and have access to the eternal youth of the Norse gods.

"I have two different trees growing, but they have yet to bear fruit. I am hoping they will flower soon."

"You still have plenty of time."

"I know, but this body is not so athletic as it once was. I will need to find a new body if the apples don't come soon. The trees are magical and may take longer than normal to produce anything."

"I can brew Immortali-Tea if you want," I say. "Return your body to its twenties and give you more time to wait on the tree."

"You can? Mr. O'Sullivan taught you how to do this?"

"Yes. You'll need to set aside a block of time to get it done, because there are side effects, but it's not insanely difficult."

"Let us speak of it later, then. You are here for your father."

"Yes, where is he?"

"I do not know. I cannot divine his location. The raksoyuj possessing him has defenses."

Orlaith, who is unable to squeeze under the canopy of

the umbrella, shakes herself and sprays water in all directions. <Go inside now? Under roof?> She has an excellent point, and I pet her and shoot her a quick private apology.

"Might we be able to find someplace dry to talk more?" I ask Laksha.

"Of course. This was simply a convenient place to meet. You found it easily, yes?"

"Yeah, it's quite a landmark."

"Good. Follow me." Laksha begins to walk away from the entrance of the shrine, and I'm faintly disappointed that we won't get to talk inside. But then I remember that Atticus will come here looking for me.

"Wait," I say. "Can we leave a message somehow for Atticus? Tell him where to find us?"

She looks over her shoulder at me. "Mr. O'Sullivan will be coming?"

"Yes. I don't know when, precisely, but I'm sure he will get here eventually."

"You have not gone your separate ways?"

"Well, no, I never wanted that. I had a crush on him, if you remember, even before you told me he was a Druid. Turned out the feeling was mutual."

"I see." The rain falls uninterrupted by our voices as she digests this, the susurrus of the earth's business always continuing, heedless of human concerns. Then, "Can you not simply call him? Text him?"

"He's not on this plane right now."

"Surely he will call you when he returns?"

I grin and shake my head ruefully. "Nothing is sure with Atticus."

"There is no way to guarantee he will get any message at the shrine," Laksha says. "Is there no other way to contact him?"

"I'm not sure . . . Oh! Duh. Yes, there is. Hold on a moment." Looking down at my feet, I see that we are standing on a cobblestone path, but an expanse of grass waits a few yards away, flirting with the edges of the temple walls. "Let me talk to the elemental for a minute, and then we can go."

"I will wait here," Laksha says, and I nod my thanks and skip over to the grass. Orlaith follows, shaking herself again.

<What happens?> she asks.

I'm going to speak to the earth and then we can go someplace dry.

<Good plan! Talk fast?>

I will do my best.

Since I've never spoken to this elemental before, I feel a bit nervous about introducing myself without Atticus around. But I access my Latin headspace and speak through my binding to the earth: //Greetings / Harmony / New Druid visits//

The reply fills me with euphoria but also inspires some introspection. //Welcome / Fierce Druid / Harmony / Enjoy my lands//

I blink. Atticus told me that the elementals were calling me something like Fierce Druid, but I had yet to hear it—or feel it, I suppose—until now. Elementals don't use words, of course, but I could feel that the image or concept of "Druid" had been modified to imply ferocity when applied to me specifically. Did they know something about me that I didn't? Why wasn't I Nice Druid or Mellow Druid with a Lovely Singing Voice?

//Druid comes here soon// I say, using the unmodified concept that they employed for Atticus. //Must see him / Query: Tell him my location upon arrival?//

//Yes//

//Gratitude / Harmony / Query: What shall I call you?//

//Self is of the river humans name Kaveri//

I smile in recognition. Thanjavur was in the delta region of the Kaveri River. //I will call you Kaveri / Harmony//

After that detail is attended to, Laksha leads us through a maze of narrow streets to a modest dwelling about a half mile away from the temple. Thanjavur has trees and patches of unpaved earth scattered throughout, and there is a small vegetable garden in the front of Laksha's house, sufficient to serve as a place marker for Kaveri.

Once inside, Laksha fetches towels for us all and invites me to change into a robe while she throws my clothes into a dryer. That seems like an unnecessary delay to me.

"Won't we be leaving soon?"

"There is time enough to get dry." I give her my clothes, put on the robe, and get Orlaith toweled off to the point where she's just wet instead of dripping. Laksha makes me a cup of hot chai, then takes us to a room she calls her craft room—a polite term for witchcraft. There are circles on the floor, one of salt and another painted with what I fear might be dried blood. After cautioning to avoid the circles, Laksha guides us past them to a mahogany table on the far wall and lights a few candles. Shards of pottery with raised Sanskrit letters are arranged on the table, pieced next to one another to form lines of text. Orlaith puts her nose at the edge of the table and snuffles a couple of times.

<Smells bad,> she says, and then sits down.

"This vessel was unearthed not far from here," Laksha says, pointing at the shards. "Your father was drawn to a dig north of town, and these writings are what alarmed me so. They say, 'Keep sealed for all time. He who opens this prison will die, and rakshasas will plague the land.' Then there are some praises to Shiva at the end."

"That's it? Nothing about who or what was inside?"

Laksha shrugs. "It does not say, but we can make inferences. If he has power over rakshasas, then he must either be an *asura*—one of the higher-powered demons that rivaled the Vedic devas—or a raksoyuj. *Asuras* tend to take on their own physical form, while a raksoyuj must possess others. Your father is possessed, so a raksoyuj is the most likely—"

"Wait. Why must a raksoyuj possess others?"

Laksha looks uncomfortable at my question. "How much do you know of the Hindu cycle of birth and rebirth?"

"I guess just the basics: The body dies but the spirit doesn't. Spirits return in new bodies, and each one is trying to become pure enough to return to the source, right?"

"Precisely. And each lifetime will have few or no memories of past lives. These words suggest that the prisoner's original body is long gone but his spirit never moved on in the cycle. It was trapped in this container instead. He was trying to prolong this particular existence by possessing others."

I search her face for emotion and find none.

"Forgive me for saying so, but that sounds an awful lot like what you are doing."

"I know," she replies after a pause, her voice soft and haunted. "We are very similar. In this thing I see the end of a path I nearly walked. I am not sure the path I took is much better."

"All right. What's the difference between you and this raksoyuj?"

"I possess the body only. I have no traffic with the spirit. I push the occupying spirit out and take over— simply hijack the body. But he controls both the spirit and the body."

"Didn't you do that with me?"

"No, I shared space in your head and found unused pathways and corners of your brain to inhabit. I did not read your thoughts unless you wished to speak to me, and with rare exceptions, I only took control of your body with your permission. What he's doing is enslaving your father. He knows what your father knows, remembers what he remembers. In outward appearance your father will look the same. But his behavior is quite different now."

"What is he doing exactly? You said he's spreading pestilence."

"Yes, this is the end of the second day. The numbers of the ill are growing, and the hospitals are already strained. Doctors are confused, but people sense that the disease is unnatural. Earlier this afternoon—outside town—a woman was burned for being a witch."

She doesn't smile after she says that, though I wait for her to do so. When the silence lengthens, I prompt her. "You're kidding, right?"

"I am completely serious."

"Oh, gods. Was she a witch?"

"I do not think so. She was poor and unmarried and therefore a target. I dress like a wealthy married woman for a reason."

"That's terrible. Can't believe it happened today."

"It is easy for me to believe. Fear ignores the pace of modernity."

"How is he spreading the disease?"

"Do you know what a rakshasa is?"

"I have a general idea. It's a demon of some kind, isn't it?"

"It's not a demon in any Judeo-Christian sense. It is the rebirth of an especially wicked human into a sort of cursed half-life. They can shape-shift at will into almost anything organic that they wish—including noxious vapors. This is maya, the power of illusion. Your father is summoning rakshasas and commanding them specifically not to eat people or yank out their hearts or any number of other things but to cause this fast-moving disease that perplexes doctors. Hundreds have fallen ill in the past two days. Those who were infected first have now died. Tomorrow this will escalate and become international news, as hundreds turn to thousands."

"So we find him and then you can push the raksoyuj out, right, leaving my father intact?"

"If it were that simple, child, I would not have had to call you. I cannot exorcise the raksoyuj without killing your father in the process. And even if we were to sacrifice him for the greater good—which I'm not suggesting—the raksoyuj would simply possess another body, much as I would. Like me, it is a difficult thing to kill. It needs to be bound and contained again or else destroyed on the spiritual level."

"Can you do either of those things? Because I can't."

"I cannot bind him. I may be able to destroy him if conditions are right. We will need help."

"Whose?"

"We need a Shakti—a divine weapon—to counter this aggressive spirit."

The garden of sarcasm is watered with impatience, and mine chose that moment to bloom. "Are those on sale somewhere?"

"I do not mean a sword or a spear. I mean a devi. A goddess. I speak of Durga."

"Not sure how I can help, then. I don't have her email and she's not on Twitter."

"I will take care of contacting her. It's already begun." Before I can inquire what she means by that, she continues, "I was hoping you would have some method to find your father."

I think of asking Orlaith to pull a bloodhound act using the shards as a source, but she's a sight hound, and after the heavy rains my father's scent would be near impossible to follow anyway. "Has anyone tried to track him through his cell phone?"

"I pursued that early this morning through an acquaintance on the police force. His cell phone no longer transmits a signal. Perhaps you could ask the elemental to help?"

"That won't work, unfortunately," I explain. "Humans are just creatures bereft of identity to elementals—they're part of the ecosystem. They recognize individual Druids only because we're bound to them. Kaveri would have no way to distinguish my father from any other man in the area."

"Divination, perhaps?"

"I can try. I'm not very skilled at it. Atticus didn't dwell on it very much during my training, and I seriously doubt I would succeed where you had failed."

"I see. Might you have a way to heal those who are ill, then?"

"Perhaps. Would that help me find my father?"

"Quite possibly. If you expel the rakshasas, he may seek you out."

"Expel them?"

"Was I not clear? The illness is not viral or bacterial but a direct result of the rakshasas inside the victims. It is a supernatural cause, and medicine will have no effect. But your healing is magical and therefore may be of some use."

"So each victim has been invaded or inhabited by a rakshasa?"

"Correct. That is why your father is still somewhat limited."

"But there are already hundreds of victims, you said."

"Yes. He calls more rakshasas every day. Grows stronger every day."

"Gods, all those people. How long before you can get Durga involved?"

"I am practicing austerities and making offerings. When she will appear is of course up to her. But I am confident she will come. This raksoyuj is ruining dharma, and the devi will wish to restore balance."

"She'll show up in the middle of Thanjavur on a lion and she'll have extra arms and everything?"

"I imagine she would prefer to manifest out of sight of the general population. We should attempt to draw your father out to a rural area."

"Fine. Can we go now? Take me to someone sick on the edge of the city. I can't stand doing nothing."

Laksha nods. "Yes, we can go." She pats the folds of fabric draped over each hip and then gives an embarrassed smile at my raised eyebrows. "Still have my knives. It is a nervous thing—I always check before I go out, even though I know they are still there. I need a couple more things." She grabs sticks of incense and small jars of unguents and two miniature gongs with mallets, and all of those disappear into the folds of her sari. I begin to think she might have pocket dimensions in there.

My clothes aren't completely dry, but neither are they dripping wet. I shiver at the chill and resign myself to getting cold and wet again, bidding farewell to the robe as a brief interlude of warmth and comfort. Laksha gives me an extra umbrella and we step back into the rain, Orlaith trotting along beside us.

Laksha leads us in silence through the rain. Water pounds our umbrellas and sluices underneath our feet as we follow a sinuous path through the city. We continue on muddy trails along the ridges of rice paddies to a sad collection of hovels that struggle to live up to the name of *shelter* but completely own the word *ram-*

shackle. The people who live here work too hard for too little comfort.

Laksha knocks and a tired, worried woman opens the door, blessing us with a whiff of incense before the rain sweeps it down to the ground. Moans of pain arise from the darkness behind her, only a hint of candlelight ameliorating the gloom. Her eyes take in Laksha and they widen somewhat before she bows and clasps her hands and a stream of musical language bubbles forth from her lips. Laksha responds, gestures briefly to me, and then the woman opens the door wide and steps aside, inviting us to enter.

The modest living area stretches unbroken into the kitchen on the back wall. A battered couch that was once orange hunches against the wall to our left, hoping we won't notice it, and two doors to our right probably lead to a small bedroom and a smaller bathroom. The moans are coming from one of them.

I ask Orlaith to wait on the floor by the couch, and we follow the woman to the bedroom. A teenage boy writhes there on the sheets, his brow clammy and his breathing labored. Incense battles with the stench of illness, and the storm pounds the roof.

Laksha puts her hand to the boy's forehead, and he twitches. She holds it there for a few seconds and then moves her hand to the center of his bare chest, over his heart. Nodding, she glances at the rain-spattered window and withdraws. "The storm is good. It dampens the spirit like it would dampen mine. And the noise is annoying. We need to increase both the water and the noise."

"I understand how noise can be a nuisance, but what does the rain outside have to do with anything?" I ask.

"The rakshasa in this form," she says, pointing to the boy, "is a thing of the air—or, more properly, the ether. It drowns in water. We need to get him into a bath." She turns and speaks in Tamil to the woman—presumably the boy's mother—explaining what needs to be done. Together, we lift the poor thing out of bed and support him as we stagger into the bathroom. He's wearing a pair of shorts, and we just leave those on as we try to tumble him gently into the tub. He's so out of it, he can barely function.

Laksha kneels next to the tub and turns on the water. The boy jerks and then spasms intermittently, whimpers once, but his eyes don't open. The mother and I hover behind, and the helplessness I feel in this situation can be only a fraction of what she must be going through.

While the tub fills, Laksha begins to pull out all the items she stowed in her sari. She has the mother light incense and rests the miniature gongs and mallets on the side of the tub. Her voice rolls out of her in a chant as she removes the lid from a small jar with a sweet-smelling unguent in it—sweet, but so powerful and cloying that it makes me cough. Laksha dips a finger in the paste. While the water rises to cover the boy's abdomen, she writes on his forehead and continues to chant. That causes a convulsion and elicits a little cry of alarm from the mother. Laksha frowns, as if the boy's reaction disappoints her. Perhaps she had been expecting something more; regardless, she keeps chanting, then picks up one of the miniature gongs and indicates through gesture that the mother should do the same. They start to bang the crap out of them, and the din is enough to set my teeth on edge.

And that, of course, is the point. The noise, the smells, the rising water—all of it is supposed to force the rakshasa to leave the boy. But this particular rakshasa is strong and doesn't want to let go. Still, the clamor of gongs and chanting has its effect: The boy shudders, seizes up, and his eyes snap open, except the pupils have rolled up into his head and all we see are the whites. An inchoate roar surges out of his throat, and it's not merely the sound of a teenage meltdown. His arms, suddenly imbued with strength, grip the sides of the tub, and he attempts to get out. Laksha pushes him back down and flicks a glance at me, suggesting that keeping him in there is now my job. She has a gong to bang and chants to yell. She can't do it all.

<Granuaile all right? Very loud.>

I'm okay. Stay in there no matter what you hear.

<Okay.>

Stealing a glance at the mother as I kneel down and set Scáthmhaide aside, I see that she's crying. I would be too. And I remember that the thing that has my father is much worse than what has the boy. If we can't handle this rakshasa, how can we hope to prevail against the raksoyuj?

Keeping the boy in there is more challenging than I thought it would be. He fights me actively, and I get slapped as well as splashed. The water level is up to his chest now, and he doesn't like it at all. Laksha interrupts her chant to explain why he's suddenly so animated when he was such a dead fish before.

"The rakshasa was attacking his heart chakra and slowly divorcing him from life. We have forced it up into the head. It's now possessed the boy. It's here, at the sixth chakra," she says, pointing at the bindi placed just slightly above the spot between her eyebrows.

We couldn't very well submerge the boy up to that point. We had annoyed the rakshasa significantly, but it wasn't sufficient to drive it out.

"See what you can do to heal him now," Laksha says, but I am unsure how to proceed. I have not done much direct healing of others, and I am cut off from the earth here. Healing his symptoms would not cure him of the possession, in any case. Anything I did to help his body now would simply be undone by the rakshasa as soon as I stopped, and I would have to stop soon without an energy source. I have some stored in the silver end of Scáthmhaide, and I use that in an attempt to relieve him directly. His breathing clears up, but that's about all. He's still very much in the grip of the rakshasa. We need something more to address the possession, and I realize it is hanging from my neck. Cold iron is the antithesis of magic, and though Laksha might call it maya, what the rakshasa is doing is still magic, regardless of its flavor.

I remove my necklace and wrap the gold chain around my fist before slapping the cold iron amulet against the boy's forehead and holding it there. The reaction is immediate and terrifying.

His roar becomes a screech, and his hands lock around my wrist and try to pull it off, but this boy's weakened body is no match for me. His mother boils over with worry and she begins to scream behind me. Oily smoke belches out of his mouth, nose, and ears, forming a cloud above the boy's head, and this is what Laksha had been waiting for.

"Yes! It's leaving him! Once it's all out, thrust the iron into the middle of the cloud!"

My amulet is not made of an overwhelming amount of iron. I can cast around it, after all, though it always requires extra energy. I've tried casting with the amulet off, and it's far more efficient to do it that way. It's undeniably a damper on magic, and combined with the noise and smells and the water, it's enough to break the rakshasa's hold.

The cloud of greasy vapor slithers above me—toward the mother, who's blocking the exit and making all kinds of noise—and once it stops billowing from the boy and he slumps back into the bath, Laksha urges me to move. Rising to my feet, I thrust the cold iron into the cloud, and it reacts with a sort of jellyfish ripple, then it curls in on itself, like a spider in water, cold tendrils of it closing around my fist. Abruptly, it gushes toward the floor in front of the toilet—directly to my right—and the vapor solidifies from the ground up into a humanoid form sheathed in black. Then the face appears—a nightmare made flesh, with bloodshot eyes and an obscene red tongue lolling over a gaping maw of sharp teeth. It is the rakshasa's true form, a portrait of corruption like Dorian Gray, temporarily robbed of its ability to shift or cast illusion by cold iron.

Instinctively, I draw back, but there's hardly any room to maneuver—the tub is directly behind me. The rakshasa lunges for my face, but a flash of steel darts between us and slides across skin that is quite solid and real, opening a slit that splashes blood onto the floor. The demon clutches its throat and turns those horrible eyes to my left in time to see Laksha drive her knife blade into one of them. It topples backward, its knees buckled by the toilet, and dies, gurgling, in a sitting position—an image that I file under THINGS I NEVER WOULD HAVE SEEN IF I HAD KEPT BARTENDING.

The boy regains consciousness with a gasp and asks for his mother. She rushes to him in relief and shields his view of the room; with an exchange of gestures, Laksha and I silently agree to remove the body. I put my necklace back on but realize I'll have to leave my staff here for the moment. As we enter the living room, cradling the corpse, it occurs to me that we might be violating some kind of taboo—we may have made ourselves untouchable. I'm not an expert on the caste system or to what extent it's observed anymore, so I ask Laksha about it.

"Is it all right for us to handle the dead? I mean, are we tainting ourselves somehow in the eyes of others?"

"I think she will overlook it," Laksha replies, tossing her head back to indicate the mother. "And no one else will see. Which is vital. The sight of a real rakshasa will cause panic and draw the attention of the authorities."

Seeing that we are headed for the door, Orlaith gets up and moves out of the way. *You're a good hound,* I tell her. Aloud, I ask Laksha the all-important question.

"What are we going to do with him? It's still raining."

"That's a blessing. Everyone is indoors."

"There's no convenient burial ground."

"He should be burned far away from here, but that's not an option. We will choose a place where no one will try to grow anything."

That place is a well-worn path between houses, a sort of alley, now a muddy trench. I contact the elemental Kaveri and ask her help in burying the rakshasa's body, explaining that we might be doing this sort of thing all night to help people. She parts the mud for us far more quickly than I could do it myself, and we drop the dark corpse of the demon into the resulting grave. The mud flows back over him and the problem is solved—no witnesses.

Orlaith, who had followed us out of the house, is struck with the procedure's practical application for dogs. <So fast! Bury bones like that?>

Your paws do the job admirably on their own, I tell her.

"One down," Laksha says. "Now that we know what works, perhaps we can do the next one a bit quicker. It won't be long until we draw your father out. And in the meantime we are saving people. This is good karma."

A tight smile on Laksha's face suggests that the last point is perhaps the most important to her. I cannot blame her for wishing to do others well, but I do wish there was a quicker way to find my dad.

"What did you use as a focus when you tried to divine his presence?" I ask her.

"The shards of the canister that held the raksoyuj. It was the object he most recently touched."

"Ah, but that wasn't really his. It was a thing of the raksoyuj. Might a different object be more effective, one that was more closely tied to him?"

"It might," Laksha agrees. "Do you have such an item with you?"

"No," I say, "but I might be able to get one. Let me think about it."

Laksha darts into the house to retrieve what I suppose must be called her exorcism kit, along with my staff, and to offer a hurried farewell to the family. I squat down next to my wet hound and scratch behind her ears, trying to think of something that might hold a stronger psychic signature of my dad than the shattered remains of that clay vessel.

When I was growing up, he'd send me little trinkets and cards for my birthday and Christmas from wherever he was, and I'd go into my room and open them in private and cry because he was always so sweet and loving, albeit from a distance; to me, that was infinitely preferable to the coldness of my stepfather up close. He continued doing this even into my adulthood, never forgetting me, always letting me know that he was thinking of me and that he loved me. From a distance.

I still had some of his gifts back at the cabin, but the most recent one was more than twelve years old now. The gifts had stopped coming, of course, when I'd faked my death to disappear and begin my apprenticeship in secret. Would any of them have a psychic signature strong enough for Laksha to find, when so much time had passed and he was possessed by something with its own magical defenses? Emotionally I wanted the answer to be yes, but rationally I could not imagine that the odds would be good. Laksha's approach of killing rakshasas to lure the raksoyuj would probably work better. And it would keep me busy while I worried.

When Laksha reappears with Scáthmhaide, she asks if I've thought of anything useful.

"No," I say, shaking my head. "Let's go play exorcist."

CHAPTER 5

I have noticed over many centuries of relationships that a corollary to love is worry. They sort of come together as a matched set, and it's nigh impossible to ditch one without the other. I don't mean worry in the sense of a constant hand-wringing or an outward show of anxiety but a silent panic, always there but flaring up on occasion until one chokes and cannot see through a sudden veil of tears, panic that what you cherish most will be scarred or lost or taken away forever.

I worry about Granuaile a lot.

That's not to suggest I lack confidence in her abilities. She can handle most anything. But Laksha Kulasekaran is one of the few things she might not see coming in time to defend herself. I'm sure Granuaile thinks Laksha would never hurt her. I used to think that way about Leif Helgarson too, right up until he betrayed me.

At their cores, Leif and Laksha are the same: They must prey on humans to ensure their continued existence. They are predators, and we mustn't forget that.

When we shifted to a banana grove near Thanjavur, Oberon passed judgment without much deliberation.

<Wauugh! So this is what meatless air smells like? I don't like it!>

Oh, come on, it's not that bad. I thought the air was pretty clean, due to what had obviously been a good shower overnight. The ground was soft and I could see standing water in places below. The morning sun banked off the surfaces and glinted in my eyes.

<You think I'm being a drama hound, don't you?>

Maybe a little. We have to find Granuaile and Orlaith, and meatless air isn't registering high on my threat dial. The temple is a couple miles away, so let's go, and stay close, okay?

<Okay,> Oberon said, loping along beside me as I descended from the grove, <but how far do you think it is to the nearest sausage? I ask merely to gauge the depth of my peril.>

I imagine you would have to travel many miles.

<Miles to go before—hey! That was in that Tarantino movie, right?>

Which one?

<*Death Proof!* The deejay was talking to Butterfly, and she said, "And I have promises to keep, and miles to go before I eat.">

Ha! No, Oberon, it was "miles to go before I sleep," and the movie was actually quoting a poem by Robert Frost.

<Well, Robert Frost was obviously not writing for hounds. "Miles to go before I eat" is much more edgy.>

The Brihadeeswara Temple was built in 1010 by the Chola emperor, and I figured it hadn't moved very far since then. But when I checked in with the elemental Kaveri, just to let her know I was visiting, she responded with the news that she knew precisely where Granuaile was and she would lead me to her. Going to the temple was no longer necessary.

A tightness in my chest relaxed with the confirmation that Granuaile was still alive. We found them to the south of the city in the rural farming district, walking wearily along a ridge bordering a rice paddy. Oberon and Orlaith said hello to each other and began to play.

"Thank you for coming," Granuaile said, giving me a quick hug. I think both of us would have shown more emotion had we been alone—well, I know *I* would have. Laksha was capable of truly frightening magic besides her already-creepy body-snatching, and Granuaile wasn't protected from it as I was, so myriad worst-possible scenarios had run rampant through my mind, like kobolds in a mine shaft. What I wanted was to squeeze Granuaile close and say how glad I was to see her, but instead I gave a tight nod to Laksha, which she returned, and then replied to Granuaile as if I'd never been worried.

"Of course. You look wiped out. What happened?"

"We've been working all night, exorcising these demons in an attempt to lure my father out of hiding. So far it hasn't worked, and we are exhausted. We decided to take a break and continue after we're rested."

"Good plan. Catch me up; I'll walk with you." The hounds trotted behind us, making happy growling noises and nipping at each other.

Granuaile recounted their night and explained their exorcism process to me, and I asked for clarification on one point. "Why is water effective again?"

"The rakshasas are of the ether, and their powers are drowned in it."

Something about this was familiar. "But they have to be submerged for this to work, or would taking a shower be sufficient?"

Granuaile looked to Laksha for help, and the witch supplied the answer.

"The rakshasas are attacking the heart chakra, so they must be submerged, preferably up to the neck."

"But telling everyone to take a bath wouldn't solve the problem."

"No. The rakshasa would merely move to the head until the victim got out of the tub—and that's more for comfort than necessity. Surrounding it with water cuts off its access to the ether but doesn't kill it. It is the same as when you are cut off from the earth."

"Oh, okay," Granuaile said, nodding her understanding, and I did the same. Those were terms we could understand.

"In other words, the water wasn't affecting them once they moved to the heads of the victims?" I asked by way of confirmation. "They had access to the ether, and so it was the noise, the smells, the chanting, and the cold iron that drove them out?"

"Precisely," Laksha said. "But it was a close thing."

"Right. So that's not going to be enough when you find her father. Anything that can summon and control the rakshasas down to the method of how they kill their victims is going to require something more than what you've managed so far. Is the raksoyuj also a thing of ether?"

"Yes. Even more so. It cannot take its own physical form, like the rakshasas it summons, but rather must possess a body."

"In theory, then, water magic would harm it?"

"What are you thinking?" Granuaile asked. "Involving Manannan Mac Lir?"

"Indirectly, yes. Well, maybe. Laksha, let us say that I know of a weapon made of ice that will not melt and that holds an edge like steel. It is made of water and bound by water magic. Would such a weapon harm the raksoyuj—say, if applied to the proper chakra?"

The witch's eyebrows climbed up her forehead. "Such a weapon exists?"

"Yes. Five of them, maybe more."

"You never told me Manannan had something like that," Granuaile said.

"He doesn't. Gaia lets him draw energy from the water, but his magic is still of the earth." I addressed

Laksha. "And I should probably confirm: As far as affecting the raksoyuj goes—and I'm asking because you are more familiar than I am with them—this would be different from getting stabbed with an icicle, right? Or anything that I bound together with the power of the earth? Because I can smoosh ice together into whatever shape I want, and so can any other Druid, but I can't make it hold an edge and I can't prevent it from melting. That's a different kind of juju from mine."

"Yes, I think you are right," Laksha said. "If these weapons are truly forged with magic born of water, strikes to the fourth and sixth chakras—the heart and the third eye—should break its hold. It would be forced to leave the host."

Granuaile raised her hand. "I have a problem with this plan to stab my father in the head and the heart."

"No, no," Laksha said, a rare smile blooming on her face. "We are merely severing the ties, fouling the chakra points with water magic so that the raksoyuj cannot hold on. Breaking the skin will be sufficient. You will have to draw blood and he may scar, but he will heal, and he will not be able to be possessed again."

"Then what happens?" Granuaile asked. "I mean, after the ties are severed?"

"The raksoyuj will be forced to leave your father, and it will try to possess someone else—but I will not allow this. I will fight him in the ether and I will win."

That was bold, but Granuaile asked what I was thinking.

"How do you know you'll win?"

"I have been doing this for quite some time now. He has never had to fight out of body, but I have."

I didn't think that necessarily guaranteed a win, but I kept my mouth shut. I also tried to conceal my elation over the fact that Laksha was teaching me how to defeat her, should it ever become necessary. She was a creature of the ether too.

Granuaile decided to let Laksha's assertion pass without comment and asked me, "So where do we get these five ice knives?"

"I doubt you'll be able to get more than one. You need to go to the Himalayas and ask a yeti."

Oberon broke off his play with Orlaith to interject, <That sounds like a game show! ASK A YETI! My first question is, "Can you thaw a steak or only freeze it?">

"You're being serious?" Granuaile asked. "Because you told me the bigfoot thing was one of your shenanigans."

"Yes, Sasquatch is dead, if he was ever real to begin with. But yeti have been around for about twelve hundred years now, and they speak Old Irish."

"What? How is that possible?"

"Not a word of this to anyone else, okay?" I held up a finger. "I need an oath from both of you."

"Wait," Granuaile said. "Before you say anything, did you make a similar oath?"

"Fudge. Yes. Yes, I did. But I think he'll grant me an exception in your case. It shouldn't take long. Wait here?"

"We will wait in my home," Laksha said. "We are tired and need to eat."

<You'd better tell Orlaith there won't be any meat for breakfast.>

"Ask Kaveri to direct you to the house when you get back," Granuaile said. "And hurry. If I have to go to the Himalayas and back to beat this thing, I want to get started."

"I'll hurry," I promised, and together with Oberon I jogged to the banana grove and shifted planes to the tree nearest to Manannan Mac Lir's estate in Tír na nÓg. We were fortunate enough to catch Manannan as he was walking from his hog pens back to the house. A mild look of concern settled like weights on his expression when we flagged him down.

"Siodhachan. Well met, I hope."

"Well met, Manannan Mac Lir. I must speak with you in private. Could you shroud us from ears and eyes?"

The mild look of concern deepened into worry, but he spoke the binding that provided us with a small bubble of soundproof air and shook out his Cloak of Mists to hide us from lip-readers. His estate was infested with faeries who lacked discretion at best and were outright spies at worst.

"I come to ask you to grant an exception to my oath. I need to tell Granuaile the true story of the yeti." He listened in silence as I explained why Granuaile needed a yeti ice knife, and he gave me permission to tell her and Laksha, provided they took the same oath of secrecy.

"You're going to need something. Come with me." He led us back behind his hog pens, where there was a butcher shop, and on the way told me the quickest way to get to the yeti. He wrapped up a few pounds of the miraculous bacon of youth in brown paper and handed it to me. "They'll be expecting that." He gave Oberon a ham bone with plenty of meat on it and another for Orlaith. My hound could barely contain his excitement.

<Oh, she's going to be so surprised! No soy burgers for her, no way!>

When we shifted back to India after saying our farewells, I listened to my paranoia and paused by the tree, waiting to see if anyone had followed us. A flying pixie with yellow wings shifted in after a minute and flew right into my chest. She rebounded, and her face had time to register her death before she crumbled to ash, destroyed by my cold iron aura.

"Damn. I wanted to question her first."

\<Works for me. I can give the gift of ham that much sooner. Come on, let's go!\>

I smiled at my hound. *All right, off we go.* Kaveri directed us to a modest house in the city, with a vegetable garden in the front yard, and I did my best to quash my worries on the jog there. It was a gorgeous morning, and Oberon quite properly observed that it would be a shame not to notice how good we had it right then.

\<Look, Atticus, we have food and sun and each other, and soon we will be with pretty girls who like us. I hope you're paying attention. You shouldn't be missing this.\>

You're right, Oberon, I shouldn't.

\<I think life is like a ham bone if you live it right. You enjoy it and then you bury it when you're finished. If you don't enjoy it and you let it go to waste, you still have to bury it, so you might as well savor everything you can.\>

That's truth.

Laksha answered the door when I knocked, and she invited us in.

\<Will you have Clever Girl tell Orlaith I brought her this food?\> He had both ham bones in his mouth, with the meaty parts hanging out to the sides.

Of course. I relayed the message and Orlaith came over, tail wagging, and barked a greeting. She opened her mouth and grabbed on to the one on Oberon's left. He let it go and she set it down on the floor briefly, then delivered a couple of licks to the side of his muzzle. He was so excited about this that he dropped his bone and barked.

\<Atticus, she kissed me! Did you see that? She loves me!\>

Yeah, I saw it, buddy, but I'm not sure you can conclude—

\<Hail Oberon, Lord of All Meats! I am the sausage in

the morning and the bone at night! I am the bringer of beef and the singer of sweet suppertime! Mine is the chicken and the gravy forever, nom nom!>

Oberon, I think your ego is getting the best of you here.

<Don't hate the Meat Lord, Atticus. Just offer him steak sauce and words of praise.>

The two of them lay down side by side on the floor, blocking the door, and began to gnaw away, their tails wagging and slapping against each other in a joyous duel. I left the hounds to their meal and joined Laksha and Granuaile at the round kitchen table. Laksha announced that we were having fruit for breakfast. There were three lit candles in the center of a flat round platter, flickering and offering whiffs of vanilla and spice, and arranged around them were small bowls of sliced melons, bananas, and berries, each with its own set of tiny tongs. A pitcher of cream, presumably representing the fruit of a cow, waited to be poured on top of whatever medley we chose to assemble for ourselves. I went for blackberries and honeydew and thanked Laksha for her hospitality, then had them swear not to repeat the secret origin of the yeti to anyone. That chore completed, I began.

"I'll try to keep it short, since time is probably a factor here. Granuaile, I think you know that Manannan Mac Lir has had some commerce with the Norse pantheon in the past. You remember that map of the nine realms I showed you, given to him by the Álfar?"

She nodded but said nothing, her mouth full of strawberries and cream.

"Good. I bring it up because, about twelve hundred years ago, while I was still roaming the world and tethering it to Tír na nÓg, Manannan was going well beyond commerce and was enjoying sexcapades in Jötunheim."

Granuaile spoke out of the side of her mouth. "He cheated on Fand?"

"He did and continues to do so. And the same holds true for Fand. She had a rather famous dalliance with Cu Chúlainn once."

She held up a finger while she swallowed, then said, "They have an open marriage, then?"

"Not really. They try to keep their liaisons secret for as long as possible and likewise try to discover what the other one is up to. Both of them are now excellent at hiding things and finding them out."

"Ah, but Fand never found out about this thing in Jötunheim, right?"

"Right. And Manannan wants to keep it that way."

"Wait—I'm just catching on to the implications here. Does that mean Manannan Mac Lir did it with a frost giant?"

"It does. Somebody probably said *graah*." I shuddered, remembering a horrific tableau I had the misfortune to witness in Jötunheim. "And the giantess in question became pregnant."

Granuaile froze, a spoonful of blueberries halfway to her mouth. "No way!"

"Way. She had to leave Jötunheim, because the frost giants would kill anything that wasn't strictly a frost giant. And she couldn't stay in Tír na nÓg, because Fand would eventually find out. So they had the giantess come to term in the Himalayas, far away from the Norse and the Irish, and you can probably guess the rest."

"I can't believe this. You're saying the yeti are essentially Fae?"

"They're Fae in the sense that they're magically gifted and represent a hybrid of human and something else, but they're not vulnerable to iron. And the rest of the Fae don't know about them. She had quintuplets, and they were born with white fur and pale blue skin. When they grew up, they could do any damn thing they wanted with snow and ice."

"What happened to her?"

"At first she remained in the Himalayas with the yeti. Manannan visited as often as he could, and he had a trusted faery visit in his stead when he could not. Eventually, however, the faery turned out to be not so trustworthy. Once the yeti were fully grown, the frost giantess wanted out of the Himalayas. Returning to Jötunheim was out of the question. But the faery, who had become smitten and was quite eager to please her, pointed out that there were other cold places on the earth. She ran away with the faery to Manitoba, near the northern shores of Lake Winnipeg, using a tether I had made there."

"How do you know this?"

"They appeared in front of me almost as soon as I had completed it! The faery had shifted her from the Himalayas to the newest of the New World. Since Manannan had been the one to start me on the tethering project in the first place, I reported it to him."

"Oh, my gods, deity drama! What did he do?"

"He let them go, since they clearly had no plans to speak to Fand and he figured the giantess deserved what happiness she could find. He told me who they were, told me about the yeti, and swore me to the oath of silence. And my guess is that the runaway couple eventually had some Fae spawn of their own up there in the frozen north. Bit scarier than the yeti, though. I'll give you one guess."

Her eyes widened. "No—not the wendigo?"

"Aye."

Granuaile finally remembered that she had at one point been eating, but now she was too excited to continue. She dropped the spoonful of blueberries that she'd been holding in midair back into her bowl. "Holy shit. What happened to the yeti?"

"They're still there. Manannan has kept them eternally youthful with periodic shipments of his fine swine products—and they're due for another. You're going to deliver this bacon to them and get their attention that way."

"There are still five of them?"

"Yes. Aside from the fact that they're siblings and wouldn't want to go there, they can't reproduce. They're like mules. Luckily, their low numbers are keeping them safe. Scientists all say there can't possibly be a reproducing population of yeti in the Himalayas, and of course they're right about that. But the yeti are still there."

"So the frost giants don't know about them, and the Fae don't know either."

"Both groups may have heard of the yeti by now, but if so, they probably think they're just legends and don't know their origins."

"And the yeti speak Old Irish."

"Manannan taught them. Their mother taught them Old Norse when they were young, but they've had only Manannan to speak to since then, and it's been a long time."

Granuaile put her hands up to the sides of her head and then popped them away as she made an explosive puffing sound. "Pfff! Mind. Blown." She leaned forward and crossed her arms in front of her, flat on the table. "Have you been keeping other secrets like this?"

"Yes. But I can't tell you or they won't be secret."

"Sharing is caring."

"Unlike most American voters, I have built up an immunity to rhyming slogans."

She smiled. "Fine. We will table the secrets for later. What I want to know is why you aren't coming with me. Because I've inferred from your speech that you aren't."

"Oh. Well, remember the old man from the island?"

"Yeah, I meant to ask. Is he all right?"

"Yes. He's a Druid and he can fix my tattoos."

"A Druid, eh? The plot thickens. You didn't want me to meet him earlier."

"I still don't. He'd pick a fight with you inside five minutes."

"How do you know that?"

I'd kept the secret of his identity from her up till then but figured there was no use keeping it any longer. "Because he's my archdruid."

"Seriously?"

"Yep. Ornery through and through. His name's Owen Kennedy. I promise I'll introduce you later. The thing is, I feel responsible for him right now and I also feel kind of disabled without the ability to shape-shift. I thought that he could fix me up, since you're busy now, and I could also maybe smooth away some of his rough edges before you two meet. Would that be okay?"

"Oh. Well." Granuaile leaned back and considered. "I suppose it would, because I'm not sure what else you could do that I'm not already doing. But I don't know how to find the yeti."

"Take the bacon. They'll smell it. And look around in the magical spectrum. They use snow and ice to hide everything, including themselves, but it's magic and you'll spot it. Make sure to tell 'em their dad says hi." I gave her the directions Manannan had given me and wished her luck. "I'll check back at the cabin when I've finished."

"Okay, I'll leave messages there if I need to."

We turned as one to look at Laksha, who had remained silent through all this—and who also hadn't eaten anything. "I will do what good I can while you are gone and try to minimize the damage," she said. "And perhaps I will find your father. I will give you a key to this house and leave notes here for you when I am out."

Granuaile said, "Thanks." Her eyes flicked down and noticed the blank space in front of Laksha. "You're not eating because this is part of summoning Durga?"

"Yes. Austerities, ritual, and prayer will help to draw her attention."

We had little else to say once the decision was made. Oberon was reluctant to leave Orlaith and I didn't want to leave Granuaile, but in truth I was much relieved regarding Laksha's current intentions, and Owen needed a shepherd at the moment. Even though I hadn't yet been gone two hours, it was still more than the quick trip I'd promised him, and I hoped I hadn't already drained my well of goodwill with Sam and Ty by saddling them with a man who put the tank in cantankerous.

Granuaile and I parted, both worried but hopeful about the challenges ahead of us. My concerns about my archdruid proved to be well founded, unfortunately. Once I'd shifted from early-morning Thanjavur to early-evening Flagstaff, I heard growls and bellows and cheers a bit deeper in the woods north of Sam Obrist's house. Casting night vision and following the noise, I discovered a ring of men and women in a circle, egging on two combatants in the middle. One was a werewolf, and the other was Owen in his bear form. Both of them were bloody.

Sam Obrist was in the ring of onlookers, and my guess was that this was the entirety of the Flagstaff Pack. I didn't know what Owen had done or said to incur their wrath, but I couldn't let him get torn apart without an explanation.

Oberon, we need to break this up. We can't let the bear get killed.

<I'm on the bear's side? That's a new one.>

The bear is Owen. Just bust in there with me and look threatening; get the werewolf to back off but try not to engage it seriously.

I began to run toward the circle, drawing power to leap over it and into the center. <I don't get what you mean. You want me to engage a werewolf in combat jokingly?>

No, just—don't engage, but growl a lot.

<Okay.>

Using some of the energy I'd drawn, I vaulted over the crowd and into the ring, where the bear was circling to keep the werewolf in front of him and the werewolf was trying to flank and leap up onto the bear's back. A few onlookers tried to shout warnings, but they weren't in time. I delivered a kick to the rear left leg of the werewolf, hard enough to wipe him out and spin him out of range of the bear's claws.

"That's it! It's over!" I yelled, and I got defiant roars from all directions, including that of the bear. Oberon nosed his way through the crowd and planted himself by my side, snarling at the werewolf as he rose to his feet and showed us his teeth.

"Damn it! Ty, stop!" Sam shouted, but the werewolf—presumably Sam's husband, Ty—either didn't hear or pretended not to. He gathered himself to leap at me, and that was way more threat than Oberon was going to allow. Oberon threw himself at the wolf as he jumped at me, and when they collided and fell to the ground, I dog-piled onto the werewolf's back, wrapped my hands underneath his front legs, and gave him a hug.

Hugs are not normally part of my martial arts. However, in this case, it brought my silver charms into contact with the back of the werewolf's neck, and the pain of that caused him to howl and rear back from Oberon, which was precisely what I wanted. Locking my arms across his chest, I stood up, yanking the werewolf away from Oberon and telling my hound to *Let him go,* then forced the struggling creature to turn and face his alpha. I released him, giving him a less-than-gentle shove in the proper direction. The general tenor of the noise around me changed from jeers to angry shouting when they smelled the silver burn and saw the mark on the werewolf's neck fur. Everybody's back was up and they were making a lot of noise, but Sam restrained Ty from charging again, and that meant the fight was over. I tasted victory for maybe two seconds, long enough to ask Oberon if he was okay and for him to answer in the affirmative. And then my archdruid informed me that I had cocked everything up again.

"Is this how it's going to be from now on, Siodhachan?" he said in Old Irish, his tone querulous in my ear. He'd shape-shifted back to human and now stood with his hands on his hips, naked and bleeding from multiple scratches. "Every time I try to have a little fun, you're going to come along and ruin it?"

"Fun?" I said. I pointed at the werewolf. "He was trying to kill you."

"No, he wasn't. We were having a friendly match until you showed up. We can both take a lot of punishment and heal from it, and we agreed to leave throats, spines, and balls alone. And we did all that without you here to interpret for me. I think ye owe us all an apology."

I could have pointed out that my intention was to save his crotchety ass and there had been hardly any time to ask politely if he was in true danger, and erring on the side of his safety was actually a much wiser course of action at that particular crisis point, but there was no way that I would come out looking good by pursuing that argument. My best option was to admit that I had screwed up and beg forgiveness.

"I'm sorry," I said to Sam. "I misunderstood what was going on here and thought it was a death match instead of a friendly fight."

"We're a pack, Atticus," Sam replied. "If it had been a death match, he would have been facing the entire pack, not just one of us."

"Fair enough. Again, I apologize. I acted without knowing what was going on. If there's a way I can make it up to you, I will."

The forest grew quiet as everyone looked to Sam to see how he would respond. "Apology accepted." The tension visibly leaked out of the pack's shoulders at those words. "You didn't break the skin, and Ty will heal. Let Owen come back and play with us some other time and we'll call it square. It's hard to find good sparring partners."

"Easy enough. He's free to do as he wishes, honestly. I just have to teach him the language and he'll be fine. Do you have everything you need to send to Hal Hauk?"

"Yes, it's already done, already sent. You can pick up his ID in a week to ten days."

"Thank you. We'll be going, then." I turned to Owen and asked him where his clothes were.

"They're around here somewhere, waiting for you to apologize."

"I did."

"Not to me."

No one could exasperate me like he could. Drawing on my dwindling reserves of patience, I repeated my apology to him in Old Irish and said it was time to leave. He dawdled and delayed, but eventually he was dressed, his scratches were closed up, and we skipped around the world to the French Pyrenees, where he would restore my ability to shape-shift.

CHAPTER 6

Siodhachan says it's great to have a name like Owen Kennedy in this modern world. A Kennedy was President of the United States not so long ago, which I guess means he was fecking important. I should be proud that someone of my family name rose to be a great leader.

"Of course," says he, "John Kennedy was a Catholic. And Catholics were the ones who drove the Druids out of Ireland."

"Stab me in the tit, why don't you," I says.

But then Siodhachan says this JFK was a good sort as far as leaders go. All the Kennedys were while they lasted.

"While they lasted?" I says.

"John was shot to death, and so was his brother. They never caught the bastards who did it."

"Well, now you're just throwin' rocks at me stones," I says.

"Life must be a kick in the head for you right now," he replies, and he's not far off. It's more like a bucket of cold water every few seconds. The cars and the buildings and what the hell people wear on their feet these days. And fecking plumbing! Siodhachan introduced me to that modern miracle *after* he took me to the woods to drink his thrice-damned tea. I never would have thought that taking a dump could be a luxury instead of gambling with your arse every day. And when I asks him why he didn't let me use one of those toilet things to begin with, he says it's because everyone knows that a bear shits in the woods, and then he laughs like he's fecking funny. I don't know what my bear form had to do with it, but I told him a bear kicks arse in the woods too, and he'd be finding out personally if he messed with me any more.

"You should write all of this down," he says. "It will help you learn the language faster and process everything."

"Druids don't need to write anything down," says I.

"And how did that work out for us?" he says. "The Romans were able to wipe us off the earth and we never got to tell our side of it to history. Most of your time—most of my youth—it's all gone because no one wrote it down. All the world knows is based on what someone dug up out of the earth, and rocks with a few scratches of Ogham script on them marking land boundaries tell the world very little about how things really were. But the world knows about Julius Caesar and all the Caesars that followed, because they wrote everything down and it survived. We need to write if we want the world to know about us. I'll do it with you. We'll write together."

He has a point. He's still an enormous cock-up, mind, but I have to admit that Siodhachan has the occasional moment of competence. If I ignore the embarrassing side effects, that tea of his did me more good than a week of sex in a cave. I have all me dark hair and muscles again, and the ache in me knuckles is gone like he promised. And protecting himself with that cold iron aura so the Fae can't touch him—that was a clever idea.

I suppose, when I see such things, that he's done me proud. But he's also done some other things so stupid that if all the other Druids weren't already dead I'd have to kill them before they blamed me for it.

I'm told this language is English, which wasn't around in my day. Kind of a great soup of a tongue, with influences from all over Europe. He's teaching me to speak it with a modern Irish accent and spell words according to British rules. "The Americans adopted a bunch of nonsense, thanks to a bloke named Noah Webster," he says. "And, besides, the Americans don't swear as much as the Irish do, so having an Irish accent is the best fit for you all around."

"And I suppose ye think I should get an Irish wolfhound like you?"

"Can't go wrong with a hound. I know a good breeder."

"I say balls to that, lad. You get a hound and people always want to pet them. I'm going to get a monkey and let it throw shite at people. They'll clear the feck out of me way right quick."

I didn't really say that. I didn't know what a monkey was until one threw shite at me a couple of days ago, and now that I'm remembering this conversation and writing it down after the fact, I wished I'd known about them in time to be clever.

Instead, I told Siodhachan I wasn't ready for an animal companion yet. I had so much to learn right then that I'd be a poor friend to it, and I never was one to form such relationships anyway. I suppose I'm ornery. Siodhachan tells me that's the English word for my character. Or my disposition. Or some other big fecking word for the same thing. English is full of words like that.

And it's full of fancy words for the ache in your knuckles and every other pain ye might have. Siodhachan warns me that I have to watch my health and heal infections in the blood as soon as they appear. Tells me I've never been vaccinated and I don't have any anti-bodies or immunoresistance to modern disease and I'll be dead shortly if I don't monitor myself closely and break down infections. All those big words require lengthy explanations, and eventually I cut him off when he gets to modern drugs people take with side effects worse than the problem they're supposed to fix.

"Ye could have stopped at 'watch your health, nasty diseases around here,'" I says.

Siodhachan has taken me to some place in Gaul—which they call France now—to touch up his tattoos. Says manticore venom is evil brew, and he isn't lying. His skin is a mess even after he's had time to heal, and I've never seen a wound like it.

"It's the strongest poison I've ever encountered," says he, "and I'm not sure I even got a full dose, because I removed the thorn before it was finished pumping the toxin into me."

"So where did you run into the manticore?" I asks him. "Because we'd heard about them and how to tame them from Druids on the continent—they were sup-posed to be monsters from the east somewhere—but none of them ever showed up in Ireland."

And he says, "You probably won't believe me. It was in Tír na nÓg, in the home of Midhir, where it was chained up and waiting for me. One of the Tuatha Dé Danann put it there. And I figure it was the same mem-ber of the Tuatha Dé Danann that strung up Midhir in iron chains and cut his throat so that he'd bleed out, separated from the earth."

"Gods below, lad, that's a terrible way to go. Who would do such a thing?"

"That's what I can't figure out. Someone is playing me for a fool, but I don't know who. They didn't just kill Midhir at Brí Léith, but they conspired against me with the Fae, a good number of vampires and dark elves, and the Roman gods as well. I bet they told Loki where to find me a few times and sent those Fir Darrigs after us too. And it's not only me they're fooling. They're also keeping it secret from all the rest of the Tuatha Dé Danann. Either that or they're all in on it, but I seriously doubt that."

"What have ye been *doing* for two thousand years to make someone hate ye so bad?" I says.

"Hiding out, mostly. I could use your help figuring out who's after me. You'd bring a fresh perspective to the problem. And by spending time in Tír na nÓg, you wouldn't have to deal with all the shocks of modernity right away."

It's taken me a while to figure out what to call Siodhachan in this new language, but I think I have it figured out: He's a bullshit salesman. You'll walk away thinking you got something for free, but Siodhachan's a buy-now-and-pay-later sort, and the coin you pay for buying his bullshit now is grief later. I knew right away that this talk of me spending time in Tír na nÓg would be for his health and not mine. "What do you expect me to do, lad? Go ask the Tuatha Dé Danann one by one if they'd like to stick a sword in your guts?"

"Perhaps you could be a tad more subtle than that."

"What's that? I don't know the meaning of *subtle*."

"No, you never have. Might suit you, though. No one would expect it."

"I don't have enough information to make a rational decision. It's like you're asking me to order a drink according to how me nipples are feeling instead of telling me what they're ready to pour. Why don't you tell me who's killed who and why, and how they've been trying to kill you. Take your time; we have plenty. And keep teaching me this new language."

We had at least a week of work ahead of us. Most of that would be getting in direct touch with Gaia, and we could do that in one headspace and keep talking in another.

The story he told me, which he swore he'd write down soon, took up the largest part of that time. All about how he killed Aenghus Óg, then cocked up everything with the Norse, except now they had an uneasy alliance against Hel and Loki, and the Greco-Romans were standing by too, and meanwhile he was financing a shadow war against vampires and dodging the occasional batch of dark elves who were being financed to kill him.

"Oh, yeah," he says near the end, like it's something he almost forgot, "I should probably tell you that the Morrigan's dead."

I took a break from the tattoo work to give him a thorough cussing for that. But I have to admit that the week passed quickly with all the talking, and I had only a half hour's work left on his arm when he finished.

"I noticed a pattern," I says to him after taking some time to think it over. "When ye stayed hidden, nobody died."

"Well, everybody thought I was dead for a while."

"They didn't think ye were dead for two thousand years, before ye killed Aenghus Óg, and somehow they all survived. It's only when ye exposed yourself and waved your sword around that—"

"Hold on, now, that's a poor choice of words," he says.

Sometimes I have to bark at Siodhachan to make him focus. "Stop paying attention to me word choice and pay attention to what I'm telling ye!" says I, and he shuts up and gets that sullen expression on his face he always gets when I tell him how it is. "Now, ye know right well I'm in favor of solving problems through stomping on nuts, but the first rule to follow—the one ye didn't remember—is not to stomp on your own. If ye want to learn how to do it right, take a lesson from the person what's causing all your trouble lately. Who did ye say it was again?"

"I didn't. I don't know who it is."

"Fecking exactly, lad. We're dealing with a sneaky nut-stomper here. That's what you need to be."

"I'm trying, Owen," he says. "You're part of my sneaking, because you haven't revealed your loyalties or even your name yet to the Tuatha Dé Danann. They're going to be seeking your favor."

I hawked up something loose and spat to the side. "It's nonsense you're talkin' now, lad."

"It's true. I've been the only Druid in town for centuries. Granuaile is obviously on my side. But unless you told them who you were before I got there, you are still an unknown quantity."

"No, I kept my mouth shut. You can't trust the Tuatha Dé Danann, and I didn't know what was going on. But I'm sure they know who I am."

"I'm not sure of that at all," he says. "Why would they?"

"Because you're so well known, lad. How can it be a secret?"

"Because I wasn't well known back when the Morrigan put you on that island. I was just another Druid amongst many and had done nothing special to draw their attention. And the Morrigan was not the sharing type. She told Goibhniu that she put someone on that island but didn't tell him who. He had no way of knowing anything about you."

"But he knows something now, doesn't he?"

"Aye. He knows you're ugly."

I punched him in the arm where it was still tender, and he winced. "Well, then, you can bet he's been doing some investigation on top of that."

"It's been more than two thousand years since she put you on that island. That's a pretty cold case."

"And don't I know it?" I says, and I shuddered, remembering. "What a miserable fecking day that was."

"No, a cold case has an additional meaning apart from the temperature, but never mind. Tell me what you were doing when the Morrigan put you on the island."

"I was telling your mother her cooking tasted like salted shite."

"Oh. Guess you don't want to talk about it," he says.

"You guess right. What kind of favors do you think the Tuatha Dé Danann would be seeking from me?"

"They might begin with seeking your actual favor. If you pray to some and not others, you lend them more power. But they may have other ideas that they would never share with me, and they might say things to you that they would keep private in my presence."

That deserved another spit to the side. "Are ye really thinkin' they'll just spew all their secrets to me because I haven't walked the earth for a while? I'd be a fool to count anything they say as more than a half-truth. And they may tell me all sorts of things merely to see if it reaches your ears."

"Understood, but anything they do will provide us more information than we have now, which is nothing."

"What's all this 'we' business, Siodhachan? Are we sharing the same pair of pants now? Don't be making any plans for me, lad. I'm grateful to ye for bringing me here and setting me up, but I won't be running any errands for ye."

Siodhachan sighed in frustration, and it was like old times. But he collects himself and then keeps his voice civil—respectful even—as he says, "I'm not sending you on an errand. You have to go to the Fae Court anyway and present yourself to Brighid. She'd feel slighted if you didn't. All I'm asking is to be aware that someone already has Granuaile and me on their list of people they'd like to kill, and you might be added to it. If you happen to learn of a way to keep us safe, I'd appreciate knowing about it."

"Aw, Siodhachan. That was so sweet, you'll be having me thinking ye want to get into me pants after all."

"Gods below, are you finished yet?" His irritation was clear.

I stabbed once more with the ink-stained thorn, and the soft green glow of Gaia's guidance faded. His bindings were whole again, and his skin returned to normal, with a bit of assistance from Herself. "Aye. All done. Ye can shift to a dodgy otter and get eaten by an eagle if ye like."

Can ye believe he didn't even thank me for my help?

CHAPTER 7

Oberon had been so patient while we fixed my tattoos that I declared we needed to hunt before we did anything else. Owen thought it a fine idea but decided to be our spotter instead of joining in. In the earliest gray of dawn, I shape-shifted to a hound and he assumed his bird form, a red kite, before taking wing and searching for game. After a few minutes he gave a screech to the east and we ran over to see what he had found, and it was a small herd of deer.

Owen and I shifted back to human after we brought down a buck, and we waited until Oberon had eaten his fill—neither of us was particularly fond of eating in our shape-shifted forms. Owen practiced speaking English with me to fill the time. He could understand the flow of speech pretty well now, but speaking is always tougher than listening. He was nailing the accent, though, and once he achieved fluency he would fit in fine.

It was as we were getting dressed again, back at the binding site, that we were surprised.

\<Atticus, someone's coming. Over there in the trees.\>

I squatted down by reflex to minimize my silhouette, and Owen did the same without knowing what had alarmed me. We were squinting toward the tree line when a tiny, delicate woman wearing a rich red-and-white kimono appeared from behind an alder, perhaps fifty yards away. Seeing that I had spied her, she bowed. I inclined my head but kept my eyes on her. Aside from the fact that she was something of a visual non sequitur—an outfit like that belonged in Kyoto, not the Pyrenees—there was something off about her. Unprovoked, Oberon growled and then barked aggressively.

Oberon, what's wrong?

<That's not a lady, Atticus!>

Okay, thank you. I'm warned of her, and she is warned of you. Please hush so that I can hear her if she speaks.

She had a narrow face, high cheekbones, and large, close-set eyes. Those eyes were currently fixed on Oberon, and her entire frame seemed to quiver, the way frightened animals sometimes do. Her black hair was twisted and piled atop her head, held in place with jade pins, and these blurred in my vision with distance and her shuddering fear.

Oberon, I need you to retreat out of sight. Let her see you leave.

<But why?>

I think she wants to talk but she won't while you're here, and I would really like to know what she has to say.

<Don't trust her, Atticus.>

I won't. I don't.

<Okay, then.> Oberon turned and trotted away until the underbrush obscured him completely, though he'd gone only thirty yards or so. I rose and bowed to the woman, and she nodded in return but did not move toward me for a full minute. Her eyes focused behind me where Oberon had disappeared. Perhaps she was making sure he wasn't coming back. During the course of that minute, her shaking gradually calmed and she

regained her composure, and Owen rose and stood next to me.

"Who the feck is that, Siodhachan?" he whispered. "Never seen a woman like that."

"And you probably never will again. This is a treat. Just watch. It's safe, I think." I could have checked her out in the magical spectrum, but there was no need. Judging by clues of her behavior, I thought I already knew what she was. Owen didn't, and I heard him speak the words to cast magical sight. I doubted it would tell him much beyond what Oberon had already said: That lady wasn't really a lady at all.

Finally satisfied that it was safe to draw closer, she approached another ten yards, then twenty, before stopping. She bowed again and spoke Japanese in a soft, ethereal tone. Owen quietly breathed, "Balls," frustrated that he couldn't understand.

"Begging your pardon, honored sir, but may I speak with you briefly?" the woman said.

"It would please me if you did. This one is called Siodhachan Ó Suileabháin." At the mention of my name, Owen shot a questioning glance at me. I didn't have time to explain, unfortunately.

"Then you are he whom I seek," the woman said. "This unworthy one is called Fujiwara-no-Kuni. We are much alike."

"How is that so?"

"We are both bound creatures. We serve that which is greater than ourselves. And we do not always show the world our true face."

I gave her a small smile. "I serve Gaia. Whom do you serve?"

"I serve the celestial and radiant Inari, who wishes to speak with you on matters of great import, provided your will and convenience be untroubled."

"This one is honored and grateful for the invitation. Where should I seek an audience?"

"Seek her at Fushimi Inari-taisha near Kyoto. Do you know of it?"

"Yes."

Kuni pulled one of the jade pins out of her hair and flourished it with a graceful twirl of silken sleeve before tossing it to me gently. I caught it and held it still, away from my body.

"Place that at the foot of any kitsune statue around the shrine and call my name," she said. "There are many statues spread across the mountain. I will come and usher you to Inari herself."

"I understand and will visit very soon. May I ask, however, how you knew where to find me?"

"You may. This I am permitted to answer, but I must begin with a question. Do you remember a dream you had featuring the Vedic god Ganesha?"

"I remember very well," I said. He had instructed me to leave Hel alone and delivered a not-so-subtle threat should I choose to ignore his orders.

"I was instructed to say that, in the dream, Ganesha mentioned he represented certain other parties. The one I serve, the sublime Inari, is one of those parties. And another of those parties is omniscient. He can find you regardless of your iron protection. My mistress wishes to speak with you more about the issues originally raised by Ganesha."

"Understood. Thank you for your trouble. I wish you and your mistress harmony, Fujiwara-no-Kuni."

"Good health and good fortune to you, Siodhachan Ó Suileabháin. This one apologizes for not speaking to your companion. Please accept this small gift as a token of my respect for you both." She bowed and then abruptly shrank into her kimono, which fluttered to the ground. A white fox with five tails leapt out of it and, with a flash of fur, disappeared into the forest, leaving the kimono behind.

"A five-tailed fox!" Owen exclaimed. "Why'd it have five tails? Does it have five arseholes?"

"No. Well, I guess I really don't know—uggh, gods, I hope not! I never thought about it before. But never mind! That was a kitsune, a messenger of the Shinto gods in Japan. The number of tails indicates its relative power. Five is not the most powerful, but neither is it weak." I silently let Oberon know it was okay to return now.

"What did she want?"

"I have been summoned to visit the goddess Inari. Well, I was invited, but such invitations are really given with the expectation of attendance. Willing to spend some more time with werewolves?"

Owen shrugged. "Sure, they're fun when you're not around."

I ignored his gibe and said, "All right, let's go back to Arizona and I'll present you to the Tempe Pack. The alpha there, Hal Hauk, handles my legal affairs, and if you decide you like him, he can handle yours too. He's well connected with packs around the world."

"Sounds like the werewolves kind of run things now."

"No, not really. They have no interest in running anything but their own territories. I prefer dealing with them because they're human most of the time and have largely human priorities. And if I want something from them, all they want is money. When you deal with witches or vampires, they always want favors instead."

"You won't find me dealing with witches or vampires."

"I don't imagine I will. Come on. Let's grab that kimono and I'll introduce you to the horrors of the internal combustion engine."

"Make sense, damn you."

"That robe is called a kimono. The kitsune left it for you."

"She did? What am I supposed to do with it?"

"I imagine it will make a great gift." The silk had whorls of darker red in it, subtle layerings of color from fire-engine scarlet to burgundy, and was bordered at the edges in white with textured grass blades in cool grays.

"Oh, ye want me to give it to ye, is that it? Well, feck off. It's prettier than three pairs o' tits, and I'm keeping it."

Since there was no way to shift directly into the Phoenix metro area—a limitation I appreciated very much when I was hiding from the Fae—we shifted back to Flagstaff, and I rented a car there to drive down into the Valley of the Sun. It was an opportunity to introduce him to modern materials like plastic and rubber and asphalt.

Owen planned to visit the Tuatha Dé Danann after he'd acquired his ID, and I told him that he should get up to Sam and Ty's place somehow when he returned and call me from there. Dropping him off on Mill Avenue in Hal's care, I wished I could stay and enjoy lunch with them, but Inari was waiting for me. I turned directly around and drove back the way I came.

Even with the delay, I was able to keep that appointment in Japan in not quite six hours. I never did tether too many places there to Tír na nÓg, which often forced me to make some long trips into the cities when I had reason to visit in modern times, but one of the few places I had tethered in the old days happened to be Mount Inari in Kyoto. It had been my good fortune to spend time in the country during the dawn of the Tokugawa shogunate, and I thought Nijo Castle, with its fascinating nightingale floor, was worth keeping an eye on. I tethered an area near the top of Mount Inari because I could see even then that space was at a premium in Japan and the valleys would all be developed soon enough. The only safe place to tie up was on mountainsides.

Parts of Mount Inari were developed anyway, but the developments were Shinto shrines and Buddhist temples rather than residences, and the trees had been left alone, apart from what was needed for the slim paths through them. The largest and most famous of the shrines was Fushimi Inari, with its hundreds of vermilion *torii* to usher the faithful up the mountain. Walking the paths underneath those gates could take an hour or two. When I shifted to the mountain with Oberon, we arrived near the top. Back in Arizona it had been late afternoon, but here above Kyoto it was already dawn of the next day, and wan light filtered through the canopy of trees. We threaded our way through the forest until we found one of the shrine paths and followed it down. At a place where the path crossed another, it was watched over by two kitsune statues. These statues were often carved of gray stone, and the kitsunes were sometimes depicted holding a key to the granary, a scroll, or a ball in their mouths. The one I chose held a scroll, emphasizing the kitsune's role as a messenger of Inari; it was supported by several levels of pedestals, blocks rising like a layered wedding cake, high enough so that we had to look up at the statue. Since Oberon had missed my conversation with the kitsune, he wasn't quite caught up on what we were doing, other than visiting a shrine. When he took in the kitsune, his ears pricked up with interest.

<Atticus, is that supposed to be a statue of a hound?>
No, it's a kitsune. A fox.
<Oh. Is that a sausage in its mouth?>
No, it's a scroll.
<A *scroll*? Okay, I just lost all respect for that fox.

Every canine knows you only put food or toys into your mouth.>

Is that so? You used to fetch my newspaper for me.

<Well, yeah, but that was in another country, and, besides, you wouldn't make me breakfast until I did.>

Perhaps this kitsune will get a treat after it delivers the scroll. Did you think of that?

<No, but if that's the case, the artist made a terrible decision choosing his subject. The awarding of a treat would have been much more worthy of a shrine.>

I needed Oberon to entertain himself while I concentrated on summoning the kitsune, so I said to him, *Think long and carefully on this before you answer, because it will literally be set in stone. If there was a shrine to Oberon the Irish Wolfhound and you were sculpted with a single treat in your mouth, what would that treat be?*

<Only one treat? Well, uh . . . that would be . . . >

Take your time.

Oberon swayed on his feet, physically rocked by the magnitude of the query. <Whoa. That is a *very* serious question, Atticus. I'd better go lie down over here and consider it.>

Go ahead. I'll wait.

With Oberon situated, I pulled the jade pin out of my pocket and placed it at the base of the statue, keeping my fingertip in contact with it as I spoke.

"Fujiwara-no-Kuni, it is I, Siodhachan Ó Suileabháin, here to see Inari as promised. I await you here at the base of this statue." I kept my eyes on the face of the statue for several seconds, then I let go of the pin, turned, and sank down until my back rested against the base of the pedestal. I didn't know how long I'd have to wait. It might be quite some time. Considering that I had met Fujiwara-no-Kuni in the Pyrenees only six hours ago, it was silly to expect her to be waiting for me in Japan now. Unless she had some method of traveling quickly, as many messengers of the gods do.

Turned out that she did. Perhaps twenty minutes later she walked up the path from below, wearing a white kimono this time with a cherry blossom pattern. As before, she stopped some distance away, not wishing to get too close to Oberon.

<Atticus, it's that same lady who's not a lady!> he said, springing to his feet. He was startled because he'd been so deeply absorbed in his meditation on treats.

I know. But she means us no harm. Do not growl or bark at her, and do not leave my side, okay? It would be rude.

<Okay.>

The kitsune bowed deeply before speaking. "Welcome to Japan, honored Druid. This one will take you to Inari. Please follow me. We will walk for a short distance."

"I will follow. *Arigato gozaimasu.*"

We trailed after the gray bow of her obi down to the bottom of the mountain, actually leaving the grounds of Fushimi Inari and walking a block away into the neighborhood surrounding the shrine. There were modest single homes with patios or gardens ringed by bamboo fences and tiny cars parked underneath overhanging second stories. During the walk, Oberon shared with me his musings.

<Atticus, the question you asked me cannot be answered.>

It can't?

<No, it's a Zen thing.>

What? Who's been teaching you Zen?

<Clever Girl. She says I'm Zen sometimes. And what you have posed to me is this thing called a koan.>

I know what koans are, but I don't follow.

<Look, Atticus: What is the sound of one snack happening?>

Ohhh, yeah. You're right, Oberon, that's very Zen.

Fujiwara-no-Kuni took a right, leading uphill once more, and then stopped in front of an interesting building that did not look like a residence at all. It looked more like the walls of a compound. A rock foundation rose from the sloping sidewalk to provide even ground for the interior; above this, the walls were covered with thin wooden planks, stained brown and weathered with deep grooves. The canted roof was covered in gray tiles, but this covered only what amounted to a thick wall; the center was open, as the tops of trees could be seen peeking out from inside. The kitsune bowed to us and raised her right hand to indicate the structure.

"This is Ōhashi-ke Teien, the private garden of Ōhashi-san. My mistress awaits you inside. Enter, please." She bowed again and backed away, and I ducked my head at her in thanks. A sign outside the door indicated that this was something of a tourist destination, originally built in the early twentieth century. We were entering far earlier than its posted hours, however, and, indeed, apart from our presence and the chirping of morning birds, the street still slept.

Step in quiet and careful with me, Oberon, ears and eyes open.

<Are you expecting an ambush?>

Pretty much all the time. It's because I like to be surprised with peaceful welcomes.

This surprise proved to be an especially peaceful one. Ōhashi's garden had twelve stone lanterns of differing styles in it, each nestled amongst carefully sculpted hedges and trees and flowering vines spreading their leaves along the walls; two *suikinkutsu* fountains provided a pleasant echo of falling water. Two gravel paths dotted with stepping stones wound through the garden, and where they intersected was a large round temple stone. A small shrine rested in one corner, and in another was a wee building constructed in the style of a teahouse but which was more of an arbor, a place where one could take shelter from the elements yet still enjoy the garden. It had a circular window with white paper and a fine network of bamboo over it.

A beautiful woman in a red *yukata* tied with a white obi stood on the opposite side of the garden. It was a bit late in the year for a *yukata*, which was normally a summer garment, but she seemed comfortable. She bowed to me, flicked open a fan in front of her face, and gestured to the arbor.

<Atticus, she's not a lady either.>

I know, buddy. It's okay.

Inari waited inside the arbor, kneeling on a tatami mat. Though sometimes she manifested as a male, in this instance she had chosen a female form, resplendent in a kimono of lavender overlaid with a deep-blue floral pattern. I asked Oberon to wait outside the arbor and I entered, taking a place across from Inari on the mat. She beamed at me and bade me welcome, expressing gratitude for my time. We traded pleasantries, as custom demanded. Being a deity associated with rice, she did not have tea to offer but rather sake, and she wasn't pulling any punches: It was the undiluted kind, called Genshu sake, 18 to 20 percent alcohol.

She noted that Granuaile and I had recently spent time in Japan to heal. That was only a few weeks ago, when we had spent time in a Tokyo *ryokan*—a more apt description for the traditional lodgings than *hotel*—and made frequent visits to the *onsen*. "Did you find the earth replenishing?" she asked.

"Yes, very much so. Thank you."

After we both had taken a sip of our sake and the opening niceties had been thus punctuated, we could move on to business. The goddess adopted a posture of stillness, cup held in one hand and resting in the palm of the other. When she continued to speak, she switched from her native Japanese to English. "Ó Suileabháin-san, we have heard of your troubles with the Olympians and congratulate you on solving that particular problem."

I liked how she phrased that. With the aid of Pan and Faunus, Artemis and Diana had hunted me across Europe, and I'd barely survived—hence the need to heal in Inari's country—yet she presented it as if I'd solved a brainteaser in the Sunday paper. I wasn't sure who *we* were, but maybe she had adopted the royal *we*.

"It is not entirely solved," I said. "Diana still wishes to destroy me. But I suppose the rest of the Olympians are at least loosely allied with me now."

"In truth, we are relieved. It is a fortuitous sign. But more must be done."

I felt that I had better clarify the pronoun before I spent the entire conversation in uncertainty. "I'm sorry, but I do not understand. Who's *we*?"

"All of us," she said, which didn't clarify at all. "But now the stakes are being reset. Our adversary is scheming in a more clever fashion."

"Our adversary in Tír na nÓg?"

"I speak of the Norse god Loki. He is recruiting the darker figures of several pantheons to his side, and now you must actively recruit as well. You are a free agent, whereas most pantheons cannot act unless it is specifically in their purview to do so; they are reactive, in other words, to threats from outside their own belief system. Do you see?"

"No," I admitted.

"If a boy in Bangalore asks Ganesha to intercede on his behalf, I cannot interfere, and Shango cannot answer the prayers of a girl in Osaka who prays to me. So while we are aware that Loki plots against us, we are largely powerless to act until he directly threatens our territory. Human agency—human urging—is necessary for almost any action we take. And most humans are not even aware of what is happening."

"And yet you are permitted this meeting?"

Inari smiled primly. "I can share sake and converse with whomever I choose."

"Why do you not choose one who worships you, then?"

Her smile widened. "I assure you that I have."

"Fine. Where is your hero or heroine now?"

Her eyes flicked to the garden gates. "Nearby. Protecting this place. You would not have seen them coming in."

Oberon overheard and spoke up from outside the arbor. <Does that mean she has ninjas, Atticus? Does she?>

Shhh. I need to concentrate.

"All right," I said. "Who is Loki recruiting?"

"He is speaking to the darkness almost everywhere. But before he acts directly, he begins with pestilence to weaken us. And if he cannot spread disease directly, he will do so indirectly. I am a scion of good health and prosperity in Japan; I am therefore a target. Removing me allows disease to spread more rapidly and creates instability. It is a prelude to more forceful maneuvers."

Granuaile and Laksha were dealing with disease-spreading rakshasas in India, and the coincidence was worrying, because it might not be a coincidence at all. Was Loki's hand involved there too? I recalled that when we were on the run from Artemis and Diana, he had shown up in Poland and shape-shifted into a blue-skinned Vedic demon. Why take that particular form unless it had been fresh in his mind? And if it was fresh in his mind, what had he been doing in India recently?

"I think I see what you mean," I said, "but I am not sure what you wish me to do."

Inari opened her mouth to reply, but angry shouting and the zing of drawn steel interrupted, followed closely by roars and a tremendous impact that shuddered the wooden floor. I stood and darted out of the tiny arbor, drawing Fragarach in anticipation of meeting something large and aggressive.

<Atticus, what was that?>

Probably the ambush I always expect.

Four huge, red-faced oni—horned, bearded, and tusked—tore through the walls of the garden, swinging spiked iron clubs to smash the puny critters drinking sake in serenity. Two black-clad swordsmen, presumably Inari's chosen heroes, chased them in. I scrambled for the back wall and Oberon automatically followed me, but instead of focusing on the oni, he was riveted by Inari's heroes.

<Whoa! Atticus, I think I see the ninjas! Do you see them too?>

Those aren't really ninjas, Oberon.

<Aw, dang it! Well played once again, ninjas. Well played.>

Watch out for the red giants. I cast camouflage on my hound in hopes that they wouldn't be able to target him. I also tried my best to focus on the oni rather than the show Inari was putting on. While I hoofed it to give myself some space and time to set myself, she barked a short command, as animal trainers sometimes do, something like "HUP!"—and then she erupted through the roof of the arbor, an effortless leap during which she drew her katana. At the zenith, she hovered impossibly for more than a second, long enough to make me think gravity had been suspended in her area. It was temporary, however, for a large white flying fox with nine tails materialized in motion underneath her and swept her away in a dizzying spiral of silk and fur that confused the oni even more than it did me.

Remembering the woman who had pointed me to the arbor, I glanced at where she had stood and saw her *yukata* puddled on the ground. Of course, she was now the flying fox.

The oni swung and whiffed as they tried to bat Inari out of the air, and that slowed their charge. That allowed the two swordsmen to close the distance and slice through the tendons at the backs of two of the oni's knees. They made almost identical slashes, but the creatures fell very differently. One fell forward, doing no harm to anyone but himself as he was impaled upon a stone lantern, but the other collapsed backward, crushing the swordsman underneath him. The remaining two kept trying to track and lay into Inari, ignoring me altogether, and I felt a small tremor of existential vertigo as I realized that I wasn't the target for once. The oni thought me insignificant, and as such it behooved me to make sure they dismissed me at their great peril.

Stay back, I told Oberon, and charged silently at the nearest oni as he twisted his neck around to follow the flight of Inari. These guys wore actual loincloths but apparently had missed out on decades of laundry commercials that shared the secret to keeping their undies stain-free. They were savage hulking brutes but still vulnerable to speed and steel. My attack wasn't the sporting kind, but assassins rarely expect sportsmanship since they don't practice it themselves. He never saw me coming, so the sword I thrust underneath his sternum and up into his heart was quite the surprise. He spasmed, dropped his club, and began to topple forward. I didn't have time to yank out the sword, so I tumbled to my right and let him fall on it. Now weaponless, I looked up to see that the attention of the last oni standing had been drawn by my ambush on his comrade. His spiked club was already on its way down, aimed at my head. All I could do was throw up my forearms and hope he didn't turn me into paste.

Something hit him in the chest, however, as he swung, and that caused his arm to jerk forward in reaction. The club crashed down next to my left shoulder, one of its spikes opening a gash there. I rolled away, pushed myself up, and played some parkour using the slain oni's body as a launching point. I put the body between myself and the other one, then whirled around to check his position as Oberon's voice said, <Atticus, are you okay?>

Yeah. Was that you?

<Yep, I took him down.>

Thanks, buddy, but get away and let Inari finish him. The goddess was circling around as if she was lining herself up for a strafing run.

<Yikes!> A blur of gray color near the oni's chest signaled Oberon's hasty retreat, and Inari sailed off the back of her fox, sword held high until she whipped it down to chop through the oni's neck. A spray of blood fountained from the throat, ruining Inari's silks and revealing Oberon's position once it landed on him. <Auugh! Now I smell like liquid ass!>

Behind me, a roar of dismay heralded the end of the final oni who had been hamstrung by the black-clad warriors. The surviving swordsman had dispatched it while it was unable to rise from the ground. Wicking the blood away from his blade, he sheathed it and strode over to Inari, promptly falling to his knees before her and prostrating himself. A stream of profuse apologies flowed from his mouth, along with a demand that she take his head for his failure to protect her.

"Rise," she said, and he did but kept his eyes lowered. "Which one are you?"

"This unworthy one is Tsukino Hideki."

"No one survived outside?"

"Only myself, Radiant One. We killed two more oni out there."

"You have done well, Tsukino-san. Resume your vigil."

"*Hai.*" He bowed again and, silent and deadly, slipped outside the breached walls. The giant nine-tailed kitsune took up a position on Inari's left, sitting up straight on the temple stone, much like the statues outside her shrine.

Oberon, come to my left side please, and do not even think of messing with that fox. That's not merely a kitsune; that's a tenko—more than a thousand years old.

<Don't worry, I won't. Flying foxes are even more unfair than flying squirrels.>

I dispelled his camouflage, and the tenko watched him trot over to me. The poor hound's coat was matted with blood.

"You see the problem, Ó Suileabháin-san," Inari said. "I recognize these oni. They lived on the slopes of my own mountain in peace for centuries, out of sight of humans. It would have never occurred to them on their own to attack me here. Loki is whispering and giving the darkness ideas. But we cannot move against him based on whispers."

"And I can?"

"Yes. It is time for you to act."

"Act how?"

"As you see fit. Ganesha impressed upon you the need for circumspection years ago. There is no longer any need for such caution."

"Why not? What's changed?"

"The Olympians are engaged on our side. Had you acted earlier, they never would have been."

"Are you saying you could not have recruited them on your own?"

"That is what I am saying. Again, human agency is required. For some actions we need a plea for intercession."

"Forgive me, Inari, but that sounds faintly ridiculous. I now gather that you are part of a consortium of gods working together. Ganesha is one and I know there are others. At least one of them is omniscient and capable of finding me wherever I am, regardless of my cold iron aura."

"Correct."

"So then you *are* capable of acting together without human agency."

"No."

"Loki is hardly acting at the behest of humans. Nor is Lucifer or Iblis or any other deceptive deity you wish to name."

"True, but that does not disprove my point. The darker powers are fundamentally different. They were conceived from the beginning as free agents to sow chaos and behave in their own self-interest. But about deities such as myself, humans believe differently. They believe that we follow rules and so it is true. Their faith is a fence we cannot climb. In the normal course of events we are confined to ministering to our own people. But, in this case, our collaboration was specifically urged by a singular human who has faith in us all. Someone you know."

"Who?"

Inari tilted her head to one side and said, "Do you remember Rebecca Dane?"

CHAPTER 8

Memories of warmth do nothing to combat the cold; they only distract me from the work that must be done to keep from freezing. Had Atticus not taught me the binding to elevate core temperature and do the same for Orlaith, we would have frozen to death by now.

The yeti are not in their cave when we arrive. Though we follow the directions Atticus provided, I have to locate the cave using magical sight, since the yeti have thrown up a veil of snow over the entrance. To the naked eye, there is nothing to the mountain but snow-covered rock, but Fae eyes reveal the whorl of magic around an entrance ten feet tall and at least as wide. It lets Orlaith and me pass through, and what greets us inside is not a natural cave; it is more of an indoor palace—not hewn, but obviously made by the Himalayan elemental in accordance with Manannan Mac Lir's instructions. I discover this once I cast night vision and see the stone table against the left wall with three candles and matches on it. I light them all and then take one with me as I step deeper inside, all the while calling out in Old Irish, "Hello? Anyone here? I brought you some bacon," operating on the theory that there are few sentences more friendly than that.

The entrance opens onto a long rectangular hall with stone counters lining it on either side. These have plenty of additional candles on them, and I light them as I walk along the left wall. A rectangular fire pit, recessed in the ground but rimmed with a lip of stone, lies closest to the entrance. It has a spit crossed over it and various iron grills, pokers, and tongs arranged alongside. I would bet that those pieces were made by Goibhniu but Manannan never told him where they would be used.

On the counter opposite me, across the pit, five stone plates sit with a fine dusting of snow on them. There are also a couple of large serving bowls and a platter waiting to be filled with food. I see giant three-tined forks but no knives.

Proceeding deeper into the hall, lighting it as I go, I come to a beautiful five-sided oak table, carved with bindings of health and harmony around its edges. Creidhne's work, no doubt. The high-backed chairs, too, are oak, no arms, but proportioned for very tall and very wide people. Something akin to a polished marble chess board sits in the middle of the table, but there are forty-nine squares instead of sixty-four. It's a fidchell game, the old Irish version of chess, and the pieces are miniature ice sculptures of remarkable beauty. Parts of them are clear ice, parts are purposefully cloudy, swirling through the forms in thin ribbons, and parts on the surface are a frosted blue, creating additional depth and texture and reflecting light in unexpected ways.

Much larger sculptures of similar artistry sit on the long table lining the opposite wall. Five representations of the Tuatha Dé Danann, at least two feet tall and finely detailed, stare at me with—*ahem*—cold expressions. I recognize, from left to right, Flidais, Manannan Mac Lir, Brighid, the Morrigan, and the Dagda. An interesting selection of the pantheon: hunting, the sea, fire and creativity, the Chooser of the Slain, and a god of fertility. The Dagda's inclusion is curious for a group supposedly incapable of reproducing. I theorize that the yeti are praying for bounty elsewhere—amongst the animals they prey upon, perhaps. I wonder if the statues are unmelting and bound with water magic, like the ice knives, or if they are made of mundane ice. I smile at an idle thought: What would an unmelting ice sculpture of the Dagda, hand-carved by a yeti, bring at one of the New York auction houses? I suppose the identity of the artist would be most difficult to establish.

I wonder why their mother never taught them to worship the Æsir—or, if she did, when they converted.

A high arched passage beckons to more rooms beyond. I feel hesitant, however, to stick my head through it.

"What do you smell, Orlaith?" I ask.

<Smells old.>

"You mean like old people?"

<No. Old smells. Long time gone. Smells are old.>

"Huh." The news worries me but fits with the thin coating of snow I see around the room, little lines of white powder tossed about by the odd circulation of air. It does circulate, somehow; there must be vents scattered about.

Leading with Scáthmhaide and triggering no ambush, I step carefully through the arch and discover a twisting hallway, which leads to the left and curls around clockwise. To the right is a door, barred closed with a plank of wood on a hinge, crossing the jamb and fitting into a bracket. Checking it out in the magical spectrum, I perceive no bindings that might be booby traps. That doesn't mean there isn't a mundane trap attached to it, though. The staff serves me well again; using the end of it, I flip up the plank from its slot and thereby free the door. It puffs out a smidge but doesn't open, and nothing dangerous leaps out.

"Smell anything through there?" I ask Orlaith.

\<Dead wood.\>

Her nose is on target, for it turns out to be a room full of firewood, oak and birch and juniper—hauled up from who knows where, since we are above the tree line. Cords of it, stacked and waiting, fuel for the fire pit in the other room. Where is the food? Another door, through the fuel depot, provides the answer.

The room is bigger than the dining hall we first entered, and it might be the world's largest natural walk-in freezer. Carcasses of boar, yak, and musk deer hang from hooks—hooks made of solid ice, which droop from the ceiling like frozen scorpion tails. A butchering station, notable for its lack of anything sharp, offers evidence of past activity but shows no signs of recent use. A hole in the floor, presumably for refuse, tells me nothing except to watch my step.

I scan the room in the magical spectrum to make sure I'm not missing something important, but fail to see anything beyond the impressive provisions. There are no other doors, so we retrace our steps back through the wood storeroom and out into the hallway. I follow its curling path, asking Orlaith to report on anything she hears or smells that would indicate we are not alone here. While I am still worried about possible traps, I no longer think the yeti are home. I hope, however, that I will find an ice knife somewhere that I can borrow.

The hallway reveals five bedrooms and a sixth room that serves as a bathroom. There's no plumbing, of course; it's simply a hole in the mountain. But the bedrooms reveal a bit more about the yeti. The rooms themselves are simple cubes of space where solid rock used to be, but the furnishings—a bed, table, and chair—are crafted entirely of ice. Furs are piled high on each of the beds, and more rest on the seat of each chair. But the styles of the furniture vary widely. Four of the yeti have tried to outdo one another with whorls and patterns in the ice, but one of them must value simplicity or feel incapable of competing against the others, for everything is of the clearest, most translucent ice I've ever seen.

Each room also contains three rectangular blocks of ice attached to the walls like paint canvases. These have been carved or etched or bound in breathtaking fashion, revealing new surprises depending on what angle you look at them from. The exception is the canvases of the Zen yeti: One ice painting is entirely pale-blue frost, another is clear with a cloudy white circle off-center to the right and a smaller blue circle nestled inside of that, and the last is a white expanse with nothing but a clear horizontal stripe running across it about a third of the way down from the top.

And in the midst of this wonderful dwelling made of rock, water, iron, and wood, the one thing that does not belong is the iPad sitting in the middle of the Zen yeti's bedroom table. It's an old model, but the gray plastic and silicone rectangle is an artifact of our time, our world, an anachronism in a place that shows no other sign of technology beyond the Iron Age. Somehow its presence is sinister to me, a tumor ready to metastasize and attack all life. That's a silly notion, of course, for the only life here is my hound and me, and a single iPad is unlikely to turn into Skynet all by itself, especially without WiFi or a source of electricity.

I check the iPad and am unsurprised to discover that it's dead, its battery drained and no method available to recharge it. What did the yeti see before the device died? Could that explain their absence somehow? More likely the yeti took it from a human mountain climber as a curiosity and its presence is of no significance.

"Whichever yeti calls this room her own," I tell Orlaith, "she seeks peace. I hope we meet her first. If we meet them at all, that is. I'm sorry to find it empty."

\<Not true! Full of food.\>

"And mystery. Where have the yeti gone and when are they coming back?"

\<Eat first. Get warm. Think later.\>

"It's a hierarchy of need, isn't it?"

\<Higher what? FOOD, Granuaile.\>

I smile down at my hound. The concept of a hierarchy does not translate well into emotions or images without a need to worry about one's place in it, and the word is meaningless to her.

"Yes, I suppose we might as well have a bite since we have to wait."

\<Wait long?\>

"I hope not." I'm already worried that I'll never find them. "Are any of the smells more recent in here?"

\<No. Still old.\>

The problem with Orlaith's assessment is that she, like Oberon, has tremendous difficulty with concepts of time and numbers. Old, to her, might mean anything from years to a matter of days. The point might be moot—what I really need to know is when or even if the yeti will return—but I want to have a more accurate idea regardless. I set my weapons and the package of bacon on the table, strip out of my clothes—shivering despite my raised core temperature—and bind my shape to a black jaguar.

After a sneeze, I smell something like ape and woman and honeydew, frosted flowers floating brittle over old resentments and bones of frustration, gnawed on and discarded but not forgotten. I smell the furs and the tanning oils used to make them, and, more faintly, I note wood smoke and ash from fires put out days ago and lingering scents of cooked meat and grease.

Leaving the Zen room and padding down the hallway to the main hall, I intend to take a good sniff around the fire pit and try to figure out how long ago it was last used. Orlaith follows me, tail wagging.

<Go hunt now?>

I answer her mentally in the jaguar form, idly wondering if I sound different to her this way. <No, just having a look around. We will eat something from the freezer when I'm finished.>

<Okay!>

Though I'm no expert, my best guess is that the pit was used a couple of days ago, not a very long time at all. Orlaith must think *old* means anything past a nap or two. But if they were here a couple of days ago, the yeti's absence is easily explained by a hunting trip or . . . I don't know, maybe they ski? Or thought they could use a vegetable side dish and went down the mountain to get some broccoli?

<I've smelled enough. Keep a lookout here for me? Let me know if you smell or hear anyone coming?>

<Where you going?>

<I'm going to shift back to human and start a fire while we wait, then we'll put on something to eat.>

<Good plan.>

<I thought you might approve.>

Shifted and dressed, I haul wood out of the storage area, along with some kindling, and use a candle to ignite it in the pit. A wide, yawning hole in the ceiling above the pit—unnoticed before, while I was more worried about what might be waiting in the hallway—acts as a chimney, and no doubt its egress is well disguised on the mountaintop.

I grab a musk deer carcass from the freezer and then thank all the gods below that Atticus isn't around to see me try to spit it. We cooked a lot of things over open flames during my apprenticeship, but we never actually put anything on a spit. It's an awkward business, and I realize that the movies never show you the spitting of raw meat. They always show it to you when the job has already been done and it's almost ready to eat. Orlaith, sensing that I'm upset about my flailing incompetence, is so sweet that she tries to make me feel better.

<You do good, Granuaile,> she says. <I can't do it at all.>

For the record: Cooking a frozen animal on a spit in a frozen yeti cave while you're thinking about freezing takes a really long time. And all of it is time I do not feel I can afford while my father is possessed and people are dying in Thanjavur.

But it does give me the opportunity to review what I have seen. According to what Atticus told me, the yeti have been around for centuries. The bacon I brought ensures they will live yet longer. But what do they do for fun? Aside from carving the occasional ice sculpture and playing the odd fidchell game, how do they not go mad—especially when one considers that they're siblings? I saw no reading material in my exploration of the cave. No card games. No evidence of The Settlers of Catan. Maybe they spend most of their time out of the cave, frolicking in the snow, animating snowmen and playing war games with them. That would be pretty fun, honestly. If I had their talents, I'd make a giant snow berserker and call him Snowdor. He'd have a Chill Blade of Harrowing and Hoarfrost Armor of Eternal Winter and—sweet gods below, I never should have let Atticus get me into gaming. But sometimes, when taking a break from my training, we'd fire up the PlayStation and slay digital monsters for a few hours, and inevitably it had colored my thinking.

I force myself to stop daydreaming of the ass-whupping Snowdor would deliver to his icy enemies, but because I still need something to distract myself from worrying that this delay will doom my father, I work with Orlaith on forms of the verb *to be*. I've noticed she often leaves it out of her sentences. I think we've scored a breakthrough when her ears perk up and she says, <Someone *is* coming!>

I clap a couple of times and say, "You are such a smart hound! You did that very well!"

<No, is not practice. Someone *is* coming. Real. Now.>

"Oh! I think we should go behind the table, in case they get angry at trespassers." I suddenly feel like Goldilocks caught eating porridge when the three bears come home. Perhaps I should update the old tale to "Redhead and the Five Yeti."

I grab Scáthmhaide and hurry behind the table, the only available cover in the hall should the yeti throw or shoot before talking. With that in mind, I start to talk— yell, really—in Old Irish, so that they won't be surprised by my presence.

"Welcome home! I come from Manannan Mac Lir to bring you bacon! I am Granuaile MacTiernan, a Druid of Gaia! Please come in and warm yourselves! I have a fire going!"

<Not moving now. Or they move quiet,> Orlaith reports.

I repeat my friendly greeting and hope it carries well enough to be understood. We are some distance away and catercorner from the exit now, so there is a small sort of foyer outside my vision into which the yeti can step without my seeing them. I still know when they do, however, because the ambient light from outside darkens perceptibly, indicating the presence of something huge blocking it.

A flurry of snow blows into the room, some of it hissing and melting as it drifts near the fire pit, and then a solid mass of snow above eye level moves cautiously around the corner. A half-moon peeks around the stone.

"Hello!" I say. "Well met!" And I reiterate that I'm a Druid sent by Manannan Mac Lir, father of the yeti. I hold up the paper-wrapped package of bacon, then toss it gently onto the table.

The figure that steps out of the entrance and into my view appears to be my daydream of Snowdor come to life. It is an almost shapeless goliath of white powder, humanoid in figure but lacking features—except for the significant fact that it stands close to eight feet tall. It holds still, perhaps waiting to see if I will attack, and when I do not, its head turns slightly to take in the fire nearby.

"Oh, yes, sorry about that," I say. "We didn't know when you would return, and we were cold and hungry. I will of course replace all the wood and game that we used."

The head turns back to me, and then a transformation begins. The figure remains still but sheds mass, as snow flies away from it like full-body dandruff at the mercy of gale-force winds. The snow escapes out the side of the mountain, leaving in its wake the true form of the yeti. It's not as bulky and not quite as tall, but it is still the progeny of a frost giantess—and I use the pronoun *it* only because I don't know if I'm looking at a male or female. My immediate guess is that it's a male, because of the thicket of white fur dangling from the cheeks on down. It can't be called a beard, can it, when the hair on the face is of the same thickness and consistency as the rest of the, uh, pelt? Maybe I should call it a mane. Its . . . well, let's say *his* mane is gathered, braided, and looped through little circles of solid frosted ice, partly in a practical fashion to keep his nose and mouth clear of hair, but partly in an aesthetic arrangement that makes his face and neck wink with blue reflected light. Above the cheeks, the skin is a pale blue around deep-set dark eyes. The brow is white-furred, as is the forehead and all else, save the lips, palms, and tips of the fingers, which are also pale blue. He doesn't have claws, but he does hold an exquisite knife in his right hand—no doubt the ice knife I had come to find.

Shaped like the khukuris employed by the Gurkhas of Nepal, it looks heavy and larger than something that could creditably be called a mere knife. It's a knife that deserves modifiers like *damn big* or even *huge fucking*. And unless it's a trick of the firelight, it shines from within along the top of the blade. The blade itself is a translucent blue along the cutting edge, frosted opaquely on the flat, but along the blunt edge it's clear and smolders with a disturbing, unnatural red. I privately note that he had hidden it completely in snow until he saw I did not intend to attack.

He doesn't trust me, however. He doesn't smile and say howdy or welcome or gosh I'm glad you got dinner started. Instead, in a low thrum of a voice, he says in Old Irish, "Prove you are a Druid."

He can't see most of my tattoos, since I'm wearing a coat, but I show him the back of my right hand so that he can see the healing circle and the triskele.

"That is only ink. It is not proof. Remain where you are, but summon a piece of this wall to your hand." He points to the wall behind him, the one opposite me. I nod at him, acknowledging the request, but hold up a hand, palm out, asking him to wait.

"Okay, I'll need to remove my shoe."

I have some energy stored in the metal knots of Scáthmhaide, but I don't want to reveal that, and the point here is to prove that I'm a Druid and bound to the earth. Despite my elevated core temperature, my toes alternately leap up and curl in their attempt to shout, IT'S COLD, DAMN YOU, as they touch the frigid stone floor. But I draw power from the Himalayan elemental, focus on a fist-sized portion of the wall opposite, and begin my unbinding. It's odd to speak the words in front of someone who can understand them besides Atticus, but of course it's not the Old Irish language that makes me a Druid—it's the binding to Gaia.

A fault line in the shape of a sphere appears, and then I bind the rock to the skin of my palm to make it fly across the room into my hand. A simple test of unbinding and binding, but not something that could be performed by many magic users apart from Druids. I hold up the baseball-sized hunk of granite for the yeti to see, and his lips spread in a satisfied grin. The teeth are somewhat sharp, but I wouldn't characterize them as serrated razors or treacherous fangs or anything. I unbind the rock from my palm and set it down on the table.

"Good enough?" I ask. "Because I'd like to put my shoe back on before my foot freezes."

"Yes, good enough. Welcome to our home, Druid, and thank you for making the journey. I am Skúfr Jötunson, third eldest of the yeti." I blink in surprise at the name, and then I realize that they have followed Old Norse instead of Irish naming conventions, which makes sense, considering their mother. But instead of using a patronymic or matronymic surname, she chose to call them *giant's son*.

"I am grateful for your welcome. Though you may have heard me shout it before, I am Granuaile MacTiernan, and this is my hound, Orlaith."

She wags her tail at the introduction and says, <Hello, Nice Furry Person.>

Yes, he seems nice, doesn't he? But he can't hear you.
<No magic?>
He has magic, but it is very different from mine.

Skúfr waves for the others to follow, then comes farther into the room. "Come on, she's a Druid sent by Father. Say hello."

One by one, four more yeti come into view, the snow shedding off them and revealing their features. Most of them have ice rings about their face, but each is different from Skúfr's.

The first to enter is as tall as Skúfr and carries a musk deer over his left shoulder, confirming that they had been out hunting.

"I am Erlendr Jötunson, the eldest. Welcome." He has far more ice rings in his mane, so many that some of them clink against one another. "Please excuse me while I store our kill." He moves past Skúfr to visit the freezer, and I see that his ice knife has the same disturbing red glow to it.

The third yeti introduces herself as Hildr Jötunsdotter, second eldest. There is nothing in her voice to indicate that she is female, nor do I see any physiological differences. Whatever the yeti have or don't have swinging between their legs, it's hidden behind a curtain of white fur, and Hildr, at least, has no breasts bigger than those of her brothers. Hildr's mane decoration falls between Erlendr's and Skúfr's, and I hypothesize that the number of braids and the complexity of their grooming is a marker of age as much as personal preference.

The fourth yeti, also fourth eldest, lends some weight to the idea. He has only two braids on either side of his face, and he introduces himself as Ísólfr Jötunson.

The last to enter is both the smallest and the youngest, with only a single braid on either side of her mouth, simplicity itself. I bet privately that this is the Zen yeti.

"I am Oddrún Jötunsdotter," she says. She's a full head shorter than her siblings but still towers over me. "Welcome. Can we offer you refreshment?"

"Yes, that would be great," I say, suddenly aware of my thirst. I had brought a canteen, but the water inside was a solid block of ice now.

"We have mead and water," Oddrún says.

I request mead for me and water for Orlaith. Oddrún

asks Ísólfr to take care of Orlaith's needs, while she takes long strides across to my side of the room, stopping in front of the counter where the stoneware rests. She lays her ice knife on the counter next to the plates and then squats down and pulls aside a panel of stone, revealing a hidden cupboard that I might have discovered had I looked any closer. She retrieves a small cask of mead and a mug of horn, then slides the stone panel closed. While she's working on pouring me some mead, my eyes are drawn to Ísólfr, who has put his knife down on the far counter and extended his right hand, palm up, toward the cave entrance. As I watch, a flurry of snow flies into the space above his palm and hovers above it like an upside-down tornado. More snow keeps coming in, feeding it, and the bottom of the funnel begins to pack together and solidify, then harden into a bowl of ice, which clarifies until it is largely transparent but with swirls of decorative white flurries in it. Snow fills the bowl, then Ísólfr waves his left hand over it and it melts to clear water.

"Your hound will need to drink this before it freezes again," he says.

We move out from behind the table, and he puts the bowl down in front of Orlaith while Oddrún offers me a mug of mead. It's delicious to an almost unbelievable degree, and I wonder aloud where it came from.

Hildr grins and answers me. "Father buys it from Goibhniu and sends it to us."

Orlaith laps up her fill, and the yeti invite me to sit at the table. Erlendr returns from the freezer as I seat myself, and I remember that I should be paying attention to the food.

"I will take over cooking," the eldest yeti says, picking up the package of bacon. "Thank you for bringing this. I'll be right back."

He disappears again, and the four remaining yeti sit

at the table with me, once they all fill their own mugs of horn with Goibhniu's mead. Orlaith lies down next to my chair, and my head spins a bit over how strange and wonderful my life is now. I am drinking mead with the yeti in the Himalayas. And they're very polite hosts.

But not especially talkative. They all look at me, expectant, but I am not sure what they're waiting for.

It turns out to be Erlendr. They must not have wanted him to miss anything, for Hildr speaks as soon as he returns carrying an armful of wood. "We have never met a Druid aside from our father. Always he sends one of the Fae when he cannot come himself, and he has not visited us in person for more than a hundred years. Does your presence here mean that the secret of our existence is now known in Tír na nÓg?"

"No, you are still very much a secret," I say, "but I have been let in on it. I confess I have come with hopes that you could help me."

The yeti exchange glances, and then it is Oddrún who speaks next. "We could use some help as well. Perhaps we could exchange aid. What is it that you require?"

"I need an ice knife."

Skúfr snorts. "That is all?" His hand shoots toward the cave entrance, much as Ísólfr's had when making a bowl for Orlaith, and in a few seconds he summons snow and shapes it into a serrated knife, similar to the kind you'd find in a steakhouse. He lays it on the table with the handle facing me. "Done."

"No, that's not what I meant. I need a knife like yours. One that won't ever melt."

They all lean back, and Erlendr, who was inspecting the musk deer on the spit, whips his head around to stare at me. I fear I might have crossed a line.

Seconds tick away and I remain silent, afraid that I will make it worse if I add anything else. Finally Oddrún says, "She doesn't know what she's asking."

"Clearly not," Erlendr says, and holds up his blade. "She thought this was an ice knife." They all kind of snort in derisive unison, and this succeeds in making me feel stupid.

"I do beg your pardon. What is the proper term for the weapons you carry?"

"They each have a name," Hildr replies, hefting her own aloft, "but in general this is a whirling blade, not a mere ice knife."

"A whirling blade. Very well." I cannot fathom why this is a better name for a knife made of ice than *ice knife,* but I'm not going to criticize them for it.

Ísólfr says, "Brothers and sisters, perhaps it is not too much to ask when you consider what we will ask in return."

Erlendr stalks over from the fire pit and looms over us. "It is too soon to think of that, brother. First we must ask why she thinks she needs a whirling blade."

"Yes," Hildr agrees. "We do not make them for others."

I take a long swallow of mead for courage and explain that my father is possessed by a spirit of the air and I need a weapon crafted of water magic to free him. "My earth magic is insufficient. My archdruid suggested that I speak to you, and Manannan Mac Lir agreed, and it was he who sent me with your shipment of bacon to speak of it." Dropping their father's name couldn't hurt. Or at least I hoped it couldn't. After I said the words, it occurred to me that they might be upset with him if he had not paid them a visit in a hundred years.

"Father knows of her problem and he knows of ours," Oddrún says, looking up at Erlendr, "and he sent her here. I think we are answered."

Erlendr and the other three yeti grunt their agreement

as a chorus. I notice that they are not creatures given to lengthy debate.

"Propose the exchange, then," Erlendr says, and they all turn to watch me as Oddrún speaks.

"We will craft a whirling blade for you, tailored to your size and named according to your wishes, as a service of water magic in exchange for a service of earth magic. We can move what lies on top of the mountain but not move the mountain itself."

"What are you asking? You want me to move the Himalayas? I can't do that."

"No, I speak of the sort of movement you have already demonstrated. Our cave is not a natural one; it was created by our father. He spoke to the earth and said he needed a room that looked so, and it was made as he said. We wish you to do the same."

"Oh, you need another bedroom? I am sure I can arrange that." I would speak to the elemental and it would be finished within the hour. This was good.

"No, not a bedroom. Something significantly larger. What we need may sound strange or unnecessary, but I assure you it will prevent us from going insane. We are so very bored, you see." The other four yeti nod to confirm that they are all bored.

"I can imagine."

"Good. We have expressed this sentiment repeatedly to faeries sent by our father. Through them, we asked him to visit us or, failing that, provide us with something new to do in the snow and ice, since we cannot mingle with humans. And the faery returned with something he called an iPad. Are you familiar with iPads?"

"Ah. Yes," I say, encouraging her to continue.

"This iPad had images inside it. Images that moved and made sound."

"Videos of some kind," I venture.

"Yes. Recorded images of a game called hockey. Humans play it in cold climates. Two teams skate and slap a puck around in an attempt to score goals."

"I'm familiar with the game. It's somewhat violent."

"Yes!" Skúfr bellows, hammering both fists against the table and startling me. "A violent game played upon the ice! We were born to play it!"

"But we need a place to play," Hildr says.

My jaw drops open as it dawns on me what they want. "I'm sorry. You want me to build you a hockey rink?"

"Inside this mountain, yes," Ísólfr says. "Underneath where we sit. The faeries cannot do this. Only a Druid can. And you are a Druid."

"Okay, wait, let me clarify something. I can't do it either. Only the Himalayan elemental can."

Oddrún shrugs away this annoying detail and says, "Accomplish it however you wish. We know you can make it happen. We propose a whirling blade for a hockey rink in the heart of the mountain."

"Gods below, I don't even know how big a hockey rink is."

"We do," they chorus, and Oddrún adds, "Father's faery told us all the rules and regulations."

"But what about nets and pads and sticks and everything?"

Erlendr smiles at me and backs up so that he is opposite the door. "We have already thought of this. Our style of hockey will be ice hockey in its purest form." He holds his arms out from his sides, and in moments he is obscured by a small snowstorm pulled from outdoors through the auspices of his magic. When it clears away, he is padded in snow and has a helmet, a stick in his hand, and a pair of skates made entirely of ice. It's a neat solution, because I doubt they'd be able to find any equipment their size otherwise.

"Well, if I can get the elemental to agree, then I'll do it. Hockey rink for whirling blade."

Toothy smiles all around and toasts to health and hockey. Erlendr announces that the musk deer is at least partially edible and uses his whirling blade to slice off a few juicy hunks. There are only five plates and now seven of us including the hound, but with the yeti's permission I unbind a new plate for Orlaith and one for myself from the wall. They grill me about the NHL and which teams are the best. I feel woefully inadequate, since I know so little about the sport and can remember only some of the team names.

They are unimpressed with the Toronto Maple Leafs. "Who fears a leaf?" Skúfr asks, and I assure him that no one does. At least no one I know. Atticus makes a habit of mocking Toronto whenever he can, but I think that he has reason for it due to some unpleasant episode he had in the 1950s, when he lived there under the name of Nigel. He's never explained to me what precisely happened, and I make a mental note to ask him.

"You would probably like the Colorado Avalanche," I tell the yeti.

They grunt and nod. "A fine name! Worthy of the sport."

After we have eaten our fill, Oddrún says she will begin to craft my blade while I'm working on the rink. While still seated at the table, she summons snow above her right hand, condenses and shapes it into a crude ice knife, then asks me questions as it floats there. Did I want my blade to be shaped like theirs or of a different design? How large? Serrated blade or no? I opt for a blade in the style of a military fighting knife, no serrated edges or sawing teeth. She balances it and makes the handle thin and grooved so that I can wrap leather around it. Along the top of the blade on the blunt side, a transparent tube of ice waits like a thermometer lack-

ing mercury. She lets me hold it to see if it feels comfortable, albeit without the leather wrapping. It seems a tad
light to my hand, and I say so.

"That is perfect. It will be heavier soon. You can go
start your work now. I have what I need." Oddrún takes
the knife back and floats it above her right hand again,
but this time the tip is pointed directly at her. She passes
her left hand over the top of it, left to right, and the
knife twirls clockwise. Another pass and it speeds up,
and after a final pass it is moving so quickly that it
blurs.

"What are you doing?" I ask.

Erlendr answers. "The whirling begins. We will each
take a turn before it is finished. Come with us." He and
the other yeti move toward the door, their turned backs
indicating that the subject of the blade is closed. I'm not
sure what he means by *the whirling*—I think there is
some significance there that I am missing—but I don't
wish to be rude and persist in my questioning when the
yeti are so clearly ready to move on. "We will show you
where to build," Erlendr says. "We want it separate
from our home."

With an uncertain glance back at Oddrún, I leave the
table, and Orlaith takes her place at my side. I grab
Scáthmhaide on the way out, and the yeti lead me
downhill "the slow way," once they discover that I cannot ski. What they consider the "slow way" is in fact
quite convenient. Walking single file, with Erlendr and
Hildr in front and Ísólfr and Skúfr in back, they use
their skill with snow to create a firm, level series of steps
for us and then disperse it back onto the mountainside
after we pass, leaving no trail behind us.

Seeing their complete mastery of their element, I ask
them, "How did humans ever manage to spot you?"

Hildr snorts in amusement and says, "Sometimes we
would leave a footprint or let them see one of us on

purpose. We were bored. But we stopped doing that once they came hunting us and we were forced to eat them. We felt badly that they would die for our sport."

"Plus they didn't taste very good," Skúfr adds, "and they were scaring away all the animals we do like to eat."

I try not to shiver at that but then go ahead and do it, because it's cold, after all, and somehow it grows colder as I realize I'm all alone with four large creatures who have eaten humans in the past. The yeti hunters were hunted by the yeti and were probably hung on hooks in the freezer and then roasted slowly over the same fire pit we just used and, oh, gods, let's think about hockey instead.

We descend about five hundred yards from the yeti cave and some additional distance to the west. Once we burrow inside I imagine the rink will indeed be below their living area above. I don't know why they chose this particular spot for the entrance, but, like their cave entrance, it is in an open area, completely covered in snow and therefore unattractive to mountain climbers, who prefer bare rock in which to lodge their pitons.

I myself would require bare rock if anything was to happen. I couldn't talk to Himalaya through all the snow. Once I explain this, Erlendr clears a space for me and I remove my right shoe, exposing my foot to the cold again. Himalaya is willing to help but would like my aid in preserving musk deer, tigers, and the Himalayan black bear, all of which are endangered and frequently poached. Feeling guilty about our recent meal, I pass this on to the yeti, who agree to stop hunting musk deer altogether and do what they can to protect the tigers and black bears from poachers.

They give me dimensions and describe what they want, and I relay these ideas to Himalaya in images through our bond. I'm a little uncertain, so it goes

slower than when Atticus asked Colorado to build him
a road or had Sonora create a cache for him to store his
rare-book collection. Still, the earth begins to shift and
move, and a tunnel forms in front of us, like a navel of
rock growing deeper. We follow along, and soon it becomes clear we'll need some light. Hildr and Skúfr run
back to the cave "the fast way" to fetch candles and
matches, and once they return, they set them up at in-
tervals so we won't be tripping in the dark. I come up
with the idea of creating little niches in which to place
the candles, and they congratulate me for being so sen-
sible.

I realize much later, in the midst of an epic yawn, that
it must be far past my bedtime, but I can't imagine taking
time out to sleep when who knows what could be happening back in Thanjavur.

We create more than a simple rink. There's a track
around it, penalty boxes, players' benches, and stands
for spectators, because the yeti insist that they will have
an audience someday. We design a lighting and ventilation system for the top of the stands and circling the
rink. The yeti will continue to use candles but will back
them with mirrors to reflect more of the light to the
middle of the rink. Inefficient but effective. Ventilation
shafts to the outside provide airflow and a source of
snow and ice for the yeti. At some point, Orlaith chooses
a spot in the stands and curls up for a nap.

When the yeti pronounce themselves satisfied, they
spend about ten minutes summoning in snow and trans-
forming it into a floor of solid ice. They alter the crystal
structure of the ice to achieve that frosted blue look,
and thus they give the ice its face-off circles and blue
lines. Forgoing the goals and sticks and everything else,
Skúfr runs back to the cave to get Oddrún. She looks
exhausted when she arrives, but she brightens up when
she sees the rink. They all waddle awkwardly out to the

middle of the ice, whooping with joy. As soon as they encase their feet in custom ice skates created on the spot, they promptly fall on their asses, laughing and giddy.

"Oh, this is powder!" Hildr says, and for a moment I am unsure what she means.

"The best powder ever!" Ísólfr agrees, and then I get it. They're talking about snow and equating powder with something excellent. Achievement unlocked: I have learned yeti slang.

"You know what our mother, Freydís, would say right now?" Oddrún asks the others, beaming up at the rock ceiling.

"She'd say, 'Graah!'" Skúfr says, and they all laugh again.

Though I hate to interrupt, I do have an emergency to attend to. "If you're satisfied," I call from the players' bench, "then perhaps I can take the whirling blade and bid you farewell?"

Five incredulous yeti heads raise up from the ice to regard me.

"The whirling blade isn't finished yet," Erlendr says, and though he doesn't add, "you idiot," it's implied in his tone. "Oddrún has just finished her piece of it, and I must do mine next."

"I don't understand."

"Clearly. Let us return to the cave."

Leaving the others behind, Erlendr dissolves his skates and shuffles off the ice, then leads Orlaith and me back to Castle Yeti. It's dark outside, but I cast night vision and can see well enough. Inside, there's a freshly laid fire and a much larger animal roasting. It looks nearly finished. How long had we been gone?

The whirling blade sits on the oak table. It appears perfectly serviceable to me, and I say so. "All I need to do is wrap leather around the handle."

"It will melt as soon as you leave the mountain. It's not ready."

"When will it be ready?"

"After each of us works on it. Four more days."

"Four more *days*?"

"I do not understand why you are upset. We told you it was a thing of great value. Such things are not made quickly."

"Explain what you're doing."

Erlendr sets his whirling blade on the table next to mine. "Aside from the size and shape, what's the difference between these right now?" he asks.

"That red glow. Mine doesn't have one."

"Indeed. Do you know what that is?" When I shake my head, he continues. "It is the energy needed to keep the ice from melting in warmer climates and to keep the blade sharp and shatterproof. That energy is slowly drained and must be replenished."

"Replenished how?"

"With the blood of your kills, of course."

"What?"

"When you stab something with a whirling blade, you are not merely damaging organs and tissue. The tip drains some of the target's energy through the medium of blood, the water of life. It creates a magical vortex within the body and siphons it."

"Are you saying it steals their spirit?"

"Not the whole thing, but a fraction of it, yes. A spirit in solution. And what we are doing right now is creating that vortex and providing a temporary energy source. That is why Oddrún was so tired when she joined us at the rink. We each contribute a fraction of our magic to the whirling blade, and once you make your first kill, that will be returned to us. We will remain drained until you do so."

"Oh, gods below. I didn't realize . . . I don't know if I want a weapon like that."

Erlendr huffs, impatient with me. "Do you wish to have a magical blade capable of freeing your father or not?"

"Yes, but . . . won't this kill him? Steal his spirit?"

"Earlier, when you spoke of your need for this whirling blade, you described cutting the skin and drowning chakra points with water magic. That is clever, and we think it will work. Just don't stab him with it."

"What if I accidentally nick my finger with the tip?"

"Don't do that."

"Holy shit."

"Were you not a Druid, we would not consider giving you one. We know you will use it responsibly."

"What happens if it runs out of energy?"

The eldest of the yeti shrugs. "Then it is no different from an icicle. It will melt as soon as it's exposed to temperatures above freezing. If you wish, you may use it to save your father, kill a very small animal with it, and leave it in the sun. The kill will release our energy back to us, and then it will not be long until the animal's spirit is used up and the blade is destroyed."

"Gah. So until I kill something with it, I'm draining your energy?"

"Not in any permanent sense. We imbue it with the elemental frost magic we inherited from our mother. It won't drain or expire, because the potential for frost exists wherever there is water in the air, and it is maintained by our will. Our power is diminished, however, until the first kill frees it from the blade."

"Could I simply return it to you and let you get your energy back without killing anything?"

"No. This magic has a price."

Of course it does. All magic has a price. The question is never whether you can afford it; it's whether you truly wish to pay it. When I draw energy from the earth, the elemental passing it on to me is drawing it from the life of its ecosystem. My speed or strength or healing is paid for in the diminished health of all its plants and animals. What makes it bearable is that the drain is distributed and shared so that nothing is destroyed, and they will renew themselves in the ordinary course of the world turning. My responsibility in this contract of mutual protection is to defend the earth from predatory magics, but it's difficult for me to see these whirling blades as anything but predatory.

It's not that ending a life is anathema to me, but damaging a spirit, great or small, and then consuming it for my own ends—that's an unwholesome tea to swallow. Making choices like that must stain you on the inside somehow. It's why I chose the path of a Druid rather than pursuing the path of dark witchcraft that Laksha once offered me—which she so desperately wishes to escape now. And, as I stand there with Erlendr staring at me, waiting for a response, I am struck with the idea that perhaps the yeti feel stained without realizing it. Their pursuit of art through ice might be their attempt to balance the ugliness of these blades with beauty. Or perhaps they do not feel anything of the sort and I am merely projecting my sympathies.

"I've changed my mind, Erlendr. I don't want a whirling blade. Let's forget it."

The ice rings in his mane clink together as he shakes his head. "We cannot stop now. It must be finished and used or Oddrún will be forever diminished. You see that the vessel is somewhat blue. That is her."

I look closer at the transparent glass in the knife and see that some of the clear interior is indeed filled, a slightly darker blue against the frosted blue of the blade. I had missed that earlier.

"Fine. Finish it and use it yourself. I want no part of it."

A great weight of weariness settles about my neck and shoulders. This entire trip has been a waste of time, and I won't be able to save my father after all. It's odd how a profound sense of one's own foolishness tastes like bile. Erlendr doesn't move or say a word, and the only sound is the hiss and pop of the fire. A single tear escapes down my left cheek, and Orlaith thrusts her head under my hand, making me realize that I must be communicating some of my distress to her.

<Granuaile sad? No need. I love you.>

I kneel and lay Scáthmhaide on the floor, wrapping my arms around Orlaith's neck and giving her a hug.

I love you too, sweet hound.

Erlendr shifts his weight uncomfortably, and his mane rings tinkle like wind chimes. "You must be tired," he says. "Why don't you rest, and we will speak more later. You can use my room. The furs are warm and you won't be disturbed."

It's true I am very tired. In fact, I might actually qualify for the phrase bone-weary. I don't even know what day it is; I've been awake continuously since I jogged into Ouray and got that phone call from Laksha. I want to get back to Thanjavur, but after a nap I'll be better able to deal with whatever horror awaits me there.

"Okay," I say, unable to muster anything more eloquent. "Lead the way."

He shows me into the first of the bedrooms, wishes me restful slumber, and closes the heavy stone door behind me. I crawl onto the furs, burrow underneath them with Orlaith, and, with an arm draped around my hound, worry about my father until sleep takes my cares away.

CHAPTER 9

This Hal Hauk lad is more than he seems. I mean beyond the werewolf business. Or maybe that's precisely it. In the first few seconds I can tell that he is an older, tougher dog than either Sam Obrist or Ty Pollard, and he hides it extremely well. He is all manners and easiness on the surface, but there's a punch in the teeth waiting to strike under that suit and handshake. I get the feeling he would rather avoid fights if he can, but once he's in one, he'll pound and tear you until you're bloody paste, and that's the kind of lad I admire.

Siodhachan introduces the two of us and then he putters away in that horrible car he rented, off to visit a country where women dress in colorful robes and turn into foxes with five tails. Are they women first and foxes second, or is it the other way around? He called her a kitsune, so I guess that's not human. I'm not too clear on what exactly I witnessed there. I must investigate that country when I can.

Hal walks me up to his office, a second-floor suite off Mill Avenue, situated on a balcony that overlooks a red brick courtyard. In the middle is a solid sphere of stone with water bubbling out of the top. It cascades down the sides into a pool, but the level of water never rises. How is such a thing possible, I wonder? Are werewolves water mages?

The door of his office is made almost entirely of glass, and black letters floating on the surface say MAGNUS-SON AND HAUK, ATTORNEYS-AT-LAW. Siodhachan told me that the Magnusson fellow used to be the alpha but died in Asgard, killed by the golden boar of a Norse god. If he was tougher than Hal, I would have liked to meet him.

There are pictures of wolves on the walls of the office, but they are somehow idealized and not a true likeness. I learn later that they are called *paintings*. There are sculptures too, cast in bronze. A woman with an un-naturally pale face and lips the color of roses sits behind a gigantic block of wood, and I cannot imagine why. When I ask Siodhachan about it later, he says that she is probably something called a receptionist. She smiles at Hal and says, "Good afternoon, Mr. Hauk," and he grunts at her as we walk down a hallway to the left and enter a room lined with shelves of books. He sits behind a large block of wood and invites me to sit in a chair on the other side of it. He presents me with a driver's license, a birth certificate, and a passport. From what I can tell, I will never need to use these things for their intended purpose—I will never drive or check in at an airport in other countries. But together they establish to modern humans that I was born forty-three years ago and am therefore permitted to work in this country and participate in the international banking system and be taxed until I die. There is also a fictional work history that I am supposed to memorize.

"So I take these in to a bank and they give me money?"

"No, the money is paid to you in return for work that you perform. What that work might be is up to you. If Atticus is willing to support you for a while, let him. He can afford it. Are you hungry? Let's go to lunch and bill it to him."

I chuckled. "I like you already."

He takes me to a pub called Rúla Búla, claiming that it's Irish. I had no doubt that it was, but in my day the Irish didn't have fecking pubs; they had fires. Still, I like the place. It's furnished in wood and smells of whiskey, and the people are ready to pour you plenty of it. Hal recommends a particular whiskey, and I order it along with lamb stew. He tries to talk me into ordering the famous fish and chips, but that involves a process called frying, which I don't understand. Stew is something I understand. I'm glad people still eat it.

"So what are your plans?" he asks me.

"I need to absorb and adjust more than anything else," I says. And, of course, at the time of that conversation I wasn't all that fluent in English yet. In these writings I am making myself sound more clever than I actually was at that point. But whatever I said made sense to Hal.

"Where are you planning to do that?" he asks. "I mean, I presume you will be on your own for a while. So where are you going after this lunch?"

I shrug. "I have to go to Tír na nÓg and say hello to the Tuatha Dé Danann. And while I'm there, I have to figure out who's trying to bend over me apprentice."

"You mean Atticus or some other apprentice?"

"Siodhachan, aye. I know he's been a proper Druid now for longer than I've been alive, but I still think of him as me apprentice."

"And you were speaking metaphorically about the bending-over thing?"

"Aye. But it's not all that far from the truth if ye think about it. If the Tuatha Dé Danann haven't changed much since the old days, then there will be lots of drinking and sweating underneath the blankets together. Probably won't learn a thing while I'm there."

"Not much of a detective, eh?"

"What's a detective?"

His eyebrows shoot up and then his mouth spreads into a huge smile, which tells me I'm in for something. "It's someone who looks at a crime scene and figures out from clues who could have committed the crime. If they're successful, they accuse someone and try to prove that they are guilty and deserve to be punished. It's my job to defend the accused and prove that they are innocent—or at least cast doubt on their guilt."

"You'll have to define a lot of words for me there," I says, and he smiles again and spends the rest of lunch giving me a basic introduction to criminal justice. Then he says to hell with it, I'll call it a day, why don't you come over to my house and I'll show you the most famous detective in human history.

"He lives with you?"

"No, he's a figure out of stories. Think you'll like it."

I see no reason to refuse, because while meeting with the Tuatha Dé Danann is necessary, it's not an urgent business. Hal settles our bill with a rectangle of plastic called a credit card, says I'll need to get one of those soon, and then we walk to his car: a wee silver box, low to the ground and more pleasing to the eye than the thing Siodhachan rented. The paint job matches his tie, and I remember Siodhachan saying something about how the leaders of werewolf packs often wear silver for symbolic reasons. Sam Obrist didn't, but maybe I caught him on his day off.

When we get in and fasten the seat belts, he presses a button on the steering wheel and then says, "Call office." I'm wondering if he's talking to me when a ringing noise comes from the middle of the car, clicks off, and then a woman's voice says, "Magnusson and Hauk." I try to conceal my surprise and casually look around the car to see where she might be hiding. There's no room for anybody in the car but us.

"Nicole, it's Hal. Clear my schedule for the rest of the

day, please, and invite the pack over to my place at their convenience to meet Owen Kennedy."

"Absolutely, Mr. Hauk," the woman says. Where was she? Behind the console? Siodhachan said there was an engine in the front part of a car underneath the hood, and this was supposed to give the car its animating force, but her voice seemed to be coming from there. Then I realize that this is the voice of the woman with rose-red lips in Hal's office.

"Thank you." There's a beep, and then he looks over and smirks as he puts the car in gear. "Don't worry. She's part of the pack."

That wasn't my worry at all. My worry was that my ignorance had me stuck in a bog when everyone else was on dry land and dancing to pipes. It's no fun being stuck in a bog.

Hal's house is perched on a hill of granite and sandstone that the locals call Camelback Mountain. Big sprawling place with a swimming pool in the back. He talks to the house as he walks through, and lights come on even though it's not dark outside yet, then strange music plays, using instruments I have never heard before. He gets me a cold beer in the kitchen and leads me to a room with couches and a large-screen television.

"You've seen one of these before?" Hal asks, and takes off his coat but leaves the shirt and silver tie. I reply, yes, they had some smaller ones in that brewery in Flagstaff. "Good. I'm going to show you a chap who uses his mind, his vast knowledge of facts, to deduce what is going on around him. Might strike you as Druidic. Maybe." He speaks into the air, and the music stops and the television turns on. It's like he's creating bindings but without any help from the earth, following no laws of Druidry. The magic of these people is a wonder.

Siodhachan tried to explain some of it to me—made

me say *electricity* and *technology* three times each. But he pointed out that I can make their magic technology work without understanding exactly *how* it works, and this is largely how people function now. That idea—the idea that you can use magic without knowing how it works—is fundamentally different from how Druids do things. There is no way to perform Druidry without knowing how first. To even attempt it would be dangerous. I am beginning to think that much of what these people are doing in the name of convenience might be dangerous also. Magic does not happen free of cost.

Hal explains that the show is called *Sherlock* and that it was made some years ago by the Britons, some tribe from the island next to Ireland that rose to prominence after my time. A Roman outpost called Londinium grew into a huge city called London, and this Sherlock Holmes solves crimes there. Except not really.

It opens with explosions and people diving to the ground, and Hal says that's how modern humans conduct wars, with guns and with vehicles that carry bigger guns around on them. So this war veteran, John Watson, joins up with Sherlock to solve crimes.

The plot of the first episode involves phones—more modern magic—and the sending and receiving of messages on them. I keep making Hal stop the show and explain what I'm looking at.

"Do I need to get myself one of those fecking phone things?"

He considers and then says, "I wouldn't imagine you'd need one in the short term."

"Good. If you had said yes, I would have shat kine."

Sherlock's a clever lad, no doubt, and I think that Hal is right: He takes a Druidic approach to his problems. Unlike Watson and the other people around him, he pays attention to how things work and how humans behave.

"What did you think?" Hal asks after it ends, and I wonder aloud if there are any more of these shows. He says, aye, there are more, and he puts on the next one. I don't have to interrupt him quite as much this time to ask questions, but we are interrupted by the arrival of Hal's pack members, who trickle in as they get off work and make their way to Camelback Mountain. The first to arrive is a healer, but they're known as doctors now and you're supposed to call them Doctor before you say their surname. He's a handsome lad named Dr. Snorri Jodursson, and I can tell he spends more time than he should styling his hair. He doesn't have a wedding ring—something Siodhachan said I should look for— and once I meet more of the werewolves, I notice that almost none of them do. Apparently, only shallow, informal relationships with humans are allowed, to preserve the secret of the pack. And when a human gets too close to the truth or starts to notice how the werewolf is never seen during full moons, the relationship is over. If the human persists, then the werewolf in question is uprooted and sent to join another pack—new identity, new job, the works. On a somewhat regular basis, entire packs trade territories with another. A werewolf who wants a lasting relationship must find one in the pack, therefore, or perhaps with another creature of the magical world that already knows about them and is used to keeping secrets. Dr. Jodursson's hair tells me he isn't looking for a lasting relationship. It's flashy and indicates that he might belong to a tribe of modern men that Siodhachan told me about called the Douchebags.

Turns out the doctor is a big fan of *Sherlock* too. His favorite character is the woman who works at the hospital morgue. I cannot stand her. I am not sure if this reveals more about him or me.

One of the things Siodhachan told me to expect after meeting the fox lady from Japan was a greater range of skin tones and bone structures than I was used to seeing in the old days. He was nervous about it, like he expected me to disapprove of the way Gaia had created people.

"Is there something wrong with them? Are they witches? Abominations?"

"No, no," he says.

"Why are you so worried, then?"

"I . . . well, you see, history . . ." Then he stops and shakes his head. "Never mind." He smiles, relieved now, and says, "That's perfect."

Punch me stones if I know what he was talking about. But I finally get to meet a variety of people, once the rest of Hal's pack shows up. The core of his group is from Iceland, of "assorted Scandinavian stock," he says, but over the years the pack has taken on new members from everywhere, transplants from this part of the world or that. Efiah is a tall woman from someplace called Côte d'Ivoire; Farid is originally from Egypt, where his brother, Yusuf, is the alpha of the Cairo Pack; and Esteban is a small, quick man from Colombia. I have to admit that me heart beats a little faster when I meet one of Hal's original pack, a tough woman named Greta with braided yellow hair that falls down to her waist. When Hal introduces me as Siodhachan's archdruid, her eyes flash with anger and her mouth presses together as if she's biting her tongue. It can't be me causing a reaction like that, so it must be Siodhachan.

At first I think maybe he's broken her heart at some point, but then I remember him mentioning her in that endless story of his while I was fixing his tattoos. Greta had been there at Tony Cabin and was wounded by the Sisters of the Three Auroras, who had kidnapped Hal and used silver weapons when the pack came to rescue him. She watched several of her pack mates die that day. And later Siodhachan had taken off to Asgard with her alpha, Gunnar Magnusson, and come back with his body. She had good reason to despise him, and now I had just been introduced as the man who taught him everything he knew. Fecking wonderful.

Siodhachan's advice about disguising my loyalties from the Tuatha Dé Danann comes back to me, and I figure it might be wiser here as well. I couldn't deny any connection with him, but it would be best to bury any notion that I thought him incapable of doing any wrong. We pause the video and I announce my need for another beer. Everyone congregates in the kitchen around an island of granite, and I tell them stories of Siodhachan's greatest cock-ups back when he was me apprentice, asking them to forgive me poor skills at the language. When I tell them about that one time with the goat and the Roman leather skirt stolen from Gaul, they laugh so hard that some of them cry, and Greta simply gives up trying to stand and falls down on the floor, rolling around and laughing until she's gasping for breath. She almost drops her beer and creates a minor tragedy, but thank goodness she has the sense to hand it off to Hal before she loses it completely.

This is reassuring to me. Amidst all the fancy plastic and unnatural materials of the modern world, some things still endure. Goat shenanigans are still fecking funny.

The sun set without me noticing, and it feels wrong when I finally figure it out; you can't tell time well inside these modern buildings. Farid asks Hal if he should throw together some dinner. Hal says, sure, Farid, dazzle us. Farid raids the refrigerator and recruits Efiah to help him. He's a chef at some restaurant that specializes in "Sino–Mexican fusion cuisine." I have no earthly clue what that means and they chop up vegetables I have never seen before, but when the food is finished, it tastes good to me. We drink more and the wolves all share how they were first transformed. Most of them admit that they shat or pissed themselves when they were first bitten and that at the beginning they considered the moon's light to be a curse, but with the gift of the pack and the fullness of time they came to view it as a blessing.

I nod and approve: This should be the nature of power. It must always be acquired at great personal cost. Thus the Druids have the *Baolach Cruatan,* and the twelve years of training, and the three months of binding to the earth. After the dinner, we are faintly exhausted from entertaining one another and ready to be entertained by other means. We return to the sitting area and spread ourselves around. Farid brings around glasses of whiskey, and I enjoy the sound of ice clinking against glass. Greta sits next to me on a couch and answers my questions in a low voice, and I keep asking them so that she will keep talking. Laughter swirls around the room like the ice in me drink, and though there is much in this time that confuses and worries me, I have to admit that I like werewolves. They're hearty and loyal and believe in the many benefits of recreational arse-kicking.

After the second episode of *Sherlock* concludes, everyone goes into the kitchen for refills or visits the bathroom or goes outside for a smoke. Greta remains with me on the couch.

"So," she says.

"So."

"You're not a smart-ass know-it-all like Atticus."

"Ha! You mean Siodhachan? He's a thief, is what he is. Robs you of your patience within five minutes of meeting him. The fact that he's still alive is a testament to me restraint. I wanted to thrash the shite out of him on so many occasions, and only did it maybe ten percent of the time, heh heh."

Her eyes twinkle, and her mouth, which had been drawn tight in disapproval at our introduction a few hours ago, relaxes and widens in a smile. "Yes, I think it's true that he's a thief of patience." She looks down and her expression twists at a sudden thought, and she spends a bit of time involved with some kind of internal struggle. I wait in silence until her eyebrows fly up and she shrugs, as if to say, "To hell with it." She moves closer to me, puts a hand on my shoulder, and whispers in my ear. "Tell me: Is it also true that you haven't had sex for more than two thousand years?"

From my point of view, of course, it hadn't been that long. But I didn't need Siodhachan to tell me that she had just made the first move.

"It sure feels like it," I says.

CHAPTER 10

I wake up in the furs, with tremendous pressure on my bladder, and shuffle to the yeti privy to take care of business. I quickly discover that it is the coldest seat in the universe. It's not really designed for wolfhound use, so I promise Orlaith we'll go outside as soon as I'm finished.

When I emerge into the main hall, Erlendr is tending yet another animal over the fire and Hildr is sitting at the table with the whirling blade spinning in the air in front of her.

"Erlendr, how long was I out?"

"A little over half a day."

"Oh, my. You're already finished with your, uh, whirling?"

"I worked through the night while you slept. Hildr has just begun. If we work around the clock instead of only the waking hours, we can complete it in two days instead of four."

"I see," I say, careful to disguise whether I think this news is good or not. It's easy, because I'm not sure at all how I feel. "Excuse me, I need to take Orlaith outside."

I had thought of an alternate scenario, in which I used the whirling blade to save my father and then returned it to the yeti to destroy in whatever manner they chose. It would be nice to believe that I would not be responsible for what happened then. But I know that by merely asking them to make it for me, I have become responsible. Walking away at this point would not change the fact that some creature would have its spirit splintered at my behest.

Against that I had to weigh my father's spirit. What would happen to him if I did not free him from the raksoyuj? Would he be consumed? Or would he die and go wherever he believed he would go? I am not sure what he believes, actually, and though it's completely illogical, I feel like a terrible daughter for not knowing something so basic about him.

The cold outside is much worse than in the cave. The constant fire has warmed it up in there a noticeable few degrees, and as such I think it better to make a decision inside and not linger where I could turn into an Otter Pop.

When Orlaith is finished, we return to the fire pit and warm up while staring longingly at the roasting meat.

"It's ready. Are you hungry?" Erlendr asks.

"Yes, we both are."

"Sit. I will bring you some."

There is an oddness to being served by a yeti—I mean, beyond the bare fact that I am being served by a yeti. It's the juxtaposition of a warm domestic act of friendliness on the one hand with a whirling blade designed to inhale the spirit of a stabbing victim on the other.

Erlendr puts a plate in front of me and another down on the floor for Orlaith.

<Yay!> is my hound's only comment as she attacks her breakfast.

"What do you wish to accomplish today?" Erlendr asks, sitting down at the table and ignoring his sister.

My eyes flick to Hildr and the blur of a weapon hovering in front of her.

"I'd like to save my father," I say.

"The blade will not be finished in time to do that today. But does that mean you have reconsidered?"

"Yes. I think there is no escaping my responsibility for its creation. I might as well save my father too. But perhaps I can kill something very small with it to return your elemental energy. Like a mosquito."

"I doubt that will work. But a small rodent should suffice."

After he finishes eating, Erlendr excuses himself to get some rest, since he worked on the whirling blade all through the night. Ísólfr and Skúfr come out and join us, while Hildr stays in her zone. The day only gets stranger from there. The yeti teach me how to play fidchell, and I teach them how to play charades. And then, struck by inspiration, I say, "Tell me about snow," and their faces light up with joy. They take me outside, eager to share the beauty they have discovered, like children explaining butterflies to adults.

They say things like, "Snow is the form to which all water aspires, for only as snow is it unique and at rest," and "Vapor is distant and water cuts away at the earth, but snow is the blanket that protects us."

They create puffs and eddies of snow that take brief shape as animals or plants and then scatter. Ísólfr leads me to a sheer cliff face where he has composed ice poems. Skúfr doesn't seem to think them important or even worthwhile, but he reevaluates once I express approval. Ísólfr has written five short poems on the wall in blue ice, where the snow cannot rest. They're written in Old Irish, and each letter sparkles in the weak sunlight. The type is even kerned well, if I'm not mistaken, and that takes it to another level of artistry. I memorize one, to be translated later and preserved for posterity, so:

Mountain home of frost in exile,
Shroud the yeti in secret snows.

Let men whisper and wonder
And never find that which is hidden:
Graah.

Ísólfr puffs up with pride when I tell him the poems are beautiful, and Skúfr inexplicably becomes jealous.

"I was the one who sculpted the figure of Brighid," he announces. I hasten to assure him that it is a brilliant piece of art. "Shall I make you a snowman?"

Before I can answer, a figure of snow begins to rise out of the drift. Not a marshmallow-looking thing but a real human figure—legs and hips and everything.

"Oh, cool!" I say. "Can you make him hold a huge two-handed sword and wear a cloak with feathers all around the shoulders?"

"Of course," Skúfr replies, pleased that he gets to show off a bit. I demonstrate the pose I want and the yeti obliges me, giving the snowman a nice mane of hair at my instruction, including a lock that droops fetchingly in front of one eye. He even creates eyebrows and a thin blue frosty beard that hugs the jawline.

"Can you write something for me on the ground in frost letters, but using English?" I ask him.

"If you trace it out, I will do so."

I scrawl a phrase in front of the snowman's feet, then back away as Skúfr changes it to blue ice and fills in my foot and handprints, smoothing out the surface of the snow.

"Oh, that's perfect! I love it!" My cell phone's battery is long dead, so I haven't a prayer of capturing an image. "I wish I had a camera. I want a picture of me talking to him."

"Does he represent someone you know?" Ísólfr asks.

"No, he represents a character from one of my favorite stories. A handsome fictional man. On several occasions, a beautiful redhead tells him what I have written there."

"What do the words say?"

"They say, 'You know nothing, Jon Snow.'"

By the time the day is finished and it is Ísólfr's turn to work on the whirling blade, Skúfr asks me to give the weapon a name.

"Each whirling blade is unique and has its own identity. I must have a name when I begin the final phase."

The temptation to be flippant and thereby blunt the sinister nature of the whirling blade is strong. If I named it Usul, I could ask it to tell me of its homeworld and promise that its water would forever belong to my sietch. Or I could name it Yoda, firmly aligning it to the light, except that Yoda would never have anything to do with a blade that glows red. I blurt out, "Fuilteach," without knowing precisely why it came to mind when I thought I was traveling a safe but silly thought path. In modern Irish, it means *bloodthirsty*.

"It will be called Fuilteach, then," Skúfr says, and bids me a restful sleep. I use Ísólfr's room this time, since he will be spending the night working on the blade.

I managed to occupy the day with other thoughts besides what was transpiring in India, but the worries come back to me once I'm snuggled up with Orlaith. It takes me hours to drift off, and I don't remain asleep for a full night. When I wake, Ísólfr is still working and looks very tired. No other yeti are in the main hall, so I feed the fire and wander outside with Orlaith for a while.

When I return, Skúfr is awake and Ísólfr is finished. He staggers up from the seat, stiff and weary, and Skúfr extends a steadying hand.

"Sleep, brother."

Ísólfr is so wiped out he can manage only a half-hearted grunt in reply, and a twitch of his fingers serves as a wave goodbye.

As Ísólfr leaves and Skúfr sits down at the table, I take a look at Fuilteach in progress. The transparent tube of ice at the top of the blade is now nearly full with pale-blue energy.

"Do you have a name for that thingie there?" I ask, pointing to the tube. I hope he'll say something nice, like *energy gauge*.

"That's the soul chamber," Skúfr says, and I wince.

"Of course. Look, I'm going to leave for a while and return tonight. Happy whirling."

Orlaith and I exit before any of the other yeti can awaken and delay our departure. The journey down to the tree line, where we can shift away, is only an hour's slog through the snow. I want to take a hot shower and renew my acquaintance with vegetables, so we shift back to the cabin in Colorado, where nightfall is beginning to get serious about its darkness and Steller's jays are talking about how they would have eaten all the worms today if they hadn't become so tired, but they would totally eat them all tomorrow, you just wait.

Atticus hasn't been back—not that I expected him to be. I plug in my cell phone and turn it on to discover the date. It's now October 25. Owen is probably not finished with Atticus's tattoos yet, though they should be wrapping up in a couple of days. I scribble a note to Atticus with the date and time and let him know that, as far as giants who used to eat people go, the yeti are quite agreeable. And then, to mess with him, I add that the invention of hockey might be more crucial than anyone previously believed.

Orlaith and I finish our interrupted trip into town, returning to the leather shop. I buy some rawhide strips and some unfinished pieces to fashion a makeshift scabbard for Fuilteach. I'm going to put a piece of shaped stone at the bottom to make sure that the tip doesn't accidentally punch through and steal a shred of my spirit.

Once we return to the cabin, I shift to my jaguar form and run and play with Orlaith in the forest for a while, keeping my claws in and nipping her gently when she wants to tumble. After a shower, a salad, and a brief nap, I bundle up for the return to the Himalayas, making sure to include a set of throwing knives, since I'll probably be getting into some trouble after I leave the yeti.

On the way up the mountain, I briefly consider asking one of the Tuatha Dé Danann for help in locating my father, but I'm afraid of what their help will cost. The price of getting a whirling blade is already too high. Making deals with deities has gotten Atticus in more than a little trouble, and I wish to avoid that if I can. I hope Laksha has thought of something.

Skúfr is nearly finished and the other yeti are all seated at the table, engrossed in a game of fidchell.

Oddrún welcomes me first and asks what they all must be thinking: "What's the name of the blade? Skúfr can't stop to tell us." Once I share it, they make noises of approval.

"I want to make clear," Ísólfr says, "that you are welcome here anytime. Please visit whenever you wish. And we have made you a gift."

"It was my idea!" Hildr says. She flashes her teeth, reaches down by her feet, and then produces an ice box, which she places in front of me. It's a beautiful, shimmering thing, and inside is a leather scabbard proportioned to Fuilteach's dimensions.

"Oh, you saved me some work! Thank you!" The leather strips I brought with me serve to tie it to my left thigh, and once I have it on, Skúfr groans, sighs, and then allows the whirling blade to stop whirling.

"It is finished." He lowers his hand and the blade descends to rest on the table. "Fuilteach is yours."

The soul chamber is full blue now. Using more of the leather, I wrap the bare handle and then carefully slip it into the scabbard, thanking the yeti all the while for their hospitality and help. They assert that meeting me was pure powder and wish me success in freeing my father. I give them all hugs, because I'm going to make a T-shirt that says I HUGGED A YETI and I want it to be true. But after the farewells, Orlaith and I scamper downhill to the trees as fast as we can manage.

Thanjavur is very different when I return. There are police, or perhaps army troops, in plain sight, wearing masks to ward off contamination. Anyone on the streets is likewise masked and presumably subject to search and curfew and all the other measures governments take to exert control and institute a quarantine. If the blight had been a traditional virus, then it quite probably would have spread far beyond the city by now, but since the rakshasas were the source, it had contained itself to the local area. Of course, rakshasas wouldn't respond at all to modern medicine. I shudder to think how many more must have died while I was gone.

I shed layers of clothing that were necessary in the Himalayas but stifling down here, then cast camouflage on Orlaith and use the bindings carved into Scáthmhaide to turn myself invisible. Keeping a hand on my hound to guide her, I thread my way through the quarantine to Laksha's house, only to find that it has been burned down. The smell is awful, even to my human nose, and smoke still rises from some of the beams. Had my father attacked her or sent a rakshasa to do this? Or had some portion of the townsfolk decided that she was a witch and needed to burn?

"Oh, gods," I breathe, and whip out my cell phone, unable to believe that she's trapped inside. My call goes directly to voice mail. "Laksha, I'm back in town and looking for you. I hope you're okay. Please call or find me."

If her body is in the ruins, I won't find her without drawing attention to myself.

<Now what?> Orlaith asks.

I don't know what to do now, but I flail and grasp at something just to get us out of the neighborhood. *Let's go south, where we last saw her. She seemed to know people in that area and might be around there somewhere.*

We exit the city. The agricultural areas do not look much different but somehow feel neglected already, as if the fields sense that they are fallow in the minds of those who used to tend them. The air trembles and ripples around me, disturbed by what floats in the atmosphere. The sun sets as I run next to Orlaith, and I cast night vision.

Laksha is nowhere to be found near the last two houses we visited, and Orlaith says her scent is either missing or "very old." But at the first house, where we stabbed the rakshasa in the eye and buried him in an alley, a group of people cluster together and speak in hushed, urgent voices. As I draw closer, I see that the mother of the boy we saved is crying, wiping tears from her cheeks as she speaks. She stiffens suddenly and her eyes flick in my direction, but then she relaxes and resumes talking, her tone suggesting that she is tired and would like to go inside. She begins to hug people and wave farewell, and I guide Orlaith toward the door of her home, around the edge of the group. We flatten ourselves along the front wall, unseen, and wait for her to open the door. The neighbors leave one by one, and as the woman turns to open her door, she says in clear but accented English, "Follow me inside, Granuaile."

"Laksha?"

"Come inside." She turns the knob and pushes open the door but leaves it ajar so that we can dart in behind her. Orlaith follows close on my heels, and Laksha closes the door once she hears Orlaith's paws on the floor. I drop the invisibility and camouflage and tilt my head at the woman.

"Is that you in there?"

"Yes," Laksha says, and pulls out her ruby necklace from her sari. "I'm possessing this woman for the time being. I need a new body. Selai Chamkanni has been proclaimed a witch, and they burned her house down while she was still inside."

"Who are *they*?"

"This very woman was responsible," she replies, pointing to herself, and then gestures angrily at the door. "Along with those friendly people out there and others who helped burn my house down."

"Why?"

"The boy we saved was taken over by a new rakshasa the night after you left, but this time it did not linger. It came in under the door in a foul fog, showed itself to the woman, then deliberately attacked and killed her son in front of her. I can see her memory of it. She blamed me, thinking that I sent the rakshasa."

"But that—"

"—Makes no sense, I know. Grief can make us do terrible things. Still, she and her friends caught me by surprise. They surrounded the house and set it on fire, and there was no way to escape without marking the body of Selai forever as a witch. So I tossed my necklace at this woman, left behind the body of Selai, and took over this woman's mind. It is not the friendly arrangement that you and I enjoyed. I would like to find a more willing vessel. But I don't think there will be time for that."

"You know where my father is?"

"No, but I know who does. Were you successful in acquiring a yeti ice knife?"

I don't bother to correct her on the name. I draw Fuilteach from its sheath and hold it up as an answer. She steps closer, her eyes losing focus as she employs her own version of magical sight. She doesn't see bindings the way a Druid does, but whatever she sees, she can interpret correctly. Her eyes refocus and she looks awed.

"That is an extremely dangerous weapon. Did the yeti tell you what would happen if you use the tip?"

"Yes. I won't use that on my father."

"Good. Are you ready, then, or do you need to rest?"

"Ready."

Hidden from view again with my bindings, Orlaith and I follow her out of the house. She leads us east until we reach Nanjikottai Road, a route that runs north–south. We trace it south until we come to a bus stop, but Laksha makes a disgusted sound. "We have missed the last one," she says, looking at the sign. "We will have to walk."

"How far?"

"Only a couple of miles. We can afford the time. South of here is the Thanjavur Air Force Station and a government high school. And once we pass through the village of Nanjikottai, there will be nothing but fields for some distance. I have been able to determine that the rakshasas are coming from the south, so your father must be summoning them from somewhere down there."

"Who's this person who knows where my father is?"

"The devi, Durga."

I blink. "You've spoken with her in the recent past?"

Laksha shakes her head. "Not yet. But I think I will soon. The raksoyuj has drawn her attention, and my prayers regarding him have also been heard. I can feel her watching, benevolent and kind."

Statements like that defy commentary, so I keep my mouth shut. She might be right, after all. Though they rarely deign to manifest on the earth, the gods can and do watch us when we are up to something interesting. Aside from a few of the Tuatha Dé Danann, however, I wouldn't call them benevolent and kind. Maybe Durga would prove to be so.

My education on the Hindu pantheon suggested that Durga was a great protector of humanity. In the old Indian epics, she is not shy to employ her many weapons, slaying rakshasas by the score and smiling all the while, as if to say, "Sorry, fellas, you're living this life the entirely wrong way, so let me help move you along to the next one." She smiles because she is restoring balance, never acting out of anger or malice. And, as Laksha pointed out, this business with the raksoyuj certainly qualified as the sort of thing to which Durga would attend.

We walk mostly in an uncomfortable silence, not only because of our tension and worry but because the insects and animals of the area seem to sense it too. They are all silent, and our footsteps sound abnormally loud. The occasional passing car is magnified to a roar, and its lights blind us in the darkness until it passes.

<Feels wrong here,> Orlaith says.

I feel it too. A fight may be coming, and they may have weapons. Please do not attack. I can fight well. Instead, guard my back and warn me if anyone approaches from behind.

<Okay.>

Laksha leaves the side of the road and walks southwest, directly into a recently harvested field. Its clumpy dirt and severed stems wait to be plowed soon with a winter crop. Once we cross that field and stand on the raised berm that borders another, I can see a lone house perhaps two hundred yards away, maybe more. Surrounding it on all sides are more fields, suggesting that the owner of the house farms all this land. At night, no one from the road would see Laksha here—not that they would even look at anything but the road in front of them during a night drive.

Halting and taking her ruby necklace out of her sari, Laksha clasps it around her neck. "Fighting this woman is tiring." I had not seen any evidence of a struggle, but I have no doubt the woman is fighting Laksha with all her spirit. "Once I leave her head, I will not return. I will preserve myself in the necklace instead. If you would be so kind as to take it from her and then lead me to a hospital, where I can find another comatose person willing to become my vessel, I would be indebted to you."

"Of course. What now?"

"Now we let Durga know that we are ready and hope that she is ready too."

"Forgive me for asking, but how do you know you have a direct line to the goddess?"

"Your question is not offensive; it is a good one. Durga is unlike the other devas in that she is completely independent of the male. She is no one's wife or consort and is not associated with domesticity. She is a warrior alone. And thus she listens to those who are like her. Nontraditional women, shall we say. Like myself."

Laksha kneels down on the berm and draws a circle around her. She produces a small candle and a book of matches from her sari and lights the candle. I expect a chant or something next, but before Laksha can begin, Orlaith startles beside me and her voice fills my head.

<Hey! Big cat! Behind us!>

I whirl around, staff held defensively, and look into the yellow eyes of an enormous lion no more than six feet away. Even though I'm invisible, he's staring directly at me. And so is the goddess astride him.

Stay still, I tell Orlaith. *It's fine.*

Durga is represented in art with varying numbers of arms, but tonight she has manifested with eight. In six of these arms, she wields the trident of Shiva, the sudarshana-chakra of Vishnu, the thunderbolt of Indra, the spear of Agni, the mace of Kubera, and the sword of Yama. She raises one empty hand in greeting and nods ever so slightly at me.

"Laksha, I think she's ready," I say.

Laksha spins around on her knees, gasps, and gushes a stream of words that I can only imagine are praises and thanks. Durga waits until Laksha pauses for breath, and when she does speak, I hear the words both in an unfamiliar language and in English. Her voice is a calm contralto, warm and comforting, like hot tea with honey.

"Druid. Witch. You are closer to evil than you know. The raksoyuj is in that building," she says, pointing with the trident at the farmhouse we had spotted earlier, "and he is surrounded by rakshasas. He knows I am here and even now orders them to attack us. See where they come."

Dark shapes boil out of the house and form ranks. It will not be an undisciplined mob rush, then, but a coordinated attack. Far more of them appear than should be able to fit inside the house. In a matter of seconds, there's an army of demons mustered between my dad and me. I've never been in a battle of this scale before.

I grip Scáthmhaide tightly and boost both my strength and speed.

"Ready," I say.

Durga's lion roars and leaps forward, in a charge at their center.

CHAPTER II

Back in 2010 I had sold Third Eye Books and Herbs to Rebecca Dane for the absurdly low price of $1.72, setting her up in pretty fine style with a functioning business, and I also gave her a first-edition copy of *Leaves of Grass* to auction off for a nice chunk of capital. The revelation that she was somehow responsible for the meddling of a multi-pantheon conclave in my life thus rocked my socks—or would have, if I had been wearing any. Inari refused to tell me anything more of substance beyond that, however, and I must admit that it tested my patience. Like many people, I don't appreciate being manipulated so baldly that I can see the string of the puppeteer. Her entire conversation with me boiled down to, "Do something about Loki. Because Rebecca Dane," and she wouldn't tell me anything else about what had worried the gods so much that they felt they had to nudge me into action.

"The future is a many-forked path," she said, "and only you can choose which one to follow."

"I know that. What I don't know is what waits at the end of those paths."

"Victory or death. Choose well."

<Does anybody really need to think that one over?>

She means I should choose my path well, Oberon, and the paths won't be clearly labeled VICTORY *or* DEATH.

<Never go in against a Druid when DEATH is on the line! A-ha-ha-ha-ha!>

You do remember that the Sicilian who uttered the original version of that sentence died?

<Oh, yeah. I withdraw my ill-chosen pop-culture allusion.>

"Thank you for inviting me to speak with you, honored Inari," I said, pressing my palms together and bowing. "It has been most enlightening. I will retrieve my sword and take my leave." She didn't reply but nodded her head at me, serene and still, as if posing for a portrait next to her kitsune.

Turning the oni over onto his back nearly tore a muscle in mine, and Fragarach, when I pulled it out of his guts, was fouled with juicy juices and in dire need of a de-goring. The Uncompahgre River near our cabin would get that started.

"Farewell," I said, bowing again and receiving no reply. Oberon and I stepped through the ruined doors where Tsukino Hideki stood watch. The bodies of two more oni and four more swordsmen lay in pools of blood in a very public street. I cast an uncertain glance at Tsukino-san, and he bowed to me.

"Do not worry. Inari will not allow this to be seen. All will be hidden and the damage repaired before anyone walks this street."

Thus reassured, Oberon and I trotted back to the top of Mount Inari, where we shifted to our cabin in Colorado.

I found a note from Granuaile dated October 25 waiting for me on the kitchen table. It was a couple of days old, but she didn't mention her father and didn't ask for help, and it sounded as if everything had gone well with the yeti, so I didn't need to worry about her.

<Atticus, I kind of feel icky. Can I have a bath?>

"Absolutely. Let's go."

<But you can't ever tell Orlaith I asked for a bath. It would be unhoundly.>

"I'm not sure that's a word, Oberon."

<It is now. And you also have to promise never to tell her about my poodle addiction.>

"Your poodle addiction? Really?"

Oberon drooped both his head and his tail. <Yes. I am a poodler, Atticus.>

"That's not even a thing!"

<Is too. And the first step to recovery is admitting you have a problem, and I have a problem. With poodles.>

"Oberon, where are you getting this? You don't have a problem."

<Oh, see? Right there! You're enabling me, Atticus! We both have to stop. We should go to meetings.>

"I can't believe what I'm hearing. Tell me where this is coming from."

<People in crime dramas are always being ordered by judges to go to meetings about their addictions. So there has to be a Poodlers Anonymous meeting somewhere.>

"All right, look, I promise never to tell Orlaith about your addiction. You're over it now, right? No more poodles for you?"

<That's right!>

"Okay, then, you are no longer a poodler, we don't need to go to meetings, and you may consider your secret safe." I turned the bathtub faucet on and placed the plug in the drain. "I won't tell her you asked for this bath either." Oberon hopped in and I searched for the liquid soap. He would need a good scrubbing to get all the blood out of his fur.

<Will you tell me a story about ninjas this time, since we almost saw one?>

"I would love to, Oberon, but I never knew any ninjas, and they tend to keep their personal histories a secret."

<But you know lots of secrets.>

"True, but not those." At one time I had been pre-pared to tell Oberon the story of a samurai I had met personally in the sixteenth century, before Tokugawa solidified his power, but decided against it because that fellow had met a bad end and Oberon tended to take these stories to heart. I could, however, tell him about another warrior who had lived and died with honor. "What would you say to a story about a real samurai sword master, perhaps the greatest who ever lived?"

<That sounds good! What was his name?>

"Miyamoto Musashi. Or, if you want the Western order for names, Musashi Miyamoto. In Japan they usually give the family name first."

<They do? What's my family name, Atticus?>

"Well, you can have mine, if you want."

<I don't know if that would be right. We are not re-lated. Didn't I ever have a family name?>

"No, I don't think you did."

<Does that mean I can make one up?>

"Sure."

<I want my family name to be Sirius!>

"So when I introduce you to people, you want me to say you're Oberon Sirius?"

<No, I want you to do it the way they do it in Japan. I am Sirius Oberon. But they can just call me Oberon.>

I stifled a snort of amusement. "Got it."

I turned off the water and dug into Oberon's fur with soapy hands. I had to keep him occupied until I was finished or he would shake himself and soak me.

"Miyamoto wrote *The Book of Five Rings,*" I began, "and before you ask, no, one ring did not rule them all. It was a collection of instructions on swordsmanship and musings on strategy, spirituality, and life, which people still study today. And he's considered an author-ity because he defeated at least sixty men in personal duels and even more in war. He began his violent life at age thirteen and died an old man at peace."

<How was he at peace?>

"It was common for samurai to try to balance their violent lives with art and meditation. Miyamoto enjoyed painting and calligraphy and even architecture. He urged people not to study the sword only, because there is so much more to life than learning how to end it. There was a certain fatalism to the samurai way of life and an emphasis on dying well."

<Dying well? I don't get it. If you are already dead, how do you know you did a good job getting that way?>

"Dying well actually meant that you had lived well, because few samurai believed they had rewards waiting for them in the next life. Regardless of whether they were Shinto or Buddhist, they knew they would pay a price for killing others. So it was necessary in their eyes to make their lives as beautiful as possible to balance the ugliness. They wished to die with honor. They lived according to a code called bushidō."

<What was that like?>

"They valued courage, of course, but also loyalty and honesty and benevolence, among other noble values."

<Were they vegetarians like those people in India?>

"No."

<Okay, then, that's noble.>

"But Miyamoto Musashi was not the typical samurai. For many years he was rōnin—masterless—and remained outside service for much of his life, pursuing excellence in strategy and the art of the sword. He even invented his own style of fighting, called *Niten Ichi Ryu*—fighting with two swords. He became so good at what he did that he changed martial arts forever."

<So he's kind of like you!>

"What?" I have been called many things but never an

influence on martial arts. The idea was so novel that I stopped scrubbing in surprise.

\<I mean he invented new stuff and nobody could beat him. You made up that amulet and no one can beat you.\>

"Oh. I . . . Well, I'm not unbeatable, really."

\<*Man,* this tickles!\>

"No, Oberon, wait—"

Too late. He shook himself and sprayed the entire bathroom with nasty, bloody, hound-flavored water and soap. I took the brunt of it.

"Auuggh!"

\<Sorry. I thought you were done.\>

CHAPTER 12

A car engine wakes me—someone next door going to work at sunrise. Next door, I should say, to Greta's house, which is located on the north side of Camelback Mountain in a town called Paradise Valley. The noise rouses her, too, and she shifts against my side and drapes a thigh across mine, regarding me with sleepy eyes and a lazy smile. We don't say anything, because I think we're both wondering why we're there and what to do next. Or maybe it's just me wondering that.

I mean, I know how I got there: Greta invited me to her bed. But I don't know why she did it. I'm not a pretty man like Siodhachan. And considering how she feels about him, I'm surprised she wanted anything to do with me, his archdruid.

Before I take another step down the emotional path—it's a rough walk, always choked on either side with thorny bushes of self-doubt and feelings I'd rather not feel—I decide to accept the night for the gift it was and be grateful. She would explain or not, as she wished.

I stretch and yawn and then she takes a turn at it, demonstrating that she's a fecking expert at stretching.

"Have ye got one of those fancy toilet things in this place?" I ask. When we came in last night, I didn't see much of her house. We were paying attention to each other and little else.

"I wouldn't call it fancy," she says, "but, yes, I have one in the bathroom."

"It's all fancy to me," I says. "Ye don't know how good ye have it."

"Oh, yes, I do," she replies. "I was around before the toilet, you know."

"Ye were?" Me jaw drops and she grins, pleased to have surprised me. "How long do werewolves live?"

"If someone doesn't end us through violent means, somewhere between four and five hundred years. We don't start showing our age until the last fifty or so." She tilts her head, looking smug. She expects me to ask her how old she is now, but I'm not going to fall into that trap. For once in me life I see a chance to be nice, and I take it.

"I like what you're showing, regardless of your age," I says, and she hums with pleasure as I leave the bed to search for the bathroom. I think the term for her home might be something like *swank* or maybe *opulent*. It is decorated in earth tones, and the furnishings are all of natural wood, aside from the occasional cushion. The floors are hardwood too. There are many more rooms than she needs. When I return to the bedroom she is gone, but she comes in behind me.

"I used the other bathroom," she says.

"How many are there?"

"Four."

"And you live here all by yourself?"

"Yes. But the pack visits often and I'm able to put them up, and my house is also used to board visitors from out of town."

"What is it that you do, exactly?"

She shrugs. "I do lots of things. Whatever the pack needs."

"I hear everyone has to have a job these days. What's your job title?"

Her mouth quirks up at one end. "I don't have a title. Enforcer, perhaps?"

"Is that what you tell humans when they ask you?"

"No. I tell them I'm a government courier. Often out of town, you see, and lots of secrets; can't tell them much because they don't have security clearance."

"They believe that?"

"If they don't, they won't be seeing me again. Among people who have dealings with wolves I'm sometimes called the gamma. I am number three in the pack, behind Hal and Esteban."

"Oh. Does that mean you could be alpha somewhere else if you wanted?"

"Maybe, but I don't want that. I'm content where I am. Lots of benefits and none of the responsibility."

"I see. What is it that you enforce?"

"I'm the primary enforcer of the territory's boundaries. And if someone is messing up our territory—vampire, witch, whatever—I'm the one who lets them know they need to calm their shit down."

"Sounds dangerous."

"It can be. More often it's drudgery. I do the criminal stuff for the pack, like getting your fake IDs. I have to do all the shit jobs too, which mostly involve your apprentice."

"Ah, he's like a sick baby, isn't he? Spewing his mess everywhere."

"That's a good analogy," she says, and flashes a grin at me. "But let's not talk about him. Are you hungry?"

"Aye. Can ye maybe teach me how to cook in these kitchens? I saw some of what Farid did last night, but I couldn't follow. All I had in my day was an open fire."

"Sure. That'll be fun."

She teaches me how to make coffee and then demonstrates the arcane procedure for making something called French toast. After she sprinkles powdered sugar and pours syrup on it and I take my first bite, I have to admit it's the most delicious breakfast I've ever had. I couldn't imagine any of the Gauls of my day ever making something like this, but I suppose the modern French must be a very different tribe, and I keep all such thoughts private.

"What's next for you?" she says around a mouthful of toast.

"I have to go to the Fae Court and tell the Tuatha Dé Danann that I'm walking the earth again. It's the kind of courtesy that only matters if you don't pay it."

"Oh, so you'll be back tonight?"

"It might take longer than that," I admit. "I expect I'm going to be invited to dine a lot. They need to find out where I stand and what I know so that they can decide what role I'll play in their power games."

"Sounds familiar. Seems like werewolves think of nothing else."

"The funny thing is, I don't think they ever knew about me in me own time. Druids were everywhere back then. But now that I'm one of only three, I suddenly matter. I don't suppose ye could drive me out of here to where there's some trees? Siodhachan says there's nothing tethered to Tír na nÓg in this area and I can't make me own tethers. We have to go somewhere called Payson. Or near it, anyway, up to someplace called the Mogollon Rim."

She nods and says, "All right. That's about an hour and a half away, but I'll do it on one condition."

"What's that?"

She leans forward, her blue eyes intense and her voice low. "Run with me in the forest, as wolf and bear."

I blink, surprised at the mildness of the request. "Gladly. That's no hardship."

"Good. What are your other forms?" she asks, leaning back and dropping her eyes to me right arm, where the shape-shifting bindings are. The designs give a good idea of the basic creature, but the specific animal is not always obvious.

"Ah. Me hoofed form is a ram. And then there's the bear, a red kite for the winged form, and in the sea . . . well, it doesn't really matter. I can count on one hand the number of times I've shifted to that form. I'm not fond of it."

"Why? What are you in the sea?"

"In English it's called a walrus."

Her eyes nearly start from her head, and she quickly covers her mouth so that she won't spit anything out. She struggles to swallow her last bite and then gasps when she finally manages to choke it down. Slapping her hand flat against the table, she says, "*You* are the walrus? Of course you are. You're the walrus. Goo goo ga joob! Ha! That's perfect!"

"Goo goo ga what? What's that mean?"

"We'll listen to the Beatles in the car and it'll all become clear. Come on, teddy bear. Let's do the dishes."

"Wait. What's a teddy bear? I'm a black bear."

"Don't knock it. People like to cuddle with teddy bears."

On the way up to Payson she tells me a bit about her history. She'd shared last night that Gunnar Magnusson, the old alpha, had originally bitten her and brought her into the pack, but she hadn't revealed the circumstances surrounding it.

She'd been living on a farm some distance outside Reykjavik. During a full moon, a small band of men, recent arrivals from Norway, had invaded and slain her father and brother. Greta hid in the barn, but it was only a matter of time until they found her. Gunnar and Hal, hunting beneath the moon's glow, heard the cries of battle and arrived before the invaders could find and violate Greta. They tore out the Norsemen's throats and then had to decide what to do with her. There weren't supposed to be any wolves in Iceland, and their presence needed to remain a secret, so their choices were to kill Greta or make her a werewolf like them. Gunnar bit her, then he and Hal stayed until dawn, when they could shift and explain what had happened. Gunnar shifted, Hal stayed in his wolf form, and Gunnar told Greta that she could choose death or choose the pack. The pack would offer her a violent life, but, he promised, she would never get so close to death again.

Gunnar and Hal became her father and brother after that. And Gunnar's promise held true for centuries: She never came so close to death again, until the night that the Polish witches almost killed her in the meadow around Tony Cabin—the night Aenghus Óg opened a portal to hell. She blamed Siodhachan for that, for the deaths of the pack mates who didn't survive that night, and for Gunnar's death in Asgard as well. Siodhachan had told me as much, but it was far different when it came from Greta's perspective. To her way of thinking, Siodhachan had done her serious wrong, and for the life of her she could not imagine why Hal would continue to have dealings with him.

We're driving past a sign that says SYCAMORE CREEK when tears escape from her eyes and run down her cheeks. "I think sometimes about all the other packs in the world, who have never met Atticus O'Sullivan. How they still have their alphas. How they never had to watch their pack mates be killed by silver." She sniffles and takes her hand off the steering wheel to wipe irritably at her cheek. "And I wonder why it was my pack that had to suffer." She shakes her head. "I'm sorry. I don't mean to dump on you."

"Dump away, love. It's all I'm good for. I don't have an answer for you, though."

"No, I don't need an answer. I guess I just needed a release. Thanks."

"You're welcome." A minute passes without any words. A mile underneath the car's wheels, during which I realize that I am probably no more to her than an exercise in mental health. And I am fine with that. She has suffered long enough. If I can bring her to a semblance of balance and that is all, then I have done Gaia's work here.

Then she says through a sob, "I miss them."

"Yes. It's our duty to remember the dead. And our duty to let them go."

She weeps in silence, aside from another sniffle or two, and then she gasps, "Oh, shit! The dead must be, like, everyone you've ever known. Owen, I'm so sorry."

"Ah, not to worry. Everyone's gone but Siodhachan and the Tuatha Dé Danann, but I'd already outlived most of the people I knew and didn't get along with the rest. But I remember them all."

"What do the Druids believe about death?"

"I don't know what you mean. I mean, it happens."

"Right, but what happens after death?"

"Feck if I know, Greta. I haven't died yet."

She laughs and says, "No, I mean, do you believe in an afterlife? A paradise?"

"Oh, aye. Once the Tuatha Dé Danann agreed to leave this world to the Milesians, they created nine planes, of which Tír na nÓg is the largest. There's also Mag Mell and Emhain Ablach and others. But I can't tell you where I'll be going, or where anybody else goes, or what will happen when I get there."

She drives us up to this Mogollon Rim, the very southern tip of the Colorado plateau and another elemental's territory, and takes a left at a sign marked WOODS CANYON LAKE.

"We're up on the Rim now," she says. The road is

paved for a few miles, until we get to the turnoff for the lake, but she keeps going and it becomes dirt. "Most everyone turns off at the lake, so after another five miles we won't see anyone. Great place to run around."

She's right about that. It's mostly tall ponderosa pines mixed with the occasional juniper, and the undergrowth isn't bad at all—only sage and something she says is called manzanita. She pulls over and we get out of the car, and I enjoy the silence after the slam of the door. No industrial hum here. I say hello to the elemental, and it welcomes me. Through it I am able to discover that there are bound trees within easy running distance.

"Let's get out of sight of the road before we shift," she says, and together we jog into the trees until the car and the road are out of sight. I can pretend it's old days again.

"Have you ever seen a werewolf shift?" she asks me.

"Aye. Saw a lad in Flagstaff do it. Ty Pollard."

Her face lights up. "Oh, I know Ty! Sam's husband. Nice fella and good to have at your shoulder. Anyway, I'm glad you've seen the change before, so you won't be shocked." She pulls off her shirt and adds, "It's not a pretty sight."

"Well, *those* are pretty—"

"Ha! Stop. You know, my wolf is going to want to play with your bear. And when I say play, I mean fight. You up for it?"

I grin and say, "Yes. That's what I was doing with Ty."

"Throat and spine are off-limits."

"Those are the rules," I agree, as she continues to undress and I get started doing the same.

"My wolf is going to be pissed. Changing during the day with the moon out of phase is painful. I mean more than usual."

"Understood."

"Talk to you later." She smiles and winks at me and then, free of her clothes, winces as the transformation begins. Bones snap and shift underneath the skin, threatening to burst through in places, and she falls to all fours. The worst part has to be the knees popping and reforming in the other direction for the back legs. I feel a bit guilty as I mouth the words and bind my spirit to the shape of a bear, a process that Gaia has made quick and painless for us. We are her creatures, and our bodies are hers to shape as she wishes.

Greta's wolf is powerful and angry, as she promised. She growls once low in her throat and then launches herself at me. I stand up, take her charge in the chest, and then we tumble, clawing and snapping at each other. She gets in a good bite on my left chest, near the crook of my arm, and I'm able to rake my claws down her left ribs. She makes a few superficial scratches, but her claws aren't like mine. We disengage and face off. She barks, I bellow, and then her aggression dissolves and she wants to play in a different way. She splays out her front legs and lowers her head to the ground while her tail rises and actually wags. She barks once and then takes off deeper into the forest. I give chase, surprising her by closing the gap on the straightaway, but I'm not nearly so agile. Every time she changes direction, I lose ground. We run for ten minutes, top speed, then she leads us into a meadow, where we scare a small herd of elk that had bedded down for the day. She's not interested in hunting them, though; she turns and faces me, tongue lolling out, happy, and then begins to circle me and growl again. It's back to fighting.

Our second tussle lasts much longer than the first, and we mess each other up pretty good. There's no audience, no one to stop us, and it's savage. She takes plenty of punishment and delivers it right back. We stagger away, bleeding like lambs, both trying to give the impression that we're ready for more, but in truth we're maybe ready for a break. We're panting, too concerned with breathing to waste anything on vocalizations, and that's a reliable sign that we have worn each other out. She walks up to me, ears and tail up, nonaggressive, and sits down, her bloody muzzle raised to look at me. I sit too, then decide to go ahead and lie down on my right side to draw more energy for healing. She slumps over onto her left side so that we're lying in the meadow facing each other.

I hurt in places I didn't know were places. Somewhere, Siodhachan had picked up a binding to shut off pain, and he taught it to me, but I don't use it now. Greta doesn't have a binding like that. It wouldn't be fair.

Gradually our breathing slows and our eyelids grow heavy. I see hers flutter closed a couple of times before mine do the same.

I awake later to popping and crunching noises as she shifts back to human form. We lost a few hours, judging by the sun, and I feel warm and much better when I shape-shift myself.

"Thank you," Greta says. "I needed a good fight."

I lack skills for expressing emotions other than anger and impatience. I feel them quite often but rarely communicate them. All I manage to say is, "Me too."

Her eyes trail down my body. "You heal well."

"A good thing, that is. So do you."

"Ready to go back?"

We walk to where we left our clothes—a decent hike, during which she talks a lot and I grunt in all the right places and try to think of something appropriate to say. I'm uncertain if she wants to see me again. I still think our time together might be more about her past than about a present attraction. Her rate of speech might indicate her own nervousness about where we go from here, but, if so, why exactly is she nervous? Is it a sign that she likes me and wants to share everything, or is it a desperate bid to fill the time so that I won't ask to turn a dalliance into something more?

She finally stops talking when we reach our clothes, yet I'm not ready with anything to say. I must look as scared as I feel, because, after we're dressed, she examines my face for a few moments and then smiles in an attempt to put me at my ease.

"Thanks for listening to me ramble on," she says. "You're quite good at it."

I have never been accused of being a good listener before. It was probably a result of my discomfort with the language. Or else it emphasized how much this jump forward in time has changed me.

Greta throws up her hands and lets them fall back down to slap against her legs. "This was fun."

"Well—yes. It was." Unexpected and very welcome fun.

"I know you have to go now, but feel free to visit again." She comes closer until her nose almost touches mine. Light dances in her blue eyes. "You know. If you're free. And if you feel like it."

"I will." I nod at her, relieved at the invitation. "I like you." Gods below, you'd never think I came from a family of bards. If me uncle had heard me say that shite he would have taken me balls because I wouldn't be needing them anymore.

"Good. Let's leave it at that." She kisses me quickly on the mouth and heads for the car, with me standing there stunned. She's almost out of sight before I can compose a sentence.

"Balance and blessings go with ye!" I call after her. She doesn't answer, but I'm sure she hears me.

I shake my head, trying to clear it. I desperately need

to find me own balance. I have so much catching up to do.

First on the list is catching up in Tír na nÓg, because I can speak Old Irish there and not sound like I took a hammer to me skull.

The elemental tells me to run toward Woods Canyon Lake, where Siodhachan has tethered a tree. He said he'd spent hundreds of years tethering the world to Tír na nÓg, back when kings were grinding their people to early deaths and using priests to tell them it was the plan of their god and it was not their place to question. It kept him busy and away from Aenghus Óg in the short term, but in the long term it ensured that he'd always have somewhere to run if anyone else came after him. If I had to point to one thing he's done that's a hundred percent good, that project would be it.

My thinking is that I need to be training Druids again—it's me mission, really—but it will be quite some time before there are enough of us to matter. In the meantime, this ability to travel around the entire world instead of just to Europe will make our wee numbers as effective as possible.

When I find the proper tree, I shift directly to a place on the edge of the Fae Court. It's nighttime there, and no one is around except for a few guards. One of them, a flying faery dressed in some kind of silver and green bollocks, yells at me to state my business. My patience disappears right away.

"Why don't ye state yours first?" I says.

"I'm doing my assigned duty, guarding the Court." He draws a sword on me and opens his mouth to demand my business again, but I interrupt him.

"From what, I might ask? Are ye afraid someone will drop their pants and water the grass? There's nothing to guard, lad. It's a meadow!"

"Someone could craft an ill binding while no one is

looking. And sometimes messengers arrive at all hours from other planes. Now, who are you?"

"I'm the man who's wondering who taught ye to talk like that. Are ye serious, lad—'ill binding'? The Fae used to be a proud folk who spoke plainly and dressed sensibly. Now look at ye!"

He points the sword at me. "State your business or be gone!"

"My business is with Brighid, First among the Fae. I'm a Druid of Gaia long gone from the world, here to announce my return."

He shrinks back. "A Druid? Not the Iron Druid?" That physical reaction to the mere idea of Siodhachan tells me an epic or two. Me apprentice was right: He wasn't popular here at all. As much as I hated to admit it, it would be best to take his suggestion and pretend I didn't know him.

"No, lad, I'm fresh out of iron, and mixing iron with Druidry sounds dumber than having a swim with the Blue Men of the Minch. Would you let Brighid know I am here, or let someone else know who will then speak to her?"

"I require your name to do that."

"Eoghan Ó Cinnéide."

"Wait at the foot of her throne. She will receive you there when she is ready." He uses his sword to indicate an iron chair on a small mound of dirt.

"Fine." I brush past him and prepare myself for a long wait. I'm sure it's hours until daylight and Brighid might take her time waking up. I plant myself in front of the throne, legs crossed, and take off me shirt so that the tattoos will be plainly visible to anyone who wishes to check me out in the dark. It won't reveal anything except that I'm telling the truth about being a Druid.

Less than an hour has passed, I'm guessing, when an orange globe of fire drops from the sky into the iron throne, startling me. A wall of it spreads out from the impact and I roll backward, away from the heat. When I look back, Brighid is sitting on the throne, and the small hill is circled by a ring of fire. She is dressed simply in a belted blue tunic and wears a golden torc around her neck.

"I am told you are Eoghan Ó Cinnéide," she says.

"Yes."

"I can see that you are bound to the earth, so you are who you say you are. My son, Goibhniu, tells me that you spent two millennia on one of the Time Islands."

"Yes."

"He also says it was the Morrigan who put you there and Siodhachan Ó Suileabháin who removed you. Will you tell me why?"

"I've been entrusted with a message from the Morrigan in the event of her death. She told Siodhachan where to find me, knowing that he would bring me back into the normal flow of time."

"Then we have much to talk about."

"Aye, Brighid, we do."

CHAPTER 13

Perhaps deities spend more time talking things over in whatever realm they reside. I have noticed, though, that once they are on earth, they have a very specific to-do list and waste no time getting to it. It's disorienting to go from passive observation to full battle in the space of a few seconds, with no time to discuss objectives or strategy or tactics. I have to scramble to take up a position on the left side, and Laksha brings up a very tardy flank on the right. When Durga and her lion meet the vanguard of the rakshasas, I understand the true meaning of Shakti, a divine weapon. The demons are bowled over as the lion keeps plowing through them and Durga lays about her with her weapons, tossing some of the demons into the air and crushing others, cutting and spearing and painting the air and ground with blood and viscera.

For a second I feel entirely superfluous; Durga can surely take care of everything by herself. But the rakshasas keep pouring out of the house as fast as she slays them. A growing roar from behind me earns a glance, and I see that another army is advancing from the city. The raksoyuj has called all the rakshasas back to defend him, giving the city a respite from ruin while giving us a significant problem.

Out of the corner of my eye, I see Laksha spread her

hands in front of her and fall forward into the dirt, life-
less. She wasn't hit by anything, so I presume she's left
the woman's body and intends to do battle in the ether,
working her way through the rakshasas until she gets to
my father. I hope the woman has the good sense to stay
down and play dead, or she won't have long to enjoy the
sole possession of her faculties.

Before Laksha can fight the raksoyuj in the ether,
though, I have to get him to leave my father's body.

We are going inside the house, Orlaith. On my heels.
<On them.>

The rakshasas are collapsing in toward Durga, not
even realizing I'm on the field. I don't know if they can
pierce my invisibility the way the devi can, but I doubt
it occurs to them to look for me. I swing around farther
left to avoid them, hoping to sneak into the house and
do my duty with Fuilteach before the raksoyuj realizes
there's a threat other than Durga.

I'm still a hundred yards away from the house when
the nature of the battle changes. A different sort of
demon starts to pour forth from the door and take
shape in the yard—blue-skinned, many-armed, glowing
with power. I stop to reassess and realize that they
look like the form Loki took that time he tried to mess
with Atticus in the Polish onion field outside Jasło. My
guess is that they are probably not rakshasas but more-
powerful demons called *asuras*. They carry themselves
differently: They move like masters-at-arms, while the
rakshasas have all the martial skills of a coked-up peas-
ant armed with a spoon.

And in the midst of this phalanx walks my father, his
eyes glowing blue and his accustomed expression of
academic detachment twisted into malevolence. It's
been a very long time since I've seen him, of course, but
my heart sinks at how old he looks now. His hair has
gone white and wispy and it's retreated from the top of

his head, and the well-defined jaw of his younger days has faded as the skin under his neck sagged. I tell myself that I can deal with his age; it's his expression that makes me recoil, and I realize that I have never before seen him look angry or favor me with any expression more severe than indifference.

Now he's looking at Durga with the kind of leer that would inspire anyone to either run or empty a full clip into his chest, and it horrifies me. He bellows something incoherent, and the *asuras* surge forward, long swords in their fists. The flash of steel against their blue skin makes them seem like a frothy wave, building to crash upon Durga. It washes and flows around her and the lion, drowning out the black rakshasas, and clouds condense and roil overhead where it was a clear night minutes ago. The army of rakshasas behind me grows closer and I pull Fuilteach from its sheath, resuming my run around the flank, target now in sight. I will have to clear a number of the demons out of the way before I can reach him, but everything still seems possible and the problems solvable—until suddenly they aren't.

Twirling Scáthmhaide in my left hand only, I aim for throats, crushing the windpipes of unsuspecting rakshasas. I slash open the necks of others with Fuilteach, spinning as I advance to add force to my blows. Black blood gushes like oil, and bodies fall with toothy snarls onto the field. At first it is easy work, a deadly caper through opponents as skilled as training dummies, but soon the ones closest to my father become aware that something that isn't Durga is approaching on their flank and they turn, slashing the air with their blades at an unseen foe. My father doesn't notice; his eyes are locked on the seething tumult surrounding the goddess.

I need two hands on the staff to parry the attacks of the rakshasas and then the three *asuras* who guard my father, so I sheathe Fuilteach and wade in. I knock aside blades, slam the demons in the gut to make them bend over, and then finish them with a blow to the head or throat as they are momentarily robbed of breath.

Orlaith defends my back a couple of times, judging by her growls and the panicked howling that abruptly chokes off behind me.

I find that my staff alone cannot break through the defenses of the *asuras*. They present an impenetrable flurry of steel, with their four arms weaving blades in front of them, and they are far more disciplined than the rakshasas. It's an excellent counter to a single weapon. To create an opening, I flick a small throwing knife at their faces, not particularly caring where it hits and knowing it won't be fatal. All it does is cause a flinch, an interruption of their defenses, and I take advantage of that to shoot the shaft of Scáthmhaide into their throats. I feel something wet on my arm, look down, and see that I've been cut somehow. No matter; I'm high on adrenaline and the earth's energy, and there's only a single *asura* left between my dad and me.

The demon's reach is incredible, and he's using all of it now that he's seen his companions fall. I drop down into a squat and swing Scáthmhaide at his ankle, cracking it loudly against bone, then rise from my crouch as he falls to the ground. He's there for less than a second before I shove my staff into his nose and pile-drive it into his brain—a tad more vicious than I would normally be, but he was keeping me from my dad. A small voice in my head wonders if this behavior in battle is why the elementals have been calling me Fierce Druid, but I can't answer it.

Dad—or the raksoyuj—turns, finally aware that something threatens nearby, and I wonder where his pupils have gone. His sockets are like blue Christmas lights. If I dwell on it, however, I will miss my chance—

the ravening cries of the rakshasas from the city are
growing louder.

I whip Fuilteach from its sheath, hold it so that it is
upside down in my fist—a grip better for slashing than
for stabbing—and lunge forward, before the thing possessing my dad can process what's happening and I can
nurse any doubts about what I'm doing. I drag the sharp
blade across the center of his chest, opening up a rent in
his shirt, and the skin beneath that blooms blood. And
that's as close as I ever came to saving my father, because I never got to make the second cut to the chakra
above his head.

In retrospect, I can see the chess moves, if not the mo-
tives behind them. The blight of the rakshasas draws
Durga to earth; Durga's presence draws out the raksoyuj and the *asuras*. The summoned clouds provide
cover from satellites so that humans never see that demons and gods still do battle on this plane. And then,
when the tide of blue demons manages to slip through
Durga's defenses and wound her lion—as an anguished
roar testifies—the devi can no longer slay with patience
and kindness. The lion's roar comes almost simultaneously with the roar of the raksoyuj after I cut him.
Eager to press my advantage and make the second cut
on his brow, I get caught on the temple by my father's
raging, flailing arm. He's far more powerful than he
should be, knocking me backward and setting off popping light flashes behind my eyes. I tumble over Orlaith,
hitting the ground hard, and my window of opportunity shuts forever. From the ground, I see Durga leap up
into the air and hover, seven arms low and one held
high, the high one clutching the twin bell shapes of Indra's thunderbolt. The third eye on her forehead opens,
and with it comes destruction.

Lightning lances down into the *asuras* surrounding
Durga's lion, throwing them back and charring their

skin, and then a single massive bolt is thrown at my father. It doesn't destroy him or even knock him off his feet, but it burns away his clothing without igniting any of his skin. Wreathed in blue fire, he looks pale, wizened, and skeletal, and he shouts something in a deep, throaty rasp that's not his own.

I scramble to my feet and backpedal, because I'm starting to feel the shock coming up through the ground and there is palpable, searing heat radiating from him. I back off a good fifty yards on sheer instinct, grabbing a fistful of Orlaith's coat and urging her to run with me, before I remember that I still have work to do. But the devi continues to pour power into her strike, and I can't get any closer to make that second cut; it's already like putting my face down in front of a four-hundred-degree oven and opening the door.

<What happens?> Orlaith asks, but I don't have time to explain.

Stay with me, I tell her, and then I shout at the devi, "Wait, Durga, I can separate the raksoyuj from the man! I just need one more chance!"

The sorcerer possessing my father is immensely powerful—he could not withstand such a barrage of elemental fury for even a second if he did not have legendary defenses—but he is not so powerful as perhaps he thought. It is already clear that whatever he sought to accomplish by forcing Durga to visit the earth won't be happening. The arrogance and malevolence on my father's face slowly drains away, and the blue glow in his eyes fades too, as the body begins to quiver under the strain of the assault.

"Please stop! I can fix this!" I plead.

But the devi continues to punish him with lightning. It swirls and crackles around him, and his movements grow more jerky and involuntary. I drop my invisibility and call out to him.

"Dad!" I cry. "Can you hear me? It's Granuaile!"

His head twitches in my direction, the blue lights wink out, and his eyes return to brown, and for the briefest instant I see confusion, wonder, and kindness in them as he lifts a hand toward me, recognizing his daughter. And then the devi's energy overwhelms the raksoyuj, and my father is torn apart in a violent explosion of meat and bone, atomized into a red mist that evaporates completely, leaving nothing where he stood but ash and a rising trail of smoke.

CHAPTER 14

When I drove down to Tempe for the second time in as many days, I took comfort in the knowledge that I could stay a few hours and enjoy myself. I had missed Mill Avenue more than I realized. Crunchy unwashed people still inhabited the corners, selling hemp jewelry and singing badly in hopes of scoring enough cash to buy their next dime bag or "wicked nommy sammich." Feeling insouciant, I joined a pungent pair in a raucous ukulele rendition of an old Tom Petty song, loudly informing passersby that, regardless of their relationship status, their living conditions need not resemble that of a refugee. I gave them forty bucks afterward for letting me sit in, and they couldn't believe it.

"Thanks, brah!" one gushed, but the *brah* kept going as he stared at the twenties until it became a manic laugh: "Ha-haaah! Ha! Haaah! Yeah! Wooo!"

His companion said, "Dude, you are motherfucking solid. *Solid*, man! We are going to get the best sammiches ever thanks to you!" He turned to shout at two college coeds who were strolling by with shopping bags from a shoe store, eager to share what he had just learned. "This dude with the dog and the sword is hella cool! I'm not kidding, okay?" They cringed and hurried past, and I figured I should leave before the praise of my newfound fans got any more effusive. I gave them both quick bro hugs and wished them harmony before heading to Rúla Búla to meet Hal.

<Atticus, I don't think I've ever seen humans get that excited about sandwiches before. Where's the sandwich shop they like so much?>

I don't know, buddy. I doubt the sandwiches they're thinking of are anything special. It's more like those two guys are special.

<Well, I share their enthusiasm for food, and I was thinking I should contribute something legendary to the world in that area. I will master food like Miyamoto Musashi mastered swords and you mastered iron.>

That wasn't the obsession I'd expected Oberon to take away from last night's bathtime story, but I could live with it. *You want to learn how to cook?*

<No, I want you to cook and let me coach you on the taste. Because you have thumbs and I have highly tuned senses. Together we will develop Sirius Foods, and I'll have my own line of premium meats, like Oberon's Eight-Spice Triple Boar Turbo Sausage and Oberon's Chop-Licking Beer-Braised Hogaggedon Brats.>

Sounds like a thrilling odyssey of arterial plaque.

<We will show Abe Froman what it means to be Sausage King! And don't try to tell me he's not real.>

We met Hal on the patio because it was a nice day, even in late October, and a camouflaged Oberon would have more room to stretch out underneath the table. It was a high top with an umbrella over it to provide shade during the hot months. We ordered some draughts and the glorious fish and chips, along with some bangers for the hound. Hal was in a good mood.

"That archdruid of yours is quite the character. We had lunch here yesterday and I took him home to meet the pack. The stories he told!" He chuckled. "You and that goat!"

"Aw, no—I'd forgotten about that; thanks a lot." He

looked as if he was going to laugh some more about it, so I asked him a question to forestall him. "Where is he now?"

"Don't know. But I bet Greta does."

"Why is that?"

"Well, he left my house with her."

I didn't quite know how to take that news, because Greta was not fond of me, so I filed it away for later and made no comment. Frankly, it made me uneasy—but it wouldn't be politic to reveal my uneasiness to Hal. I changed the subject instead.

"Remember Rebecca Dane, the girl who runs the old shop now?"

"Sure, I remember."

"I'd like you to do a full background check. And I mean full. I especially want to know if there's anything magical about her house or if she has any ties at all to the paranormal community here. And maybe she has abilities we never suspected."

Our food arrived, and we paused while the server asked us if we needed anything else. Hal waited until she was out of earshot before answering. "I know you're serious about this, but I can't imagine why. There was never any indication she had a magic hobby on the side."

"I agree that was the case back then. But I have reason to believe that we may have been duped." My dream from Ganesha had come shortly after the sale of the shop, so if Inari was correct in assigning her culpability, she had done something back then to set events in motion. If it was just prayer, why had Rebecca's drawn attention and inspired action when so many others were—and are—ignored? "I'll go see her after we're through here, but I'd like the check done to make sure."

He drummed his fingers on the table once and gave a tight nod. "All right. What else?" I put a plate of bangers and mash on the seat next to me so that Oberon could slurp them up from underneath the table.

"I need you to liquidate more money to pursue my private vampire war. It's been quite effective."

Hal cleared his throat before picking up his fork and digging in. "Yes, well, I don't mean to cast a shadow on your joy, but I should probably interject here that financing wars is expensive and your accounts are not inexhaustible."

"True, but I have more accounts," I said. Hal stopped chewing his first mouthful. "I never told you about all of them, and they're all bigger than the ones I've been using so far."

Hal growled around his fish, "What were you saving it all for?"

"For dodging Aenghus Óg. And for the day when I needed to hire a small army of implacable vampire-killing mercenaries."

"How do you manage it all? It must take enormous time. I know, because I spend quite a bit looking after the assets you've told me about."

I shrugged and dipped a chip in ketchup. "I have a trustworthy person looking after things for me. You'd like him, Hal. His name is Kodiak Black."

"Kodiak? Is he some kind of bear shifter?"

"Yes, but don't call him a werebear. He gets cranky about that."

<Atticus, how many other great big bears do you know that you haven't told me about?>

There's only Owen and Kodiak. I promise.

"Wow. I've heard of those bear boys," Hal said, "but I've never seen one. Where'd you find him?"

"Up in Alaska, where all the yummy salmon run in the summer. He's into fresh fish, as you might imagine."

"Huh. Does he tell regular folk his name is Kodiak?"

"Nah, he tells them his name is Craig. I'll give you his email address."

"All right. Hey, speaking of mail and vampires, I have something for you." Hal reached into his jacket and withdrew an envelope from his breast pocket. He handed it over, and as soon as I took it, his face contracted into a look of guilt, which triggered my suspicion, albeit far too late.

"Hal? What is this?"

He looked down at his food. "'S a letter," he mumbled.

"Hal?"

"You've been served. Sorry."

"Aw, I can't believe this!"

The envelope didn't look like an official letter, but the neat script on the outside was familiar. I tore it open and yanked out a sheet of lavender paper, folded in half.

Dear Mr. O'Sullivan:

If you are reading this, then you must have survived the pursuit of Artemis and Diana and it is fitting that you be reminded of our agreement. Though Loki escaped our custody after only two days, under the terms we discussed—where a full month of captivity equaled a full year of a vampire-free Poland—you are bound by those terms to keep Poland vampire-free for a pro-rated span of time in payment for services rendered. By my math, two days of captivity equal approximately twenty-four days of vampire-free Poland. I will expect your purge of the vampires to begin at the agreed-upon time.

Kind regards,
Malina Sokołowska

I looked up from the signature into the uncomfortable eyes of my attorney. "What the hell, Hal? You just served papers to one of your clients on behalf of another?"

"Well, it's not like a regular server could find you. And that's not your normal legal document."

"Have you read this? We never agreed to pro-rating my services or hers. The deal was that one month equals one year. She didn't keep him a month, so the contract's null and void."

"That's what you want me to tell her?"

"Well, what do you think?"

"I think the pro-rating is implied. Otherwise, you get into definitions about what a month is, precisely. If she kept him for only thirty days, would you say it was null because she didn't keep him for thirty-one? And what's the incentive for her to keep him beyond a month if her efforts are not going to be rewarded? You should have called me before agreeing to it."

"I was naked in an onion field, Hal, with two huntresses on my tail. I didn't have the time or the phone to call my counselor."

"I bet Malina had a phone. All you had to do was ask."

"Come on. Help me out here."

He sighed. "I don't think we can convince her that she's owed nothing. But maybe I can reduce the time. The spirit of the contract is that you somehow free Poland of all vampires—and I notice there's no language in your contract regarding how you would prove you did so. Maybe I can get her to agree to a shorter time period than twenty-four days or maybe get her to agree to the elimination of a fixed number of vampires—which would be wise, my friend, because what if she invites all the world's vampires to Poland right before you're supposed to go in there and kill them all? One way or another, though, I think you're stuck doing something."

"All right. See what you can do for me and let me know." I slapped some money down on the table, enough to cover the check and then some. "Hopefully you and Kodiak can get to work soon—I'll shoot him a message to let him know to expect you—but liquidate what you can in the meantime."

"Good enough." We shook hands, and he told Oberon to keep me from making any more deals in the future.

<Tell him I would like to agree to that, but I need to speak to my attorney first.>

Attaboy.

"Oh, and, Hal?" I said as I stood up.

"Yes?"

"If I were you, I'd rebuild my firm's security from the ground up, using people I knew to be completely incorruptible. Leif Helgarson has been listening in on all your calls, and I wouldn't be surprised if he has a Trojan horse in your computer files as well."

"What? When did you learn about this?"

"Soon after I called you from Calais. Leif's people heard all of it and told him everything."

Hal's outrage turned his voice into a growl. "And you're just telling me now?"

"It's because I just remembered. All this talk of vampires, you know. And you know how Leif is. He's probably got his fingers in the pies of everyone with whom you've ever associated."

The Old Norse profanity that flowed from Hal's mouth at that point exceeded anything I had heard before in that language.

"Sorry," I said, and headed for the door, with Oberon trailing behind.

<He sounds angry, Atticus,> Oberon said.

He is.

<I wasn't paying attention to your conversation. Did you tell him how terrible it is to have a citrus air freshener in his car?>

No, he's angry about something else.

When we returned to Mill Avenue, my bros were gone, no doubt doing serious damage to monster nommy sammiches. I ducked into a souvenir shop on the way to Ash Avenue and picked up a Sun Devils hat, which I pulled low to hide my eyes. It wasn't much of a disguise, but since my hair was much shorter than it used to be and eyes are often key to recognizing someone, it would at least cast some doubt on my identity. And, besides, Rebecca hadn't seen me in more than twelve years and wasn't expecting me. I'd just be another half-baked college kid looking to restock my incense, until I demonstrated otherwise.

The shop looked almost the same as when I'd left it, save for a new coat of paint and a bewildering array of flyers advertising local events and services papering over a portion of the window next to the door. Checking out the building in the magical spectrum, I saw no wards or enchantments of any kind.

You okay to chill out here while I go inside? I asked Oberon.

<Yeah, I'll just take a nap.>

Okay, holler if anyone tries to mess with you. I took off Fragarach, and Oberon lay down on top of it, guarding it well.

When I opened the door to my old shop, I was hit with a complex mixture of scents—tea and sandalwood and paper and ink. A low, throaty moan from a bamboo flute skirled above the sounds of a gentle waterfall, the kind of meditation music to which people liked to do their yoga. It was pure nostalgia for me, and I missed the years of tending the shop in a semblance of peace and harmony.

"Hello, welcome to Third Eye," Rebecca said from behind the tea counter. I grunted in response and didn't make eye contact. Instead, I turned toward the bookshelves, making it clear I intended to browse and keeping my back to her.

The books for sale were still centered on religion and philosophy. The ones on the shelf locked up behind glass, however, were prominently labeled as RARE and FIRST EDITION. I'd never labeled mine, because I did not particularly want people to browse tomes of summoning and enchantment, but Rebecca must have discovered that there was a fair bit of money to be made from collectors of more-pedestrian volumes. Scanning the titles, I saw that she still had a few of the books I had acquired for her originally, but most of it was newer material now. It reminded me that my cache of magical texts was still buried and encased in iron and stone near the Salt River.

Rebecca would never sneak up on anybody. She still wore a ludicrous amount of silvery jewelry about her neck and wrists, religious symbols from most every religion people had heard of and quite a few that people hadn't, and I heard these clicking and tinkling together as she moved behind me.

"We have quite a fine assortment of rare books if you're interested," she said, coming to a halt at my right shoulder and admiring the spines. "Can I help you find anything in particular?"

"I don't suppose you have any first editions of ancient Edgar Rice Burroughs pulp?"

"I'm afraid not, but we do have a signed first edition of Heinlein's *The Number of the Beast,* which is practically a love letter to Burroughs."

"Seriously? That would be outstanding."

"Great, I'll get it for you." She had an assortment of keys dangling on one of those curly plastic wrist thingies nestled in amongst her other jingly bangles and bracelets. She was like a set of mobile wind chimes.

I gestured vaguely at the source of the noise and said, "That's quite a collection of necklaces. Couldn't decide which one to go with, eh?"

"Well, I guess I *have* decided," she said, speaking at twice the normal rate of most people. She might have been suffering the side effects of too much caffeine. "I've decided to believe in them all."

"Really? Isn't that contradictory?"

"People believe contradictory things all the time," she replied. "Anyway, it's not as contradictory as you might think. Religions are kind of like clothes. There are all sorts of them and some are more fashionable than others, but at the end of the day they all serve the same purpose: They keep you from being naked."

"Religions keep you from being naked?"

"Spiritually speaking. Most of us seek the divine, and most of us prefer not to be nude in public."

I smirked. "Well, we don't have any data to support those assertions, but I imagine that would prove to be accurate."

"Of course. At their roots, the faiths are fundamentally the same the way that clothes are the same. And that's because we recognize that there is a certain power in faith. Even atheists believe strongly in their own rectitude, and that gives them power."

"I believe that's true."

Rebecca smiled at me. "And what else do you believe?" She removed the Heinlein first edition from the case and put it in my hand.

I took off my hat and returned the smile. "I believe, Rebecca Dane, that you are the best possible owner of this shop. I'm Atticus. Remember me?"

She gasped and held her hand up to her throat. "Oh, my gods! Mr. O'Sullivan!"

"You don't have to be that formal."

"Sorry, it's just that I thought you were dead and I'm so glad you're not and I've always wanted to say thank you for the store and ask you why you did that and—oh! Do you want it back now? Is that why you're here?"

"No, no, it's yours," I assured her. "But I did want to talk a bit. Might we have some tea?"

"Of course! Have a seat, I'll be right over." She bustled back to the tea station, making such a racket as she went that she drew the attention of everyone else in the store, each of them with tiny smirks of amusement on their faces. There were only three other people, and two of them made their choices and paid for their purchases while Rebecca was busy boiling water. She made us some Irish Breakfast tea, a blend that didn't mess around on the caffeine front. I doubted she needed to be any more wired, and another shot might take her into the territory of those professional disclaimers who spoke at three hundred words per minute at the end of commercials, but at least our conversation promised to be high energy. We chatted about the store and her plans to open another location down in Tucson, and she asked about my beauty regimen, because I looked far too good after twelve years.

"Are you, like, using a mud pack or cucumbers or something because, oh, my gods, I gotta get me some of whatever you're on, you look *fantastic,*" she gushed.

"I put on a guacamole mask every night. Avocados are the secret."

"Really?"

"No, I'm just kidding." I grinned at her briefly and then tapped the table to indicate a change of subject. "I wanted to ask you a question that might sound a little strange. Think back, if you will. Was there ever a time, shortly after I left you the store, when you prayed for me to many gods?"

I expected her to roll her eyes up and think about it for a while, or maybe express some curiosity about why I would ask such a thing, but she answered immediately. "Oh, yes, definitely," she said. "It was right after Hal sold me the store. I was worried about you."

"This might be an unrealistic request, but can you remember any details of that prayer and to which gods you prayed?"

"Oh, absolutely, that's no problem." Maybe the caffeine was speeding up her memory access as well as her speech. "I prayed more than once. Nine times, actually, to a group of nine gods."

"Why nine?"

"It's a magic number—"

"—Amongst the Tuatha Dé Danann," I finished with her.

"I prayed for your deliverance and guidance in accordance with their divine will," Rebecca said.

"Exactly that? I mean, you didn't ask for anything more specific? And thank you, by the way."

"You're welcome. I'm fairly certain that was it." That would allow the gods to work together but give them freedom to do whatever they wished. Remembering the second part to my question, Rebecca continued, "And I prayed to Jesus, Ganesha, Odin, Inari, Buddha, Guanyin, Shango, Perun, and Brighid."

"Brighid? No shit?" I said. "That is so *very* interesting."

More than interesting, actually. As the implications filtered through my head, it was more like world-rocking. If Brighid had known about all this since Rebecca had prayed twelve years ago, then the First among the Fae had never been fooled by my fake death at all. On the contrary, she'd played me. Again. She had stood there in the Fae Court, pretending to be outraged as she said, "I was told you died twelve years ago," but that is a very different thing from "I *thought* you died twelve years ago."

And it wasn't just Brighid who had allowed me to feel more clever than I really was. Perun had been watching over me in person while pretending that I was doing *him* a favor. When I first met him before the raid on Asgard, he gave me a fulgurite to protect against Thor's lightning. And when Coyote had assumed my shape to allow a group of thunder gods to "kill" me and thus give me time to train Granuaile in peace, Shango had gleefully joined in the slaughter, knowing it wasn't me all along. Damn. Filthy godses are tricksy, Precious.

Seeing that I was more than a little gobsmacked, Rebecca said, "Oh, I can see that nearly made your head explode. I'm dying to know why you asked and what's going on, but I don't want to be rude, and, besides, I have a customer." She excused herself to tend to a tiny, lost-looking man hovering near the register with a couple of books.

As I viewed the past through these new lenses, the most shocking revelation was Odin's involvement. Exactly when—and why—had he agreed to participate in my deliverance and guidance? Because, unless I was mistaken, he had to have known about this prior to my invasion of Asgard with Leif Helgarson and others. He lost Thor, Heimdall, Ullr, and Freyr that day, not to mention Sleipnir on my previous solo raid, when he'd tried to kill me. Perhaps he could not have known in advance who would die during that encounter, but he definitely accepted it afterward. Why? What did he and the other gods hope I would accomplish that was worth all that?

With a sense of dizziness, I realized that I was but a single piece on a very large chessboard and that these gods had been pushing me around while I thought I was exercising free will. I immediately berated myself for sloppy thinking, because of course I *had* been using free will—they were just supremely skilled at influencing and predicting my decisions. But if I wanted to run a tad further with the chess metaphor, I had two questions: Who were the gods playing against, and how close were we to the endgame?

CHAPTER 15

I know that time continued to tick away after my father died, but it's difficult to put a figure on how much of it passed before I became aware of anything besides the ruin of his body. It may have been only seconds, or it may have been minutes. Orlaith brought me back.

<Granuaile? Water is on your face.>

My father is gone.

<I know. Mine too. Fathers gone a lot.>

I clutch at her words, desperate to find anything that might distract me from the horror I'd just witnessed. *Did you know your father?*

<Yes. Humans called him Seamus. Played with his pups. One night I go to sleep and think I play with him tomorrow. But when I wake he is gone. Everyone sad. Like you.>

Yes, I am very sad now, Orlaith.

<I am sad with you. But also worry! Because people fight. And you not move for long time.>

That tears my eyes away. Durga's lion lies to my right, surrounded by the blackened bodies of the *asuras;* he is alive but wounded. The devi herself is behind me, dancing gracefully through scores of fallen enemies and pursuing the last few rakshasas, demoralized now that the raksoyuj no longer holds sway over their actions. Durga's weapons flash—Indra's thunderbolt most visible among them as it continues to flicker and torch fleeing targets—and I can tell it will not be much longer before she has slain them all.

I look down at Fuilteach, still gripped tightly in my left hand, its soul chamber glowing blue and a thin film of my father's blood along the cutting edge—almost the sum of his remains now. All that time and effort wasted. If I had a rakshasa in front of me now, I would have no trouble splintering its soul with the tip.

"Whoa," I say aloud, recognizing the anger rising. Carefully, purposefully, I sheathe the whirling blade and then use my left hand for a much better purpose—petting Orlaith. I dispel her camouflage so that she'll be a little more comfortable; there is no immediate threat now. My eyes mist over as I glance back at the small pile of ash that represents the end of Donal MacTiernan.

"I'm so sorry, Dad," I say, and before the emotions overwhelm me again, I shake my head and assign myself a task. "I need to understand how this went so wrong, Orlaith. Help me find Laksha?"

<Easy. She is still on ground.>

Orlaith leads me over a field of hewn and battered bodies, some of them cooked from lightning, and it's only thirty yards before I can no longer contain my nausea. I retch until my stomach is empty, then signal Orlaith that it's okay to continue.

Laksha—or, rather, the body of the nameless woman whose son we saved—is still facedown in the field. When I turn her over and check for a pulse, I find none. She is dead, though there is no apparent cause. Perhaps Laksha did it, or perhaps one of the multitudes of rakshasas did it before Durga destroyed them.

My eyes flick down to the ruby necklace, Laksha's focus and onetime home. Perhaps it is her home again.

"Laksha, are you in there? We have to talk. It's safe now."

I get no response, no silky Tamil accent echoing in my ears. It occurs to me that if Laksha had been near my father, floating in the ether about his head when Durga struck, she might have been killed in the same firestorm. She said that she was a thing of the ether like the raksoyuj, and what killed him could have killed her too. Gritting my teeth, I remove the ruby necklace and put it in my pocket, feeling abandoned by everyone save my hound.

"Druid," a voice says.

Looking up, I see Durga standing before me. I must have lost some more time, dwelling in shock. Her weapons are gone. She holds a conch shell in one hand, a lotus blossom in another. The others are empty but held out in different gestures that I know are significant, because I've seen them in art before, but I don't know what they mean. Her third eye is closed, and her normal ones are pools of serenity.

"I know that man was your father," the devi says. "But there was no earthly way to sunder the sorcerer from him, short of death."

Thinking that she cannot possibly possess all the facts, I protest, "I have a knife forged of water magic. I thought if I cut him at the proper chakra points, then it would have . . ."

I trail off when the devi shakes her head. "Wishful thinking. It would have annoyed him—it did annoy him—but it would not have worked. The raksoyuj bound himself very tightly so that he could not be killed without also killing his innocent host. Your father was a victim, but I was the target."

"Why?"

"We were very old enemies."

"So Laksha lied to me about the water magic?"

"No. The witch thought she spoke truth. And against

a lesser spirit she would have been correct; the knife would have worked."

The words are no comfort to me. "Is she dead too?"

The slightest twich of one of the devi's hands indicates the necklace in my pocket. "She dwells in the rubies. Weakened but alive."

I cannot hold back my question any longer, impertinent though it might be. "Why did you let it go on for so long? All those people who died in Thanjavur . . ."

"Yes. Refusing to kill one innocent man—your father—meant the death of many others. Innocents would have died regardless of my action or inaction. Do you wish to judge me?"

I look down at her feet. "No."

"There were other paths by which this could have been avoided. I hoped we would walk along one of those. But it was not to be."

"What other paths?"

"Do not torture yourself with what might have been. You may have occasion to wonder at the weapons I brought with me today and the shape of the *asuras,* but the choices of the past cannot be changed. Know this: Your father is free of the raksoyuj. And all the answers he sought in his life, he has them now. One day, so shall you."

"He knows *why*?"

"Yes, he knows that too. Go now, Druid. I must cleanse this place."

Unsure of what to do but feeling that some gesture of respect is needed, I clasp my hands together and bow.

"I wish you peace, Durga." It feels inadequate, but she accepts it.

"You have my blessing," she replies, and these are not empty words, for I take a breath and the roiling inside me calms down somewhat.

Come on, Orlaith.

<Okay. Go where it smells good?>
Yes, let's do that.

With my mouth pressed tightly together and with tears leaking out of my eyes, I run with Orlaith to the road first and then head north toward the tethered banana grove. As soon as we turn, a great thump in the air heralds the ignition of the battlefield, a cleansing fire erasing all evidence of what occurred. I do not stay to observe, but I imagine that anything that didn't burn got swept up into the sky, like at the end of *Raiders of the Lost Ark*. The privilege of Druids, I suppose, is that we get to witness the works of deities on earth without our faces melting afterward. Our bond to the earth sets us apart from the rest of humanity.

Yet I am humbled by the limits of power. We all seek it, and there is no denying I have found a goodly measure. But no gift of Gaia could have saved my father, and in the end, no weapon crafted by the Tuatha Dé Danann or the yeti could set him free. And, yes, I will write it down, for it should be written: Never in my life did I possess the power to make him love me more than he loved his work.

Perhaps that was the power I sought all along. I suspect that many of us, if given the chance to make one person in our lives love us more, would have no trouble in choosing where to point a finger. We are all needy, all vulnerable, all terrified that perhaps that person has an excellent reason to withhold affection. We shape our purposes to make ourselves worthy and often do not see until much later how it was love—or perhaps the lack of it—that both picked us up and dropped us off at crossroads.

I can see what happened to me now. Before I knew what Atticus was, I could have become a witch like Laksha. She would have taught me. She had offered without me ever asking. But I asked her what other sorts of magic existed and learned of Druids. And when Laksha spoke of earth magic, I knew that was what I wanted. The mysteries of the earth—that stuff my father was always digging up—I would master it. Master it and say, "See, Dad? I'm worth your notice after all." Always was, really.

But that was a fantasy. He would have noticed me, all right, but only as he would have noticed a fabulous new excavation tool. Love can and does push the levers of power, yet there is no power that can force one to love another. It is a thing freely given and just as freely accepted or rejected. It is by degrees of love that we wither or blossom—and I suspect that this holds true in both the giving and receiving.

I run faster, hoping the exertion will purge the poison building anew in my mind. I know about the stages of grief and that the second one, anger, is trying to assert itself—it's difficult to linger in denial when I saw my father die and had its reality confirmed by a goddess. I fear what anger might make me do—what I've already thought of doing—especially with the power at my command. Yes, it is by our loves and hatreds that we are shaped and manipulated.

Gasping for breath—I draw no power from the earth, craving the exhaustion—I remind myself that, though my father is gone, I cannot wither now. I am loved by Atticus and Orlaith and by Gaia herself, and with such nourishment as that, I cannot choose but blossom.

And how can I bear to see another wither if it is in my power to help her be whole again? Yes, there is someone I can help—that is a power I *do* have. My mother has thought me dead for twelve years. But the very good reasons we had for faking my death are moot now, and I can't stand the thought of her enduring the pain of that deception for another second. I will go to her and say, "Mother, I am home, and I love you. Please forgive me and hold me and make me hot chocolate like you used to. With extra marshmallows." So many fucking marshmallows—like, a tide of them that completely hides the cup underneath a tiny mountain of puffy white lumps of sugar.

It is the middle of the night in India, so it would be sometime in the middle of the day back in Kansas. Orlaith and I shift to Tír na nÓg, and then I have to spend some time figuring out how to shift home. Wellington is fairly flat and devoid of proper forests, and there aren't many tethers in the area. I settle for something down near the border with Oklahoma, the northern range of the Osage Hills, about forty miles away from Wellington. I could do with more running. This time I would let the earth help me, though, and Orlaith too.

Much of the run is spent trying to remember events from my youth to prove to my mother that I am who I say I am, because I suspect she won't believe me at first. The police never found my body, of course, but she had to believe I was truly dead after such a long time with no contact.

I had checked up on her periodically through intermediaries, and once, about halfway through my training, Atticus and I visited in person, only to find she was out of the country at the time.

As for my stepfather, I intended to say very little to him. I still despised him and wished to take apart his oil business, as I'd always planned, but that could wait until I'd seen Mom and let her know about Dad. And me.

It's midafternoon when Wellington appears on the horizon. I slow down to a normal jog once I'm in sight of windows, and, after some thought, I decide to cloak my passage through the city. Though some of my old acquaintances might not recognize me right away, people would surely remember the tattooed redhead with a giant hound running alongside and a strange staff in her hand and would ask around until they discovered who I was. Returning to my mother was one thing, but returning to the rest of the world was quite another in legal terms. I would have a lot of official questions to answer and perhaps a bit of trouble if I tried to resurrect Granuaile MacTiernan. Better that the world thought of me as Nessa Thornton.

Mom lives on a gigantic estate, thanks to my stepdad. I lived there for a year myself before I left for college. It's walled and gated and tricked out with a passive security system and a real live dude manning the gate; a golf cart waits next to his booth so he can drive to the house and back if he needs to do so.

I decide to play it straight and see if I can talk my way in, and if that fails, I'll go ninja. Dropping my invisibility and Orlaith's camouflage but adding camouflage to the whirling blade, I approach the booth and steel myself for the confrontation.

The security guard is older and carrying the weight of too many beers and wings on game days. That doesn't stop him from looking me over as if I'd be lucky to have him. He ignores Orlaith and thereby confirms that he's an idiot.

"Can I help you?" he drawls, voice syrupy with condescension. I can almost hear him tack on *little missy* to the end of his sentence.

"I'm here to see Mrs. Thatcher."

He doesn't say anything for a few seconds, just sucks his teeth with a wet squidgy sound, letting me know what he thinks about someone like me visiting someone like Mrs. Thatcher. "Do you have an appointment?"

I don't know why, but that question stops me. Of course I don't have an appointment. I haven't made an appointment of any kind since I began my training. Appointments are something from another time—another life. Now that I'm here, confronted by the prospect of explaining everything to her, I can't see how it ends well. People who live in a world with appointments aren't prepared to acknowledge that the world is sentient, that magic is real, or that they have created gods by the power of their faith. The world slid into the paradigm of science and skepticism centuries ago, and shaking my mother loose from that would frighten her more than anything. Even if she accepted that I was Granuaile—an uncertain outcome—she'd think me insane when I told her I was a Druid.

And then what would I do to prove it? Shape-shift in front of her? Ask the elemental to grow a rosebush in her backyard inside a minute? She would think it all a hoax or a dream before she would accept the truth of my binding to the earth. The conflict would cast a pall over my homecoming and choke off any chance of me saying what needed to be said and her hearing it.

The impulse, the raw need to see her, is still pure, though, and will bring me a small sense of harmony, but it should not go beyond that. Seeing her, and being seen in turn, is the thing itself. I must accept that a storybook homecoming is impossible. So I do not need to deal with this round man and his teeth-sucking. There is a better, simpler solution. Imperfect, and not what I truly want, but better than risking the dangers of the truth.

I turn and jog back into town without answering the guard, leaving him to his condescension and casual misogyny.

In one of those soulless big box stores, I find a black jacket and gloves to cover up my tattoos and pick up a flower arrangement in a white vase, oranges and yellows and dark-green leaves with tiny white blossoms like snowflakes sprinkled on top of it. The walk back to the estate is slower, because it's difficult to jog with a flower arrangement, but once I reach the wall, I make sure I'm unobserved and cast camouflage on my hound and myself. Then I unbind a portion of the cement block, which allows us to slip through.

The land of the Thatcher estate is expansive, with gentle sloping flats of tall grass punctuated by stands of timber planted purposefully long ago. In the distance, the white house rests on the light-brown plain like a dollop of cream on caramel. Orlaith and I might trip some motion detectors on the way to the house, but cameras won't pick us up until I drop the camouflage, and the guard won't alert the house until he sees something. My mother won't think anything of me suddenly arriving at the door—deliveries were always waved through without comment by the guard.

I ask Orlaith to wait for me at the edge of a small copse perhaps a hundred yards from the house. I leave my weapons with her and promise to return soon. As the sun hovers low over the horizon, I dispel camouflage, stride up to the house, and ring the bell.

My mother opens the door, and I cannot help but catch my breath when I see her hair, dyed red now, presumably because she'd gone to gray recently. She's smaller than me, kind of petite; I got my height from Dad. She wears jeans and a salmon tank top with a white button-up shirt hanging open on top of it, and her eyes—green like mine—do a quick scan before locking on my face. Then she gasps as her jaw drops. She still has her freckles, and when I see them, the tears start to well in my eyes. I think hers are filling, too, and a stillness stretches as we absorb the shock of seeing each other—until I remember that I'm not supposed to be her daughter and I'm missing my cue.

"Delivery for you, Mrs. Thatcher," I say, and thrust the flowers toward her.

"Oh. Thank you," she replies, and wipes at her cheek before reaching out to take the vase. Her fingers lightly brush against my gloves, and now I wish I hadn't worn them; I would have cherished the contact forever. She cradles the vase in her hands and gives a tiny embarrassed laugh. "I'm sorry to seem so surprised," she says, "and I hope you'll forgive me. It's just that you look like the spitting image of my daughter."

"Yeah? That's a funny coincidence," I say, sniffling and sweeping a hand across my eyes to clear them of tears. It's only a temporary fix, I'm sure, but I try to hold myself together. "You remind me so very much of my mom. Probably because of this red-hair thing we have going." I wag a finger between us, pointing at our heads. "I haven't seen her for a long time."

"Oh, honey, I'm sorry to hear that. And I know how you must feel. It's the same for my daughter and me." She takes a deep breath and tilts her head to one side, studying me, her bottom lip quivering a bit before she speaks again. "You know, she'd be in her thirties now, but I swear you look just the way she did the last time I saw her."

My throat tightens, and I struggle to get the words out before I lose all remaining vestiges of self-control. "Would you mind—I mean, I haven't spoken to her in forever, it seems like, and I'm never going to get to now, but there's something I've always wanted to say to her. Would you let me say it to you instead? As a favor? Would you mind?"

"No, honey, of course, you go right ahead." And she stands there, waiting, holding the flowers but unconscious of them.

Through a blur of fresh tears I manage to say, "I miss you so much. And I love you." I sob once, and so does she, and my throat is so constricted with emotion that I have to whisper the last. "Goodbye, Mom."

Something shifts in her expression, perhaps a recognition that I am more than someone who merely resembles the daughter she thought long dead, and she reaches out to me, the forgotten vase of flowers slipping from her hands and shattering on the threshold. "Granuaile?"

I want nothing so much as to be held again, but I can't rush into those arms. It would lead to all the questions I cannot answer. No, I had said what I'd come to say, so I choke on another sob, back away three paces, spin on my heel, and run from the house, except it's more of an awkward, loping stagger. My chest is heaving and I can barely see, because I'm crying so ugly—ragged whimpers alternating with convulsive shudders of grief.

The door clicks shut behind me, dimly heard, my mother no more able to step forward into my world than I am able to step back into hers. Atticus had warned me of this, when I first began my training; he'd said that becoming a Druid would mean giving up my family, so abandon all ties, ye who enter here—but I didn't fully understand then. To achieve my goal at the time, I had blithely traded some pain in the distant future, unable to fathom how much it would hurt when it came time to pay that particular bill. I thought it would be like homesickness tempered with the wistful hope that someday you could go home again—intense, to be sure, but endurable so long as you knew it would end one day. But now I see that it's terrible and irrevocable. As large and wondrous as my world is now, it will forever be a world without my parents. And it stings especially that I consciously chose this fate—it isn't something that happened to me. I made it happen. Now Dad is gone and Mom lives in a headspace with no room for magic in it. No room for me.

When I approach the stand of timber, reeling and weaving, Orlaith hears me long before I hear her, and her voice enters my head before I spy her narrow body scissoring through the tall grass toward me.

<Granuaile sad again?>

She comes to me, ears up, and I fall to my knees and wrap my arms around her neck, bawling.

Yes. I miss my mom.

<But she is in house. Over there.>

I can't talk to her. Can't tell her the truth.

<Why?>

It's like there's a giant river of time and circumstance between us and I can't figure out how to cross it safely. It's too dangerous for both of us.

<Oh! I understand maybe. Time is hard. I think time is most hard thing in world. Oberon is bad at time too.>

I'm sorry to be such a downer, Orlaith, but I need to cry for a while.

<Okay, Granuaile. I will stay and wait. Sad you have no time with your mother. But you can have all my time.>

I hold her hard and cry for my lost mother and father until the setting sun, conspiring with my exhaustion and the wind sighing through the treetops, sends me adrift into a dreamless sleep, the two of us sprawled out of sight in the tall grass.

CHAPTER 16

Brighid doesn't want to talk in the Court, where anyone can hear us, so she leads me to her own private residence and a room she calls the Iron Hall. It's a grand name for a very small chamber, not much more than a closet, but it has a beautiful round table, a pair of stools, a cask of dark beer, and two glasses waiting inside. The walls, door, floor, and ceiling are all covered in solid black iron.

"Casting a binding to keep our conversation private can conceivably be countered," she explains, "but iron cannot. We will not be overheard here, and we can speak in comfort for as long as we wish. I needn't be so formal either, where no one can see me. Would you like a beer?"

"That would be grand."

She pours for us both and we clink glasses. *"Sláinte."*

It's wonderful stuff, something Goibhniu probably brewed, and I praise it before we return to business.

"Tell me of the Morrigan," Brighid says.

"Right. It was more than two thousand years ago when the Morrigan approached me with a deal. I was seventy-two and had no nuts left in me sack. There is nothing worse than being old and miserable and hurting everywhere. I don't recommend it. It was a cold-ass day in the darkest part of winter and she drops down from the sky, all naked and sexy, and I get annoyed that she's blocking me view of the sunset—that's how bad it was. Ye can die now, she says to me, or I can put ye on a Time Island, where ye might get to continue your life in some distant future. A far distant future, she says. And in that future, ye might get to be young again. All I had to do was deliver a message. I took the deal, o' course, and here I am."

"And the message?"

"It made no sense when she made me memorize it, because I didn't know anything about these other pantheons, but here's what I'm supposed to say, from the Morrigan's own lips to your ears: 'Brighid, I am dead now, either at the hands of the Olympians or by Vedic demons, and a great danger gathers among the Norse. I have seen terrible futures, and I tell you three times, the difference between life and death lies with the Svartálfar. Recruit them to our side at any cost.' "

When I fall silent, Brighid frowns. "That is all?"

"Aye."

"Tell me everything else she said or did."

"There's not much else. She opened a portal behind me and said I would owe a great debt to Siodhachan, and then she pushed me through as I was about to tell her how I felt about that."

"And Siodhachan knows nothing of this?"

"No. The message was for you, and you can tell him or not, as ye please. But he's spent some time telling me about recent events, and I had to pretend to be surprised when he told me the Morrigan was dead."

"I see. You have done the Tuatha Dé Danann a service. What would you have in return, Eoghan Ó Cinnéide?"

I hadn't expected a favor. I thought getting to extend my life was payment enough, but it would be a shame to pass on an opportunity like this.

"I have a question," I says, "and I would like ye to answer it truthfully in that three-part voice o' yours. Ye have my word I won't repeat it to anyone."

She eyes me warily and gives the faintest of nods. "Ask."

"What do ye know about the death of Midhir?"

Brighid sits up straight with a jerk, and her eyes light up all blue. She speaks simultaneously in three different registers: "Nothing. I did not even know he was dead, nor did I realize anyone wished to kill him."

She couldn't lie with that voice. I can safely cross her off the list of suspects.

"He's been dead for at least a couple weeks now, maybe more. He's hangin' upside down in his bedroom, strung up in iron chains with his throat cut."

I catch her up on some of the things Siodhachan shared with me while I was touching up his tattoos—and I reveal to her that I'm his archdruid, figuring it's safe to do so now that I'm sure she doesn't have it out for him. When I finish, she sighs and says, "You've given me much to think about and much to investigate, but I will need to keep this secret until I know more. Therefore, you will present yourself formally at the Court this morning, say nothing of these things, and I will welcome you and give you my blessing to follow your own desires. What are they, by the way, now that you have discharged your duty to the Morrigan and to me?"

"I'd like to get back to the world and take on apprentices. We need more Druids."

She looks surprised at first but then relaxes with a happy sigh. "I will have no trouble blessing that. It is precisely what I would wish myself."

"Would it be rude of me," I says, "to ask if I might dine with you and your boys? An informal thing, of course."

"Not at all. I invite you now."

"Excellent."

She leaves me in the care of a steward while we wait for dawn. I'm able to grab a few hours' sleep before it's time to go to Court and pretend this is the first time we've spoken. I feel hundreds of eyes on me, judging and calculating and scheming already. I am judging them in return. In front of the Court, Brighid invites me to dine with her and a few others, and my acceptability is immediately established. Manannan Mac Lir extends an invitation to join him the next night, and I accept. I catch more sleep after that in preparation for the evening, and I have no doubt that Brighid is investigating Midhir's estate as I do so.

Ogma joins us for dinner, which consists of some magnificent whiskey and some other things that I don't remember but which were chewier than the whiskey. I'm paying far more attention to my company than to the food. Ogma sits on my right and Brighid to my left; facing us across the table are the brothers Goibhniu, Creidhne, and Luchta. They're all dark-eyed and mischievous, but I think it's the good-natured type of mischief they prefer. They seem to have made a wager amongst themselves as to what kind of weapon I'd ask them to make, even though no such idea had crossed me mind. Their disappointment when they learn that I have no epic project for them to tackle is so profound that I feel guilty.

"Wait," Goibhniu says. "I know how to settle this. Eoghan, when you fight, what is your preferred weapon?"

"Well, I like to fight with me fists, if ye can believe it," I say. "Especially now that the ache in me knuckles is gone."

Creidhne whoops in victory. "That's it! Brass knuckles! That's my job, brothers! Victory is mine!"

"What's all this, then?" I ask.

They confess that they cannot wait for more Druids to walk the earth, because we offer them new challenges as craftsmen.

"Goibhniu and I had such fun crafting Scáthmhaide for Granuaile," Luchta says, "that we were a bit sad when we finished it."

"I was left out of that project entirely," Creidhne says, "but this will make up for it. I'll take your measurements after dinner and we will speak of what might be done."

Apparently I'm not to be given a choice in the matter. These boys are artists who love life for the beauty it shows them. They spend their days wondering how they can be creative rather than destructive. I have always secretly admired such people and their vision and wished I possessed a quarter measure of what their eyes perceive. I cross them off my list.

"So what do you do to keep yourself busy these days, Ogma?" I ask. He's big and bald and fond of gold hoop earrings. At first I think that's a tempting target for an opponent, but then I realize he *wants* you to reach for them and see what happens.

"These days I dance among the planes on behalf of Brighid, an ambassador of the Fae. Not the sort of heroic thing I was used to doing in the old days, but the other pantheons need to know the Tuatha Dé Danann are serious, and sending a liveried faery to represent us somehow doesn't have the same gravitas."

"Ah, I see. And you're scouting, of course, while you're there. Wherever you've been going, I mean."

He looks at me, I think, for the first time. He'd been avoiding eye contact and until that moment had given the impression that sitting down to table with me was a duty rather than a pleasure. Suddenly, dinner was interesting.

"Of course," he says, a small smile tugging on one side of his mouth.

"Because if ye want to lay the hurt on someone, it's best to know where they're hiding their soft bits."

"Precisely."

I raise my cup and says, "To punchin' 'em in the pillows," and he smiles heartily at that and drinks with me.

"Do you know of the Wendish gods?" he asks.

"No, I don't even know the Wendish people."

"They have largely disappeared as a distinct ethnicity, assimilated into Germanic and Slavic cultures," he says. I don't know those peoples either, but I hold me tongue and let him keep going. "Their pagan shrines were attacked and destroyed by surrounding Christians. They have been out of any significant worship for centuries and they're very weak, so I cannot imagine why they would want to pick a fight with us. One of Brighid's faeries went to their plane recently, however, and never came back. I went to investigate and just returned."

And as he speaks of Wendish strengths and weaknesses on their plane, I can see that he's a fine military mind, but it is straightforward thinking and lacks subtlety. He has no ideas about how to outthink and outmaneuver them, only about how to overpower them. It's not that his ideas aren't fine—I admire them and can't find fault—it's just that they are of a particular flavor, and it's not the one I'm looking for. Ogma is clever, but he's not a mastermind; he's the competent guy the mastermind sends in to pound your organs into jelly.

I stay the night at Creidhne's place after he's finished measuring me hands and making molds and so on, and as I drift off to sleep, I catch myself wondering what

Greta is doing. Even in my subjective timeline, it has been a long while since I cared enough about anyone to wonder such things. I wonder next if I might be the only man who ever made a deal with the Morrigan and came out ahead.

CHAPTER 17

After concluding my chat with Rebecca Dane, I fled north to Flagstaff, grabbed a slice at Alpine Pizza on Leroux Street, and then drove my rental car to a winding forest road behind the mountains on the north side of town. I planted myself in Lockett Meadow underneath a stand of aspens, to think of how best to act now that Inari and her cabal o' gods had given me the green light to do as I wished. But I couldn't focus. Lockett Meadow is a popular place, and since the first snow hadn't fallen yet, there were other people around—only nine hardy campers, mind you, but that was enough distraction for me at the moment.

Every so often I have to get away to a quiet place to think, take my brain somewhere that the noise of the modern world cannot be heard, and seek clarity in an unspoiled environment without a hint of cell phone service. Rebecca Dane's revelation required a good long think, and I knew just the place. There's a waterfall in Glacier National Park that they call Bird Woman Falls these days, reachable by car in the summertime only but reachable by me year-round via plane-shifting. I'd bound the trees there long before it was a national park or the falls somehow became associated with a bird woman. It has a view of Heaven's Peak, snowcapped and jutting defiantly above the clouds. Once I'd shifted there with Oberon, a breathtaking panorama of natural beauty was spread before me, and I didn't have to share it with anyone. Going-to-the-Sun Road was closed off at this time of the year, so there was no traffic passing below the falls at all. The only noises were the companionable rush of the falls and the friendly whispers of the wind in the trees. I was all alone with my hound.

For five whole minutes.

"*Hola, amigo,*" a voice called from behind me, just as I was proposing hypotheticals to myself. Startled, I rolled left and turned, old instincts taking over, and searched for the owner of the voice. A short Latino man with a wide smile waved at me, a gold wristwatch band shining on his arm. He also had a gold crucifix on a thick chain hanging around his neck, and this rested on a button-up linen shirt that was entirely out of place on this cold mountaintop in Montana. Of course, I wasn't dressed for the weather either.

Oberon barked once, as startled as I was. <Atticus, who is that? How did he sneak up on us?>

I don't know, buddy.

The stranger's smile was friendly and infectious. He had large, kind eyes. A thin, wispy mustache rested on his upper lip, but a fuller beard ran along his jaw, and his dark hair was long and gently wavy, tied back in a queue. I looked down at the bottom of his chinos and noticed that he had made the impossible decision to wear flat sandals. I wear sandals most everywhere but get strange looks for it—especially in a place like this, where one expects to see hiking boots.

"*Hola,*" I replied, on my guard. He continued to smile and speak in Spanish.

"*Es un placer volverte a ver, Siodhachan.*" Then he switched from Spanish to English, speaking with a subtle accent in a rich, confident voice. "To answer the question you were thinking, I did not hike up here at all.

I used . . . other methods. The last time we spoke, we enjoyed fish and chips and a very fine whiskey together in Arizona. I also healed a rather grievous knife wound, after which I gave you some advice that you chose not to follow."

Whoa. I squinted at him. "Jesus? Is that you?"

He laughed and put his hands in his pockets. "Well, during this particular visit I suppose you should call me *Jesus*," he said, pronouncing it the Spanish way, *hay-suse*. "But, yes, it is I. Do you not like this body I have chosen to wear? I got it from a delightful Mexican woman living in Whitefish. Her name is Gina and she worries about her son a lot, prays that he would love me the way she does. Very few love me as purely as she does, however." He removed a hand from his pocket and swept it from his chest down toward the ground, presenting himself like a game-show prize. "This is how she sees me, and I tell you truly, I like the way she thinks. It is an uncommon visualization, and I appreciate the modern quirks. I have this wristwatch, for example. I do not truly need it, and Gina herself is unsure why I'd have one, but she thought it would look nice on me and I cannot argue the point."

<Atticus, you know this guy?>

Yes. He's the Christian god, Jesus. You weren't with me the last time we met.

Jesus was always quick to identify himself using things only he and I would know, so that I wouldn't hurt myself looking at him in the magical spectrum. Most of the old gods seared my sight a little with the bright white of the magic suffusing their bodies; one of the current A-listers like Jesus would probably blind me if I tried to check him out.

"It is good to see you, indeed," I said, returning his smile and stepping forward to shake hands. "A very pleasant surprise."

"Shall we sit and have a drink? This time the drinks are on me." He reached into his right pocket and pulled out a tall bottle of amber Milagro, an extra añejo sipping tequila, which could not possibly have been waiting there before. From his left pocket he produced two small crystal goblets lined with a gold frosting along the rims, which also could not have been clinking around in there previously. He handed them to me while he uncorked the tequila.

<Whoa, this guy is pretty slick, Atticus. What else do you think he has in his pockets? Maybe a thick salami for me?>

I almost dropped the goblets. *Gods, Oberon, it's a good thing no one can hear you. It's not polite to ask if a man has a big salami in his pants, okay? Especially this guy.*

<Why? What does he have against salami?>

Laughter bubbled forth from Jesus as he poured two generous shots for us. "I like your hound, Siodhachan." He turned his head a bit to address him. "Hello, Oberon. I can hear what you say as well, and I tell you truly, I have nothing against salami itself. It is best to know when to keep your salami in your pants and when to pull it out, however, and even my priests have had some difficulty with that issue. Fortunately for us, there is little doubt regarding the right course of action in this situation." He pulled a long soppressata from the same pocket that had produced the goblets. "I imagine this should take the edge off your hunger. Siodhachan, would you oblige us both and unbind the casing so that he may eat it?"

<Oh, great lakes of gravy! Thanks, Jesus! Atticus, why didn't you introduce us before?>

Jesus laughed again. "You are welcome, Oberon. And, if I may answer, I rarely visit, so your friend did not have the opportunity to introduce us before now."

I unbound the casing so that it fell away from the meat, and Jesus gave it to Oberon. With my hound happy, the two of us strolled back to the edge of Bird Woman Falls and sat cross-legged on the ground with our tequila, admiring Heaven's Peak. We said cheers and clinked glasses.

"This particular drink did not exist the first time I walked around on the earth," he said. "But, then, neither did Mexico exist as a nation. Have you not noticed, Siodhachan, that for all we lose and regret in the long course of history, there is always something new to love?"

"I have." The tequila was certainly new and lovable, a smooth mellow burn down the throat, not like the sharp punch of blancos. We might have licked our chops, except that Oberon was doing enough of that for all three of us.

"So tell me why you are here, Siodhachan," Jesus finally said.

"I was going to try to figure out what you are up to, because I learned that you are one of the heavy hitters in a gang of gods that was asked to look after me. You're the guy who told Inari where to find me in the Pyrenees."

Jesus finished his drink and poured himself another, topping off mine while he was at it. "I have always appreciated your ambition."

"Ambition?"

"Yes. You may have heard before now that I tend to work in mysterious ways. To try to figure out my designs is ambitious."

"Shall I simply ask you what they are instead? Jesus, what do you have planned for me?"

"The irony of all those people saying that I have a plan is that I do not plan so very much. Other gods have their plans as well, and so does every creature walking the earth, and they all have free will. It ensures that virtually no one will ever get to say, 'It's all going exactly as I planned.' Instead, let us say that I can see multiple futures and prefer that certain ones come to pass while others do not. It so happens that your decisions and your actions play a vital role in ensuring that the best futures of a poor lot come to pass."

"I remember you saying something similar to me before. You also said that had I remained meek, I would have inherited the earth."

"Yes."

"That haunts me."

"I understand. But if I may make a suggestion, my friend, let it rather instruct you. We are far past the time when everything might have turned out well. We are now in crisis management, hoping that things will turn out badly instead of much, much worse."

That was a sobering message, even under the influence of fine tequila. "But Inari said I must act now, not remain meek. Move against Loki and Hel."

"She did not expressly say that. She said you are free to move against them if you wish. You are also free to do nothing. We merely removed our injunction. I thought that may have not been made clear enough by Inari; hence, my visit."

That was a mite exasperating, but I understood his position. Free will is hardly free if you go about commanding people to behave as you wish. Still, Jesus wouldn't be here if he didn't hope to help me somehow. He could have had Brighid or Odin tell me, or Inari could have sent a kitsune or used any number of methods to clarify that I could do whatever I wanted. So this was my chance to ask him anything. I could perhaps nibble at the edges of this problem until I could see a way to take a larger bite out of it. "What about your adversary?" I asked. "Does he not have a role to play?"

"He is indifferent in this matter, which is fortunate for us. Ragnarok is not his preferred apocalypse, you see. His ego requires that things go according to *his* plan, and thus he is already thwarted. He is sulking and sitting this out, as are the dark forces of some other pantheons who do not wish to follow Loki's orders."

"Good news. Speaking of which, maybe you could give me some more. What ever happened to the widow MacDonagh? Hel told me her soul went on to the Christian lands, but I'm not sure I should trust Loki's daughter."

"You should not. But in that particular case she spoke the truth. Let it not trouble you; Katie is at peace and with me."

I sighed and felt lighter. That burden had been taken away. "Please give her my love. I miss her."

"I will. She misses you too. You were a blessing to her in the sunset of her life."

We started in on round three, and I felt the buzz coming on. Jesus didn't appear to be affected by the drink at all. I began to worry that I would fail to ask the right question. You always think of the perfect thing to say after the moment's passed, and I could sense that this moment would end soon. So of course I asked something pointless.

"Jesus, why involve Inari at all? Why didn't you visit me earlier?"

"She wished to meet you. When you had need of healing and could literally go anywhere in the world to do it, she was flattered that you chose Japan. She likes you."

I didn't think she had expressed any affection for me, but said, "All right. What I can't wrap my head around is your ultimate goal—the nine of you together. You're obviously working toward something big, but I don't know what it is. I mean, Odin has sacrificed a lot.

Heimdall and Freyr and Thor, all dead, his Valkyries too—"

"Is Thor truly dead?" Jesus interrupted.

"What? Are you kidding me?"

"I am asking a question. You know that certain members of the Irish pantheon have been able to act from beyond the veil, and you suppose that the Morrigan can as well. Their active worship by humans gives them the power to manifest at will, even though their flesh has passed on. And I, too, am an example of this truth. I died more than two thousand years ago, yet here I sit, drinking tequila with you. I can manifest when I wish in any form chosen by a worshipper—I am a god created in many images. Why do you suppose it would be any different with Thor? He is still actively worshipped throughout Scandinavia and in pockets of Iceland. The same is true for Heimdall and Freyr. So what has Odin lost, truly?"

If Odin could still count on Thor to come back and fight in Ragnarok but had also recruited me to fight in his place, then he had snookered me pretty good. It made me wonder, though, why Thor hadn't shown up yet—to bash my head in, if nothing else. "But . . . where is Thor? Valhalla?"

"That's a question you should ask Odin."

"Oh!" The answer came to me—or at least part of it. Thor probably wouldn't show up at all until it was over. Those dead gods were lying low as a matter of long-term survival. It would be impossible to return *after* Ragnarok if large portions of their believers were wiped out. Odin had them on a Die Now, Live Later plan— and he'd been open with me in sharing his hope that I would die horribly in Ragnarok, as a matter of justice. And if he himself fell in the final battle, why, then, Thor and the others would remain and carry on if they just sat it out. Since the old prophecies of the Norns weren't in effect anymore and Odin didn't know who'd be left behind afterward, he wanted insurance that *someone* from the Norse pantheon would survive.

I realized I'd gotten sidetracked. "Okay, okay, sorry. Back to your ultimate goal."

Jesus shrugged. "It is not so very complicated. There's a big fight coming, and we want the good guys to win."

"I remember that you said I had a whole lot of pain coming."

"Yes." The kind eyes turned to me and filled with sympathy. "I am sorry, but it is still to come."

It had already been cold on that mountaintop, but I shivered for the first time.

CHAPTER 18

There is a certain desolation to waking up alone, especially when one is emotionally vulnerable, and I wake up missing Atticus. So much has happened to me since he's been out of touch, and I don't think his tattoo will be finished until later today or maybe tomorrow. My father's death replays in my head, and waves of regret and anger and helplessness rise up, crashing against the inside of my eyelids. I open them and let the sunlight streaming through the grass burn the negativity away. The waves will keep coming unless I distract myself, though, so I take action. Rolling over and pushing myself up, I find Orlaith curled next to me, and I wake her with a nuzzle and a squeeze.

Good morning, sweet hound.

<Granuaile! Hello! Happiness! Need stretch.>

I'll stretch with you. We stretch together, arms and legs, a thoroughly delicious exercise, and not for the first time I reflect on what a blessing it is to have a hound. Already she is helping me through this, showing by example that life goes on and it is a thing to be enjoyed.

<Go for a run?>

Yes. We must definitely run.

I was far too wrecked to manage it last night, but now I really need to escape this property. I was fortunate not to have run into my stepfather, and I didn't want to risk meeting him now. I pick up my weapons, then we run the long miles back to the Osage Hills, where we can shift away. Orlaith and I are both famished by the time we get there, and I take us back through the tethers to our cabin above Ouray, where the first order of business is breakfast.

Once I sit down at the table, I see the note I wrote for Atticus before I went to pick up Fuilteach. It's a hopeful note, so I leave it alone. Let Atticus find it and feel that hope, as I did, that all would turn out well. There is no need to burden him with worry.

I'm sure Atticus will have plenty to do with his archdruid when his tattoo's finished, anyway. The two of us would catch up soon enough, the threads of our lives intertwined once more, and we would both be stronger for it.

In the meantime, I still need some answers regarding my dad, and perhaps I can get them. Laksha had mentioned in passing that the vessel containing the raksoyuj had come from a dig north of Thanjavur. Maybe some answers will be waiting for me—like, why was he there in the first place? He'd never been a particular expert on artifacts from the Indian subcontinent. Had he been looking for this thing intentionally, or was it an accidental find? And even if I can't satisfy myself that this was all accidental, the very least I can do is try to help out somehow as the city recovers from what must seem like the most mysterious plague ever.

I shower and pack a small bag, including a touchpad and my passport for the Nessa Thornton identity. I throw Laksha's necklace in there as well, even though I haven't heard from her yet and am not sure what to do with her. With Scáthmhaide in hand and Fuilteach strapped to my left thigh, I shift with Orlaith back to that familiar banana grove outside Thanjavur.

It is strange to be back in India so soon. It is a raw wound into which I have plunged my fingernail before the scab can grow. The smell of the air is enough to bring prickly tears to the corners of my eyes. Unfortunately, the time difference means it's already dark here; it's the end of the day rather than the beginning of it.

I speak to the elemental Kaveri in hopes that she can tell me where the humans are digging in the earth to the north of town. After casting night vision on Orlaith and myself, I follow her directions to several sites. The first four of these are merely construction of some kind, but the fifth is an archaeological dig. Noting its location, I set off with Orlaith in search of lodging. We find a hotel, and I camouflage her through the lobby; once in my room, I flip open my laptop and start to look for news.

English newspapers report in subdued tones the miraculous overnight recovery of every ill person from what health officials had worried would be an unstoppable pathogen. Though I never saw the headlines while it was getting worse, I presume they made much more noise about people growing ill and quickly dying. Doctors are still baffled about what caused the disease and caution that it might not be over and people should continue to take basic precautions against contagion.

I do a search for my father coupled with the key word *Thanjavur* and discover a brief article reporting him missing a week ago. His disappearance was flagged by a couple of members of his team who were in India on a short-term visa. They were colleagues of his from the university. That might be an angle worth exploring.

More searching on the university and its archaeology faculty. It appears that the department chair—who would presumably be the one to approve such digs and perhaps help secure grant money—is still in the States, teaching classes for the fall semester. I remember the name: Michelle Liu. She's an old friend of Dad's who preferred the lecture hall and the cozy office to the heat and dust of digs. They often published findings together. I think they kind of had a deal: She'd minimize his teaching responsibilities and the agony of academic bureaucracy, and he'd brave the mud and the icky bugs to dig for treasure. Each thought the other one was doing all the dirty work. I'd drop her name if I had to; I figured I had enough to proceed now and a safe place to keep my stuff.

"Ready to head back out?" I ask my hound. Orlaith is curled up on top of the bed, hogging all of it.

<Nap first.>

"You've been napping already. Come on, let's go, unless you want me to leave you here."

<No, go with you!> she says, and climbs down off the bed, her tail up and wagging. I leave my bag in the room and put a Do Not Disturb sign on the door. I take my weapons, though. I'll need Scáthmhaide to snoop around.

It's after midnight when we return to the dig, and I approach the trailer sitting off to the side with the hope that it contains an office instead of sleeping archaeologists. I camouflage both of us, to be safe, and gently try the door. Locked.

I've not done it before, but Atticus told me that you can bind tumblers into the unlocked position with very little trouble. Despite his assurance, it's quite troublesome for me; I'm not so accustomed to free-form binding as he is, and I can't actually see the tumblers. I don't know how to target them without visual aid, and we haven't had time since my binding to the earth to go over Breaking and Entering for Druids. After ten frustrating minutes, I give up and unbind the entire metal doorknob and lock, letting it melt away out of the hole. Problem solved.

"Stay here and let me know if anyone comes?" I whisper to Orlaith.

<Okay. I watch.>

The trailer contains three desks, a mini-fridge, and a garbage can stuffed full of empty soda bottles and sandwich wrappers. No slumbering archaeologists.

I turn on a light and dispel my night vision, figuring that Orlaith will let me know in time if anyone comes to investigate. I can't imagine that anyone would, besides the archaeologists themselves, and they're surely sacked out in a hotel somewhere.

It takes little time to discern which desk is Dad's. Two are messes and one is neat. And the papers on the neat one are covered with my dad's tight, crabbed script.

They're not interesting to me—catalogs of artifacts found and reports on soil composition and radiocarbon dating and so on. I try the drawers of the desk, only to discover that they're locked too. I don't waste time but unbind the lock right away. I find what I'm looking for in the bottom drawer: Dad's personal diary. I skip forward to the last couple of entries, beginning with one dated October 3:

> *I am in India now, drawn by a call from a former student about a very odd discovery. It is a sealed clay vessel with Sanskrit markings on the outside, warning that it should not be opened. We will, of course, be opening it in the interest of science. I have never seen its like before; this may turn out to be a stunning discovery. Have spent the day preparing samples for the lab. Cannot wait for the results.*

I skim through the rest of that paragraph, because I know how it ends. But I do wonder who the mysterious former student is and what happened to him, because this indicates that my father didn't find the vase himself—as Laksha told me—but rather had it given to him. I would dearly love to speak to whoever was responsible for that. In the entry of October 4 I get a clue:

> Nothing new today in terms of artifacts, but Logan claims to have reliable information about location of the Lost Arrows of Vayu. He says they must be buried somewhere near here, north of Thanjavur. If I didn't have this magnificent find sitting in front of me, I would dismiss it as the worst kind of silliness—arrows supposedly crafted by a god of the wind, imbued with magical properties? Ridiculous. And without a credible source of origin, as far as I can tell, though he tried to argue that these arrows influenced the creation of fabled weapons owned by Thor and Odin. But perhaps there are some arrowheads of historical significance buried out there, which we can creditably say were made in honor of the god rather than by the god himself. After we publish our work on this vessel—Ray has taken to calling it "the Sorcerer's Urn"—perhaps we will get additional funding to look for them.

No entries after that. I have two names to inquire about now—Logan and Ray—and a search to run about those arrows. I take the diary with me and leave everything else untouched, though I do scan the tops of the messy desks to see if I can determine to whom they belong. Hard copies of memos and emails reveal that one belongs to Chirayu Parekh—who might be Ray—and another to Miriam Vargas. I'd come back to the dig at dawn and try to catch one or both of them before they got to the trailer and realized it had been burgled.

Okay, my favorite hound, I say as I exit the trailer. *Nap time. Let's go back and get you snuggled into bed.*

<No nap for Granuaile?>

Maybe later. I need to work on a problem for a little while. Durga's suggestion that I might have occasion to wonder at the weapons she brought two nights ago comes back to me. I think this might be the proper occasion. The mention of the arrows makes me realize that she hadn't brought a bow with her.

When I get back to the hotel and run a quick image search of Durga, I discover that she is often depicted as having a bow, and the stories that delve into the gifts given her by the gods of the Hindu pantheon do include mention of Vayu's arrows. However, I cannot find any specific mention of the bow in the stories, beyond a symbolic religious meaning. Vayu's arrows, then, must be the important weapons, and she had come without them. Perhaps because they truly were buried somewhere north of Thanjavur? If so, why? And why did she not simply explain?

When I review the last entry, Dad's journal makes another connection for me. The idea that Vedic culture influenced the Norse somehow is certainly true in my own experience: The *asuras* I'd seen surrounding my father were blue-skinned and four-armed, like the shape Loki had taken when he confronted us in Poland. I remember thinking at the time, what the fuck, why is he blue, but it never would have occurred to me to think it was anything but the product of his own derangement. We had the Olympians to worry about, and Loki had to be put on the back burner. And now all I can think is, what if that was my big clue—my one chance to walk the path to which Durga alluded, where none of this happened?

I hide my face in my hands and mutter, "Oh, shut *up*." Orlaith hears me and raises her head from the bed.

<What? I didn't say nothing.>

I was talking to myself. And watch out for double negatives.

<I meant I didn't say no nothings neither. Um. Yeah?>

I know it is pointless to speculate and torture myself with what might have been, but I expect I'll take a good long while doing it. Later. To prevent a spiral of second-guessing and self-recrimination, I'd try to grab a few hours of sleep to get myself adjusted to Indian time, so I could begin again at dawn. I'd search for this Logan guy, and when I found him, I'd ask where he got that urn.

It's an excellent plan, and the flaw doesn't become clear until I stop Ray in the morning, before he makes it to the trailer and sees that the doorknob is gone. I am so very smooth: I tell him my name is Beverly Childress, drop Dr. Liu's name, and say I've been hired by the university to investigate the disappearance of Donal MacTiernan. My American accent in this place gives me instant credibility with him.

Indian-born but educated in America, Chirayu Parekh is an adorable if slightly doughy man with glasses and a mustache imported from the seventies. Like many people from overseas who spend any time in the United States, he had grown tired of repeating his name over and over again and had hacked it down to Ray to simplify it for the 'Mericans. He carries a leather messenger bag in one hand and a cup of coffee in the other, and he's very eager to help once he checks me out and decides that he wants me to like him.

"Mr. Parekh, in my preliminary investigation we came across a student of Dr. MacTiernan's named Logan, who was working here on site," I say. "Can you tell me anything about him?"

"Oh, sure, that guy. Kind of tall, blond, sort of kept

to himself. Or at least kept away from Miriam and me. He hung around with Dr. MacTiernan a lot."

"Where can I find him?"

"I'm sorry, but I don't know."

"All right, what was his last name?"

"I don't know that either. He was always just called Logan."

I try to hide my irritation, but I'm uncertain that I manage it. "Will he be joining you here at the dig today?"

"No, I don't think so. He disappeared at the same time Dr. MacTiernan did. But we couldn't report it, you know, because we didn't know his name."

I frown at him. "We? You mean Miriam Vargas doesn't know either? How do you let someone work on a university-sponsored project like this without knowing his name?"

Ray begins to panic at the implication that he screwed up somehow. "Well, Dr. MacTiernan vouched for him and he knew his stuff, so who was I to question? I mean—"

"This man may be responsible for Dr. MacTiernan's disappearance. Can't you think of any way to find out his name?"

I fear that the opposite might be true—that my father, once he was possessed by the raksoyuj, caused Logan to disappear—but I can't share that with Ray.

"Well, no, I mean, I hardly even think about living people; it's not in the job description of an archaeologist, you know—"

"Walk me through how you first met Logan, please, Mr. Parekh."

"Oh, well, when Miriam and I arrived, he was already here with Dr. MacTiernan, who introduced the guy as Logan, a former student of his. Hey, should we maybe talk more in the office?"

"No, I'm almost finished. You flew in from the States?"

"Yes. Dr. MacTiernan flew in from a dig he had going in the UK, so he got here first."

"And this was on October third?"

"Right."

"You were called in by Dr. MacTiernan?"

"Indirectly, yes. He called Dr. Liu at the university and asked her to send someone who could help with Sanskrit. She tapped us and we packed our bags. We were going to publish together."

"There was a vessel here, wasn't there, with Sanskrit markings on it? That's why he needed you?"

Ray is taken aback by this. "Yes. How did you know?"

"Dr. Liu informed me," I say. "Where is that vessel now?"

"It disappeared with Logan and Dr. MacTiernan. We think one of them took it."

"That's my suspicion also. Was the vessel unearthed here?"

"That's what Logan claimed. He said he dug it up here and showed us a depression in the earth where he'd excavated it. But we just got lab results back on the soil and material samples Dr. MacTiernan sent off, and it looks like it didn't come from here at all. The lab says it was buried originally somewhere in the west, probably in Gujarat."

"Interesting. Thank you for your time, Ray. I'll let you know if I find anything."

"What? That's it? Hey, you want some coffee?"

I wave goodbye at him without answering. With Orlaith at my side, I put some distance between us, before he can discover that the office has been invaded and remember that he really isn't that good with people and probably should have questioned me a bit more. No doubt he'll get some grief later from Miriam for being so trusting. Poor Ray.

As soon as I'm out of sight, I cast camouflage on the two of us and we jog down to the house south of Thanjavur in which my father—or, rather, the raksoyuj— had been staying. I'd never gone inside to check it out, and if Logan had disappeared with Dad, then maybe he had been there too. Maybe he's still there—and dead. Or maybe I'll find a clue to his whereabouts. It seems as good a place as any to begin.

Except it's no longer a place. When I get down there, I can't find it anywhere, though I'm sure I recognize the field in which it stood and where everything happened. And then I realize that Durga had probably wiped it from the earth as part of her cleansing ritual. The earth had been scoured clean. No evidence of rakshasas or *asuras* for humans—or even me—to find.

I don't know what to do next. If Logan's body had been in that house, it wasn't there anymore. There might be an immigration officer who could tell me all the Logans that had entered India in early September or early October, but I couldn't just smile and lie my way into accessing that information. I might be able to try approaching Dr. Liu back at Dad's university, posing as an investigator hired by his family, but she'd be far more skeptical than Ray. Besides, even if she could access Dad's class rosters for the past twenty years or so, privacy laws would prevent her from handing out names of former students without serious legal paperwork signed by a judge.

One thing I do know is that the "Sorcerer's Urn" didn't disappear with Dad or Logan. It was somehow found by Laksha, and she was still someone to whom, in theory, I could talk. She'd need a mouth for that, however, since she's clearly not interested in jumping into my head anymore.

I return to the hotel to consult my laptop again, because it's easier to mask than cell phones or other wireless gadgets. I grab us some lunch, and Google tells me about the Raja Mirasdar Hospital in Thanjavur and provides me with a map. After I retrieve Laksha's necklace and stuff it into my pocket, we set out to find Laksha a new body.

We circle the hospital campus a couple of times and pick out a nice tree under which Orlaith can stretch out and take a nap. I camouflage her and then ask Kaveri if she would continue to keep Orlaith hidden while I am inside and cut off from the earth.

Using the binding carved into the length of Scáthmhaide, I melt from sight and enter the hospital in search of a suitable host for Laksha.

She hasn't spoken to me at all since the disaster in the field, and I'm both hurt and relieved by it. She could have taken up residence in my head again but has chosen not to. I wonder if it's because she's too weak or if it's because she doesn't want to face the questions I have for her. Either way, I don't want the responsibility for her life in my pocket anymore, and since she seemed partial to choosing a young woman's body before, I'm hoping to find one here.

Searching the hospital for comatose patients takes me a while. I don't understand the signs near the doors, which are only occasionally printed in English alongside other scripts. But a few floors and many dead ends later, I find some comatose patients. Two are men, one is a very old lady, but the last is a tall woman in her thirties with sallow skin and lank, stringy hair. Most of her chart is meaningless scribbling to me, but some vitals are also typed in Roman script, such as her name: *Mhathini Palanichamy*.

Deciding that has a nice musical ring to it and that I don't have nearly the patience for an extended search that I had years ago when we found Selai, I pull out the ruby necklace and settle it about Mhathini's neck. Once I remove my hand, it becomes visible and looks so very out of place against a white hospital gown.

Checking again to make sure I'm the only conscious person around, I bend lower and speak to the necklace, feeling somewhat silly even though no one can see me.

"Laksha, it's Granuaile. You're resting against a comatose patient who will serve as your new body. I'm going to leave the necklace here, so if you want to make sure you retain control of it, slip into this woman's body right now and wake her up before I go."

I wait a full minute and nothing happens, so I lean down again and say, "Right now, Laksha. You have one more minute and I'm leaving. I won't know what will happen to the necklace then."

With fifteen seconds left, the eyelids flutter open and the beeping of the heart-rate monitor speeds up. I drop my invisibility so that she can see me.

"Welcome back."

"Whur . . . mur? Er. Nur?"

"Pardon me?"

"Cur. Tur!" Her hand rises from her side, IV and all, and points first at her mouth, then twirls around her head. Her expression twists in frustration.

"Ah. This woman must have suffered some serious brain damage to the speech centers, I'm guessing. She probably has aphasia. Can you understand me all right? Thumbs up or down." I get a thumbs-up. "Good. Looks like your motor skills are fine. Shall I assume that you can fix the speech problem with time?"

Another affirmative. "Excellent." I'm disappointed that we can't speak right away, but I can hardly blame Laksha for the problem. "I will give you that time and we'll speak later. You have ways of finding me, so I trust you will do that as soon as you are able. We need to talk."

"Whur mur nur?"

"Your name is Mhathini Palanichamy. Is that what you were asking?" Thumbs-up. I hear footsteps approaching in the hall, which heralds the arrival of medical staff responding to a change in her vitals. "You're still in Thanjavur. I'll leave you to the business of starting over." I wink out of sight just as a nurse enters and exclaims at the sight of Mhathini's open eyes. I slide past her and sigh in relief once I get out into the hall, glad to have that burden off my back. I don't know if Mhathini is still in there, sharing space with Laksha, or if she has moved on, but I suppose I will find out later.

I pick up Orlaith and spend the remainder of the afternoon trying to find some way to help the city recover from the rakshasa plague. The language barrier hinders me, however, and that, coupled with perhaps a dose or two of paranoia and xenophobia—or else a fear of big dogs—makes us unwelcome.

It's been a completely frustrating day, and after a desultory dinner I curl up in bed with Orlaith and my father's diary, working backward through the entries in case they include any mention of Logan. I don't find anything about him, but I do find something else: an entry on my birthday.

> *Granuaile would be thirty-three years old today.*
> *I wonder what kind of person she would be. I*
> *wish . . . well, it's far too late for wishes, isn't it?*
> *Far too late to make anything better. There's only*
> *time for regrets now. Lord, I miss her.*

I feel as if I've fallen from two stories and landed gut-first on a pommel horse, the air completely gone from my lungs, and when I breathe in again, it's so very painful that the noise wakes up Orlaith.

<Granuaile?>

It's okay. Go back to sleep.

I trace the words with my finger, trying to contact my dad through the ink he scrawled there months ago. I know exactly how he felt, because I'm feeling it now. There's so much time for regret ahead of me, days and months and years of it. I put the book down, turn on my side, and drape an arm across Orlaith, hoping to sleep away some of that time.

I resolve to track down a possible site north of town for the Lost Arrows of Vayu. If this Logan person is still alive, he might be attacking the earth with a shovel somewhere.

When I wake up, a gray Saturday in India, I shoot off a text to Atticus before I hop into the shower, to let him know he shouldn't worry about me. To my surprise when I emerge, he's answered, asking if my father is okay.

His death isn't something I wish to consign to a text message, so I say, *You don't need to worry about him either,* and then he does his Shakespeare thing, sweet man, kissing me with a line from *Troilus and Cressida: The strong base and building of my love / Is as the very centre of the earth.*

It is a game we play, sometimes, to answer one poet's words with another's, so that both the bards and we converse. The reply has to make sense in context, of course, but you score bonus points if you use a quote that contains one or more words from the previous one. I send him two lines from Whitman: *Far-swooping elbow'd earth—rich apple-blossom'd earth! / Smile, for your lover comes.* And then I amend that with, *As soon as I can, anyway. Don't wait up.*

CHAPTER 19

The estates of the Tuatha Dé Danann are proper castles, but they rise straight out of the turf like gray mountains, no walls around them like the few human-built ones I've seen on earth. They're never besieged, so that makes walls unnecessary, I suppose, but I know the true reason the Tuatha Dé Danann don't build walls around them: They want people to lose their shite and fill their pants when they gaze upon the glory of their architecture, and it makes me laugh. Binding stone together into a seamless tower doesn't impress me. Show me what ye can do when there's no wall between us, and maybe then I'll offer my respect.

When I shift to the trees ringing the pastures of Manannan Mac Lir's estate, I see that he's worked some blue stones in with the gray here and there, swirling patterns of it, and mixed in are some shiny reflective bits of shell, which Siodhachan says is called mother-of-pearl. There's plenty of that around the entrance to his castle, and it's worked into the tiles of his floor and his interior walls as well, which I think is a terrible idea. It keeps flashing and winking at me, and I can't tell half the time if that's a piece of shell or a pixie wing in the corner of my eye—which I guess must be the point. It's a kind of camouflage for them.

His place is fecking lousy with faeries. Flying about

the grounds and hovering near the ceiling and hiding
under furniture, walking around in livery of two different kinds because some of them serve Fand and some of
them serve Manannan. Manannan's are in blue and
gray and tend to be water Fae of some kind or other.
Selkies and sea horsemen with big eyes looking around
for their ocean but seeing only stone and the small dead
bits of other creatures that swam in it once upon a time.
Fand's lot favors maroon and gold and a soft fabric
called velvet, and they're the ones that make me nervous, because she has the fliers. Pixies and assorted airborne irritants, and plenty of the large, man-sized Fae
who look as if they have bones made of willow sticks. If
I breathe heavily in their general direction, they'll fall
over. But I see that some of them have weapons, oversize bronze needles they use instead of swords.

I notice that their eyes fall to my throat when they
first see me and then relax only after they confirm that
there's nothing there. They're looking for iron. Two of
them greet me at the gate and lead me inside to an inner
courtyard that has both a tethered tree and a deep pool
of salt water.

"What's that for?" I ask, pointing at the pool. It can't
be for fishing.

"The Lord Manannan sometimes comes and goes
that way. He opens a portal underwater and swims directly into the earthly oceans."

That was handy. If the pool was deep enough, he
could shift away—or not—and no one here would
know whether he had truly left, without diving in to
make sure. And he could also return but not surface
until he chose.

There are white benches distributed around the pool,
along with sculpted hedgerows and flowering plants.
Two figures rise from one and approach. I think I might
know who one of them is, but not the other. Best to wait

for an introduction. One is a red-haired woman in a white tunic edged in green bindings around the collar and sleeves, and the other is a giant man with coppery curly hair and a thick beard. He has a leaf stuck in his hair on the left side of his head, but I don't think it's my duty to point it out to him. I had seen them both at the Fae Court yesterday, but they had slipped away after my audience and I never got to speak with them.

"Eoghan Ó Cinnéide," my escort says, "may I present Flidais, of the Tuatha Dé Danann, and Perun, thunder god of the Slavic people."

I'd been right about the woman. The huntress was wearing a knife at her hip inlaid with green stone, something Siodhachan had mentioned in his story. "It's an honor," I say, giving them both a tight nod. It might have been more proper to bow or take a knee or something, but if they truly want their arses kissed, they'll have to force me to do it.

"Pleased to meet you, Eoghan," Flidais says, her face a polite mask. It's a bit pink and puckered here and there, as are parts of her arms; she had been burned by Loki and then driven mad by Bacchus not so long ago, but her physical recovery was almost complete and she wasn't drooling on her boots. Perun smiles underneath his beard at me.

"Is honor to meet another Druid. I am liking Irish peoples very much."

"You've been visiting for a while, then?" I knew that Loki had set fire to his plane and he was something of a refugee, but I wondered what he would say to a stranger.

"Yes, I am guest here." Just the basics, then.

Flidais takes his hand and says, "He's my guest."

"Oh," I says, understanding. Siodhachan hadn't told me about this relationship, so it might be a new development. Or perhaps he thought it wasn't important. Knowing Flidais's reputation, I could imagine that Perun had been a very recent guest of hers in the forest, and the leaf in his hair indicated that he'd had a good time. She had to have seen the leaf before this moment, though—it couldn't be missed—so she had left it there on purpose. But what purpose, exactly? Was this merely a practical joke on her lover? Was she marking him as hers? Or was this a pointed message, either to me or to our hosts? Since Fand was her daughter, Flidais might enjoy making her uncomfortable with small tokens of promiscuity. I wouldn't find out unless I waited and watched, so I says, "Well, peace and balance to you both."

Flidais sees that I notice the leaf and say nothing. She winks at me with her right eye, so that Perun can't catch it, before giving me a pleasant grin. "Manannan and Fand await us in the dining room," she says. "Shall we go?"

"You are in for meal of memory," Perun assures me, and saws the air with his thick hands. "No one sets a table like Fand and Manannan."

He's not exaggerating. I've never seen so much food, and there's only the five of us at the table. The strangest thing is that it all seems to be for display instead of for eating. We each get a faery who puts full plates in front of us and takes them away after a couple of bites, only to produce a new dish to sample—but none of it comes from the food already on the table. The plates are brought out from the kitchen. Another team of faeries is in charge of drinks, keeping our glasses full of whatever we wish.

"We will bring any libation you desire," Fand says as soon as I'm seated, and though I don't know what the fecking hell a libation is, I guess that it means a drink. I decide to test her on it.

"Can I have a shot of whiskey, something aged at least twenty years?" Siodhachan told me such drinks are rare and expensive because people typically can't wait that long to drink what they've distilled. But Fand is sincere.

"We have nothing so old here," she says, "but it will be fetched immediately from Ireland." She turns to find a faery dressed in her livery and nods at him. "Please bring us a selection as soon as you can manage."

The faery, who I guess is some kind of steward, bows deeply and says, "Yes, my queen," then withdraws, presumably to pop off to earth to steal me a few bottles.

Distractions aside, once I'm settled at the table it's difficult not to stare at Fand. She possesses a rare beauty, though it's a bit cold, like the sharp peaks of snowy mountains against a pure blue sky. And the more I think about it, the more apt it is. Mountains inspire no sexual desires in me whatsoever—a blessing to be sure, because I can't think of anything so useless as humping a mountain—but I'm always ready to stare at them and be grateful that they are there to be seen. Fand is like that. Stunning and inaccessible.

I tear my attention away from her with some effort and address Manannan. He's making an effort to appear relaxed, but he's gripping his flagon a bit too tightly for that. It's full of something delicious that Goibhniu brewed, so he can't be disappointed with his beer. Something is bothering him and he would rather be elsewhere. "What's occupying your time these days, Manannan?" I asks him.

He snorts. "Better to ask what isn't. I'm looking after the sea and the dead. Also searching the oceans for evidence of Jörmungandr and trying not to bash in the heads of Poseidon and Neptune, who are supposed to be helping but are failing."

"Ah, I've heard the Olympians can be difficult."

He snorts again. Dinner will be a festival of snorting

at this rate. "That's putting it very mildly," he says. "They're ignoranuses."

I don't know what that word means, but Perun doesn't either, and he asks about it before I can.

"An ignoranus," Manannan explains, "is someone who's both stupid and an arsehole."

"This is great word!" Perun exclaims. "I know many peoples who fit this word in perfect way! Very useful!" He turns to me. "Do you agree, Eoghan?"

"I do. I'm sure to use it myself. Shall I assume, then, Manannan, that you've had no luck in finding Jörmungandr?"

"Not yet. He must have reduced his size considerably. But he will have to bulk up if he wants to do any damage, so we must keep looking to have the earliest possible warning."

The faery steward returns with several bottles of very good stuff and presents them to me, but he saves the best for last. It's a bottle of something called Knappogue Castle 1951, which he says was distilled in Tullamore and aged in sherry casks for thirty-six years before being bottled in 1987. Now that we're in 2022, fewer than a hundred bottles are left in existence. It's the rarest Irish whiskey available, and I remember hearing of it. Rúla Búla in Tempe had a bottle at one point. Siodhachan told me he bought a shot of this for the Christian god, Jesus.

"Aye, I'll have that. Just leave me the whole bottle, there's a good lad." Because if you're going to drink stolen whiskey, you might as well have the stuff that gods drink.

Seeing that I'm pleased, Fand favors the steward with a smile and a nod. "Well done." The faery is so overcome by this small scrap of praise that he looks on the verge of tears as he bows and backs away.

"What do you do, Fand," I asks her as I pour myself a shot, "while Manannan is out doing this and that?"

"I manage the estate. And I see to numerous errands on Brighid's behalf. Right now many of the Fae are out looking for signs of Loki, and I'm coordinating the search."

"Has he been spotted?"

"He's proven to be as elusive as Jörmungandr, unfortunately."

"Huh." I savor the golden burn of the whiskey in my throat and consider. "Has anyone tried to divine him? Or Jörmungandr?"

"We get nothing," Flidais says, and Fand agrees.

"What about people in his own crowd? I'm new to the Norse, and maybe I don't know their capabilities, but doesn't this Odin have some way of finding him?"

Manannan answers. "He has a throne called Hlidskjálf, from which he can see most anything, but he cannot see into Hel. Mist cloaks her entire realm."

"And you'd know a thing or two about hiding in mist, wouldn't ye?" I says, grinning at him.

Before Manannan can answer, Flidais says, "We are quite anxious to meet Loki again." She nods with a cold promise that the meeting will be unpleasant. "Believe me, when I find him, he'll have an arrow through his throat."

"I believe ye with all me heart," says I, and I pour another round and hold up my glass, proposing that we drink to the swift yet painful death of Loki.

"*Da!* Swift and painful death!" Perun booms, his beard quaking with emotion, and the others chime in and we turn up our glasses with enthusiasm.

I should pause to add that I'm not in the habit of drinking to anyone's death. Usually I'm fond of drinking to peace and health, or drinking for no reason at all. This seemed like a special occasion, though.

Conversation continues to swirl around courses of food and drink, and I mentally record it all to sift through later.

Actually, that's probably not what I'm doing. The information I'm taking in is more like a giant load of shite that I'll sculpt into the truth. An ugly truth, no doubt, of considerable stench. And a bit wobbly on its feet, because that's what I am after drinking half the bottle and eating more than I ever have in me life.

When a faery has to save me from flopping facedown into a slice of pie a couple of hours later, I know it's time to leave. I bet it's a universal truth: You eat your pie or go home.

I deliver slurred compliments on the hospitality of my hosts and lurch unsteadily from the table. I manage to grab the remainder of the bottle as two faeries help me out of the castle. They have the good sense to lead me to the reeking pigsty, where my stomach forcibly ejects its contents into the mud.

"Ah, thash mush bedder," I tell them. "Have ye goddanywadder?" I lean against the fence and wait for one of the faeries to return with a skin of something that isn't whiskey. Perun and Flidais appear outside the gate, wish me farewell, and wander off in their own drunken stupor to the eastern pasture. While me poor head spins like a hound getting ready to sleep, I ignore the remaining faery and start letting the evening's events slush around in the old skull. My dinner companions weren't a group like last night's, where I could easily dismiss them all as the mind behind the secret war on Druidry—for if you're trying to kill the only two Druids around at the time, what else is it?

When the faery I sent away returns with some water, I tell him and the other to piss off, I'm recuperating, and I can't do it with them hovering about. Left alone, whiskey in one hand and water in the other, I try to stagger with dignity back to the trees and away from the stink of the hogs. The staggering part is easy; the dignity is tougher.

On the show Hal let me watch, that detective Holmes narrows his eyes or talks too fast to demonstrate that he's being brilliant and solving the case. Or he lies down on a couch with patches on his arm that deliver chemicals to his brain. These particulars serve to make him look like a clever addict, but it's not a very keen insight into the workings of genius. Or the workings of Druidry. What Sherlock does is train his mind to remember details, access them as needed, and then spy the hidden pattern in them. It's like spotting animals in clouds: The vapor's the same for everyone, but sometimes you're the only person who can see what's floating there, because you have the proper angle and the imagination to see it. And that's the magic of Sherlock Holmes—his talent for synthesis and discovery. Anyone can train the mind to absorb and recall; that's the bulk of a Druid's apprenticeship, after all. Making sense of it is another skill entirely, and I'm not sure if my thinking, outdated by two thousand years, will be any help here—especially when it's swimming in whiskey.

I drink half the skin of water and pour the rest over me head to achieve something like a refreshed buzz instead of minimal consciousness, and I think: The trouble with this group is that they're all sufficiently sneaky to have pulled it off. Manannan's out there in the sea all the time now, supposedly, but who's to say he really is? Fand's faeries can't keep track of him out there, and he can shift where he likes. And Flidais disappears for long stretches into the woods or even to other planes—no one knows where—and she has all the guile of a hunter, as well as a thunder god at her side these days.

Three more steps bring me to the edge of the trees ringing the estate, and it's there, quicker than I had any right to expect, that the answer jumps out of my fogged mind and shouts "Balls!" at me.

When Siodhachan first explained the subtleties of modern cursing to me, he was careful to stress the importance of vowels. "There is a time for fecking and a time for fucking, Owen," he said, "and a wise Irishman knows which is which."

I don't know if I'm wise, but I do know when the situation demands a vowel change. "Well, fuck me standing," I says to the trees, before I use them to shift back to the woods outside Sam Obrist's place. "What are we going to *do*?"

They don't have an answer for me, but the way they're swaying in me vision suggests that there's a mighty wind blowing. Either that or it's the whiskey's fault.

CHAPTER 20

I would have returned to my cabin in Colorado, except that Owen was going to show up eventually near the house of Sam Obrist after his trip to Tír na nÓg, and I had to return the rental car in Flagstaff anyway.

After Jesus had bid me farewell and gifted me with the glasses and the remainder of the tequila, I wasn't any closer to figuring out how best to proceed. I had more doubt than resolve, and a faint but growing worry about Granuaile. As it grew dark Friday night, I thought perhaps I should give her a call. I shifted back to Arizona, where there was cell service, and was about to punch in her number when she texted me and told me not to worry about her. She was still in India, and it was Saturday morning there. I didn't know how things had turned out with her dad, and she said not to worry about that either, so I was left with the luxury of time to decide what to do next.

I dreamed up several different courses of manly, decisive action with muscles and swords and copious grunts of exertion, but I wasn't sure which of the gang of nine gods would deign to join me, if any. Jesus had hinted pretty strongly that I was on my own, which made any action extremely risky. After a night spent under the stars, I leavened my meditation on Saturday with long runs through the Coconino National Forest with Oberon, during which he informed me of his plans to write a book like Miyamoto Musashi's, except his would be called *The Book of Five Meats.*

Only five?

<You have to leave room for sequels, Atticus.>

Oh, yes, I didn't think of that. Miyamoto divided his book into five rings, or ways—The Way of Fire, the Way of Earth, and so on—and each way taught something about his approach to martial arts. What will your five ways be?

<The Way of Poultry. The Way of Beef. The Way of Seafood. The Way of Deli.>

That's a good way to group them, Oberon. Seafood and Deli encompasses a wide range of meats. I'll be interested to hear what you have to say about head-cheese. And the last?

<The Way of Sausage, of course. I will begin your instruction now.>

Please do.

<The perfection of life, like the perfection of sausage, is achieved in its flavor. It must vary in taste and spiciness if it is to nourish us and be cherished in return.>

I think you're on to something there, buddy.

<Though it may at first be fine, the same sausage every day palls with time.>

Oh, that's a winner. In addition to the warning against the dangers of routine, it has both rhyme and innuendo.

<It does? I mean *of course* it does; I totally planned that!>

My phone eventually rang on Sunday afternoon. It was Sam Obrist's number, but Owen was on the other end of it.

"Siodhachan?"

"Yes?"

"Come to Sam's house so I don't have to talk to this unnatural piece of shite anymore."

"What the hell, Owen? Sam is not an unnatural piece of shite!"

"What? Gods blast it, I was talking about this fecking cell phone, not Sam!"

"Well, you should choose your words more carefully, then!"

"Ye really need to shut your hole about me word choice. Or do I need to remind ye that this isn't my fecking *native language*?"

"Blow a goat!"

"You've already blown them all!"

"I'll be there soon!"

"Fine!"

I pressed the button to end the call and saw that Oberon was looking at me.

<Well, that escalated quickly.>

I breathed out a long sigh and tried to relax. "Yeah, somehow my conversations with him always do."

When I got to Sam's house, I had to endure more hazing along the lines of "Fun's over, boys. Siodhachan's here." Owen left them a half-finished bottle of whiskey, and the unsteadiness of his gait indicated he might have drunk the other half recently, but eventually we were able to shift to Colorado. It was his first visit to the place, and he made some effort to say nice things about it. Perhaps that was his apology for snapping at me earlier. Or perhaps it was an apology for what was to come.

A pronounced chill heralded the early onset of winter, and the birds were beginning to notice. As the sun sank below the jagged ridge of the San Juans, many of them spoke loudly of leaving soon for the south—or anyway it sounded that way to me—and at least one pair said, to hell with it, we're leaving *now*. Sitting outside in canvas sling chairs with glasses of stout in hand, Owen and

I listened to the song of Gaia in silence and spent a half hour pretending there wasn't anything to talk about. Then, without preamble, Owen cleared his throat and broached the subject he'd been avoiding ever since he got back. "Look, Siodhachan, the good news is that it's not Brighid."

"Oh, I know. I found that out recently through a different source, but I'm glad to hear it confirmed."

The archdruid nodded, uncomfortable, looking disappointed that there was little reason to dwell on the good news before he had to get on with the bad.

"All right, keep in mind that I haven't any proof," he said. "Someone else will have to get that. All I have is circumstantial evidence, though I'm convinced I'm right. I'll walk you through it. All the business with the Fae assassins and the vampires and the dark elves started after you came out of hiding and presented yourself at the Fae Court, am I right?"

"Right."

"So it was that appearance that triggered everything. We know it's not Brighid, and you can eliminate all the Fae, because they don't have the connections outside Tír na nÓg to pull this off. So it had to be one of the other Tuatha Dé Danann."

"I'm with you so far."

"Now you look at Brighid's boys, and they have no motive. They're into their respective crafts and they're actually happy you're back, because you make life more interesting. Ogma is spoiling for a fight, but he's the sort who will pick one with you and leave the subtlety to others. If he's after you, you'll know it. Same thing with Flidais. If she wanted ye dead, then you'd be dead already with an arrow in your eye, and besides, she came to your aid against those huntresses. Nearly all the others who might be able to do this sort of thing are long gone. So, by my figuring, that leaves only two of the Tuatha Dé Danann with the power to do this: Manannan Mac Lir and Fand."

"No."

He slapped his chair arm with his free hand. "Fecking *listen,* boy! They're both incredibly good at keeping secrets, but only one of them had the opportunity to do this. And with all his responsibilities as master of the sea and being the only remaining Irish god looking after the dead, Manannan Mac Lir doesn't have the opportunity. Nor does he have the motive."

"You're saying it's Fand? What motive does she have?"

"She's the Queen of the Faeries, Siodhachan! The faeries who can't stand cold iron, who hate and fear you more than anything in all the worlds, and who, I might add, you have killed in vast numbers over the years, by your own admission."

Stunned, I managed only a lame protest. "But Fand has been so kind to us. . . ."

My archdruid lost what little composure he had left. "Of course she has, you giant fecking tit! You had the favor of the Morrigan and her husband and even Brighid, so she had no choice but to smile in your face! But she hates your guts in sympathy with all the Fae who love her so. The Fae both respect and fear Brighid, Siodhachan, and they follow her, but it's Fand that they adore. And the very last thing Fand wants, lad, is another Iron Druid. One is far too many for her, don't ye see? So both you and Granuaile had to go, but go without anyone figuring out who was responsible. Manannan was often not at home, and her mum was off having thunder sex with Perun in the forest, so Fand had plenty of time to scheme and leave and come back without anyone being the wiser. She met Granuaile at the Fae Court when you introduced her, which means Fand knew her name and shook her hand, maybe swiped a hair or two or something to help her with divination, and that was all she needed. She could track you through Granuaile and send in the assassins of one kind or another almost immediately, but it took her some time to set up that arrangement with the Romans and shut down your ability to shift planes."

"So she was the one who killed Midhir and Lord Grundlebeard and left that manticore in his home. . . ."

"Aye. And that manticore told ye he was captured by someone masked, with an odd voice, correct?"

"Correct."

"I'll bet ye three grandmas and all their cookies that she was masked like that when she killed Midhir. That way, when Manannan arrived to take Midhir's shade away to wherever he was bound, Midhir couldn't tell him that Fand had done the deed."

"Gods, Owen. She's Manannan's wife and Flidais's daughter."

"I know, lad." He burst into a wide grin and leaned back into his chair, taking a sip of Guinness and smacking his lips. A line of foam trailed along the bottom edge of his mustache. "Oh, that's right delicious, that is. But you're fecking doomed, and that's no lie."

"I don't think that's necessarily so."

"Oh? And why is that?"

"Because I can see where she's coming from. If someone was out there killing people I cared about, I'd be going after them myself. I can't blame her, because I'd do the same thing in her position. There has to be something I can do to fix this."

"Ah, so you'll be lyin' down and presenting your belly, then, and askin' her to kill ye straightaway, because she's justified?"

"Of course not. But this isn't a kill-or-be-killed situation yet. We can still talk."

My archdruid scoffed. "Aye, lad. I'm sure she talked

to Midhir for a nice long while before she wrapped him up in iron and cut his throat."

"I'm in a very different position than Midhir was. I just . . . don't . . . want to jump to violence."

"Why not? It will solve the problem, and you're good at it."

"No. Every time I think I've solved a problem with violence, more problems grow in their place, like a hydra."

"A hydrant, ye say? One of those yellow things ye pointed out to me?"

"No, a hydra. Greek monster. Cut off a head and two grow back in its place."

"Oh. Well, then, ye don't cut off its head. You take out the heart or the kidneys."

"Yes, Owen, that's my point. I'd rather approach this a different way."

"All right, approach it on your knees if ye must. I'll be tellin' ye I told ye so later."

I quelled the retort on my lips and instead replied with, "Tomorrow's Samhain. Celebrate it with me here?"

Owen took his time in responding, wondering if perhaps I had an ulterior motive, but finally he said, "Aye, lad. I'll do that."

"Good. With any luck, we'll be celebrating it with Manannan Mac Lir."

CHAPTER 21

The brief text exchange with Atticus leaves me feeling much better and hopeful that the day will yield something positive. After finishing breakfast, I let the hotel know I'll be staying another day or two, then return to the banana grove simply because we won't be bothered there. Once situated in the grove in the lotus position, I close my eyes and stretch out my thoughts to contact the elemental Kaveri. The conversation goes on for hours, long enough that Orlaith lies down for another nap, but gradually we isolate a place underground where a chamber existed in ancient days but is now filled in.

Kaveri explains that it is a //Place of magic / Long dormant / Dangerous / Slivers of air trapped inside//

It might not be the resting place of Vayu's arrows, but a place of magic sounds interesting, and in lieu of any other leads on Logan, I ask Kaveri to lead us there. We trek north from the grove until Kaveri tells me to stop in the middle of a rice paddy that's lying fallow for the season. We are all alone.

//Here// she says. In front of my feet, a black square of earth opens up, crumbling away like a sinkhole. A pungent scent of dirt wafts skyward, and steps leading down into the dark beckon me forward to discover wonders or uncover horrors. Something about it disturbs me, and I hesitate.

Orlaith?

<Yes?>

I don't really want to go down there, but I feel that I must. You should probably wait here for me. The elemental said it would be dangerous.

<I go with you. I am dangerous.>

In truth I wouldn't mind her company, but I can't bear to risk her. Oberon got hurt once when he was trying to protect Atticus from a vampire, and it nearly destroyed us both. *I know you are, Orlaith, but it is smarter to have you wait here so that you can come help me if needed. Please stay. I will return as soon as I can.*

She doesn't like the idea one bit, but she obeys, ears drooping. I pad cautiously down into the black, step by step, and tell myself that the foreboding I feel means nothing, because this space was solid earth a few moments ago. There can't be anything down here that can hurt me. But I also remember from my education in horror movies that girls who wander alone into dark places without a flashlight tend to make messy ends. Halfway down—and it's a long stairwell that Kaveri has made, for the chamber is deep—I cast night vision and hope the ambient light from the surface will guide me below.

At the bottom, it's clear that the ambient light won't suffice, even with night vision. I ask Kaveri to open a trench and she complies, creating a narrow slit in the overhanging earth through which sunlight can filter and provide some weak illumination. It's a large room for ancient days—forty by forty, I guess, with only pieces of the original walls and floor mixed in with the earth. It makes me wonder how Kaveri remembered this shape—but I don't get a chance to take a closer look at anything, because the light begins to fade almost immediately. The trench isn't closing, but something dark is passing between it and the rest of the room, as if someone put the entire room in a black bag.

//Query: What is happening?//

//Old creature wakes / Long hidden / Forgotten / Hates light / Air//

I almost cry out for Orlaith but quash it because I don't want her to run into this. Something unseen slams me backward, something fingerless and formless but undeniably exerting force, pressing me into the hard earthen floor. And it continues to press, crushing air out of my lungs but also crushing everywhere else—my legs, arms, and head—a claustrophobe's nightmare.

There is nothing to fight and no leverage to gain. It's like being in a compactor, I suppose, but without the hard walls of steel and the astromech droid at the other end of a communicator who can shut it down. This is more of a soft but inexorable weight, like a pillow pressed down by a very credible hulk, and the smothering darkness and weight serve to fuel a rising panic inside. I'll be smooshed soon, if I don't finagle an escape. I cast magical sight and see no change at all—only pitch black and nothing at which to strike, nothing to bind. Yet something is undeniably attacking me.

I cannot raise my arm to deliver so much as a blind punch. I use the limited strength stored in Scáthmhaide's silver metalwork, because none of my tattoos currently touch the earth—one of the few pieces of remaining ancient stone floor rests underneath my right arm where my tattoos wrap completely around the biceps, so I'm cut off. I quickly discover that even my boosted strength is insufficient to win freedom from this oppressive weight. But in struggling to lift my arms, I find that some lateral motion is possible.

My collarbone snaps—the first of many bones to go. It will be only seconds before my stronger bones give way and then I collapse like a submarine that dived too deep, fragments of calcium swimming in a skin bag full of bloody soup.

I move my left hand to the side of my thigh. An epic effort from my thumb flips off the thong holding Fuilteach in its scabbard. I draw the whirling blade, and the edge is immediately pressed into the dirt as it comes out, the pressure increasing every second. Once the blade is free, I try to angle the tip upward by using my wrist, but my wrist snaps instead. So does my right one, and my shins follow, low down near the ankles. Then my nose. I don't have breath left to scream, and I can feel my throat is ready to cave in, anyway. My fingers are pressed so tightly around the hilt that I can feel the stress fractures spreading, and they'll snap soon. Everything will. Having no other option and grinding my teeth against the pain, I shove the knife back down in the direction of the scabbard, except it's lower now and won't go in. But against a creature that somehow blankets its victims, any thrust is a thrust into its body. The tip of the whirling blade punctures something, the air pops audibly back into the room, and the pressure lifts.

The darkness shrinks away and light from the trench returns, but I can't move beyond a twitch and to take in gasping lungfuls of air. Too much is broken, and my entire body is bruised. But I'm alive, for the moment. Letting go of both Fuilteach and Scáthmhaide, I flip my right forearm over so that I can get some contact with the earth and begin to heal, and I also check on my hound.

Orlaith?

<Okay, I come down?>

No. Please stay.

<Okay. I will stay.>

I need to make sure it is safe first. I ask Kaveri: //Query: Any more old creatures here?//

//No//

So the threat is gone. Truly gone. I don't see a body of any kind, but my range of vision is limited. When I try to raise my head, my neck doesn't want to move. It's not paralyzed, just strained beyond functioning at the moment. I'll have to wait.

My ears are ringing as if I'd just enjoyed a metal concert, and they'd need some healing, no doubt, but nothing had torn loose.

Paying closer attention to my condition, I realize that more bones had broken than I first thought, and almost everything, including my skull, has stress fractures. My entire body would be a giant bruise for quite a while, and though I could heal my bones in miraculous time, I wouldn't be moving or climbing those stairs out of the room soon. Thinking of the stairs, I worry that someone will stumble across them during the day and investigate—especially if there's a large hound loitering nearby. I would have difficulty explaining what I was doing down here and how I had come to be injured so badly. Before I can invite Orlaith to join me, however, she speaks up with a note of surprise.

<Hey. Tall man comes.>

What? Orlaith, is he nice? I hear the soft mumble of a male voice, obviously talking to her, but get no answer to repeated queries and begin to worry. Then a shadow occludes the square of sunlight representing the opening of the stairwell, and Orlaith descends, saying nothing to me. Someone follows behind her, whistling.

At first I think it's a very tall person, but then, as the body keeps lengthening past the point of tall into impossible territory, I see that it's not really a person at all. And when the head finally drops into view and the hair ignites above a narrow face, and he stops whistling and laughs instead, I flail desperately with my ruined arm to find Scáthmhaide, in hopes that I can turn invisible before he sees me. I'm not nearly quick enough.

One hand blooms into flame and the other extends my way, wagging a finger. "No, no, don't get up. And none of that muttering. Try anything, move at all, and your hound will be set on fire. Refuse to answer my questions, and your hound will be set on fire. Are we clear?"

"Yes, Loki Flamehair." Orlaith steps into a corner out of my sight, ignoring me, and it's clear Loki has taken control of her somehow. "What have you done to my hound?"

"I've merely spoken to her. She will not be harmed unless you make it necessary."

Loki's gaze never wavers as he continues down the stairs, watching me carefully. It's the most disturbing gaze I have ever seen, for his flesh is still scarred and puckered around his eyes from his centuries of captivity, when a great snake's vemon dripped into them.

I don't move. When he reaches us, he squats down next to me, his booted feet purposefully stepping on Scáthmhaide to prevent me from using it if I had any thoughts of doing so. He extinguishes the fire along his arm with an unspoken command and then rests his arms on top of his thighs, letting his hands dangle down between his knees. "Excellent. Let us begin! Hello, flame-haired girl. You are the daughter of Donal Mac-Tiernan, are you not?"

"Yes."

"And a Druid?"

"Yes."

"The dabāva—how did you defeat it?"

"What? I'm sorry, I don't know what that is."

"The dabāva. The pressure. I'm sure you felt it, because your bones are broken. It's a thing of the earth, and it smothers fire. Doesn't like air very much either and tries to press it out. To paraphrase an old saying, I figured I needed to fight earth with earth. So is that what you did?"

I grow cold at the implications of his words and his presence here. He'd known about the creature waiting in the dark and had used me to defeat it. "Yes."

Loki flashes a mirthless grin at me. "Ah, you are not so good at lying as your paramour. Was it this, perhaps, that did the job?" He reaches across me easily with a long limb and plucks Fuilteach from my broken hand, lifting it and examining it close to his face, where I can also see it. The soul chamber is red now instead of blue, indicating that the yeti's magic has been released and the soul of that . . . dabāva is keeping its edge sharp and preventing it from melting. I find that I don't feel the least bit guilty about it.

"Hmm," Loki says. "An ice weapon. Work worthy of the frost giants—or perhaps even better. I've never seen anything so refined from them. But it's water magic, and I suppose that would work against a creature of the earth."

Before he can ask me where I got it, I field a question of my own. "Why are you here?"

"I'm sure you know why."

"To kill me?"

"Well . . . no. If you were O'Sullivan, I would say yes. Finding him in such a state as you are in would have been delightful. But I am here, like you, to find Vayu's arrows."

"How did—"

"—I know? You're here because of clues you found in your father's diary, isn't that right? Clues provided by a former student of his named Logan? I'm afraid that was me, pretending to be someone pathetic. I needed help getting the arrows and didn't want to promise any favors in return."

The urge to punch him in his smirking mouth builds

within me, but I can't do anything about it. Loki was behind it all. Dad never would have come here if it hadn't been for him. Loki unleashed chaos with the raksoyuj, knowing what it would do to countless innocents, and then waited for me to get here and defeat the guardian of the arrows. I decide I must take whatever small victory I can. "It didn't do you any good. The arrows aren't here."

"Nonsense. They're right over there. You just couldn't see them because of the dabāva."

I can't turn to look where he points, because it's the wall at the top of my head, opposite the stairwell, so Loki tells me to wait, and he steps out of my vision. When he returns, he squats down again and has a quiver of six arrows resting on his left side. They appear wholly unremarkable in the visible spectrum, though I guess the mere fact that the shafts haven't decomposed after all these years is proof enough of their unusual quality.

"What's so special about them?"

"These arrows were crafted by a god of the wind to pierce the heart of their target and fly true through any weather. Useful for unskilled archers like myself, and extremely useful when one may be fighting thunder gods who have impressive ranged weapons of their own."

"Thor is dead."

"Aye, but there remain some weaker versions of him, and he may yet manifest again if he can be bothered to do so. He is still worshipped by humans, after all. And there are other thunder gods too. That Perun fellow whom you have hidden from me, for example. You have him on one of the Irish planes, I assume."

I don't answer that but ask instead, "How did you know the arrows were here?"

"Some of the most interesting stories are those that are never written down. Like the time I messed with

Thor's food and he shat himself for seven days. The embarrassing episodes of the heroes often get left out of the written record, you see. India is no different. You can find plenty of stories about Durga defeating the *asuras* in the old days but very little about the details of the battles. In one of them she was facing an army of *asuras* and she shot all of these arrows right here," he says, jiggling them back and forth, "killing her targets with each one, and then she threw this quiver so forcefully at another that it plowed through his chest and destroyed him. That was quite magnificent, no doubt, but when the battle was over, she could find neither the quiver nor the arrows. That's because one of the *asuras* decided while the battle still raged to collect them all and hide them so that they could never be used again. He was a coward, you see, who saw his fellows being obliterated and rationalized fleeing the field with the excuse that his actions would weaken Durga in the future. He placed them here and set the dabāva to guard them. He died a few days ago with your father, thinking that, *this* time, Durga would surely be overcome. But cowards do have their uses."

A memory intrudes—a discrepancy. "Hey. What happened to your stutter?"

This time when he grins, it's with genuine amusement. He bobbles his head and his hair rekindles as he says, "M-m-m-my s-s-stutter?" The flames snuff out and his head stills before he continues, "I never had one. But I put on a good show, didn't I? You know how I learned English?"

"Frigg said someone taught you while you were still captive. A spirit sent from Hel."

"Yes. And that spirit she sent was a former teacher of English literature who read me *Hamlet*. Several times, in fact, at my request. Fabulous play, full of deception and assorted treachery. Do you know it?"

"Yes."

"Well, like the Lord Hamlet, once I was freed I thought it best *to put an antic disposition on.* However, *the wind is southerly,* and I do *know a hawk from a handsaw.*"

"No," I say, "you can't lie about that. I was there, and I know that wasn't an act. Atticus fooled you. On multiple occasions."

"Only the first time. I admit he is very clever and took me by surprise with that lie about being a construct of the dwarfs. But after my sleep in Nidavellir, I learned the truth of things and merely pretended to be mad and stupid. When I took the form of an *asura* in Poland, I hoped he would investigate immediately, and I had plans in place to lead him here, but I think perhaps there are too many demands on his attention. Using your father to get to you so that you would get to *these,*" he says, thrusting the quiver in my face and then withdrawing it, "was a backup that, in hindsight, should have been my first plan. It worked so very well."

He leans forward, getting in my face for a delicious taunt since I cannot smack him without healing first or putting Orlaith at risk. "If and when you get out of here, do let him know he's been played for a fool, won't you? There's no use continuing the charade at this point, and I don't want him to think too highly of himself."

He stops and waits for me to reply. "I'll tell him."

"Thank you. I see that he's forged an alliance with the Olympians, but it will not help. Ragnarok *is* coming, the world *will* be cleansed and made anew as it should be, and I *will* be bringing allies of my own. The unstoppable kind. Now, hold still, please. I imagine you are in pain enough as it is, and your hound is still very flammable." He stretches out a hand toward my left thigh, the tip of his index finger on fire.

"What are you doing?"

"I'm taking this lovely ice knife, and I see that you have a fine scabbard for it there. If you remain still, I should be able to remove it without burning you."

There are few feelings so sharp as the feeling of helplessness, of being forced to watch and endure as someone takes advantage of your weakness. It is a sting that fades very little with time, and even now, as I write this, I feel it anew, but at the time I had to bite back my frustration, unable to move as he burned through the rawhide straps fastening the scabbard to my leg. I sense the heat through my jeans, but he does not harm me, as promised. He pulls the scabbard free and shoves the knife home before rising to his feet and picking up the quiver of Vayu's arrows. He kicks Scáthmhaide away because he doesn't want me to have it nearby. He gazes at the arrows and at Fuilteach with admiration and gets lost in them for a full minute, in thrall to the power they represent.

"You've provided me with some lovely gifts today," he finally murmurs. "You know, I feel a tad guilty at taking such advantage. I didn't intend to give you anything, but perhaps I should let my kinder nature prevail just this once." He rips his disturbing scarred eyes from his prizes and turns them on me, a broad, wicked smile stretching from ear to ear. "Would you like a gift, Miss MacTiernan?"

I shudder to think what it might be. "No thanks. I'll pass."

"Nonsense. You don't even know what it is." He gently places the quiver and blade on the ground at his feet, then fumbles at a pouch attached to his belt until he withdraws a stone cylinder, etched on the bottom like a chop but with runes instead of kanji. His fingers blossom with flames, and the stone heats up in his grip, turning red around the edges of the runes so that they glow. "I think you'll like this very much."

"No, I can tell that I won't. Thanks for the thought, but please keep it."

"You still don't know what I'm offering." He crouches down next to me, right fist on fire and left waggling around like a lonesome jazz hand. "Concealment," he coos. "A cloak of sorts! The perfect gift for any young Druid." And before I can reply, his hand shoots out and presses the etched bottom of the stone into the flesh of my left biceps, searing heat wrenching a scream from my throat. He lifts it away after a second, but the deed is done and Orlaith doesn't react at all.

"There!" he says, his hand returning to normal and leaching away the remaining heat from the stone. "Now you have my mark on you. You will find that cannot be healed—not that you would want it to. It's so very attractive. And it will conceal you from divination henceforth, so that Odin can't spy on you anymore, nor can the Tuatha Dé Danann or anyone else. Except me. I'll always know where you are. But never mind that! Think of how safe you will be from the meddling of gods and witches and Ouija boards!"

"Fff—"

"Now, now, no need to thank me," he says. "It's the least I can do." He stands again, returns his damn branding chop to his pouch, and gathers up the arrows and knife.

"Farewell, Miss MacTiernan. I trust we will meet again and you will find a new way to serve me in spite of your own desire."

I know I should respond with some sort of parting shot, but I feel so beaten that I cannot even aim a half-hearted "Your mom!" at his back as he climbs the steps to the surface. I hope he tests the tip of Fuilteach with his finger.

CHAPTER 22

When Samhain—Halloween to everyone else—rolled around on Monday, I realized I hadn't heard from Granuaile for a couple of days. I figured she was doing as she wished and would call when she wanted to hear from me, but I hoped she wouldn't find a call to wish her a happy Samhain clingy or stifling. When I made that call, however, it went directly to voice mail. Either Granuaile's phone was dead or she was out of range of a cell tower. I left a brief message wishing her harmony and asking her to call me when she got a chance.

Owen surprised me by making French toast for breakfast. There was a plate waiting for me on the table when I entered the kitchen, and Oberon was sitting there, giving the food what I call the Dog Eyes of Yearning but making no move to snarf any of it. When I thanked Owen for his consideration and asked him where he learned how to cook, he told me to shut up and eat. Oberon sensed that this annoyed me and tried to provide some comfort.

<If you told me to shut up and eat, I would be totally fine with that,> he said. <You could tell me that right now if you wanted. I wouldn't be even a little bit mad.>

I gave him a smile and scratched him behind the ears, then pulled a package of maple sausages out of the freezer and dumped them into a frying pan next to

Owen's French toast operation, letting my plate grow cold. He looked as if he wanted to challenge me for the burner, but it was my house and my stove, and he could have a scrap if he asked for it.

Perhaps he was having trouble letting go of our old relationship, where he told me what to do and I jumped to obey. We watched our food fry, side by side, and said nothing. The sizzling was occasionally accented by the sound of Oberon licking his chops, and somewhere along the way I found the lack of conversation more amusing than awkward. When I was younger, my arch-druid's silences scared me more than his reprimands, but now they afforded me a measure of peace and a small victory. This was a silence he'd demanded, any-way. I put on a pot of coffee to brew while waiting for a side of the sausages to brown. When it was finished, I poured a cup for us both and gave him his without a word. He grumbled a thanks, he rather liked this coffee potion, and I nodded back with a smirk. We sat and noticed all the knife and fork noises one normally ig-nores when eating, but which become abnormally loud when no one speaks.

<Remember when I asked you if the Cold War was fought in winter and you gave me that really long his-tory lesson that had nothing to do with the weather?> Oberon asked. He had already gobbled up his sausage and watched us eat in silence for five minutes, tongue lolling out and head swiveling back and forth as we took turns shoving forkfuls into our mouths.

Yes.

<Well, this is like the Cold War but with French toast. Though I guess "Mr. Gorbachev, pass me the syrup" doesn't have the same drama to it.>

I squashed a laugh but couldn't help cracking a smile, and Owen caught it. "What's so funny, then?" he growled, assuming that I was laughing at him.

Damn it, Oberon, now I have to answer him.
<Diplomatic victory is mine!>

"Just something the hound said," I told Owen.

My archdruid scowled at Oberon and took a sip of his coffee. "The hound, eh?" he said as he put down his mug.

"Have you ever had an animal companion, Owen? At all?"

"Nah, I never have."

"Have you tried speaking to Oberon yet? You should bind with him and see what it's like. I know I suggested a companion before and you said you had reasons to remain alone, but maybe it would be good for you to see what it's like."

He squinted at Oberon. "Would that be all right with you?" Oberon barked an affirmative. "All right, then."

He concentrated and must have made contact, because I heard Oberon say, <Hi there. You have a square of butter on your forehead.>

"What?" Owen slapped at his forehead, searching for butter, and then stared at his fingertips, finding nothing.

Oberon chuffed. <I was just kidding. Made you slap your head.> And that made me laugh.

Owen glared at me. "I suppose you put him up to that?"

Grinning at him, I said, "No, he has his own well-developed sense of humor."

"Define *well* for me, lad."

I leaned forward, resting my forearms on the table. "It's not important that you think it's funny. It's important that I do. If there's anything I can warn you about when it comes to extending your life span, it's that boredom is your enemy. If you get too bored with the routine of it—the endless eating and sleeping and shitting and working so that you can eat, sleep, and shit some more—you'll do something stupid in an attempt to entertain yourself, and you'll die. Or you'll slip into depression, make the Last Shift, and live out your days as an animal. Or you'll get bitter, thinking about the past and everything you've lost, and it will turn you against people. So my free advice is to always find something to love and to make you laugh—something that will keep you in the here and now. Hounds are good at it, and they work for me. They may or may not work for you."

I was expecting a gruff denial that he needed any advice from me, its language landing somewhere between dismissive and vitriolic, but he surprised me and uttered a thoughtful grunt before asking, "Where did you learn this trick of teaching animals language?"

"It's not a trick. It's a process. But I learned it from Goibhniu. He used to have a horse named Apple Jack that he let me borrow once in the sixth century."

"Was Apple Jack the joking sort?"

"No, he was scared out of his head most of the time. Had a profound fear of goblins; he was convinced they'd get him someday."

"Did they?" Owen asked, and Oberon asked the same thing in my head.

"I don't know what happened to him after we parted. All I know is I enjoyed the companionship. Are you finished?" I held my hand out for his plate. "I'll wash up. Thanks for the breakfast."

"Aye." Owen changed the subject once I had the dishes in the sink and the water running. He spoke loudly over the noise of the faucet. "Before I fell asleep last night, ye mentioned ye wanted Manannan Mac Lir to join us for Samhain. Have ye invited him yet?"

"No, but I'll be doing so momentarily."

"How are ye going to get him here without Fand—or without her knowing?"

"I know a selkie who has his ear."

"Oh, aye," he said, and snorted. "*Everybody* knows a selkie, lad."

"It's true. I've used her to contact him on the sly before, when I was trying to keep my whereabouts secret from Aenghus Óg."

"How long will that take?"

"I don't know for sure. While I'm gone, would you mind getting the bonfires prepared for the ceremony?"

"Fine."

"Oberon will keep his eyes out for faeries and let you know if he sees or hears anything."

<I will? I mean, I will!>

We might get some extra observers. Up in the trees, down low in the undergrowth, who knows. If you sense them, don't bark, but let Owen or me know.

<Okay.>

Bidding the two of them farewell, I stripped and shape-shifted to a sea otter before using an aspen to shift to Tír na nÓg. Once there, I took a deep breath and shifted back to earth, to an underwater location: a small kelp forest growing off the southwestern Irish coast that Manannan had bound long ago. Anybody capable of shifting planes could shift there, of course, but very few would want to. It appeared to have no purpose other than birdwatching and tourism, for you surfaced at the base of Goat Island with a spectacular view of the famous Cliffs of Moher—also known as the Cliffs of Insanity in *The Princess Bride*. Razorbills and puffins and all sorts of birds nested there, whirling in the sky and diving into the waves, and the ocean was protected from fishermen to make sure the birds had sufficient feeding area. I had no intention of swimming to the surface, however; I swam straight for the base of Goat Island, where another forest of kelp and a slab of Namurian shale concealed an entrance to a subterranean passage, which opened onto a grotto the size of a ballroom.

When I broke the surface, a small titter of surprise greeted my ears. A dark-haired woman with deep-black eyes sat at an easel set upon a beach of sea-smoothed glass and gravel. Her brush was poised above a canvas of stormy blues and grays and forbidding rocks frosted with crashing surf. She was unconsciously nude and regarded me with curiosity more than alarm. Behind her, carved steps led to a raised platform of rock, where stone furnishings were softened by furs and pillows and accented by golden candlesticks, all of them blazing and lighting her living area; large torches illuminated the beach. The combined effect was impressive—her candle and fuel budget must have been enormous.

"A sea otter?" she said, her light Irish lilt floating to my ears. "Who is that? It can't be Siodhachan?"

I shifted back to human and waved at her from the frigid water. "Hello, Meara. It's been a long time."

She put her brush down and rose from the fur-covered stool upon which she had been sitting, throwing her arms wide. "It is you! Indeed it has been a long time, far too long! You're probably freezing. Come out of there and I'll get you a fur."

I swam over and crawled onto the beach, teeth chattering, while she fetched me something with which to dry off. Her smile was bright as she brought it to me and insisted on throwing it over my shoulders, and once I was enveloped, she hugged me and gave me a peck on the cheek. One of the many nice things about selkies is that they can do that and not dissolve to ash: Unlike most other Fae, they're perfectly fine around iron, since they're born in the seas of earth, or on its shores, at least.

"What brings ye to me grotto?" she said, cupping a hand behind my head and swirling her fingers through my hair. "You're not wantin' me to be lovin' ye again, are ye?"

"Much as that would delight me, I'm here on other business. And I'm hitched these days." Meara and I had been lovers for a brief time in the nineteenth century. She had a thing for art, and when I told her that I had once met Rembrandt and a brilliant up-and-comer named Vincent van Gogh, our relationship turned into a monthlong celebration of color and beauty and the kiss of brush on canvas.

"Married?"

"There hasn't been a ceremony, but it's settled in my mind."

Meara's smile was brilliant. "Ah, congratulations, then! She's human, not Fae?"

"Yes, but she's a Druid."

"Now, that's good news, to be sure!" She let go of me, stepped back, and put her hands on her hips, cocking her head to one side. "So what's this other business?"

"I need you to contact Manannan Mac Lir with utmost privacy and ask him to pay me a visit. He can't be followed or accompanied by anyone except you. It's urgent."

Her pleasant expression darkened, but she didn't ask for the specifics of the matter. She knew I wouldn't bother her or Manannan if it weren't important. "Where should he meet you?"

"Can I show you?"

"Aye, just let me fetch me skin." She dashed up to her living area and retrieved her sealskin from a heavy stone trunk at the foot of her bed, then blew out all the candles in her living area, leaving only a few bright torches blazing on the beach. I dropped the fur and thanked her for the temporary warmth, then waded into the chill lagoon with her. I shifted back to a sea otter, and she threw her skin around her shoulders and tumbled, twisting, into the water, shifting to a seal in a very different process from mine. Together we swam out of the grotto and back to the kelp forest, where we traveled the planes back to the cabin in Colorado.

Seals do not belong in high-elevation forests, but Meara didn't need to spend any amount of time there. I triggered the charm that would let me shape-shift back to human, and then I told her, "We'll celebrate Samhain here tonight. We'll have the proper fires and everything. But please tell Manannan that we have news for his ears only, with the exception of yours. He cannot be followed by anyone."

Meara gave an affirmative bark and then disappeared, shifting back to the sea and thence to find Manannan.

I sent out a mental call. *Oberon?*

<Atticus? You're back already?>

Yeah. Where are you?

<Out collecting wood with Owen. He sure does complain a lot. Whoops! Forgot he could hear me.>

I'm back at the cabin.

<Coming! Bye, Owen!> I didn't hear my archdruid's response to this, but he must have voiced some sense of betrayal, because I heard Oberon's reply: <Well, Atticus loves me and gives me bacon and belly rubs and goes hunting with me and sometimes I get poodles—but we won't talk about that, because now there's Orlaith—and all you do is talk about how he does everything wrong, when I think he does everything right, so you can just go—>

That's enough, Oberon.

<Aww. My grand finale was going to feature tapioca pudding and—>

You don't need to finish that thought. Clearly I had made a mistake by inviting Owen to bind with Oberon and then leaving them alone. I needed to get my archdruid settled somewhere else as soon as possible.

I heard Oberon coming before I saw him. He was bar-reling downhill above the dirt road that led to Yankee Boy Basin, tongue flapping in the wind of his own tur-bulence and completely happy—also completely unpre-pared, once he crossed the road, to crash into the back of Manannan Mac Lir, who shifted in from Tír na nÓg precisely in Oberon's path. The two of them fell to the ground in a tangle, making various sounds of surprise.

<Wauugh! He came out of nowhere!>

And he had arrived much more quickly than I would have thought possible. Meara had shifted in as well, dressed now in a long blue tunic with her sealskin draped over her shoulders like a cloak. Her initially widened eyes crinkled into laugh lines once she saw Oberon scamper-ing away from Manannan, tail between his legs.

<Did he do that on purpose, Atticus?> Oberon asked. <Was that some kind of joke? Because my nose hurts and it isn't funny.>

It was an accident, buddy. "Sorry, Manannan," I called to the god of the sea, who had already sprung back to his feet, scowling. "Unfortunate timing there."

Manannan slapped away some dirt on his knees and said, "A surprise but not a terrible bother. Now, what is so urgent that you have to call me away on Samhain?"

"We need to take precautions before I talk about it," I replied. "I'm sure you and Meara were very careful in coming here, but it would be wise to bind the air with a bubble of silence and maybe employ the Cloak of Mists as well."

"Easy enough."

Owen wasn't back yet—I didn't know why he'd gone uphill to gather firewood in the first place—but I didn't need to wait for him. When Manannan had drawn his cloak around us, wrapping us in mist and concealing us from outside eyes, and had bound the air so that no sound would carry past our own bodies, I pressed a big metaphorical red button and waited to see what would happen.

"Since it's Samhain and the veil between this world and the lands of the dead is at its thinnest," I said, "I'd like your help tonight in speaking to one recently departed: Midhir of the Tuatha Dé Danann."

A line appeared between Manannan's brows as he frowned. "Leaving aside the question of how you even know he's dead, why do you wish to speak to him?"

"I'd like to ask who killed him."

Manannan studied me in silence and then, quieter than I expected, replied, "No."

"Fine, then you tell me who killed him. I'm sure he told you when you came to usher him to the next world."

"No."

"We can play charades if you want. One word, one syllable—"

"No."

"Are you hiding his death because the name Midhir gave you is Fand?"

That did it. Meara gasped and Manannan's stone expression cracked. He pointed a finger at me as he growled, "Be very careful what ye say."

"Manannan, we have known each other for centuries. You know I love and respect you. I am talking about this with you first because of that love and respect. You have never been one to ignore facts."

"You have no facts."

"Midhir was killed by someone in disguise, and he claims that someone was Fand. That's a fact."

"How do you know this?" he replied, confirming for me what had been Owen's guess about the death.

"I found his body, Manannan. And the manticore chained up in his pleasure hall."

"Ah, so ye spoke to the manticore?"

"After he tried to kill me, yes. He was also placed there by someone in disguise."

"And you told no one?"

"I told Granuaile and Owen. How about you?"

"No, I've told no one yet."

"When were you going to inform Brighid that one of the Tuatha Dé Danann is dead?"

"I'm trying to learn more. I can't take this to Brighid until I know who killed him. It's the first thing she will ask, and I have no answer."

That was a poor excuse to shirk his duty, but he may not have realized it. "Fand has covered her tracks too well, Manannan. She knew you would be the first to know about it and took steps to cover her trail."

"It simply can't be true, Siodhachan!" he ground out, his voice taut and worried. "Why would she ever have reason to do such a thing?"

"Maybe I can illuminate that for you." I explained that to someone who loved the Fae so much, the possibility of another Iron Druid—maybe three, if Owen wanted to become one too—would be anathema. "She was trying to kill Granuaile and me, using Midhir to help her and to keep everything hidden from the rest of the Tuatha Dé Danann. When we escaped her net and Midhir became a liability, she killed him. I truly can't blame her for what she's feeling, you understand. There's no doubt that I deserve what she's feeling. But I do want the attacks to stop."

Manannan shook his head. "If it was Fand—and I don't think it was—I can't imagine how she hid this so well from all of us."

"Is it so very difficult?" I waved a hand toward Meara. "You have your trusted Fae who are loyal to you above all others. She has just as many, if not more.

And Midhir and Lord Grundlebeard had significant resources as well."

"Lord who? Oh, yes, I remember now. He was in charge of the rangers."

"Right. He probably told the rangers what to do, and I wouldn't be surprised if they never knew the true reason behind the orders. I'm not sure how aware you are of what happened to me in Europe recently. When you hear it, I don't think you'll be able to point to anyone else."

I recounted the series of attempts on my life that all began after I presented Granuaile at the Fae Court and announced my intention to bind her to the earth. The Fae assassins and the yewmen at the base of Mount Olympus. The vampires who on several occasions knew where I would be—not because Leif truly could trace me, as I'd originally feared, but because either Fand or Midhir had divined Granuaile's location and sent a faery to tell Theophilus. The squads of dark elf mercenaries, and, eventually, collusion with the Romans to trap me on this plane and hunt me down—which Manannan did know about, since he had been instrumental in helping us escape the continent via swimming the English Channel. The sudden and strange appearance of Ukko, the Finnish god, to spring Loki out of his entrapment so that he'd be free to mess with me some more. The Fir Darrigs who attacked Owen and me after he left the Time Island—a clumsy attack that Fand had arranged on the fly, right after she'd healed Owen.

"Now, those mercenaries must have cost quite a bit of gold, Manannan," I said. "And I'm sure she had to pay Midhir and Lord Grundlebeard for their services as well. Did you notice any large expenditures recently, perhaps explained away as necessary upgrades to the estate or something else . . . ?"

Manannan's face, up to that point a mask of defiance

and disbelief, slowly crumbled and fell like a weathered bluff sliding into the ocean after an earthquake. He pressed his palms into his eyes, as if to prevent them from seeing the truth, and when he dropped his hands, he looked shattered and desolate. He swayed, and Meara placed a steadying hand on his shoulder.

"I think I need to sit down," he said.

"Of course. We can sit inside or outside."

"Outside, but no more talk of this for a while. I'm going to remove the cloak and think."

I led him and Meara over to the camp chairs that Owen and I had occupied last night, and as Manannan dispelled the mist and air, it revealed Owen standing nearby with an armload of wood.

"Ah, there ye fecking are," he said. "No doubt the hound was plotting something against me involving pudding."

<No, but I can arrange that,> Oberon said.

Don't let him goad you, I told Oberon.

"Have ye told him, then?" he asked, nodding toward Manannan.

"Aye, he's taking it in."

"Is he, now? I figure that should take a while. Might as well fetch more wood. Where would you like to do this?"

"Down by the river."

"O' course ye would." He kept walking past us, down to the banks of the Uncompahgre River. I still didn't understand why he'd gone so far uphill to fetch wood, but since I was relatively certain he wanted me to ask about it, I didn't.

Manannan rested his elbows on his knees and hid his face in his hands, and I knew that there was nothing I could say at this point to make him feel any better. I fell back to the standard UK position for awkward social situations. "Tea. I'll make some."

The few minutes that it took to boil water and make tea gave Manannan some time to deal with his emotions and think of how best to proceed. When I emerged from the cabin with cups and saucers, he was sitting up straight and ready to talk again.

"We need to speak to Flidais," he announced.

"Agreed," I said, handing him a cup.

"Meara, will you see if you can bring her here as discreetly as possible?"

"Yes, Manannan. What if she wants to bring her thunder god?"

"That's fine with me. But no Fae."

"As ye say." She vacated her seat, walked with liquid grace to the aspens, and shifted away. I sat down next to Manannan in the chair Meara had just left, and the god of the sea took a cautious sip from his cup before placing it back down with a small porcelain clink.

"Midhir told me it was Fand who killed him, but he couldn't prove it," he said, finally confirming what we had suspected all along. "Whoever it was, they were masked head to toe. I saw the afterimage in his eyes, but there was no proof. It could have been anyone. So I didn't believe him."

"But you believe me?"

"No. Because you have no proof either. You have told me she had motive, means, and opportunity, and you have raised my suspicions and worried me that ye may be right, but I will not act without proof and cannot condone any action ye may take either."

It was at this point that Owen returned, though he didn't interrupt our conversation. He simply stood, listening, with his arms crossed. I continued without pause.

"You can't condone any action at all? What if we get the proof you need?"

"And how are you going to do that?"

"We might not be able to get proof that she killed Midhir, but there's a simple way to find out details of her scheming: Bring Midhir's shade back, like I suggested, and ask him why he was killed. What was he doing for Fand?"

"Pointless. We could not trust whatever he'd spew out."

"I didn't say we should trust him. But we should investigate what he says, try to confirm or disprove it. He might be able to lead us to proof that Fand has been trying to kill Granuaile and me."

"To nine hells with it," Owen cut in, "let's just bring it to Brighid and let her sort it out."

That elicited an explosive reaction from Manannan. He erupted to his feet and shouted, "No! You will not bring this to Brighid! She may overlook Fand's other trespasses, but she cannot ignore the death of Midhir."

Pretending I didn't hear the tacit admission that Manannan believed Fand was guilty, I asked, "Do you *want* Brighid to ignore the death of Midhir?"

"No, but I want solid proof before there are public accusations. If Brighid makes any move to imprison Fand pending an investigation, do you know what the Fae will do?"

"I imagine they'll obey the First among the Fae and abide by her decision."

Manannan favored me with the mixed look of scorn and disbelief—wrinkles in the forehead from a querulous brow, lips pulled back from the teeth in a grimace. "That's a fine imagination ye have there." He sliced the air with a hand, figuratively eviscerating my idea. "No, Siodhachan, they'll rebel. And Fand has more Fae on her side than Brighid does. More than anyone."

"Do you have a suggestion, then, on how to proceed? Because we can't simply ignore this. Brighid will find out eventually."

"She already has," Owen said, and Manannan whirled on him. "Not about Fand," he clarified, "but she knows Midhir is dead. She's looking into it."

"That complicates things."

A new voice said, "What complicates what, exactly?" We turned to find Flidais, Perun, and Meara walking toward us from the trees, newly shifted in from Tír na nÓg. Flidais wore her hunting leathers and bow, and Perun had his axe strapped to his back. He also had a leaf stuck in his hair, but since I caught Flidais winking at Owen, I assumed it was some kind of practical joke and we were supposed to keep quiet about it. We all had weightier matters to worry about, anyway.

Owen recruited Perun to collect more firewood with him—"That axe will come in handy, lad"—while I invited Flidais, Meara, and Manannan inside to go over everything again. Flidais was considerably more surprised than Manannan by the theory that Fand had been pursuing some kind of vengeance against me on behalf of the Fae, and news of Midhir's death shook her visibly—she hadn't heard.

"He and I . . . well, we had some fun in the past. If Fand killed him . . ."

"Then what?" Manannan asked when she trailed off, earning a sharp glare from Flidais. "This is the question we must ask ourselves. What if this proves to be true? Keeping in mind that Brighid is currently conducting her own investigation."

"We don't know enough," Flidais replied. "That's a chasm to jump when we get there. How do we find out if this is true?"

Manannan told her of my suggestion to bring back Midhir, and she agreed that would be best, so we stepped outside to get the fires lit and to proceed. It was only dusk, but it would be full dark by the time we got to the business of summoning Midhir, and while it wasn't midnight here, it was midnight somewhere else—close enough for Manannan to do what he needed to do.

"Where is Granuaile?" Flidais asked, suddenly realizing that she wasn't here.

"I don't know. I've tried calling her and I left her a message, but she hasn't responded."

"Have you tried divining her?"

"No. I felt that would be a little creepy."

"If you truly believe Fand is trying to kill you both, then I think it would be wise more than anything."

"She's not dead," Manannan said, trying to provide some reassurance, "or I would know."

"I'll do it just to make sure she's okay," I said, because in truth I was beginning to get worried. I became only more so a quarter hour later, when I completely failed to locate her through divination. "Maybe I'm doing it wrong—it's never been my strong suit," I said to Flidais.

"Nor mine," she said. "But I'll try too." Unfortunately, she failed to find Granuaile as well using her own methods, as did Manannan after her.

"She does have a cold iron talisman around her neck," I offered, trying to think of an explanation that didn't signify that she was in any kind of trouble.

"Aye, but she had that when you were running around Europe," Owen pointed out, "and Fand—sorry, Manannan—or someone was able to divine her location just fine."

We paused to consider, and the vision of Midhir wrapped in iron chains came back to me. Something like that would put a damper on divination. What if Fand already had Granuaile stashed away somewhere?

"There's no way to solve that problem now," Flidais said, "so we should proceed with calling Midhir and solve what problems we can."

"Is that all right with you, Siodhachan?" Manannan asked, to which I nodded. It was the pragmatic thing to do. It occurred to me that Granuaile had never said where she was or what she was doing the last time we traded texts, only that she'd join me when she could. Without a clue of where to begin searching, I couldn't hope to find her; she could quite literally be anywhere, on earth or on a different plane.

We began our rites of Samhain when darkness fell, old rituals that modern folk never got quite right, because they didn't know the words anymore and we'd never written them down, and they were a bit fuzzy on the reasons for the fires as well. I have heard people say that walking between them is a rite of purification, or that it signifies leaving the old year behind and beginning the new one, and those are harmless interpretations to which I cannot object. The fires represented any number of dualities, but amongst them were the lives of the flesh and of the spirit, the light of two worlds; between them, on Samhain, we can speak with those who dwell in the other world. We meet each other halfway and speak through the shroud that separates us.

Perun and Oberon had decided to play while we did our thing. They had squared off in front of the cabin and were circling each other. Oberon's tail was wagging madly, and if Perun had a tail I'm sure his would have been wagging too. He grinned through his beard and said, "You like to have fun, *da*?"

<He's almost as hairy as me, Atticus. Except curlier. If I wrestle with him, will we stick like Velcro?>

I think you should experiment and find out.

<YES! I WRESTLE FOR SCIENCE!> He barked once and launched himself at Perun. The thunder god laughed as they tumbled in the leaves, and I was glad they would be entertained while we performed our ceremony.

We remembered the Morrigan first, wishing her peace beyond the veil. We all got a little emotional about it— including my archdruid. It belied the Morrigan's belief that no one loved her. It might not have been love conventionally expressed, and it might not have been the sort she sought, but she was undeniably missed. And in truth, despite the death of her human flesh, she could still manifest on our plane whenever she wished; there was more than enough magic in the prayers of those who still worshipped her, ours included. I hoped she would avail herself of that opportunity and visit me again.

Midhir was a different matter. He had never been especially worshipped, and we needed him to come speak to us whether he wished to or not. Manannan took the lead on that, chanting words that were both encouraging and binding. We followed him between the fires, echoing his words and strengthening the binding, until a form coalesced out of the smoke of the second fire and resolved into a sort of negative image of Midhir, a pale hologram of swirling vapor rather than light. He looked less than pleased, and his voice was an annoyed, breathy puff of wind.

"Great. The fecking Iron Druid and Manannan Mac Lir, Lord of Denial." His eyes found Flidais, Owen, and Meara, and slid away from them, uninterested. "What do ye want?"

Manannan replied, "When I took you to Mag Mell, you claimed that Fand killed you."

"Aye, an' ye brushed me off, dinnit ye, ye salty twat."

"Never mind that. Tell me what you would have said then. Why did she kill you?"

"Because I *dinnit* kill *him*," Midhir replied, pointing at me. "Or at least arrange to have it done properly."

It took little coaxing after that for Midhir to list the full extent of his involvement in Fand's schemes—all he wanted was a guarantee that we'd never bother him again. Manannan was agreeable to that. "Just don't give us any reason to follow up. Tell us everything."

Midhir had been in charge of liaising with the vampires and dark elves, and it had been he who suggested to the vampires that snipers with infrared vision would counter our camouflage and Granuaile's invisibility spells. Lord Grundlebeard had been in charge of the rangers, as we suspected, and used them to cut off the Old Ways as an escape route. But Grundlebeard had missed a few here and there in England—probably because he never thought we'd make it that far—most notably the cellar entrance to Windsor Castle that Flidais had used to come to our aid. Midhir hastily had it blown up from the earth side so that no one could return to Tír na nÓg, but Grundlebeard had also left one open that was tied to Herne's oak, and both were unpardonable oversights in Fand's eyes. To her way of thinking, Artemis and Diana would have killed us easily in Windsor Forest if Flidais had not been there to tilt the odds in our favor. Piecing together his timeline with mine, I conjectured that Fand had taken action against Midhir and Grundlebeard while I was being snacked upon in the dungeon by little tooth faeries. If she had bothered to take a look downstairs, she would have found me there, helpless.

The two greatest bits of news I gleaned from Midhir's confession were the names of his contacts: Among the vampires, he spoke to Theophilus—which I had already suspected, but it was gratifying to have confirmed—and his dark elf contact was a Svartálf named Krókr Hrafnson, who was the leader of what I suppose must be called an assassins' guild. Most frustrating was the fact that Fand had spoken directly to the Olympians herself—an assertion that we'd never be able to prove. The Olympians were not actively trying to kill me anymore, but they weren't my friends either. They'd never confirm anything.

When Midhir finally said he'd told us all he knew and answered a couple of questions from Flidais, Manannan released him, with a promise to leave him alone going forward. The smoky outlines of his form unbound and rose in restless wisps into the night sky. Whoever said that dead men tell no tales never spent Samhain with Druids.

Meara, Owen, and Flidais were the first to leave the space between the fires, and Manannan followed after a sigh. I was about to trail after him when the Morrigan, dark and beautiful, appeared suddenly in the flames and froze me in mid-step. Unlike Midhir, she looked almost solid; she had chosen to manifest herself and hadn't been bound in any way. Her scratchy voice entered my head, and a ghostly finger reached out, chilling me as it trailed along my jaw with very solid pressure.

"Protect the dark elves, Siodhachan," she said, and then she dissolved from view, as ephemeral as mist, before I could muster a reply. I was left shouting at the fire of the next world.

"Morrigan! Wait! Come back!" I had so many things I wanted to say to her, and she hadn't given me the time. She probably already knew all of it, but that didn't ease my need to say them. I did not, however, wish to say them in front of the others, and since they had all turned and were watching me now, I subsided with a muttered promise that we would speak later.

"You saw the Morrigan?" Manannan said.

"Very briefly," I admitted. "She just did a peekaboo thing in the fire."

"What did she say?" Flidais asked.

"Forgive me, but I think it was for my ears only."

My answer didn't please any of them, but they knew they couldn't force me to share a confidence.

"Fine." Flidais affected indifference. "Tell me what you intend to do now that you've heard what Midhir had to say."

"He intends nothing," Manannan said. "We still have no proof. That's all hearsay."

Flidais shook her head. "Manannan."

"What?"

"You don't have to be a huntress to see where the trail leads. Much as I wish it weren't my own daughter or your wife who killed Midhir and plotted to kill the last two Druids on earth—I mean, the last two until recently," she amended, looking at Owen, "I don't see who else could have done it. Unless you have a theory as to who could pressure Midhir to frame Fand from beyond the veil?"

"He could simply be out to ruin my life, yours, and Fand's with a fabrication," Manannan said. "We are no true kin of his, and he has never liked any of us."

Flidais scoffed. "He'd do that and let his true killer go free?"

"He doesn't know who his true killer is," Manannan insisted, "so he's taking what petty revenge he can."

Silence fell while we all waited for Flidais to respond. It lengthened uncomfortably—perhaps on purpose, to let Manannan hear how ridiculous he sounded.

"I know how much you love her," Flidais finally said, "and that you both have taken great joy in deceiving the other in a harmless pursuit of other bed partners. I understand it is a game and you have been merry adversaries for centuries. But this deception is no game. It's murder and conspiracy and all very contrary to the wishes of Brighid. And in keeping this information from the First among the Fae, you risk making yourself an accomplice, Manannan. *We cannot blink it more.*"

That made *me* blink. Flidais had just quoted Arthur Miller—and in a context that fit well here. Reverend Hale in *The Crucible* had been telling the court that the people of Salem feared to speak the truth. I would have to ask her later if she had memorized Miller's work as an English headspace. If so, it was interesting that a huntress chose a work about witch hunting.

The god of the sea clenched his fists and shut his eyes tightly, perhaps in a final vain attempt to see no evil.

"If I may interrupt," I said, "I think we do need to go to Brighid soon. But we can wait long enough to see if I can mend a broken relationship. I can forgive Fand—I've already done so—but if she can forgive me as well, perhaps we can go to Brighid and say punishment isn't necessary."

Owen spluttered, "She gets no punishment for killing Midhir?"

"He has already paid for his role in the conspiracy, and he had nothing like the excuse Fand has for wanting me dead. As the wronged party, I can say Midhir's death was justice on my behalf and beg clemency for Fand."

"You would do this?" Manannan said.

"Aye. In the morning, I will go to Fand and ask for a truce. And if you wish, you and Flidais will go to Brighid and tell her everything, thus clearing yourselves of any collusion. You can blame the delay in informing her on the need to wait for Samhain so you could question Midhir more closely in congress with Flidais."

The two gods exchanged glances and shrugs, and then Manannan said, "Very well. But you cannot go alone. Take Owen and Meara with you."

My archdruid said, "What's this, now?"

"If Fand truly bears a grudge against Siodhachan, we can't let him go alone. You are a neutral party, and

Meara, as a selkie, will be seen as one of mine. She lends you my aegis, in a sense."

Perun, who had been waiting patiently after managing to wear Oberon out, broke into a wide grin and boomed, "Is settled, then! Let us go into this town at bottom of mountain and get shitbuttered."

Our collective jaws dropped and stared at him. "Excuse me?" I said.

"Is this not word? How you say someone is drunk?"

"Oh, you mean shit-faced."

Perun threw up his hands, thoroughly exasperated. "How is shit on face any better than my word? And why would English-speaking peoples ever think that putting shit on face is like drinking good vodka?"

"Well, I'm not here to judge—"

"Good. Then we go get shitbuttered."

"All right, but not until you take that leaf out of your hair."

Three gods, two Druids, and a selkie walk into a bar . . .

CHAPTER 23

It needs to be said: No one can completely cock up a day like Siodhachan. And I think there are few living people who can bear witness to this fact so well as I. If he's only hurting himself, then I can hold me tongue and let him go, because he might learn a lesson from it. But when his shenanigans are going to get me in trouble, I need to say something. And I know he's technically my elder many times over now, and if there's anyone who knows a thing or two about surviving it's him, but surely that doesn't mean I have to shut up about him being stupid. It just means I have to tell him he's stupid using me best manners. And not hit him while I'm doing it.

"Listen, Siodhachan, this isn't going to turn out well for us if we go in there alone," I says. "Let's bring along an army of Scottish bagpipers to distract them while we move in silent from the flanks—you know, the lads who smell like old cheese. Or maybe some of those dwarf axemen you were tellin' me about."

"We can hardly signal our desire to talk if we bring an army of anything."

"But it's not *we* who wish to talk, lad. It's only you." Of course, Siodhachan turns to the selkie to bolster his pox-ridden argument. After we drank ourselves nearly unconscious the night before, she slept in his room, while he spread out on the living room couch with his hound curled up on the floor beside him.

"Do you want to talk rather than fight, Meara?" he says.

"My lord Manannan commands it." Aye, he commanded it as the bar closed, then shifted away with Flidais and her mountainous hairy sex toy to sleep it off. Soon they would unburden their souls to Brighid in hopes that she wouldn't char them to toast. Siodhachan recognizes that Meara doesn't give a true answer, but he pretends that it's good enough, and my good sense is somehow overruled because a selkie obeys the commands of her god.

"You're perceived as a neutral party at the moment," Siodhachan tells me, "so I need you along. And Meara will be Manannan's eyes and ears and provide us safe passage."

"I hope you're right," I says, "but I'm afraid you're not. I think Fand's lost her mind once and I think she can lose it again. And my neutrality will mean about as much as a pellet of rabbit shite when I walk up there with you."

That hound of his speaks up: <So does that mean a lot or a little? What's the market rate on rabbit shite now, Atticus? And why does he say *shite* instead of *shit*? Is shite fancier somehow, or is he just trying to make it sound that way?>

"We'll go in with our eyes open, Owen."

"Speaking of going in," Meara says, "will we be shifting directly into the castle courtyard? I know which tethers to follow."

"No, but thank you for the offer," Siodhachan says. "We'll shift in using the surrounding trees, as we normally do. I want to be invited in, so that the rules of hospitality apply."

"It's going to be the rules of the battlefield, lad. We

should be going in there with a thousand naked warriors who fight like wet cats with dodgy bowels."

"You can go naked if you want," the bastard says to
me, ignoring my advice. "I'm wearing pants."

I sigh and back off for a moment. If I'm going to get
through to him, I'll need to try a different angle. And
there are things that need saying.

"Meara, would ye mind givin' us a bit o' time to talk
amongst ourselves?" I asks her.

"Aye. I'll walk the dog," she says, getting to her feet.

<She means she'll walk while I smell things, right?>
Oberon says. I don't answer him, but I assume Siodhachan does, for the hound stands and wags his tail.
<There's a fox den out there somewhere. It is my quest
to find it and see if the fox has extra tails.>

The two of them trot away into the trees, and Siodhachan is doing his best to look unconcerned about
what I'll say next.

"I'll be needin' honesty from ye now, lad. Are ye bein'
contrary with me because ye have genuine objections to
being prepared, or is it merely because you're trying to
get back at me for all those knocks to the noggin I gave
ye as an apprentice?"

"Can I say it's both?" he says. "Or neither? That's
quite the false choice you've laid out there."

"Nothin' false about it. Going in with three people
means we're unprepared for a fight, and it doesn't matter that you're the most powerful Druid who ever lived."

That makes him take notice. He whips his head
around like I'd stuck me tongue in his ear. "Pardon
me?"

"Yes, you heard me." Eye contact might be too intense for this next bit, either for him or for me, so I turn
me head and face the forest, talking in low tones but
being careful not to mumble. "I know I'm a proper bastard, Siodhachan, but that's only because I'm not afraid

to speak unpleasant truths. The truth was that you used to cock things up on a regular basis. But it was also true that you were more gifted and brilliant than anyone I knew."

There is silence for a time as I stare at the treetops and he stares at me. The intensity of his regard kind of burns the side of me face. "If you're not being sarcastic," he says, "you neglected to tell me that last part. Ever."

I shrug my shoulders. "It's why nobody ever liked me. I always forgot to speak the pleasant truths."

Siodhachan doesn't have an answer. I see peripherally that his lips tighten and his jaw clenches as he looks away and down at the ground. Silence stretches between us again, and I can see I haven't said enough. I suppose I really must have scarred him, and if I'm going to speak an unpleasant truth, I should probably begin by telling meself to stop being such a raging arsehole all the time and remember what it is to be kind.

"Look, lad," I says. "I have an apology to make that's long overdue. I'm sorry for being so free with my criticism and so frugal with my praise. I should have been more balanced, and I will try to notice out loud when ye do something well instead of noticing only your mistakes. I'll start now, if ye have no objections. I want to thank ye for pullin' me off that island. What little I've seen of this world so far looks like five pigs fucking, but it's new and different, and, damn it, I feel better than I have in so many years. There's even a werewolf walking around in Arizona who likes me, and I like her back. And I have you and the Morrigan to thank for it, which is strange, since there was a time I was sure one or both of ye would be the death of me. Heh!"

He leans forward and covers his eyes with a hand, like I'm giving him a headache, but says nothing. I probably shouldn't have said that bit about how I was sure he'd get me killed.

"Argh, I cocked up me apology, didn't I?"

"Maybe a little," he says.

"Feck it, look here: I'm sorry, Siodhachan. Truly. I'm sorry, and that's it."

"Well—"

"No, that's not it! I just thought of something else. It's me who's been your student for a while now, and you've shown me it can be done with kindness." I have to clear me throat before I can continue. It got unaccountably tight all of a sudden.

"I can see the man you've become, and it's a good man. A man who seeks peace but can win a fight once he's in one. I've never found peace meself, but I've also never felt particularly moved to search for it, if ye know what I mean. So I'm grateful to ye too, lad, for showing me that path through the woods. I think I'd like to try walking it. There might be something like happiness at the end."

He nods, letting me know that he heard what I said, but he doesn't reply for a while, maybe thinking I'd start up again. But I'd said all I wanted to say, and it felt good.

He's quiet when he speaks, and I almost don't catch it. "Thank you for all that. It means a lot to me."

I nod back at him and think he's talking about more than just the words. When Siodhachan was wee, his da got his arse killed in a cattle raid, and I was the closest thing he had to a father after that. What a shite da I turned out to be. I can't remember ever giving him a soft word until now.

"You mean a lot to me too, lad."

Funny thing happens after that. We both sigh together, as if we had laid down a burden after a long journey, and then we smile and laugh, as if we'd just escaped death. And, I don't know, maybe we had. Nei-

ther of us had any business seeing a sunrise in this age.
The gifts that Gaia gives are boundless.

I meant to ask him again to bring some help along
with us to Tír na nÓg, but I let it go. I'd try the peaceful
route and see what happened—and if it was the worst
idea ever, why, we had made a good run of it.

CHAPTER 24

I still couldn't reach Granuaile via text or voice. I left one more message on her voice mail, saying there'd be a note for her at the cabin, and then I wrote said note and put it on the kitchen table. I didn't want her to arrive unaware of the situation, so I summarized the issue in a few quick sentences and advised her to come in full ninja mode—and without the hounds. I rose and slung Fragarach across my back.

Oberon, I need you to stay here and wait for Granuaile and Orlaith. Tell her to come quickly. There's a note on the table.

<Oh, no, Atticus, Granuaile already did this to me! You don't need to leave a note *and* a hound to tell someone where you are. The note will work just fine.>

I need you to tell her the note is here. She might not see it for a long time otherwise. Your role is crucial. It wasn't, of course, but fortunately Oberon could be made to believe it was crucial by the simple expedient of linking it to food, so I added, *Plus, I will make you a brisket.*

<A brisket! Great lakes of gravy! And all I have to do is tell her to read the note as soon as she gets here?>

That's all.

<You can count on me!>

Thanks, buddy. I turned to Meara and Owen. "Ready to go?"

"I don't want to go at all," Owen said, "but I'm ready."

"Aye, I'm ready," Meara said.

After I gave Oberon a farewell chuck under the chin, we strode to our familiar trees and shifted into the grove surrounding Manannan's estate. It was a mixed lot but largely oak, with tame undergrowth and plenty of space to walk between the trees. We were on the west side of the estate, the entrance being to the south, and only three or four trees deep into the grove. Peering underneath the canopy, we could see the pasture stretched out before us, and the gray walls of the castle were visible in the distance.

Normally the birds would be chirping, but it was as silent as a classroom after a student tells off the teacher and everyone waits to see what will happen next.

"It's too quiet," Owen said, his knees bending into a half crouch. Meara unconsciously echoed his movement.

"Aye." I drew Fragarach as a precaution, figuring that I'd have plenty of time to resheathe it before we got to the gates. Under the trees, I'd give my paranoia a nice long leash.

We crept forward with mincing steps in the grass, eyes darting to the flanks and even up into the branches, but seeing and hearing nothing. Past the first rank of trees and then another, all was well, aside from the palpable tension in the air. I didn't sense the problem until I'd taken a few steps too many.

I'd been cut off from the earth—or at least what passes for earth in Tír na nÓg. As in all the planes, whatever I'm standing on is supposed to allow a strained flow of energy to course through me from Gaia, for all planes are connected to her. I stopped walking when I realized the comforting presence of her energy was not merely strained but entirely absent. Before I could say anything to Owen, he pointed through the canopy at the top of the castle, where a haze of flying faeries swarmed along the tops of the walls.

"Looks like they're ready for a fight, Siodhachan. She must know that we've figured things out."

"Owen, our power's gone."

"What?" My archdruid looked down at his foot, slow to realize that I spoke the truth. No juice was coming up through our tattoos. "Now, how in the name of seven sets of ox nuts did *that* happen?"

Four Fir Bolgs—giant ugly blokes that weren't strictly Fae but eked out an existence here now as hired thugs— stepped out from behind large oak trees. They wielded net launchers, tubular weapons with gigantic muzzles, and they shot them at us without so much as a battle cry. I tried to shout a warning, but it was only in time to make Owen and Meara look up and see what was coming. The nets blanketed us, and when they touched my skin I knew that we were in trouble. They practically punched us to the ground, for the links between the intersecting knots were coated with bands of iron. It was far too much iron through which to cast anything, especially considering the iron already dangling around my neck. Cut off from the earth and unable to cast from stored magic, we were essentially powerless humans now.

We struggled to get out from under the nets, of course, and while we did that, the Fir Bolgs dropped their net launchers and grabbed spears, which they had leaned out of sight against the oak trunks. They advanced on us with ugly smiles, and I knew we wouldn't get free in time.

CHAPTER 25

As soon as Loki is out of sight I speak to my hound, mind to mind. I can hear her breathing, but she's sitting out of my line of sight. *Orlaith? Answer me, please.*

<Huh? Granuaile! Hi! Where am I?>

The knot of worry in my chest loosens and I tell her, *You're in that hole in the ground with me.*

<Oh! How am I here? There was tall man and—hey! Granuaile hurt?> She walks into my view, towering over me, and I manage a tiny smile.

Yes, but I will heal.

Most of me will, anyway. Unlike the pain of my broken bones and pulverized muscles, the burn of Loki's brand on my arm cannot be quelled. It feels as if it's still sizzling, and I imagine that I can hear and smell the burning flesh. Tears leak out the sides of my eyes, the product of one part pain, one part embarrassment, and two parts relief that we are both still alive, but I don't make any noise. If Loki is lurking upstairs, listening, I don't want him to derive any satisfaction from my distress.

I wonder if cold iron will dissipate the magic of his mark enough to let me heal it. I am quite some time away from being able to test that, since it would involve some arm movements I don't think I can pull off. I can't put any weight on my bones yet, lest they fracture further, and I resign myself to a long wait, exchanging comforting words with Orlaith and suggesting that she take a nap by my side. I myself can't fall asleep so easily.

The light from the trench gets intense at noon, then fades as the entire day slides by in a fugue of physical discomfort and mental self-flagellation. The burn mutes itself to a dull throb over time, but the internal bashing intensifies. My own stupidity led me to walk this path instead of others, and I doubt I'll ever be able to forgive myself.

As twilight begins to creep toward darkness, however, the last dregs of my patience burn away, and that, along with an urgent call of nature, urges me to get moving. Aware that the nerve block I'm using is actually denying me feedback on what works and what doesn't, I release it—and cry out at the sudden return of agony from all my muscles. Orlaith starts awake from her snooze.

<What? Why yell?>

I unblocked the pain and it surprised me. Want to try moving.

<Okay.>

It hurts everywhere, and my body squirms to get away from the discomfort, but there's no way to escape, since each contraction sets off a new complaint. Gritting my teeth, I slide my left hand to my jeans pocket— a slow operation and one that requires me to breathe in and out quickly, but at least my limb functions well enough. I wiggle my fingers in there and succeed in pulling out my cell phone, only to discover that its touch screen is completely crazed, shattered by the pressure and therefore useless. I think of trying voice commands, but it won't turn on. So much for calling Atticus.

Testing my abs, I try to sit up, and they surprise me, letting me raise myself with only a mild complaint. Searching for the remains of the dabāva, I see nothing but a curled pile of black ribbon, like a discarded streamer or a massive accident with a cassette tape, resting on the ground near my ankle. Could that have been it? Was that the thing that had shrouded the light and tried to pop me like a wine grape?

I gasp when I look down at myself. My arms are swollen and purple, and I'm sure the rest of me, including my face and neck, is one massive bruise as well.

Sitting up turns out to be the only halfway easy thing I can do. Everything hurts so much and I feel so brittle that each movement is slow and triggers a wince. It takes me most of the remaining daylight to zombie crawl twenty feet away and relieve myself, then return to lie down again. It taxes me more than I would have thought possible.

Utterly exhausted, I reestablish the pain block and we sleep through the night, and upon waking we are vastly thirsty. I ask Kaveri to create a small basin for us in the floor and allow water to seep through. It is cool and clear and delicious. I scoop out a few cold mouthfuls before Orlaith comes over to lap up her fill, which produces considerable noise that I might normally find annoying but in this situation is strangely welcome.

<Food?> Orlaith asks once she finishes.

We could use some, couldn't we? I don't think I'm up to it, though. I still need a long while to heal. My bones aren't strong yet. Would you like to hunt? I don't know if this is an ideal area for it.

<I can try.>

Stay away from people. Don't let them see you if you can help it. Run back here if they chase you.

<You won't come?>

I can't, Orlaith. But I should be safe here. You go see if you can find something and don't worry about me.

With reluctance, Orlaith leaves and stays out for a couple hours. She returns with a bit of blood on her muzzle and lies down next to me, and we while away the time with language lessons for her. Thus I spend Sunday allowing my body to mend and my stomach to growl, trying to keep my Zen even though I am impatient to get out.

When the sun slices down through the trench once more it's Samhain, and Atticus is probably wondering where I am. Or he will, when he wakes; I have to remind myself of the twelve-hour difference between India and Colorado. While I think I might be able to join him, I don't think I want to just yet. He'd hug me and snap my collarbone again. And he would see that I've had my ass properly kicked—I'm still purple all over—and I'd have to explain. And there's the very real problem of Loki's mark to consider. Concealment from divination is, I have to admit, a great gift; I wouldn't have been able to achieve it myself without binding my amulet to my aura, and Atticus says there's no shortcut to that. It took him years to do it. But this gift of Loki's wasn't freely given—I'd firmly believe that even if he hadn't said as much. The price is that Loki can track me wherever I go. So if I go back to Colorado now, I'll potentially lead him directly to Atticus on a day when his guard is down, and Loki made no secret of the fact that he'd like to kill Atticus. It occurs to me that I might not be able to go home at all. If I want to keep Atticus safe, I might have to avoid him altogether. Or get rid of the mark.

Feeling more confident in my movements than I did before, I remove the cold iron amulet from my neck and press it against the set of runes branded into my flesh. They're red and puckered, but I can't feel them burning anymore. I reach out to the elemental for help.

//Kaveri / Query: Heal burn?//
//Query: What burn?//

I try to direct the elemental's attention to Loki's brand or mark or whatever it is, but Kaveri doesn't recognize that there is anything wrong with me now except deep-tissue damage. Examining it in the magical spectrum, I spy a soft white glow of magic within the circle but nothing I can tease at or unbind. The repeated application of cold iron to the mark has no discernible effect. What the hell had he done?

My frustration wants to have a good scream, but I bite it back. I haven't tried everything yet. Perhaps a cup of Immortali-Tea would restore me to a state where the mark couldn't cling to me. Or maybe Atticus would be able to think of something when I finally saw him.

I give some thought to the realities of travel. Loki would no doubt like to have a shot at destroying Tír na nÓg, but shifting there through tethered trees would be impossible for him since he is not bound to Gaia. I could still use them all I wished. But I could never use an Old Way again, or it would give him a path to follow. I don't imagine he can track me in Tír na nÓg, it being a plane entirely outside his purview, but he'd probably assume I was there if I wasn't to be found on earth.

<Hungry, Granuaile.>

My stomach growls in agreement. "Yeah, I think we can get out of here now. We'll have to stick to the bare earth at all times, though, because I need to keep healing."

I pick up Scáthmhaide, moving slowly. Even though I have the pain locked down, I can feel the tightness in my muscles. Now that my bones are in shape to carry my weight for a while, it's time to get everything loosened up. *Ready to get out of here?*

<Yes!>

Taking one last look around, I see nothing but the blackened spool of thick ribbon that must be the remains of the dabāva. I see no head. No limbs. No tail.

No true way to associate its physical form with the thing that nearly crushed me to death. It is simply the darkness that lives in the closet or under the bed, amplified and malevolent and much better off dead.

It takes me some time and effort to climb the stairs; I have to lean forward and half-crawl, a ladder-climbing motion, to manage it. I'm sweating and Orlaith is panting by the time we emerge into the sunlight. Kaveri obliges me by filling in the room and closing up the trench behind us, and when it's nothing more than an undistinguished patch of a paddy, I say, "Good riddance."

But, in truth, I'm well aware that I won't ever be rid of that dark hole in the ground. It will be the Colossal Bungle I replay in my mind for centuries hence, should I be fortunate to live so long. And if I should ever be proud enough to think someone else stupid, this will be a flagon of humility ready to be poured on my head.

Of course, I didn't choose to fail. Failure is rarely a conscious decision and it's often out of our control, determined by things like physics and circumstance and other people. What we can always control, however, is our reaction to failure.

I shamble in jerky movements on semi-rural roads back to the hotel, where I need to retrieve my laptop and things and check out. We disturb the hell out of everyone who sees us. Most of them give me a wide berth and try not to make eye contact. One man in particular, however, takes issue with me walking around in such a condition all by myself. Or something. I honestly don't know why he's upset, because I don't understand a word he says. Maybe he doesn't like the fact that Orlaith is not on a leash. Maybe he recognizes me from somewhere. It's conceivable that he saw me with Laksha at one point during the night we were freeing people from rakshasas, and now I'm a witch in his eyes.

His tone grows more aggressive when I don't respond to him, and he blocks my path and gets in my face a little bit, earning a growl from Orlaith. I think he interprets that as a threat I instigated, or perhaps an insult, instead of realizing that maybe he's the one being a dick. When I try to walk around him, he reaches out to grab me.

I don't even think about it: Scáthmhaide whips around and clocks him on the side of the head. There's no strength behind it and he's not seriously hurt, but now I've picked a fight, and he's the type who thinks he has to put me in my place. I'm in no shape to deal with him gracefully, so I poke him in the gut with the staff when he lunges at me, forcing him to step back, then employ a trick of Atticus's and bind the fabric covering his knees to the earth. He's forced to a kneeling position and stuck there, and now I won't have to injure him. His rage face is pretty funny, though, and I laugh and flip him the bird before turning invisible and camouflaging Orlaith. We leave him shouting in the dust as people begin to draw closer out of curiosity. All he's doing is ensuring that there will be an audience when he eventually has to surrender his pants. If I wasn't a witch to him before, I definitely am now. The one who got away. Whatever he was trying to accomplish, he failed. I can tell already that his reaction will not result in any personal growth.

We sneak past the doorman at the hotel because I imagine he might try to refuse me entrance looking as I do. Once I make it to the room and drop my invisibility, I spy myself in the mirror and catch my breath in shock. Heck, *I* would have tried to refuse me entrance. An interesting fact, however, is that my neck is fairly free of bruises in the front. The cold iron amulet in the hollow of my throat protected that part of me. Had it been

bound to my aura like Atticus, I might have been immune to the dabāva. I'm still bruised around the side of
my neck and the dabāva had restricted my breathing,
but the amulet had saved my windpipe from being
crushed even as my bones were breaking.

I gather up my things and call down to the front desk,
telling them that I'm checking out and to charge me.
Lacking the juice to turn invisible again and camouflage
Orlaith too, we walk out in plain sight. The hotel staff
is horrified by our appearance in the lobby but only too
happy to let us leave. I rest my left hand on Orlaith's
back as we walk past a gauntlet of naked stares or consciously averted eyes, and my movements are noticeably
smoother if not quicker once we leave the tiled lobby and
my toes find the spongy kept lawn outside, a welcome
balm to my discomfort. Energy renewed by the earth, I
camouflage us to avoid attention, since my experience
thus far has shown that extensively bruised women are
either shunned or accosted instead of helped.

Finding something palatable for Orlaith proves
tougher than I thought it would be, because I'd forgotten that this region is largely vegetarian. Eventually I'm
forced to admit that it would be easier to shift elsewhere
to get something to eat. In fact, we could shift to many
other places. So many that Loki wouldn't know which
one was significant. Spend ten minutes to a half hour in
each place, and then when I eventually hit Colorado, I
would spend a similar amount of time there, long
enough to let Atticus know the situation and move on.
He could move on with me. We could solve the problem
of Loki's mark together and not endanger our home.

I tweak the plan and try to factor in time. I'd take the
rest of Samhain to heal and recover my strength, but
we'd also jump around the globe before settling on
someplace to spend the night. We'd choose a place out-

doors where dawn would come a few hours before it did in Colorado, and then we'd be up and shifting around again until we arrived at the cabin on the morning of November 1, around breakfast time.

We fill the void of our bellies in Argentina, and after we are finished shifting around for the day, we spend the night of Samhain together in the Appalachian Mountains, far from all the jack-o'-lanterns and bags of candy. Upon waking, I feel significantly better. I can move without limping, albeit slowly, and the pain is endurable, like the soreness one feels the day after a strenuous workout. Gaia is so very good to me.

We flit around the globe for an hour, providing a masking pattern in case Loki is watching, until I decide we have delayed the shift home long enough. Bracing myself for the questions and the mad dash to get some supplies for a longer absence, I pull us through to the trees above Ouray.

<Granuaile! You're here already!> Oberon practically shouts in my head. He faces the tree as I shift in, almost as if he were waiting for me, and it's somewhat startling. <You must read the note on the table so that I can earn my brisket!>

"What?"

<This is all part of *The Book of Five Meats*. *Delicacies await those who perform their labors well*, it says—or it will say that when it's finished. And Atticus said my labor was to tell you to read that note right away.>

I have no idea what book he's talking about, but Atticus clearly impressed upon him the importance of delivering that message, so I say, "All right, Oberon," in hopes that he'll relax. "I guess he's not here, then?"

<Nope! He just left! Seriously! But I'm glad you're back! I'm going to play with Orlaith!>

<Oberon is here! Happiness!> Orlaith says, her tail wagging.

"You two have fun."

<Hey, Clever Girl, you look different. Are you okay?>

"I'll be fine, Oberon. Thanks for noticing."

<I was going to say something earlier, but a brisket hung in the balance. You understand.>

"Yes, I do." The two hounds collide with joy and tumble in the leaves as I head for the cabin door, and I'm actually relieved that Atticus isn't here to see me like this. Tomorrow I might look only mildly horrific instead of like a walking corpse. The relief flies away once I read the note he left.

> *Granuaile—*
>
> *Please come as soon as you can to Manannan Mac Lir's place. It turns out that Fand has been the one trying to kill us all along. She doesn't want any more Iron Druids around. It's a long story, but Manannan and Flidais are going to Brighid; I'm going with my archdruid to see Fand in an attempt to set things right. Diplomatically, I mean. Very hopeful it will go well. But just in case it doesn't . . . you might want to come ready for anything. Full ninja. And leave the hounds at home.*

"This can't be right," I say, but then remember that I really don't have time to figure out whether it's true or not. I have to get out of here, and I can't bring the hounds with me. Checking the food bowl, I see that it's full, and they have all the water they can drink in the river. If I'm gone for a while, they can hunt too, and they know this.

Dropping off my goodies from the hotel before dashing into the bedroom, I first pull out some bands, sweep my hair back, and tie it up, so that it can't easily be used against me. Then I pull out my throwing knife collection and get to work strapping them on. Holsters of three knives each hang from my belt on either side when I'm finished, and additional holsters are tied to my legs. There's also a light leather vest stashed in my closet, which Atticus gave me for my thirtieth birthday. It has six pocket slits down the front on each side of the buttons; twelve throwing stars slide inside the pockets, like mini-DVDs. I remember thinking at the time, when will I *ever* use this, but it seems like the perfect gift to me now. If I'm going full ninja, I need the stars. And against the Fae, each of these small slivers and discs of steel are lethal weapons, capable of reducing them to ash. Against a larger opponent they are most often a prelude to death; they would wound and distract the enemy long enough for me to finish them with something else.

I chug some water in the kitchen before I go outside to test the throwing motions of my arms. I'm moving all right now but haven't tried anything requiring fine motor skills yet. Choosing as my target a blackened spot on the trunk of an aspen, where a branch fell off long ago, I try three quick throws and miss with every single one. My range of motion is there, but it's tight and not as fluid as it needs to be. Taking it slow, I find that I can hit the target throwing with either hand, but rapid-fire moves are out of the question. I'll be limited in terms of martial arts too—no acrobatic moves and probably no kicks at all. Scáthmhaide will have to do most of my work for me if I walk into a fight, and it will be tight defensive sequences, nothing sweeping.

Collecting my knives and stars and returning them to their holsters, I charge up the silver energy reservoir on Scáthmhaide and cast bindings on myself for strength and speed before triggering invisibility, hoping it's all unnecessary. The hounds are twenty yards away, lying down side by side and playing by nipping at each other's ears.

"Oberon and Orlaith, I'm going after Atticus. I'll be back as soon as I can." I shift to Tír na nÓg before they can answer me.

CHAPTER 26

"Am I allowed to say I fecking told ye so?"

I think I'd be okay with those being me last words. And with a giant Fir Bolg headed this way as I'm trapped under a weighted iron net, they might well be.

The big bastard doesn't kill me, though. He just gets close enough so that I can tell he smells like bull balls and bad fish, and he gives me a wee poke in the shoulder to let me know the spearhead is sharp and he's not afraid to use it if I try anything.

Not that I can try much. With all this iron, I can't even shape-shift to a bear and make the fight interesting. The net be damned, if I could shift this close to the Fir Bolg I could probably take him down, and that spear would mean shite.

Meara's to me left and Siodhachan to me right, each of us with a Fir Bolg looming nearby. The fourth Fir Bolg has a face like a badger tearing out of a cardboard box, and when he whistles up at the nearest tree, a pixie in maroon and gold livery flies down from the leaves. It squeaks in a tiny voice as its wings hum in the air: "Is it the Iron Druid?"

"Aye," the Fir Bolg says. "Tell them as who wants to know."

He means Fand, of course. The Fae call her queen, but it's not a meaningful title in the ruling of Tír na nÓg. Brighid's in charge and everyone knows it. And if ye try to call Manannan king, he'll toss your naughty bits into the bog. But I suppose the Fae want some theatre or drama and Brighid doesn't provide enough of it for them. She was businesslike when I saw her preside at the Fae Court—powerful but not regal, I guess you'd say. The Fae in attendance seemed to hunger for a sense of ceremony or nobility, and she didn't give it to them.

The pixie whirls off toward the castle and the Fir Bolgs grunt, happy to let it sink in that they weren't waiting for just anyone, they were waiting for us specifically. Siodhachan doesn't say anything, and I can practically see him working through his options—I'm working through them too.

If we grab or trap or slap away the spears of the Fir Bolgs guarding us, there's still that extra one who can lunge in to help. And if we get skewered in any significant way, we won't be able to heal until we get out from under the nets and onto some ground that will let us draw power again.

Siodhachan still has Fragarach, I assume, because they haven't taken it from him, but neither do I see it. He might have hidden it beneath him. Clever boy. Though he won't be able to swing it around underneath a net.

Our options, therefore, are about as attractive as a slug in the sun, glistening and moist and squishy and gods damn it I hate those things. We will have to wait to see if a better opportunity develops.

It's only a few minutes until the pixie returns from the castle, though it feels like much longer. Time has a way of lengthening when you're trapped, and Siodhachan isn't filling the air with his talk. He hasn't spoken a word since he tried to warn us of the ambush.

The pixie's not alone. Four flying and liveried faeries— the willowy lads armed with bronze weapons—escort a fifth figure, who glides across the grass, a sort of sackcloth scarecrow holding an unsheathed sword pointed at the ground. A small swarm of pixies buzzes above and behind them. Once they reach us, the faeries and pixies hover overhead, while the not-so-anonymous person in sackcloth stops in front of Siodhachan. The voice is a scratchy rasp, however, not feminine at all.

"I see two Druids and a selkie. Where is the third Druid? Is she hiding, perhaps, in the woods nearby?"

Siodhachan says, "Fand, we've just come to talk to you. I know what you've done, but I'm not here to seek vengeance. I'm here to forge a peace. Can we talk face-to-face? We all know it's you under there."

"You all know, do you?" Instead of pulling off the hood or unfastening the robe, she removes her disguise by unbinding it. It dissolves to threads and falls slowly to the ground like autumn leaves, revealing a pale-skinned Fand without a stitch on. It's a threat that a modern man might miss.

Siodhachan had to explain to me that people today don't understand why the Celts of our time stormed into battle naked. They think it's because we were trying to strike fear into the hearts of our enemies by demonstrating our own fearlessness, and, sure, that's a secondary reason. But the truth is that you have to be daft to fight with clothes on when an opposing Druid can use them to bind you to the earth and then kill you at his leisure. A single Druid on the other side can take out your whole cattle raid if you come at him wearing clothes. So people learned very quickly that if there was a possibility of running into a Druid, your only chance of winning was to charge in naked with steel weapons, whose iron content defied easy binding.

A modern man might, therefore, misinterpret Fand's sudden nudity as a signal that she likes him. Siodhachan and I know that it means the opposite. And, more than that, revealing herself means she's abandoning the sneaky act. If we die now, Manannan will have his proof of her guilt as soon as he picks up our shades, and she obviously does not care. I don't know if her open defiance signals desperation or confidence, but either way I'm as disturbed as she could wish. She drops whatever she was doing to disguise her voice and returns to her normal timbre, soft-spoken yet unmistakably angry.

"Perhaps you do not understand how far I am prepared to take this. Now, I will ask you again, Siodhachan. Where is Granuaile MacTiernan?"

"I sincerely have no idea. I haven't had any contact with her for days."

"You are not a guest in my home now. I will not smile and be satisfied with lies and half-truths." She turns to the Fir Bolg to my left and grinds out a short command: "Kill the selkie."

CHAPTER 27

The danger of wishful thinking was never demonstrated to me so clearly as when Fand ordered Meara's death. I had been so sure she would be willing to talk and keep everything civil. Her behavior up to that point indicated that she wanted to avoid a direct confrontation, and it was what I wanted also. Everything should have been copacetic.

But Meara was a love of mine in days long past and, as it happened, of Manannan's in days past that. I don't know if Fand knew or if she realized it was Meara under the net as opposed to any other selkie. Regardless, selkies were under Manannan's protection, and she knew it. And Manannan would know it when Meara died. So when the Fir Bolg's spear sank through her spine and all the way through her body—over my very loud and anguished protests—I knew the killing wouldn't end with one of the kindest, sweetest women I'd ever known. It was only the beginning. Fand had gone past the point of no return, and now she had to finish first or die. It wasn't a spontaneous decision either. While I was shouting for her to heal Meara, quick, don't do this, she calmly summoned one of the faeries above her and said, "All of Manannan's Fae in the castle. Kill them now." He flew away to give the order, and she refocused on me.

"Fand, call him back, please, there's no need for that. You and I can resolve this without involving anyone else."

"What do you think we are resolving? A personal insult you gave me once? It's much more than that. It's the tyranny of iron, Siodhachan. Centuries of it, and you and Brighid are the worst tyrants of all. I'll not see the Fae diminish any more. It ends today." She raised the sword, and I saw that it was Moralltach, Aenghus Óg's blade, which Leif had used to kill Thor. I'd given it to Manannan, and she'd clearly taken it for her own. A blow from that meant certain death, for there was no healing possible from the necrotic enchantment on its blade. My aura doesn't protect against magic that penetrates the skin, and Moralltach would do that very well. If she perceived the hypocrisy of threatening me with that after railing against the tyranny of iron, she didn't show it. "I will ask you a final time: Where is Granuaile MacTiernan?"

Fand had clearly run into the same difficulty in divining Granuaile that I had last night. "Why do you think I would ever tell you, even if I knew?"

"So be it." She cocked back Moralltach and took a step forward, I fumbled for the handle of Fragarach underneath me, and that's when a slim throwing blade shucked into the side of Fand's neck, rocking her backward.

"On second thought, I think she might be nearby," I said, and then our opportunity to escape came as Fand clutched at the knife and yanked it out. The swarm of pixies and the few remaining faeries flew down and enveloped her in a protective cocoon, lifted her a few inches off the ground, and flew her back to safety, out from under the canopy and into the open field in front of the castle. I pointed Fragarach's tip through the net at the feet of the Fir Bolg guarding me and shouted, "*Frea-*

groidh tu!" freezing him in a blue aura of enchantment. Fragarach didn't care about the iron net—it was already made of iron, and I'd slipped the point through the net, anyway.

Once the Fir Bolg was caught, he couldn't move to stab me. I could move him, though, and I did, by swinging Fragarach's tip in the direction of the fourth Fir Bolg, thereby bowling him over and giving me a few precious seconds to extricate myself from the net. Exclamations of surprise and pain boomed from the left as the Fir Bolg guarding Owen got a throwing star in the eye. Something slapped his spear hand at the wrist, forcing him to drop it, then he was swept very heavily off his feet, no doubt by the invisible providence of Scáthmhaide. That gave Owen the chance he needed to scramble out of his net, and Granuaile tossed another couple of stars at the Fir Bolg who'd killed Meara. They weren't well placed, for some reason, but he clutched at them rather than worrying about the follow-up, which was seeing his spear disappear from Meara's body and reappear a few seconds later, lodged in his own guts. Just like Meara, he never had a fighting chance. It was justice.

Once free of the net, Owen cannibalized the energy of his own body to shape-shift to a bear and pounce on the Fir Bolg that Granuaile had dropped to the ground, making sure he'd never get up again. I had two of them to finish off. Fragarach's enchantment kept the one under my control on top of the other guy, so they were both trapped in a very different sort of net and were easily beheaded, one at a time.

Stealing a glance behind me at Fand, I saw that she was still surrounded by a cloud of Fae, but they had stopped halfway between the trees and the castle. She had disengaged for the moment, and it would be wise for us to take advantage.

"Let's fall back and shift out of here," I called to Owen and Granuaile, wherever she was. "We need to get some help."

"Help has arrived, Siodhachan," a rich female voice said. Whipping my head around, I saw Brighid walking toward me from deeper in the forest, freshly shifted in from the Fae Court. She was fully armored in a kit of her own making and carrying a sword so huge that it rightly belonged in the pages of manga. With her were Flidais, Perun, and Manannan Mac Lir, and also Ogma, Goibhniu, Luchta, and Creidhne. All of them were armed and ready for battle, their eyes taking in the field ahead.

Relief washed through my limbs. "I'm glad to see you, Brighid. There's a dead zone here, by the way. I don't know how, but Fand has cut off the flow of energy in this stretch of land. I imagine it doesn't extend all the way to the castle, or she wouldn't have stopped in the middle of the field to heal."

The First among the Fae paused, eyes visible through a visor in her helmet and losing focus for a few seconds as she looked at the ground in the magical spectrum. "Yes. You are on the edge of it. It continues until the pasture begins. She has slipped something underneath the sod. Looks like dead wood."

Sheets of plywood would do it. A simple maneuver, but nothing we'd ever notice unless we were specifically looking for it.

"Meara," Manannan breathed, and rushed to kneel by her still form.

"Fand has Moralltach," I warned them all. They absorbed this information in silence, and then, after a few seconds, Brighid spoke.

"Forward to the field," she said, and though it was an order we all dreaded, no one thought of contradicting it. Flidais winked out of sight, going invisible like Granuaile, while Ogma and the three craftsmen all unbound their clothes and let them fall away so that Fand would have nothing to bind. I did the same; I'd worn clothes to demonstrate my peaceful intentions, but that time was past now. Owen remained a bear, but Perun only tore off his shirt and hefted his axe in his right hand. He wore black pantaloons stolen from an eighties' music video tucked into some knee-high powder-blue suede boots, which he must have lifted from the pages of a comic book in the same era. We quick-marched across the dead zone until we could feel the earth's energy underneath our feet again, forming a company front with Brighid in the center. Brighid's voice—the voice in which she could not lie, the voice of finality—rang out across the field in three tones.

"Fand, for the murders of Midhir and numerous Fae, some in the past few minutes, surrender now and face your judgment. You cannot win."

Fand magnified her voice as well, though it did not have the three notes of Brighid's. The Fae obscuring her flew in a pattern now that let her form appear in flickers behind them, still performing their duty as a shield but lending Fand some presence. Part of that presence, to me, was the simple fact that she could speak so confidently after having a knife in her neck. She had always been amongst the best healers of the Tuatha Dé Danann, but it was still impressive.

"I disagree. I rather think you should surrender. I know you believe I've committed treason, but it is you who betrayed us long ago. You've married yourself to iron and do not deserve to be First among the Fae. And most important, Brighid, is this simple fact: The Fae agree with me. You're relieved of your throne. I'm taking it today."

It was a ludicrous statement. There was no way she could defeat all of us with a small cloud of pixies and a few faeries. Brighid took a breath and said, "You—" but whatever she was about to say died in her throat as a fountain of Fae spewed from the castle walls, a sun-blotting mass of sidheógs and sprites and bean sídhes.

None of these on their own would present a threat, no more than a single bee would offer mortal peril to a human without allergies. But a swarm of bees could take most anyone down, and many swarms of angry flying Fae were up there.

But Fand had infantry waiting too. As the drone of thousands of wings fanned the air, a horde of goblins, spriggans, and Fir Darrigs erupted from the ground outside the walls and charged us.

These weren't the goblins from the Peter Jackson films based on Tolkien. These were older creatures, earth-dwelling and given to tinkering, at home with all the metals but bereft of any true magic—I'd say instead that they had affinities. They liked their subterranean tunnels on earth hidden in the hills but visited Tír na nÓg often via Old Ways. Gray-skinned and diminutive except for their noses and ears, they didn't limp or suffer from misshapen spines or other afflictions meant to emphasize their corruption in stories. They moved quite well, though without anything resembling unit cohesion, wearing a hodgepodge of homemade armor and bristling with a wide array of weapons. They had probably been promised riches for their role in the fights, and that accounted for their presence along with the Fir Darrigs.

Noticeably absent from the army were leprechauns, though that was in keeping with their character. They're always up for shenanigans but would never engage in war, owing to their solitary natures and the fact that they'd rather annoy people to death than club them to death. I guessed that there were three or four thousand of the goblins and mere hundreds of the spriggans and Fir Darrigs. All of them looked hungry for violence.

Fand had planned a revolution for the common Fae, and I was standing with the aristocrats as the mob advanced.

"Damn it," I muttered, gritting my teeth. Neither side was going to back down, and that meant a lot of blood would be shed.

"Flidais," Brighid said, no longer projecting her voice. "I would not ask, except that we can end this quickly."

A ragged sob to my right gave me a vague idea of where Flidais stood. "Understood," she said, her voice choked with emotion. A twang, and then an arrow soared through the air toward Fand. It missed, but not because of poor aim: Fand wasn't in that space by the time the arrow arrived. She was borne into the air by the Fae and, I saw when I triggered my magical sight, by several sylphs, air-based Fae who were invisible to the unaided eye. They whirled around, forming a protective cyclone of wind with Fand floating in the eye of it, and this caused a second shaft of Flidais's to skew awry and miss. Flidais didn't have time for another, and it would have been pointless, anyway. There was a charge of infantry to break, and it would be on us in ten seconds or so. The flying Fae would get here before them. Where, I wondered, was the cavalry?

"Atticus, behind us!" I heard Granuaile call, though I couldn't see her. "Big dogs! Manannan, watch out!"

The god of the sea was still mourning Meara and would be first to meet the onrush of a pack of barghests emerging from the forest. The large black semi-spectral dogs are about the size of Oberon but with much sharper teeth and glowing red eyes—semi-spectral because they appear solid and certainly hit you and bite that way, but most weapons tend to pass through them as if they were ghosts. One of Granuaile's throwing knives demonstrated the principle admirably, passing through the body of the lead barghest as if it were so much vapor. Barghests have to be killed by hand or by special weapons like Fragarach, so, better equipped than anyone else to take them on, I turned my back on the horde to meet the barghests.

Manannan rose and spun inside his Cloak of Mists, and the barghests that entered his space came out again after a few seconds, broken. I twisted around the charge of the first one that came after me and clipped him on the back of the neck as he passed, then, with the back-swing of that stroke, tore through the face of the one following behind. Three others bounded past me to leap onto the backs of Perun, Owen, and Goibhniu. Perun was annoyed but not particularly troubled; he bowed his back under the weight of the creature, then reached up behind his head, sank his fingers into the fur, and yanked forward. The barghest was launched bodily into the vanguard of the goblin line. Owen roared and rolled his shoulders, and his barghest tumbled off in front of him; a powerful swipe of his claws—his natural hand, not a weapon—put an end to it. Goibhniu, however, was not so lucky, and when he fell facedown with a barghest on his back and a bean sídhe screeched his name, signaling his doom, I wasn't the only one who rushed to help him. His brother Luchta turned his back on the approaching horde to help, as Creidhne and Ogma shifted over to cover him. Brighid blasted the sky with broad ribbons of fire, turning the leading edge of Fae air support into ash and powdered bone and giving those that followed cause to worry about sudden climate change.

The barghest sank its teeth into Goibhniu's left shoulder and he rolled right, forcing the barghest to choose whether to let go and try for the throat or to hold on and be flipped onto its side, giving up the dominant position. It chose to let go, and Goibhniu blocked access to his throat with his forearm. I reached them a second before Luchta did, rammed Fragarach into the ribs from the side, and yanked it back out as the barghest fell over. But as I was doing that, the main body of the infantry arrived, and while most of them met wet, crunchy ends by the weapons of the Tuatha Dé Danann, a spriggan leapt high over the reach of Creidhne and landed on the back of Luchta.

Spriggans are nasty things, wood Fae on which the Morrigan based her design for the yewmen, ambulatory lumber with lots of sharp protuberances and very little photosynthesis going on. They don't have flesh so much as sap-filled green cellulose; their limbs and body are shaped like the flat ribs of saguaro cacti but always with yellow glowing eyes—the kind of eyes you see in cartoons meant to scare children from going into the forest at night.

It landed on Luchta in mid-stride, catching him off-balance, and he twisted right as he fell so that the spriggan would be thrown off, and it was, with considerable speed. It landed on its back but on top of Goibhniu, in the direction he was most vulnerable: perpendicular, as if crossing the letter *t*. The sharp spine of wood that swept back from its elbow like a stake punched through Goibhniu's chest and crushed his heart.

Goibhniu coughed blood once and died, and beheading the spriggan that had killed him did nothing to soften the blow I felt in my own chest at his passing. Luchta and I both bellowed, confirmed that his aura was fading and there was no saving him, and then threw ourselves at the Fae with abandon. Our tears washed away the blood that splattered our cheeks as we hacked and stabbed, and we knew that nothing we did would replace Goibhniu or Meara and that we wouldn't feel the least bit better by dealing death to creatures who thought they were fighting for freedom or something shiny.

Charred pixies and sprites fell from the sky, some of them still on fire as Brighid effectively neutralized their air power with a wall of flame. Off to my right, Ogma wielded two heavy maces that walloped three or more goblins at a time, and these in turn mowed down the ranks behind them so that he was clogging the charge lanes and giving himself time to swing again. Creidhne and Luchta were doing their share next to me, using magical weapons of their own craft that seemed every bit as effective as Ogma's maces at dispatching multiple opponents at a time.

Their rage was unsettling, and I wasn't sure they would know when to stop. I needed them at my side, however, or I would have been overwhelmed in short order. Fragarach was great at slicing through armor into flesh, but I couldn't handle more than one opponent at a time, and they were rushing me like it was cold outside and I was the last pair of mittens. I wasn't tired and I wasn't wounded yet, but I could see it happening soon—the numbers in front of me were too great.

To my left, between Brighid and me, was Perun, who had charged his axe with lightning. Whenever he sank it into the body of a goblin, bolts of electricity arced into the armored friends following behind, thereby always keeping space clear in front of him while adding to the scent of charred flesh and burnt ozone already present in the air from Brighid's efforts. The spriggans and Fir Darrigs didn't attract lightning and got past the bolts to visit Perun up close, but these he smacked away with powerful sweeps of his left hand; they landed far back in the ranks, to be trampled or impaled by the rest of the army.

Owen was on the far side of Brighid, raking his claws across faces and occasionally ripping out the throat of a goblin who managed to get inside his guard and take a swipe at him. Like me, he was in danger of being overwhelmed. He already had a couple of short swords sticking out of him. Granuaile and Flidais were out there somewhere, too, taking their toll invisibly. Manannan held the far left flank now, using one of the Fir Bolg spears as a weapon, and the tiny flash of his face that I spied through the churn of battle and his own cloak looked much as I imagined mine did: frozen in a grimace of pain, fighting with a mixture of grief and rage and guilt.

Yes, I felt guilt. Somehow I had pushed Fand to the precipice without realizing it, and had I not been so blind, perhaps she wouldn't be trying to pull us all over the edge with her now. I was sure Manannan felt it too—the crushing questions of how we got to this place and whether we could have avoided it, where we went wrong, and whether we would ever learn how not to cock up other people's lives in the course of living our own.

CHAPTER 28

I will have nightmares about the battle cries and death screams, raw ululations of fear and rage and murderous intent directed at Atticus, and over it all the howling of the bean sídhe. And the snarling faces, the bared teeth, and the jets of blood—some of them fountaining because of my hand—those will haunt me also. The snarls would be directed at me if I were visible, I am sure, for Fand announced that this was about cold iron, and I have a measure of it dangling from my neck. I will remember those cries, the fire and the blood, and Fand floating above the field in a cold cocoon of sylphs, until I pass from the world.

I don't know what spurred Fand to behave this way, but I feel certain this is not a fight that Atticus would have picked. He likes Fand and so do I, which is why I didn't put that knife through her eye and into her brain. I knew she could heal from the neck wound and hoped it would make her rethink. I guess I screwed up from a strategic standpoint: I had the chance to end it and flubbed it. But who among us saw this coming? Atticus said in his note that he had come here seeking peace. I suppose Fand came here seeking war, and she found it.

And Manannan still loves her. He and I are on the left edge, and I can hear him moaning and crying through his Cloak of Mists—saying, "No, stop, Fand, don't do this"—and when the mists part long enough to give me a glimpse of his face, I see torment and grief written there, not anger. He doesn't attack but rather kills anything that enters the mist. I don't think the goblins are especially after him, but he's protecting Owen's left side, and some of them try to get to the bear through him and fail. Those who choose to flank Manannan and go around to his left run into me, their feet leaving the ground when the staff they never see coming hits them between the eyes.

I can keep up with it—it's safe here—so I have to leave. Atticus is right in the center of the line, and I can tell he's barely holding on. He can't clear a path the way the gods can. Perun is taking care of some to his left and Luchta is knocking down a few to his right, but Atticus is still in trouble, and when I see how bad it is, I abandon my position, confident that Manannan will be fine, and scurry around the back to help.

Since the goblins have the weaponry to do him serious damage, Atticus is rightly focused on them, taking a risk that none of the fliers will be able to get through Brighid's defenses and take off his head. But as I run, I see a pixie slip in under Brighid's inferno and stab him underneath the collarbone with a bronze needle sword. He swats her and she crumbles into ash. He can't take time to pluck it out; he has to keep parrying and swinging at the goblins and a Fir Darrig who leaps at his head. But then a small formation of sidheóg archers follow up in the pixie's wake, flying below the ceiling of flames, and unleash a volley of miniature arrows at him, kind of like toothpicks but much sharper. I imagine they'd be foiled by a thick wool sweater, but of course Atticus is fighting naked. The arrows prickle the left side of his upper torso en masse, and many of them lodge in his face and neck, sticking out like porcupine quills. There's no serious damage, but it makes him flinch and miss the incoming swing of a goblin's axe.

I cry out a warning, but it's too late. The axe— a bronze number with notches in the blade—hits Atticus high up on his left arm, almost at the shoulder. It lodges in the bone and stays there as he falls to his right. The goblin lets go of the handle, partially because Atticus's fall yanked it from his grip and partially because he's surprised he made contact, and so he's standing there, frozen, when I arrive. I treat his head like a fungo and swing for the center-field wall. His skull crunches and he falls like timber, and I redirect the swing to clock another two goblins upside the head in quick succession. They're coming in, axes high and unguarded, thinking that they'll finish off Atticus while he is down. They go down instead.

"Get up, Atticus! I've got your left side!"

He doesn't waste time, just grunts as he pushes himself up and gets to his feet, knocking aside the thrust of a goblin sword to the right and opening the creature's throat as he sweeps left. He keeps going because the goblins keep coming, checking his swing to the left to make sure he doesn't hit me, and I do my best to lay the gobs out and give us some space. The axe is still buried in his left arm, which hangs useless at his side.

"Think you can pull . . . pull out the axe?" he says, blinking furiously as he deflects a blow from a spriggan who hopped over the lead goblin, hoping to surprise him.

"Sure," I reply, switching Scáthmhaide to a left-hand grip. "Hold on."

The staff whirls and staggers two goblins, who are in time to get caught in a chain-lightning blast from Perun. The enemy's charge slows in front of us, the goblins behind the fallen front lines realizing that something unseen is kicking their asses. They're squinting, searching for a target, and it gives me time to grab the axe handle and yank it out of Atticus's arm. It tears him up a bit, and an awful lot of blood comes with it, along with a grunt of pain, but at least now he can heal it.

As a bonus, the axe turns invisible when I touch it, so to the goblins approaching warily, it looks as if it simply ceases to exist. It exists again once I throw it at the head of the nearest one, but by the time he sees it, all he can do is duck. His buddy behind him doesn't have enough time to duck—it splits his face, and I leap in, sweeping the end of my staff up from the ground to connect with the ducking goblin's chin as he rises. He sprawls backward with a broken jaw, teeth popping out in bloody parabolas before landing on his body. That gives some other goblins ideas about where I am, and they hack blindly in my general direction. I back up and feed their throats a couple of knives. As they fall, I deliver sharp strikes to the soft bits of the next rank. Atticus is still slashing with Fragarach next to me, though the movements look jerky and undisciplined.

"Nnneurotoxin in the nnnneedles," he says. "Heal it ff. Fast if you geh. Geh. Get hit. I got lots. Sssslowing down." He steps back and barely avoids the swipe of another axeman, but that unbalances him and he takes another step and another, staggering away from the fight until he keels over backward. Fragarach falls from his hand.

"Atticus!"

CHAPTER 29

I find meself royally pissed and quite happy about it. This is the kind of battle the bards were always singin' songs about in the old days, where everybody's mad and thinks they have a good reason to be that way. Me uncle would have loved it and wrote a song for sure. He'd call it "Rivers and Lakes and Bogs of Blood" or something. Probably something else—I'm shite at makin' up songs. But I'm sure we'll be stepping in large pools of blood soon, because the goblins keep coming and I keep killing them. I'm not sure they realize I'm a Druid, with an infinite energy supply and the ability to heal quickly. They don't seem to expect me to move the way I do. They might be thinkin' I'm the average bear.

The reason I favor the form so much is that I'm damn hard to kill this way, without a lucky spear thrust or one o' those fancy hand grenades the modern soldiers like so much. If ye have a sword or an axe, there's almost no way ye can get close enough to hit me without giving me a chance to hit you first. And if ye do hit me, why, you have to hack through a few inches of fat before ye get to something that matters. So I keep my head up and out of reach as much as possible, take the odd hits here and there, and kill the fecking bastards, because a bear's strength multiplied with the earth's strength equals a one-way trip to the dirt for the lads who run into me claws.

That's not sayin' I'm havin' an easy time of it. I have three weapons stuck in me hide now, none of them feels good, and I expect there will be more before we're through. Maybe a lot more. Maybe too many.

I could die here soon. I should have worked harder to convince Siodhachan to bring help, because feck a handsome chicken if I wasn't right about Fand. But ye know what's strange? I'm lovin' the fight I knew was coming, with only one real regret: I wish Greta was here to fight alongside me. She's already under me skin far deeper than these crude goblin blades.

Instead, I have a weepy Manannan Mac Lir on me left and a fiery Brighid on me right. I don't feel sympathy for either of them, because none of us would be here now if they hadn't spent so many years refusing to see the truth.

Strategically, the truth is that we are bent over and waiting to be pounded. We Druids have incredible power, but we're not gods, and as such we'll be the first to fall. The tide of foes doesn't seem to end, and eventually one of them will push me under and I won't get up. And while the Tuatha Dé Danann might last longer, they can fall, too, against odds like this. Brighid must have come to the same conclusion, for she stops spraying fire in the sky and *becomes* the fire in the sky, rocketing from the ground wreathed in flame and on a collision course with Fand. It's impossible to miss, and as soon as she takes to the air, the crush of the charge stops, because no one wants to miss the show—it's all about whether Brighid or Fand is left standing, anyway.

The sylphs protecting Fand and allowing her to float in midair lower her to the ground as Brighid dives down to confront her. When Fand plants her feet, she still stands head and shoulders over the goblins, and on me hind legs I stand eight feet tall, so I can see them well over the horde between us.

Fand sidesteps Brighid's landing and stands unflinching as the goddess of fire attempts to barbecue her without the benefit of sauce. The sylphs bear the brunt of it, blowing the flames back and to either side. Seeing that it's pointless to continue, Brighid douses the fire and has a go at Fand with the giant sword. I don't expect it to last long, because Brighid has far more experience in battle and is fully armored, whereas Fand rarely fights and is naked. But Fand doesn't try to parry or fence; she dodges and ducks every blow, inhumanly fast—faster than Brighid, her Druidic speed aided by sylphs—and she keeps looking for an opening in Brighid's guard. Her eyes often flick to Brighid's helmet, the only place where there is a gap in the armor, and I understand. She wants to make one strike with Moralltach, a solid hit that slips through the helmet and ends it—any strike that broke the skin would be sufficient, and she would never be able to penetrate Brighid's guard any other way. The armor Brighid wears was designed and warded to fend off blows from Fragarach, which supposedly could cut through any armor, so I doubted Mortalltach would have any chance of penetrating it.

Tension rises as the duel lengthens, Brighid always missing but in guarded fashion, Fand doing nothing but dodging and waiting for an opening. Neither of them would ever tire, so it's much more a duel of wits and skill. It takes a minute of this—a long time in battle— for me to realize that something is profoundly wrong. Why haven't the bean sídhe screamed out the name of who was going to die? It's not like their predictions of death are voluntary; when they know they have to shout it, and they've been yelling their throats raw during the whole battle. Now they're silent, and it's fecking creepy.

Me answer comes in the next five seconds. Seeing

an opportunity after an overhead strike from Brighid misses and leaves the oversize sword edge in the dirt, Fand darts in and thrusts at the thin strip of space that allows Brighid to see through her helmet. Realizing that this was perhaps the only time she did not want to keep her eyes on her opponent, Brighid turns and bows her head as much as possible, and the tip of Moralltach strikes and etches a groove in the metal as it glances off. Fand tries to dance back out of range, but she had committed too fully, drawn just a hair too close. Brighid's backhand sweep catches Fand underneath her own extended right arm and draws a red line across the tops of her breasts. It's not fatal, but it rips loose a cry of pain from Fand and demonstrates that she's overmatched. So she surprises everyone and scarpers without a word. The sylphs lift her up out of the circle and whisk her away at top speed to the far pasture, where a line of trees on the other side will allow her to shift away.

Brighid doesn't have the best range of vision through that helmet of hers, and it takes her a few seconds to process that Fand has abandoned the field, leaving her army behind. By that time it's too late for her to catch up, and she has her own people to worry about, besides being surrounded by a host of the Fae in rebellion. Everyone is stunned—especially the Fae, who just witnessed their leader flee after getting scratched—but at least we know now why the bean sídhe were silent.

Brighid is the first to recover. She shoots into the sky and hovers above the field in a nimbus of flame, her three-note voice booming over our heads. "It is over. Fand is gone, and I give all Fae a simple choice: You may have forgiveness or fire. If you wish forgiveness, leave the field and send an emissary to Court tomorrow to discuss with me in candid terms how I may best serve the Fae in the future. I truly wish to be a better leader for you and am eager to hear how I can become one. If you wish fire, however, continue to fight. Choose now."

They choose forgiveness with fecking alacrity. The front line of goblins and spriggans cast nervous glances back at me, wondering if I'll be bound by Brighid's words or not. I nod and put all four paws on the ground, signaling that I have no wish to open up their bellies. The surviving airborne Fae, including the bean sídhe, disperse almost immediately, leaving the troops with no air support and only Brighid floating above them. They couldn't wait to flee. The spriggans and Fir Darrigs take to the surrounding forest, and the goblins drain into the holes in the ground from which they'd spewed. That's when I look off to me right and see that Siodhachan is down.

CHAPTER 30

I have decided that I really hate poison and I'll never use it again myself. It's not how I want to win.

The sidheóg toxin didn't deliver a fraction of the pain of the manticore's venom, but it was effective in slowing me down and making me vulnerable. And it was sneaky—the lack of pain meant I didn't realize what was happening until it was almost too late. My muscle responses dragged, and my movements became sluggish and unbalanced. My vision blurred, and I warned Granuaile about it with a mouth full of mush.

I barely avoided the swing of a goblin's axe by stumbling backward but couldn't recover from it and fell flat on my posterior, Fragarach bouncing from my grasp when my knuckles hit the ground. Granuaile shouted my name, but I couldn't answer. I knew I could beat the toxin given enough time, but the goblin who missed me wanted a second chance. He was charging after me— axe raised to chop down into my guts, and an ugly slash of a grin on his mug—when an unseen force knocked him sideways, as if he'd been kicked. He *had* in fact been kicked by Granuaile, and when he tried to get up he got a knife in the face for his trouble. Two more goblins met swift ends trying to come after me as Granuaile stood invisible sentinel, and then Brighid took the fight to Fand and everyone stopped to watch.

"Atticus, are you okay?" Granuaile's disembodied voice asked.

"Worr . . . Working on it." I hoped whatever Brighid was doing would keep everyone preoccupied for a few more minutes. My body was breaking down the toxin, but I wouldn't be turning cartwheels or even speaking clearly for a while. And then, when I had no option but to stay still and think, I felt the crushing weight of responsibility for the entire debacle.

I'd never have a beer with Goibhniu again; he'd brewed his last barrel and forged his last project in the iron and silver knotwork of Scáthmhaide. Nor would I get a chance to discuss Rembrandt again with Meara; her grotto would remain forever dark, blacker than the canvas of *The Night Watch*.

I'm not ashamed to say I shed tears for them. They deserved much more than that. And then I heard but didn't see Brighid say that Fand was gone, and the Fae army melted away like a snowman in the Mojave Desert. There was a profound lack of celebration on our side. I cast my eyes to the left and saw that Manannan Mac Lir was gone. He had plenty of spirits to escort to the next world after a battle like this, and his wife was now indisputably a treasonous fugitive. I supposed we wouldn't see him for a while. Owen and the rest of the Tuatha Dé Danann were physically fine—or at least they would be, given time to heal. Owen came up to me in his bear form and snuffled at my face to make sure I was still alive. He had several goblin weapons lodged in his body and probably needed them removed before he could shift back to human. But he moved off before I could offer any aid, apparently satisfied that I wouldn't die immediately.

The Tuatha Dé Danann were another matter. I thought they'd be emotionally scarred forever. Off to my right, Flidais dropped her invisibility and fell to her knees, weeping, and Perun rushed over to provide whatever comfort he could. Luchta and Creidhne gathered over the body of their fallen brother and engaged in some cathartic swearing as they removed the spriggan's body from Goibhniu's and folded his arms over the wound. Luchta lost it and beat the spriggan's head with his club until it was nothing but a sappy smear on the turf. Part of me wanted to go to them, all of them, and say how sorry I was, how I would never forgive myself for my role in bringing this about, but that was an atrocious idea. It wouldn't make them feel any better—it might seriously annoy them—and it would put me in their debt if I made any admission of culpability. I didn't know what else to do except weep and wonder how my overture for peace could have resulted in such ruin. Feeling small and alone but physically somewhat better, I sat up and propped myself with my right arm.

Granuaile's voice came softly from my left. "I'm here, Atticus, if you're looking for me."

I turned and saw nothing. "Where?"

"I know it's over, but I'd rather stay invisible for now. I have a lot to tell you."

Frowning, I asked, "Are you hurt?" My speech had returned to normal and I was somewhat relieved at the progress.

"Yes, but it's nothing that won't heal soon." An unseen hand ruffled through my hair. "I missed you," she said.

"And I missed you. I was worried about you, in fact, when I couldn't get in touch. But I guess you got my note. Thanks for saving me. Like, five times or whatever it was."

"You're welcome. I wasn't keeping score." Her fingers ran across my head again, and then she said, "Hey. Looks like you've been crying."

I sat forward, taking the weight off my arm, pawed at

my eyes, and sniffed. "Well, yeah, it's been a terrible day. I was hoping to broker a peace but ignited a revolution instead. I didn't want anyone to die. Not the goblins, not any of the Fae, and certainly not Meara and Goibhniu."

"Then we'll talk about that too. Is your arm okay? That axe went pretty deep."

"It'll be all right in a few days."

"Want any help pulling out all those little tiny arrows that almost did you in? You look like a mutant hedgehog."

I laughed in surprise more than mirth. "Yeah, that would be great, thanks."

As we sat amongst the ruin of so many lives and carefully plucked miniature weapons from my upper body, a strange sense of peace settled over me, the soft comfort of a small revelation that gave me hope. I'd been pushing so hard to find harmony when it wasn't there to be found. It was much better to be still and let it find me.

CHAPTER 31

Though I wish for nothing so much as a hasty departure from the battlefield, I understand that a certain amount of debriefing is needed before we can go. I cannot be certain, but I think Brighid is seething and blaming herself more than anyone else for not spying this attempted coup in time to prevent it. The sheer numbers we saw on the field are an indictment of her leadership, and while I might question many of her decisions, she is at least honest enough to admit her own failings. How many of the horde that faced us had sworn fealty to her before? Why had none of the Fae fought to defend her and the Tuatha Dé Danann from the rest? There would be uncomfortable answers to those questions.

It is a sad, tense while before Brighid can pay attention to us, since she understandably commiserates first with Flidais and then with her two sons at the loss of her third. She must feel her own flood of anguish at Goibhniu's death, but I do not think she is the sort to grieve in public. It gives Atticus time to dissolve the poison in his body and get to his feet. When Brighid joins us, she has sheathed her sword across her back, the way Atticus does, and is cradling her helmet in her left hand. Her hair, strangely, is full and perfect. Such are the prerogatives of a goddess, I suppose. I listen in silence as she confers with Atticus and his archdruid, Owen, who has had the weapons removed from his bear form and shifted to human. Visible angry wounds paint red lines across his body. I haven't met him formally yet, but I'm not particularly looking forward to it. Judging by his expression, the flag of his disposition is habitually sour, and that comports with the stories Atticus told me about him in the past. I must make allowances, however, for the extraordinary circumstances. I can expect few smiles today.

It turns out that Owen had informed Brighid about Midhir's death a couple of days ago, and, after a brief investigation, her initial suspicions had actually pointed at Manannan as the possible culprit. Discovering that it was Fand—and that she and the Fae had nursed their grievances in secret for so long—caused Brighid to wonder how she could have missed all this. And when she speculates aloud that her rivalry—no, her obsession—with the Morrigan blinded her to other problems and allowed them to fester unnoticed, I almost drop Scáthmhaide and applaud. A frank confession that the dark patches sometimes fall on her, too, is a welcome surprise, and I allow myself to hope that she will follow through and become a better leader. I know something of dark patches myself now. I feel a blossoming of respect for her, where formerly I had thought her petty and shortsighted. I think that others feel it as well—an almost palpable lifting of the mood a few notches above wailing and gnashing of teeth reminds us that we all used to be happy and maybe we would be again.

Atticus sabotages his own mood when he asks a random question: "By the way, Brighid, what happened to that manticore chained up in Midhir's hall?"

Brighid draws her brows together and says, "Yes, I remember Owen warning me about the manticore, but

I didn't see one there or find any evidence that one had been held captive, aside from the mud pit."

"No chains?"

"No."

Atticus's eyes say, "Oh, shit," but his mouth says, "All right, good to know."

"Come see me at Court in a few days, Siodhachan. I have other matters to discuss with you, but they can wait"—she pauses, and her voice drops until it's almost inaudible—"until after we have buried the dead. Go and be safe in Gaia's care."

"You as well, Brighid."

Owen decides to stay and help with all the dirty work and says he'll meet us at the cabin when he's finished. We're about to bid farewell, when the air visibly ripples behind Brighid. I have seen that too often during my training to mistake it for anything but a Druid in camouflage. And I cannot imagine a reason for anyone to be in camouflage now unless they wished someone here ill. Adjusting my hands on Scáthmhaide to a two-handed grip, I leave Atticus and pad around Brighid, swinging hard at the leading edge of the disturbance once it gets in range. A startled squawk and a dull thud greet my ears as my arms tingle with the force of contact, and this is followed closely by another impact, as the recipient of my attention hits the ground and then appears at the feet of Brighid.

The body is a naked and bloody Fand, clutching Moralltach in her right hand. I had hit her on the head and knocked her unconscious. Had I not acted, she would have surely struck at Brighid's unprotected neck. The Queen of the Faeries had shifted away, bided her time, and then shifted back in an attempt to assassinate Brighid in an unguarded moment.

I take a deep breath as it dawns on me that I just saved Brighid's life.

The goddess in question turns upon hearing the noise and sees Fand lying there—everyone does. But reminders of what Fand has cost her quickly flash behind Brighid's eyes, and she drops her helmet and draws her sword to do to Fand what Fand would have done to her.

Brighid swings down upon Fand's head, Flidais cries, "No!" and the clang of metal on metal rings out as Brighid's sword is halted by the blade of Fragarach.

Brighid's eyes flash blue and turn upon my love, who has risen and advanced in time to prevent disaster.

"Siodhachan? Do you count yourself on the side of the traitors?"

Atticus replies, "You know I do not. I invoke the ancient privilege of Druids to offer advice to leaders of the people."

"I did not solicit your advice."

"I understand, Brighid, and of course you shall do as you will. But I ask you to hear me first and consider. Fand is currently no threat. There are iron nets in the trees nearby," he says, jerking his head to the south, "and one can be fetched while we speak and render her impotent should she wake up." I admire how Atticus addresses the heart of the matter and does not waste breath on peripherals, like how Fand came to be knocked unconscious in the first place. He focuses on the present and the future rather than the past. "There is time to hear me before you make a decision," he adds.

Brighid withdraws her sword and says, "Very well." She turns to Owen and speaks formally. "Eoghan Ó Cinnéide, I ask you to fetch one of these iron nets to bind Fand while I speak with Siodhachan Ó Suileabháin." Atticus's archdruid bobs his head and moves to obey without comment. Brighid turns back to Atticus with the force of command. "Deliver your advice, Druid."

Perun walks over, bends down, and removes Moralltach from Fand's grip, tossing it aside. Atticus takes a deep breath and speaks.

"Honored Brighid, it is my opinion that killing Fand now would only exacerbate the grievance that the Fae currently hold against you. You just finished speaking to the Fae of your willingness to become a better leader, and you showed them mercy. You would therefore do damage to your own reputation by not showing mercy here. You have the opportunity to wrap Fand in iron and neutralize her while in the meantime solidifying your own power as a just and benevolent leader. And leaving an avenue open by which Fand may one day be redeemed would endear you to Manannan Mac Lir and Flidais, who have both served you faithfully already in this matter."

Brighid's head turns to regard Flidais, Fand's mother. The two of them have been friends for uncounted centuries. They worked together to put me through the *Baolach Cruatan* when I was first chosen to be a Druid initiate. Flidais had even taken a couple of shots at Fand at Brighid's request. A long history lies exposed between them, an ineffable trust and love in that meeting of eyes. And, in that moment, I know that Brighid cannot execute Fand, no matter how betrayed she feels.

Atticus makes gigantic mistakes at times. But there are also times like this one when he makes of his life a poem and achieves an apotheosis of sorts, when his years manifest as wisdom and he spies a path forward that no one else sees until he points it out. And in this case that means not allowing swords to fall where they may. Brighid swings her head back to Atticus and speaks in a soft voice.

"You counsel prudence and thoughtful consideration."

"It is no more than you would counsel yourself, were

you at Court and not on the field of battle," Atticus says.

Brighid nods. "You advise me well, Druid."

Atticus's archdruid returns with the iron net and spreads it over Fand, as Flidais draws near. Brighid speaks to him in three voices: "Go with Flidais and imprison Fand humanely in a place the two of you shall decide. She shall not have access to the Fae, but neither shall she suffer physical torment. Agreed?"

The two of them give their verbal agreement, and in Tír na nÓg such words are far more binding than a right hand over a Bible. The archdruid gathers up the body of Fand, and Flidais accompanies him to the canopy of trees where they can shift away. I don't know where they're going, but I foresee tension between Flidais and Manannan and Brighid regardless of the destination. On the one hand, Brighid can say to them both, "Fand is toast for treason!" but, on the other, the two of them could call in innumerable favors for centuries of service to the First among the Fae.

I wouldn't want to walk in any of their shoes—that is, if any of them wore shoes. I only want to be with Atticus and the hounds again. Fortunately, he is of the same mind.

"It was kind of you to hear me," he says to Brighid. "If you have no more need of me now, I will retire and call upon you soon at the Fae Court."

She bows her head at him and says, "Go, Siodhachan, and may Gaia guide your steps."

Thus dismissed, we walk toward the trees so that we can shift to earth.

"We can't go back to the cabin yet," I whisper to Atticus as we near the oaks. "We have to talk somewhere else. I promise there's a good reason why."

He shrugs and says, "Okay. I'm sure the hounds will

be fine for a little while longer. Where do you want to go?"

"Costa Rica. Can I take you there?"

"Sure."

I clasp his hand and shift us to the Monteverde Cloud Forest Reserve, a moss-covered jungle of birdcalls in the mist, redolent of orchids and the flowers of other epiphytes. Atticus smiles and draws a deep breath.

"Good call," he says. "It's been too long since my last visit."

"Okay, don't freak out when you see me."

He pauses for a few beats before saying, "You're scaring me, but all right."

I drop my invisibility and Atticus flinches the tiniest bit when he lays eyes on me, but he keeps his mouth closed for a few seconds as he assesses the bruises.

"I certainly hope whoever did that to you is dead," he finally says.

"It is."

"It?"

"Long story. Let's find someplace to sit and I'll tell you." We descend into a valley and find a couple of lichen-frosted boulders sticking up out of a river. We sit down, lean our weapons against the rocks, and—with the sounds of flowing water and treetop monkey arguments swirling around us—I pour out all that happened to me since I last saw him in Thanjavur and he suggested that I seek out the yeti: my father's death and my brief visit with my mother; Laksha's new body; the creation of Fuilteach and its loss to Loki; the Lost Arrows of Vayu, now in Loki's possession; and the indelible mark on my arm that meant I couldn't be divined any longer—a definite plus—but that also meant I couldn't stay anywhere without endangering everyone around me.

"If I stay at the cabin for any length of time, Loki will

know that's where I live and that's where you probably live too. And he wants to kill you, Atticus."

"Let him come," he says. "Loki is a shitty swordsman, and his fire can't hurt me. I've got the green light from the gods now to take him out, and Hel too."

"He might have been faking his poor swordsmanship as well—wait, which gods?"

"Nine of the biggies, plus we have the Olympians waiting outside the ring to be tagged in."

"But if he comes with Vayu's arrows, he'll shoot you and can't miss."

"Yes, he can. You fool enchantments like that by shape-shifting and removing the original target. Odin tossed Gungnir at me once and whiffed."

That's a relief to hear, but I'm not sure Atticus is taking the danger seriously. "But Loki can set the cabin on fire," I point out, "or the whole forest, for that matter. Threaten the hounds."

"Granuaile, I understand, believe me. We'll take precautions, of course—you can ward against almost anything if you really want to. But I don't think we have to worry about a frontal assault. It's not Loki's style to threaten you with something and follow through on it. His style is to say one thing and then do some other sneaky thing while you're looking the wrong way. Right?"

"I guess . . ."

"Let's not uproot ourselves because of his threats or, worse yet, live separately and alone in paranoia. I've had more than enough of that. And much as I'd like to talk him and Hel out of their desire to burn the world, recent events demonstrate that I'm absolute rubbish at diplomacy. So let's prepare instead to kick his ass, Fierce Druid," he says, and I cannot help but smile. I think a certain amount of this is bravado for my benefit, but if we are truly free now to deal with Loki as we choose, we might have some allies that he would never consider, and I warm to the idea.

"Tell me, Atticus, who would win in a fight—Loki's fire or the frost magic of five yeti?"

EPILOGUE

I am unsure why modern men are so reluctant to admit that they enjoy snuggling. When they scoff at it or claim to despise it, they're lying, of course, trying to conform to some bullshit code of machismo. Regardless of one's lifespan, there are few pleasures in it like a lazy morning under comfy blankets with someone you love. Granuaile's soft smile and the early beams of sunlight on her freckled cheeks, all healed now, were so beautiful that I suspected that my day had already been made. In fact, odds were that it wouldn't get any better, so I enjoyed the view while I could and felt grateful to be alive. Moments like that never grow old.

The moment ended, however, when the hounds demanded attention after completing their morning stretches and suggested with the force of command that we should all go running in the forest. When we didn't respond with sufficient eagerness, they leapt onto the bed and delivered a punitive slobbering.

"Gah!" Granuaile spat. "All right, Orlaith, I'm getting up! Or I will if you let me! Let's go."

We tiptoed out of the cabin together so as not to disturb Owen, who had returned from Tír na nÓg last night after a week of service to Brighid and Manannan, then gone into town and gotten hammered before crashing on our couch. The chill air of a November dawn felt bracing, and I relished a carefree romp after weeks of stress and uncertainty.

"I'm feeling a bit of Touchstone this morning," I said to Granuaile as the hounds bounded forth in a playful lope, knowing we'd catch up. She grinned at me.

"Are you, now? The clown from *As You Like It*? Go on, then, let's hear it."

I cleared my throat, placed one hand over my heart and raised the other in front of me in the likeness of a terrible actor, and pronounced with suitable melodrama: *"We that are true lovers run into strange capers; but as all is mortal in nature, so is all nature in love mortal in folly."*

"Ah, well done," Granuaile said. "Let me see." Her eyes smiled at Oberon and Orlaith nipping at each other under the trees. "I think I am in a slightly different mood. I'm looking forward to the four of us running together again, now that we are all fully recovered. And so I answer you with Whitman: *I think I could turn and live with animals, they are so placid and self-contain'd, / I stand and look at them long and long.*"

Such perfection of thought and sentiment passing over shining lips had to be acknowledged. "I love you," I said.

"I know," she replied, and then laughed because she got to deliver the Han Solo line. "Catch me if you can." She shifted to a jaguar and shot into the forest, purposely plowing between Oberon and Orlaith to trigger their instinct to give chase. I shifted to a wolfhound and joined in the fun, our tails wagging and tongues lolling as we wove through the pine and spruce and whitebarked trees and our paws stirred drifts of fallen aspen leaves.

That was one of my finer mornings in recent memory. That we lived it under the threat of Loki showing up at any time did not diminish it in the slightest.

In fact, in one sense, that may have made it even better. I have spent so much of the past few hundred years running away whenever I sensed a threat that I forgot how good it feels to be rooted. And to be rooted is not the same thing at all as being tied down. To be rooted is to say, here am I nourished and here will I grow, for I have found a place where every sunrise shows me how to be more than what I was yesterday, and I need not wander to feel the wonder of my blessing. And when you are rooted, defending that space ceases to be an obligation or a duty and becomes more of a desire. I was feeling that way about our cabin in Colorado. Snow would fall soon, vast white blankets of it, and we probably needed to find a different place to winter, but I would lay down plenty of wards on the cabin before we left. I wanted to enjoy more mornings like that one.

Even Owen, when we returned, had nothing negative to say over breakfast. I was reluctant to broach the subject of settling him elsewhere, because the pleasantness would evaporate when I did. It turned out the evaporation was to come from another source entirely: a call from Hal Hauk.

"We need to talk," he said. "The Tempe police are asking about your past again."

"Aren't I supposed to be dead to them?" I said. "Atticus O'Sullivan died years ago according to the American authorities."

"Yeah, that's why they're talking to me, because they've heard from another source that you're still alive, and they're kind of curious as to whether it's true and, if so, where you are."

"Oh, splendid," I said. "All right, give me three hours."

"How about you give me three hours instead? It's a full moon tonight and we have to get out of town anyway. Thought I'd bring my people up to join with Sam and Ty in Flagstaff. Meet you at their place?"

"All right, that sounds good."

Owen was as anxious to see Sam and Ty again as we were to leave him there. Almost as soon as we arrived, he went out to the forest with much of the Tempe pack and all of the Flagstaff pack for another round of friendly brawling with Ty. I noticed that Greta went with them, and I believe I saw her smile for the first time: It was when she laid eyes on Owen. I privately bet that he would decide to settle in Arizona somewhere and hoped that harmony had finally found them both.

Hal and Farid remained behind in the house with Granuaile, the hounds, and me. Granuaile and I sat across the kitchen table from Hal, who slapped a manila folder down on the table between us. Farid was keeping the hounds' attention in the food-prep area by marinating a massive amount of tri-tip and whipping up sundry side dishes for two hungry werewolf packs. Regardless of what news Hal had for me, at least lunch would be brilliant.

"Remember that accountant you told me about, Craig Black?" Hal growled. "The guy who's in charge of the bulk of your fortune?"

Something in my gut twisted and made a tiny noise. This wasn't going to be good. "Yes?" I said, reaching for the folder.

"Well, I tried to contact him like you said. And when I did so, I suddenly found detectives crawling up my ass."

"Why?"

"Because Mr. Black is dead, and he found a unique way to die that has the police all kinds of curious." He chucked his chin at the folder. "Go on and look. Picture's on top."

I flipped open the folder and let my eyes fall on the

glossy photo of my old friend in a close-up. Kodiak Black's corpse looked creepy but no more so than most bodies; I couldn't discern from the picture what made his manner of passing unique. His eyes were open and he was fully clothed in flannel shirt and jeans; his face was slick and puffy and unnaturally pasty, with tiny blue capillaries tracing spidery paths underneath the eyes. His dark hair looked freeze-dried and brittle, as if it could crumble and blow away with a puff of wind.

"Some kind of new disease?" I ventured.

"No, it was murder. We just don't know what killed him."

"How do you know it was murder?"

"Because the witnesses all say so. This was a few days ago up in Anchorage. He was leaving an alehouse, all smiles, when he was ambushed outside. Place called Humpy's."

That was enough to draw Oberon's attention. <Humpy's? That sounds like it's hound-friendly! Can we visit?>

The name probably has something to do with salmon, Oberon. Some types of salmon grow humps on their backs right before they spawn.

<Are you really going to crush my beautiful dream with a boring fish fact?>

"I don't understand, Hal. You're saying he was killed in public but you don't know how?"

He shrugged. "I wasn't there. Report says about ten people saw him die, not least of whom was his girlfriend, who stated he was perfectly fine one minute—he looked healthy and hadn't complained of any problems—and then he began to convulse. After three seconds of that, he fell over onto the sidewalk, his face swelled, and he stopped breathing. Total time from onset of symptoms to death was less than ten seconds. We don't know of any diseases that can do that."

"Toxicology?" Granuaile asked.

Hal gave a tight shake of his head. "It's too early to have the results back yet. They do those tests in five to ten minutes of screen time on TV, but in real life those tests take weeks to months to complete. I know the police are counting on something showing up so they can say he was poisoned, but I've never heard of a poison that turns on violent convulsions like a switch. Only thing like that I've ever heard of is epilepsy. Mr. Black wasn't epileptic, was he?"

"No," I said. "Witnesses said his face swelled up. Is this what he looked like right afterward? Because his skin looks as if he's been at the bottom of a river for a few days."

"That photo was taken at the scene, within an hour of his death. No wounds, which is why they're hanging their hat on the poison theory."

"I don't get it. Why were the police so interested in you?"

"Because I'm the counselor of record for one Atticus O'Sullivan, deceased. And when I emailed Mr. Black in the interest of starting a dialogue, I referred to a Mr. O'Sullivan, and the Anchorage police saw that when they went through his in-box in an attempt to get a clue. They asked the Tempe police to speak to me about it, and you can imagine how surprised they were to hear your name associated with a mysterious murder out of state."

"Detective Kyle Geffert is still on the force, eh?"

"Indeed."

"How did they connect Kodiak to me? He never kept any of my accounts under the O'Sullivan name, and when I emailed him myself I used an alias account."

"They made the connection because, right after Mr. Black died, a man with strange tattoos on his head and wearing a 'hideous cravat'—that's a direct quote—

approached the girlfriend, one Ayesha Salcedo, and he said to her, 'Mr. Black is dead because of Atticus O'Sullivan. Please make sure he gets this.' Then he gave her a note. She looked down to read it, and when she looked back up, he was gone."

I could almost feel the color draining from my face; the room grew unaccountably cold and I felt sick. I knew who the murderer was by the description. "What did the note say?"

Hal flicked a finger at the folder. "It's the next picture."

I looked at the next photo and saw a square of paper printed in block letters with purple ink. It said, *Atticus. We must talk. Find me. Werner.*

"Auugh! I knew it! I had this guy under my sword, Hal, and I let him go!" The mysterious cause of death for Kodiak Black wasn't a mystery at all. The very essence of his life had been drained from a distance. He had been murdered by Werner Drasche, the arcane life-leech I had set free in France. Oh, I'd find him, all right, but we weren't going to have a friendly chat. When you kill a friend of mine just to get my attention, there's nothing left to say.

ACKNOWLEDGMENTS

Whoa. Book seven. I didn't think I'd get here when I first started, so I'm very grateful to you for reading and for telling your friends about the series. This book is proof that word-of-mouth is still king. Thank you!

Many beers to my agent, Evan Goldfried, for steering the ship and untold other nautical metaphors that may or may not involve a sextant. Being an agent is nothing like being a sailor, by the way. I just wanted to thank Evan and use the word *sextant*.

The editorial team at Del Rey goes to heroic lengths to make sure my books are spiffy, and that's because they really are heroes. They're part of the Fictional Four, a supergroup defending the world from plot holes and rogue apostrophes and so on. Here they are:

THE FICTIONAL FOUR

"They're for real!"

YETI COMIX

THE HUMAN EXPLETIVE

VIKING MIKE

METAL EDITOR

DUTCH FURY

Tricia Narwani is my Metal Editor. Mike Braff, as you might guess, is Viking Mike. Sarah Peed is Dutch Fury, and April Flores is the Human Expletive. They save my life on a regular basis, and I'm extremely privileged to work with them.

Many thanks to Vidhyu Rao, whose kind and patient conversation illuminated much for me one day on a flight out of Minneapolis. Thanks also to Siva and Jesse Nattamai and to Jasmine Pues for their enlightening correspondence, and to Helgi Briem for some pronunciation help on the yeti names.

My family and friends keep me sane and loved, and I'm so very lucky to have them in my life. And doggies too. Don't forget the doggies! Peace and harmony, friends.